PENGUIN ENGLISH LIBRARY

FOUR TUDOR COMEDIES

William Tydeman was educated at Maidstone Grammar
School and at University College, Oxford. After a period pur-
suing research into the poetry of Sir Thomas Wyatt he moved
to Bangor, Gwynedd, where he is now University Reader in
English at the University College of North Wales. His publications include *English Poetry 1400–1580* (1970) and *The
Theatre in the Middle Ages* (1978).

FOUR
TUDOR COMEDIES

Jacke Jugeler

Roister Doister
NICHOLAS UDALL

Gammer Gurton's Nedle
WILLIAM STEVENSON

Mother Bombie
JOHN LYLY

EDITED WITH AN INTRODUCTION AND NOTES
BY WILLIAM TYDEMAN

PENGUIN BOOKS

Penguin Books Ltd, Harmondsworth, Middlesex, England
Penguin Books, 40 West 23rd Street, New York, New York 10010, U.S.A.
Penguin Books Australia Ltd, Ringwood, Victoria, Australia
Penguin Books Canada Ltd, 2801 John Street, Markham, Ontario,
Canada L3R1B4
Penguin Books (N.Z.) Ltd, 182–190 Wairau Road, Auckland 10,
New Zealand

First published in Penguin Books 1984

Introduction and Notes
Copyright © William Tydeman, 1984
All rights reserved

Made and printed in Great Britain by
Hazell, Watson & Viney Ltd, Aylesbury, Bucks
Set in Linotron Baskerville

TO
MY ENGLISH TEACHERS
AT
MAIDSTONE GRAMMAR SCHOOL
1946–1954

CONTENTS

INTRODUCTION

I

By ancient tradition the joyful mask of comedy must hang alongside the grieving mask of tragedy, yet in terms of human significance popular opinion still regards tragedy as the superior form. The view is widely held that whereas tragedy demonstrates sublime, uplifting, ennobling truths about mankind, comedy merely reminds us that we are fallible and often foolish, deceitful and frequently deceived, irrational and always ridiculous. Yet it should surely be possible to argue that, since fundamentally both types of theatrical experience seek to reconcile us to our mortal condition, comedy and tragedy are mutually complementary and compatible aspects of one universal process in which neither is downgraded as the inferior. Certainly, in the English-speaking theatre there have been at least as many creators of memorable comedies as of their tragic counterparts, while there are half a dozen major playwrights (Jonson, Sheridan, Wilde, Shaw, and Synge among them) whose attempts at tragedy appear anaemic beside their full-blooded comic compositions.

But despite an obvious native talent for the form – let us gloss over the fact that four of the five names cited above are those of Irishmen – the British are curiously neglectful of certain areas of their comic heritage. It is significant that, although surveys of English drama pay lip-service to their importance, the four plays making up this selection scarcely rank as familiar works, either in the live theatre or with the general reader. Critics and scholars have more often expended their ingenuity and energies on establishing fine points of authorship or dating than in demonstrating how supremely actable and well-constructed these sturdy Tudor comedies are; how vividly they convey to us the flavour of daily life in sixteenth-century England; how much pleasure their portrait of the human spectacle in its perennial quirky variety offers; how engaging, lively, touching, and genuinely funny they show themselves to be, once submitted to the crucial test of reading or performance.

Moreover, all these plays deserve to be rescued from the injustices of the academic labelling-system. For too long it has been the custom to refer to these and similar works of equal calibre as 'pre-Shakespearean' or 'minor Elizabethan' dramas, descriptions out of which it is impossible to keep the dismissive note. Such phrases tacitly ask what pleasure can possibly be extracted from stumbling through the lowland bogs in the footsteps of the Tudor pioneers when we can stand confidently on the mountain-peaks with the author of *Twelfth Night* or *A Midsummer Night's Dream*. But the answer must surely be that these plays are of interest and value, not because they preceded something more familiar to us, whose excellence they sometimes foreshadow or even occasionally pre-empt, but because they are worth our attention and appreciation in their own right. Such is Shakespeare's dominance in the field of Elizabethan and Jacobean drama that it is impossible to forget his plays entirely as we examine his predecessors' achievements, but we can at least avoid treating their work as no more than the tentative and clumsy prelude to his. Jenkin Careaway's traumatic encounter with his *Doppelgänger* in *Jacke Jugeler* is worthy of notice not because Shakespeare used the same device from the same classical source in *The Comedy of Errors*, but because its author astutely perceived and exploited the stage potential of an effective comic situation. Roister Doister is a constant delight not because his behaviour vaguely anticipates that of Falstaff or Don Armado, but because he comes to life instantly as a unique and unforgettable dramatic figure. Lyly's patterned plots and elegantly mannered dialogue have an intrinsic appeal which is based on more than their influence on *The Two Gentlemen of Verona* and *Love's Labour's Lost*. *Gammer Gurton's Nedle* exhibits a richly characterized community of low-life cre-

ations possessing a vigour which even Ben Jonson rarely emu-
lated, and which can stand comparison with similar elements
in *The Merry Wives of Windsor* or *Measure for Measure*.

Thus the appearance of these comedies in the Penguin
English Library does not represent some wayward act of hom-
age to their antiquity or quaintness or even their relevance to
Shakespearean studies. It is rather a recognition of their continued capacity to give enjoyment and satisfaction, not only
on the printed page but also in the public playhouse where
they must before long receive the acclamation they richly
deserve. The work of educated men, intended for select audiences, they also possess intrinsic popular appeal.

II

It is hard to form an adequate over-view of comic drama in
Britain prior to the emergence of these plays. We must certainly resist the tempting over-simplification that the rediscovery of classical models imposed a shape and a structure on
the chaos which was pre-Renaissance comedy, for not only
were medieval aesthetic criteria different from our own, but
our knowledge of English drama of the Middle Ages is
especially imperfect in regard to secular comedy. Yet traces
and fragments of lost pieces, along with analogous instances of
European survivals, support the commonsense assumption
that there must have been a strong tradition of popular
humorous plays in the British Isles throughout the medieval
period, even if little of it has come down to us.

One fact we must always bear in mind is that the medieval
definition of 'comedy' differed considerably from that generally current today: laughter and humour were not fundamental
to it, nor was it exclusively associated with works for stage
performance. Rather was it the term applied to literary compositions (often narrative poems) whose conclusion, as Dante
stressed in speaking of his own masterpiece *La divina commedia*,
was 'prosperous, pleasant, and desirable', whose style was
more informal and unpretentious than that associated with
weightier matters, and whose language was that of the Euro-

pean vernaculars. The 'happy ending' essential to comedy was rarely led up to through the resolution of the foolish actions of ridiculous characters, or through the creation of laughable situations from which readers could derive mirth and enjoyment. Notable examples of what the medieval mind regarded as 'comedies' appear in the *Canterbury Tales*, and they are not found amid the raucous slap-and-tickle of 'The Miller's Tale' or the *fabliau* told by the Summoner, but in the plangent narratives of the Clerk and the Man of Law, in which patient Griselda and 'faire Custance' survive years of adversity and suffering to end their days 'in heigh prosperitee'.

In the field of religious drama the civic cycle sequences and the moralities constituted 'comedies' in the medieval sense, since in these forms too might be discovered the comedic pattern leading to the vital 'happy ending'. One rejoiced in Christ's triumphant victory over death and Satan; the other celebrated mankind's ultimate salvation from the hands of its spiritual foes. To this aspect of the plays we must primarily direct our attention when considering the comic dimension in medieval Christian drama, rather than to the more superficial humour provided by Noah's wife, Herod, or the morality Vices. The laughter these figures generate must be seen as serving the artistic ends of the whole, never as outweighing them, however refreshing or liberating it may appear to a less devout age. Comedy in our modern sense is certainly a central feature of the religious drama of the Middle Ages, and it is there to be enjoyed, but within the perspective provided by the plays as complete entities, not in isolation from their more serious 'comic' purpose.

But comedy of other types there must have been, and probably secular English comedies assumed the form of their continental counterparts, namely that of the short anecdotal interlude presented semi-informally by a small versatile cast, which had as its subject some laughter-provoking aspect of everyday life, most often a piece of deception or fraud, or a confrontation between contrasted characters, variously involving a sexual encounter, a domestic crisis, or a battle of practical jokes. No doubt typical of many lost comedies of this kind is the Middle English fragment known as the *Interlude of the Clerk and the Girl* (*c.* 1300), which begins to recount how an old crone tricks the reluctant mistress of an amorous student into having sex with him. *Le Garcon et l'aveugle*, a Flemish piece of slightly earlier date, shows a young sighted rogue getting the better of an old blind one; the celebrated French farce of *Maître Pierre Pathelin* offers another variation on the favourite theme of 'the biter bit', in which the crooked lawyer Pathelin is outwitted by an apparently simple shepherd.

The early Tudor farces of John Heywood (1497–*c.* 1579), probably written between 1519 and 1528, occupy very much the same territory, based as many of them are on French originals. In *The Pardoner and the Frere* its two dishonest protagonists set up their rival 'sales-pitches' side by side near a village church and compete for alms; when the local constable and curate intervene – *Gammer Gurton's Nedle* is vaguely foreshadowed – they get beaten for their pains. In *Johan Johan* the henpecked husband of the title has to suffer the humiliation of seeing his wife entertain her clerical lover, smugly eating pie and flirting while he is forced to mend a leaky pail and look on like a menial. At the close, he kicks over the traces and drives them out.

Anecdotal and slight, Heywood's farces reveal the same need for organic structure and development as his didactic debate-dramas, among them *The Play of the Wether* and *The Four PP.* More ingenious and thoughtful than the farces, they still fail to satisfy the aesthetic sense, and in their lack of coherent organization display the primary weakness of the native form. Possibly because its authors had never felt the urge to do otherwise, English comedy in the early sixteenth century shows a preference for representative figures rather than individually characterized personalities, a fondness for digressive anecdotes and arbitrarily abrupt endings, an unwillingness or inability to sustain a complex plot, and a tendency to advance the action by serial accretion rather than smoothly developed structural procedures. Even *Jacke Jugeler*, composed under more sophisticated auspices, is not free from these drawbacks.

But the arts of the English theatre were in the process of gradual change, at least within those circles whose sensibilities were attuned to new influences. The broad jovial humour of old England was now being supplemented by a taste for the even older comedies of Plautus and Terence, the leading comic playwrights of ancient Rome. In 1520 Henry VIII watched 'a goodly commedy of Plautus' performed at court; at about the same time Heywood's father-in-law John Rastell published a translation of Terence's *Andria* under the title *Terens in Englysh*. A new and revitalizing force was about to be released.

III

How and why the late Middle Ages developed into the Renaissance are complex problems which have occupied scholars for many decades. Our task is to try and understand the attraction of the comedies of Plautus and Terence for those European enthusiasts who edited, printed, translated, performed, and imitated them so ardently, and thus passed on their enthusiasm to Tudor England. The medieval world clearly knew the work of both men. As far back as the tenth century Hrotswitha, a German abbess, had created 'Christian comedies' consciously to compete with those of Terence, and there are indications that his plays were actually staged in the Middle Ages, possibly in mime form with a single narrator reciting the lines. But the fervent excitement generated at such centres as Rome and Ferrara in the last quarter of the fifteenth century was something different. Perhaps the recovery of Plautus' twelve lost comedies by Nicholas de Cusa and his arrival with them at Rome in 1429 supplied the initial spark; certainly the aristocratic encouragement of Ercole d'Este of Ferrara fuelled the blaze. At all events, a knowledge of Roman comedy and an interest in its leading exponents became as indispensable to European men and women of culture and breeding as an acquaintance with the works of Cicero or Virgil, and twice as fashionable. Why this cult of all things classical should have arisen at all is impossible to fathom: one cannot believe that it was simply a form of intellectual snobbery or a passing craze, yet one questions the view that it represented a deliberate attempt on the part of the late medieval period to purge itself of a sense of gaucheness, of prolixity, of a lack of polish and sophistication. Were the men of the Renaissance looking for something, or did they stumble on it? Whatever the reason, the passion for Plautus and Terence seemed to them entirely justified, even if they looked on those distant writers with the eyes of their own age, rather than with those of literary historians.

Between them, Terence and Plautus were responsible for some twenty-seven surviving plays, the earlier, by some fifty years, being those of Plautus who lived from c. 254–184 BC. He made his name by adapting to the Roman stage the so-called 'New Comedy' of the Greeks, in particular the works of Disculus and Menander. Menander is credited with pioneering the use of such stock figures as the amorous but inexperienced young man, his older, knowing, Jeeves-like slave, the desirable maiden, the crusty old father, the two-faced parasite, and the braggart soldier (actually first found in the 'Old Comedy' of Aristophanes). Some would claim that Menander is important as an influence only, but too few of his plays survive intact for that judgement to be worth much. His plots are 'well-made', his milieu the world of daily events, his main topic the pursuit of love; both Plautus and Terence availed themselves of his example, despite differences of background and temperament. Plautus, an actor and a man of the people, wrote with an eye on the popular festivals or games held in Rome five times a year; Terence (195–c. 159 BC), a sensitive man of culture and refined tastes, wrote for the civic games but preferred to please a circle of like-minded friends rather than the populace. As might be expected, Plautus is less the conscious artist: his plays lack the taut, watertight, precision-engineering of Terence – he adores digression – but there is an exuberance, a relish, a sense of overflowing high spirits and a love of human variety in his best work which anticipates Rabelais or Dickens. He is the leading specialist in tricks, intrigues, deceptions, and mistaken identities. Among his most celebrated works are the *Amphitruo*, on which *Jacke Jugeler* is partly based, the *Menaechmi*, which inspired *The Comedy of Errors*, the *Miles gloriosus*, which bequeathed the Falstaff-figure to European literature, and – possibly his finest achievement and certainly his most romantic comedy – *Rudens* or *The Rope*.

Terence's surviving works number only six (not surprisingly for a man who died aged twenty-five), and include the *Adelphoe* (*The Brothers*), the *Andria*, the *Eunuchus*, and *Phormio*. Rather than repudiating the conventions of the New Comedy or the work of his eminent predecessor, Terence quietly refined the Plautine elements to a state of unequalled (few would say unmerited) polish. His neat story-lines move with a grace, a conciseness, and a credibility which the less restrained Plautus never aimed for, and his characterizations have a 'rounded' quality and exhibit a subtlety of motive and response which is all their own. The contrast between Terence and Plautus is perhaps best expressed as that which exists between an architect and a master-builder – it was no coincidence that Terence specialized in the intricacies of the double plot – and it was his genius for design that the men of the Renaissance exploited when they came to write their own plays.

Alongside performances of Latin comedies in the original and in translation and their imitation in the vernacular *commedia erudita* of such writers as Ariosto, Bibbiena, and Arentino, scholarly analysis and exegesis of the new literary discoveries also proceeded. In particular, academics helped to promote the merits of 'the five-act structure' favoured by all Roman dramatists but perfected by Terence. While it is true that no early text contains any indications of act- and scene-divisions, Renaissance critics echoed such classical commentators as Donatus and Servius in drawing attention to the firm framework sustaining the natural ease and flow of Terentian comedies, and to the three principal divisions which gave them their clarity of construction. In the *protasis* characters were introduced and the initial situation was unfolded; in the *epitasis* complications began to be developed, schemes and stratagems devised and set to work; in the *catastrophe* difficulties were brought to a head and then resolved so that harmony might be restored, often through an unexpected discovery being made. Such an orderly pattern obviously commended itself to working dramatists seeking to construct vernacular plays on the new classical principles, whereby an organic plot might be advanced through a series of planned phases organized into distinct acts and scenes.

In England, where the vogue for staging and imitating classical drama eventually arrived from the Continent in the 1510s, there was much interest in the educational value of the Roman drama, most notably on account of the fluid, conversational, colloquial Latın in which its plays were couched. Here was Latin as it was actually spoken in the streets and houses of ancient Rome; here was Latin that could be commended to pupils in whom the inculcation of a sound spoken and written style was felt to be the basis of a good education and the passport to a successful and effective life thereafter. Thus Terence and Plautus came to occupy a special place on the English school curriculum, and Tudor dons and schoolmasters encouraged their charges to engage in live performances in the original Latin as part of their vocational programme. In 1527 the boys of St Paul's School staged Plautus' *Menaechmi* under the direction of the High Master; in the following year Cardinal Wolsey was in the audience for their performance of Terence's *Phormio*. Between 1548 and 1583 at least twenty-two productions of Plautus and Terence were seen in the colleges of Cambridge alone. In schools the aim was partly to teach what one ex-pupil of Merchant Taylors' School alluded to as 'good behaviour and audacitye', that is to say, 'ease of bearing and self-confidence', but more was implied by the exercise. Moral and even psychological benefit were believed to accrue as well.

There were plenty of classical precedents for advocating the notion that comedy had a moral function to discharge. Donatus and Servius emphasized that, concerned as it was with everyday metropolitan life and people of non-exalted rank, this genre could portray with greater facility than tragedy the vices, weaknesses and follies of ordinary unheroic men and women, who by seeing their own faults held up to ridicule and amusement on stage, might be moved to rectify base traits of character or conduct. On such a basis Sir Thomas Elyot in *The Boke named the Governour* (1531) defended Terence and others from those who accused them of promoting lechery:

Comedies, whiche they suppose to be a doctrinall of rybaudrie, they be undoubtedly a picture or as it were a mirrour of man's life, wherin ivell [evil] is nat taught but discovered; to the intent that men beholdynge the promptnes of youth unto vice, the snares of harlotts and baudes laide for yonge myndes, the disceipte of servantes, the chaunces of fortune contrary to mennes expectation, they being therof warned may prepare them selfe to resist or prevente occasion . . . by comedies good counsaile is ministred.   (I, xiii)

Yet 'good counsaile' was not enough; the Tudor mind also recognized that comedy was valuable for its therapeutic function in relieving tension and promoting mirth and concord. The custom of concluding sixteenth-century comedies with a dance or a feast goes back to the classical convention in which the warring parties (usually young lovers and the parental establishment) are reconciled within a newly cemented harmonious relationship, but its presence in Renaissance comedy does not simply represent an act of blind imitation: writers shared with their exemplars the view that Comedy is Good for You. Hence all the comedies reprinted here culminate in the creation of a world where the punishment of the negligent Jenkin, the mischief-making Jack, Merrygreek and Diccon, and the insubordinate pages is sublimated to the idea that 'sport' and 'pastaunce' are not to be condemned, since they are healthful. Quarrels must be patched up, suspicions laid to rest, wrongs real or imagined forgiven; the spirit of laughter must be given sovereignty. Even in *Roister Doister* with its declared aim of ridiculing 'the vayne glorious', the principal purpose is still to disseminate 'Mirth which is used in an honest fashion', and the braggart is ultimately restored to favour. The merry man lives longer than the 'sory man' proclaims Merrygreek, and some forty years later, in *The Taming of the Shrew*, the Messenger persuading Christopher Sly to sample a 'pleasant comedy' uses identical arguments:

> For so your doctors hold it very meet,
> Since too much sadness hath congeal'd your blood,
> And melancholy is the nurse of frenzy:
> Therefore they thought it good you hear a play
> And frame your mind to mirth and merriment,
> Which bars a thousand harms and lengthens life.
>
> (Induction, ii, 133–8)

Certainly the chief purpose of *Jacke Jugeler* appears to be to make its audience 'merie and glad' in troubled times, at least according to its Prologue, for the Epilogue seeks either to impose on the piece a humourless moral or to turn it into a veiled attack on the Catholic doctrine of Transubstantiation, a *volte-face* surely never intended by its original author. This unpretentious piece has many affinities with the early Tudor interludes: its staging demands few facilities, its main mode of procedure is through speeches of narrative description interspersed with duologues of confrontation, and its plot has no pretensions to intricacy or Terentian formality. Jack's trickery requires little ingenuity and involves no complications or unexpected twists. There is clearly no attempt here to conform to 'the five-act structure' of the classicists, perhaps because the material selected did not warrant stretching so far, although even scene divisions are not indicated as they might well be. As George E. Duckworth remarks, *Jacke Jugeler* is 'a series of comic situations rather than an organically constructed comedy'.

Yet in one important respect *Jacke Jugeler* is heavily indebted to the classical tradition, for its story derives (probably directly) from one of Plautus' best works, the *Amphitruo*, his sole venture into the realms of ancient mythology. This play centres on the birth of Hercules, born of the mortal Alcumena, wife of a Theban general, and the immortal Jupiter. In order for Hercules to be conceived without suspicion, Jupiter assumes the appearance of Amphitruo, Alcumena's absent husband, while his servant Mercury adopts the shape of the general's batman, Sosia. It is the encounter between the two servants which lies at the core of *Jacke Jugeler*, though Amphitruo's overbearing character is reflected in that of Bongrace, even if his 'cresie' wife and her spiteful maid are a far cry from Plautus' upright if vocal heroine and her devoted nurse Bromia.

But for all its indebtedness, *Jacke Jugeler* remains firmly rooted in the native theatrical idiom with its extemporized structure, love of digressive inconsequence, and, above all, its avoidance of any of the sexual hide-and-seek of its source, though this may be a concession to 'little boyes' handelings' even if by present-day standards (public ones at least) some of the language may surprise us. The play's classical origins are at any rate imperceptible to all but the informed reader, while its portrait of Tudor civic life and domestic habits offers many satisfactions to anyone who studies literature primarily to obtain a fuller sense of society in past ages, and renders the piece a worthy companion in this respect to *Roister Doister, Gammer Gurton's Nedle*, and *Mother Bombie*. If its central joke is drawn out to excessive lengths when judged by later tastes, the slow draining-away of Jenkin's carefree self-assurance and conviction as to who he is merits the long wait, and his act of self-betrayal under pressure is a marvellous moment of true comic relevation. Nor should we lose sight of the more serious implications behind the trick played on the boy: the perennial issue of the nature of human identity and the sense of personal crisis loss of selfhood can engender. All in all, it is unfair to dismiss *Jacke Jugeler*, as did A. P. Rossiter, as 'an undistinguished crib'. It both anglicizes and domesticates Plautus' original masterpiece, and even if it never improves on *Amphitruo* for comic interest, the 'little boyes' who first played it must have had fun with it.

IV

It is scarcely surprising that a schoolmaster (albeit one who occupied possibly the most prestigious teaching position in the land) was one of the first English playwrights to exploit the taste for comedies inspired by the classics. Nicholas Udall was appointed Headmaster of Eton College in June 1534, after being educated at Winchester and Oxford, where in 1526 he became a Fellow of Corpus Christi College. Suspected of Lutheran tendencies, he departed in 1528 or 1529, and probably taught in a school for some years. Certainly, his first major work, completed around the end of February 1534, represents a landmark in the teaching of classics in Britain. The intention behind *Floures for Latine Spekynge* was to assist pupils to speak good idiomatic Latin rather than use the stilted phrase-book modes then current, and to read and comprehend classical authors by intelligent appreciation of spirit and nuance, rather than by simply translating them literally word for word. The author Udall chose for this novel approach was Terence, highly regarded for his command of a natural, colloquial but elegant style. Udall selected the *Andria*, the *Eunuchus*, and *Heauton timorumenos* (*The Self-Tormentor*) as subjects for a running scholarly commentary by which he sought to clarify the meaning and significance of the original phraseology for schoolboy readers. His method was to go through the texts phrase by phrase, rendering each into colloquial, even racy, English, and drawing attention to such features of grammar, idiom, and style as seemed important for acquiring a clear understanding of Terence's words. As T. W. Baldwin writes:

The influence of this little volume on the matter of translation alone must have been tremendous. For Udall aimed at nothing more nor less than to teach the boys in detail the vernacular meaning and

21

mode of rendering Terence ... he included not merely such phrases from Terence as might be most useful in speaking, but also all the difficult points where the boys might not catch the exact shade of meaning in the Latin original ...

(*William Shakspere's Five-Act Structure*, Urbana, 1947, p. 377)

Such an undertaking was obviously immensely valuable when Udall set himself to compose an English comedy on classical lines, again seeking to reproduce the spirit of the Latin rather than being content to imitate its mere letter. *Roister Doister* probably dates from 1551–3; whether it was preceded by earlier attempts is at present uncertain. It is significant that, between 12 and 24 October 1537 (such precision is possible since the birth of Jane Seymour's son, later Edward VI, is alluded to) 'A new Enterlude called Thersytes' was staged at one of the royal palaces, although this is unlikely to have been its *première*. Since the piece contains a number of Oxford allusions, it may have found favour originally with a student audience, whose average age would of course have been lower than that of present-day undergraduates. The play is classical in subject only: adapted from a Latin dialogue by Ravisius Textor, Rector of the University of Paris, published in 1530, it features as its hero a boastful soldier who derives ultimately from the Plautine *miles gloriosus*. Thersytes features in a series of virtually unconnected episodes, commissioning a helmet, sword, and armour from Mulciber, confronting his doting mother, retreating before the onslaught of a snail and running to his mother's skirts when challenged by a real soldier. A letter from Ulysses, requesting that 'little Telemachus' may be cured of worms through Thersytes' mother's occult powers, is complied with, and the piece concludes with the coward's farcical attack on his mother, and his rout by the soldier who points the moral 'That great barking dogges do not most byte... the best men in the hoost Be not suche that use to bragge moste'.

It is easy to see why many scholars support the attribution to Udall; the didactic links between his conceited boaster and the noisy 'ruffler' Thersytes are obvious, and a number of phrases (admittedly ones in common use) appear in both plays, along with possibly predictable allusions to the heroes of English chivalry. Yet Udall was not necessarily alone in seeing the possibilities of transferring classical material to a native setting, and *Thersytes* depends to a far greater extent than *Roister Doister* on the irreverent extravagance of burlesque – it is a kind of Tudor *Orpheus in the Underworld* – while the play's episodic structure is a long way from the tautly sprung plots of Plautus and Terence which Udall at least tried to emulate in *Roister Doister*. Nor does *Thersytes* as a sort of half-term holiday from dignified utterance and heroic events stand independent of its sources. If Udall indeed wrote *Thersytes*, possibly during his years in Oxford, his criteria of dramatic excellence matured considerably over the next twenty-five years or so.

Udall continued to be associated with drama: he may have led his pupils to court at some point in 1537 or 1538 to perform the play which gained him the reward of £5 from Thomas Cromwell which is recorded in the Exchequer Accounts: the piece may even have been *Thersytes*. In 1545–6 he composed a Protestant drama on Hezekiah entitled *Ezechias*, subsequently played for Elizabeth I in King's College Chapel at Cambridge in August 1564, but since lost. But his main claim to theatrical distinction apart from *Roister Doister* rests on the distinct likelihood that he wrote the proMarian morality *Respublica*, possibly the play for which Mary I ordered her Master of the Revels to provide materials in December 1554. Part of her warrant acknowledges that 'our well beloved Nicholas Udall' had previously set forth 'Dialogues and Enterludes before us for our regal disporte and recreation'. Evidently during the Christmas season of 1554–5 payments were made to Udall for 'certen plaies' seen at court, and it may be that *Respublica* was among them. It employs the techniques of such religious moralities as *The Castel of Perseveraunce* for the purposes of contemporary political comment, much as John Skelton employed them in *Magnyfycence*. While its Latinate structure and scene divisions suggest classical influences at work, Udall also employs the characteristic device of abstract personifications to defend the Marian regime with the same enthusiasm with which he endorsed Henry's work of reformation. *Respublica* is thus a typical English Renaissance hybrid.

However, it is on *Roister Doister* that Udall's reputation as a playwright must ultimately depend, for it is the only play firmly attributable to his pen. Without doubt it is an impressive achievement, even if precedents for its excellence once existed. William Edgerton suggests that it was probably presented at Windsor while Udall was a canon there in September 1552, when it was used to cheer the flagging spirits of the young Edward VI. Others argue that it dates from Udall's years as Headmaster at Eton, others that he wrote it later while in the service of Stephen Gardiner, Bishop of Winchester. Certainly the publication of its 'mispunctuated' letter (III. 4) in the third edition of Thomas Wilson's *Rule of Reason* (which Edgerton believes was printed in January 1553) is evidence that the work existed by that date, although it is not axiomatic that it had been staged before being made available to Wilson, who introduces it simply by saying that it is 'taken out of an entrelude made by Nicolas Udal'. David Bevington argues that the parody of the burial service is too mild for Edward's court to have been entertained by it, and if Edgerton's theory is nonetheless correct – the necessary singers and even actors were admittedly available at Windsor's St George's Chapel – then we have to account for the references to 'the Queen' in the extant text. Perhaps the play was revised during the reign of Mary Tudor; possibly it was hastily amended for publication under Elizabeth I.

Whatever the truth, *Roister Doister* is a fine instance of the fusion possible between native tradition and classical example. Although the model is obviously Roman – with Plautus' *Miles gloriosus* and Terence's *Eunuchus* as particular guides – its braggart and parasite are never mere carbon-copies of their originals, but rather independent creations possessed of their own distinctive traits, and perfectly 'naturalized' to form part of the English scene. If the eponymous hero owes much to Terence's Thraso and Plautus' Pyrgopolynices, he also represents the foolish knight-lover of European chivalric tradition, who goes back at least to the Provençal *pastourelle*. What is more, he is elevated from his subsidiary position in the Latin comedy to assume a position at the centre of the stage in Udall's work, and indeed this egocentric narcissist needs referring back to no literary antecedents, so confidently does he occupy the limelight. Roister Doister is the quintessential show-off, the eternal buffoon-hero, victim of his own manic-depressive temperament, buoyed up by the hot air of his own boasting, eternally deflated by the pinpricks administered by a reality which refuses to adhere to his confident blueprint, and yet never downhearted for long. He genuinely cannot understand why Custance finds him less than utterly irresistible, and his crassness, even cruelty, stems from enormous efforts to boost his own insecure ego by refusing to admit the chances of final humiliation.

The vulnerability of this comic figure is played on mercilessly by Merrygreek, less the traditional parasite who flatters his patron in order to live off him, than a descendant of the medieval Vice, a stock figure whose genius is for the manipulation and temptation of the leading character into imperilling his immortal soul. Here of course something rather less important is at stake, but Merrygreek (like Jack Juggler) performs his trickery with the same pert smartness, the same relish for his own cleverness, the same conspiratorial intimacy with the audience which can enlist them to his side. He deliberately prolongs Roister Doister's fantasies (and incidentally Custance's ordeal), but he is never called to account for his actions, but is rather accepted as embodying the nimble spirit of anarchy and confusion unleashed when men indulge in delusions of conquest. He participates as a guest in the final rejoicings, the personification of a 'merriness' which by now has engulfed everyone.

But it is not for Udall's character portraits alone that this comedy deserves high praise, though the economy of means with which such minor figures as the sardonic Dobinet, the cheerful Truepenny, the sentimental Madge, and the scatty Tibet are drawn is masterly. Equally skilful is the piece's construction, and here the influence of Roman precedent is central. *Roister Doister* is a model of dramatic 'regularity', even if it does not adhere perfectly to the traditional unities; it is practically a copy-book demonstration of the approved method of building a play, even if one comes to feel that every act signals a fresh phase in the action a little too obviously. Indeed, Udall departs from the *Eunuchus* in this particular, that he emphasizes each phase of his plot much more distinctly than does Terence. Certainly, he does not avoid all the pitfalls of his classical inheritance. Merrygreek's long opening conversation with the audience seems needless, as we are to see Roister Doister in action for ourselves, and the fact that there are precedents in Plautus, especially in Mercury's solo at the start of *Amphitruo* (duplicated in *Jacke Jugeler*), does not mitigate all the tedium.

Only in Act V, with the potentially serious misunderstanding between Gawyn Goodluck and his fiancée, reminiscent of the false suspicion entertained by Amphitruo of the innocent but pregnant Alcumena, do the action and tone cease to be all of a piece. Even here, as T. W. Baldwin points out, they provide a pleasant variant on *The Eunuch*, where it is the braggart not the rival who becomes a prey to jealousy. Further, the final obstacle to the ultimate resolution of the crisis has a 'braking effect' on a plot which might otherwise peter out after the abortive assault on Custance's house. Even this brief moment of incipient tragedy shows that English dramatists did not slavishly copy their prestigious classical models. The scholarly knowledge of the principles of play-making which Udall acquired from their study may have been vital to the finished nature of his achievement, but his own innate theatrical sense, his eye and ear for traits of character and their indication through dialogue, were things which no amount of reading in Plautus and Terence could earn him. He remains one of the important pioneers of Tudor drama.

V

Doubts may exist as to the exact nature of Udall's dramatic output, but as a historical figure he stands sharply outlined before us compared with the shadowy creator of *Gammer Gurton's Nedle*. Some of the complex arguments surrounding this man's identity are rehearsed in the introduction to the text, but it remains likely that we must search for somebody with a strong connection with Christ's College, Cambridge, where the play was 'played on stage' on some occasion prior to the text's publication in 1575. Since many Cambridge men must have felt an urge to compose vernacular dramas in the 1560s and 70s, the possibilities are vast.

But whoever wrote *Gammer Gurton's Nedle*, the central fact remains that it is an extraordinary achievement in a theatrical *genre* which in England at least had barely recovered from its labour-pains. It betrays even fewer signs of its classical antecedents than does the more derivative *Roister Doister*, so expertly is the tough Terentian structure concealed from inspection by the immense variety, vitality, and viciousness of the Tudor kitchen-sink mode. The play is like a Brueghel painting animated into spontaneous, throbbing, scabby, stinking life, but the evolution of its fantastic, farcical story-line is as rigidly controlled as anything set in a salon by Marivaux or a bedroom by Feydeau. As in *Roister Doister*, each phase of the action is geared to the Latin act-structure, so that the first act establishes the circumstances of the needle's loss, and the early efforts to retrieve it, the second finds Diccon setting Gammer Gurton and Dame Chat 'by the ears', while Act III brings them to open conflict. Fresh interest is injected at the start of Act IV by the intervention of Dr Rat, whose injury and humiliation precipitate the *catastrophe* which begins with the entry of 'Master Bayly' at the opening to Act V. This authoritative figure, unlike Gawyn Goodluck, is above the controversy, and so can dispense 'even-handed justice', although by a fitting irony it is not he who solves the play's main puzzle. That is achieved by means of the 'fortunate discovery' hallowed by ancient tradition, or rather in this case by a delicious burlesque of it, whereby the long-lost needle stuck in Hodge's breeches takes the place of the lost child or abandoned treasure which lay all the time under the noses of those who sought it.

However, few commentators have thought to make the practical inquiry as to how the needle ultimately comes to be discovered in Hodge's breeches after all. The initial picture seems clear: while Hodge is 'ditchinge' and ripping his breeches in the process, Gammer is disturbed while mending *another* pair by the sight of 'Gyb our cat in the milke pan'. The difficulty rests in getting Hodge out of one pair of torn breeches into the other which contains the needle, and I suspect that this is why the dramatist was at pains to have him foul his original pair at the end of Act II, scene 1, making it credible that he should return in scene 3 wearing the pair that Gammer Gurton 'swapt' down. True, there is no indication in the dialogue or stage-directions that Hodge does make such a change, but it appears to be the only solution to a genuine problem of staging.

Many misconceptions cling to *Gammer Gurton's Nedle*: it is said to be mere scatological farce; to involve a storm in a tea-cup; to be 'a college-man's indulgent laugh at unlearned country folk' (Bevington). The first charge seems negligible: the author is genre-painting, not glorying in excrement. Admittedly, the play offers a virtuoso display of linguistic hyperbole and extravagant behaviour, but one doubts if the playwright was guilty of patronizing his lively personages in their honest innocence, or that he dismissed the loss of a needle as trifling in itself. The emphasis is rather laid on the chain-reaction of ferocious passions unleashed by Diccon's manipulation of the domestic crisis. Not that there is much moral purpose behind the laughter: though Diccon is the archetypal sardonic 'outsider', who acknowledges no authority and is accountable to no one, his aim is not to castigate *bourgeois* society or to expose it as a hot-bed of envy and suspicion, but like Merrygreek to create 'sport' for the community's and his own enjoyment. He is an odd choice as a comic protagonist, the medieval Vice brought up-to-date and yet as far removed from Shakespeare's 'Poor Tom' as it is possible to imagine. It is perhaps significant that his lack of mental stability is never referred to or called in question, yet there is a kind of savage glee about his conduct at times, which only adds to the fascination of this dynamic and occasionally disturbing comedy.

Like the authors of *Jacke Jugeler* and *Gammer Gurton's Nedle*, and Nicholas Udall, John Lyly (*c.* 1554–1606) came to drama from an educated background, and like theirs his comedies were mainly written for private performance by youthful players. Leaving Oxford, baulked of a fellowship, he made his literary reputation in 1578 with *Euphues: The Anatomy of Wit*, whose elaborately wrought style 'influenced a generation'. Not long after he joined the household of Edward De Vere, Earl of Oxford, Elizabethan courtier, and, according to some scholars, author of Shakespeare's plays. The staging at court of Lyly's earliest comedies, *Campaspe* and *Sapho and Phao*, in January and March 1584, was part of the Earl's efforts to ingratiate himself with the Queen, and it was 'Oxford's Boys', a troupe combining the Children of the Chapel Royal, choristers from Oxford's own chapel, and pupils from St Paul's choir-school, who performed them. At other times the boys played – still under the Earl's patronage – at the tiny coterie playhouse at Blackfriars, in which Lyly had a financial interest. When the company was deprived of its base there around Easter 1584, the dramatist still retained his links with the Children of Paul's, for in January and February 1588 the boys were at court once more, presenting Lyly's *Gallathea* and *Endimion*, followed in January 1590 by his *Midas*, partly meant to satirize Philip of Spain. Such plays may have formed part of their normal repertoire at their own theatre, possibly in St Paul's chapter-house, or else were specially written for command performance. *Love's Metamorphosis*, written during this period, also reads like a play for court presentation, but there is no evidence that it was ever staged there, any more than its two successors, *Mother Bombie* and *The Woman in the Moon*. At about the time these pieces were composed, the Children of Paul's were officially inhibited from continuing their performances, and Lyly seems never to have written for the stage again. He drifted somewhat forlornly through the last decade of the century, dying in November 1606.

Like Congreve, Wilde, and Shaw, Lyly is one of the supreme stylists of the English stage, and his contribution to forging an idiom for Elizabethan comedy (much as Marlowe did for tragedy) is often underestimated. His courtly comedies, for all their elegant display of allegorical allusion and tasteful compliment, are solidly built on classical principles, and their witty supercharged dialogue complements wellmade plots and well-balanced contrasts of viewpoint. The fact that his pieces reflect a departed world of court rivalries and intrigues is now immaterial: the lyric beauty of romantic comedies such as *Gallathea* and *Endimion* transcends mere topical relevance, as Lyly puts his familiarity with classical mythology to work in creating enchanted landscapes whose appeal goes beyond their reflection of some political situation or factious controversy. Their outstanding asset remains their verbal texture; though mannered and artificial, it blends so perfectly with the dream-like atmosphere of its context that it rarely cloys as it does when we encounter its antithetical, alliterative, self-conscious obliqueness in the pages of *Euphues* or its sequel.

Much has been said of Lyly's style: its origins, its strengths and weaknesses, its influence, and its legacy. It is sometimes argued that it is only suited to a rarefied and enclosed dramatic universe intended to appeal to the exalted in rank and the refined in taste, but there is a little more to Lyly's manner than this. As Jocelyn Powell has demonstrated in a perceptive essay, this fanciful idiom invites us to take pleasure in 'the language of play' which serves no utilitarian purpose, except to delight us with the ingeniousness of its conceits, the extravagance of its imagery, and the sheer variety of a universe which supplies it with its diversity of materials. Thus

Lyly's work, while anticipating the abstruse analogies and bizarre correspondences of the Metaphysicals, also connects with the world of 'sport and play' that characterizes earlier Tudor comedies.

Mother Bombie is, of course, less specific in its appeal than that of Lyly's attested court comedies; as part of the fare offered to the less esoteric, though no less erudite clientele of Paul's Boys, it is set in the world of everyday life – actually in Lyly's native Kent – and its language rejects the evocation of mystery and magic in favour of more domesticated preoccupations. Certainly it is the closest its author ever came to writing a traditional comedy on Plautine lines: here we find the successors to the cheeky wags of *Jacke Jugeler* and *Roister Doister*; here are the frustrated lovers and gulled fathers of the classical convention; here is the last-minute sorting out of paternities which effects the fifth-act revelations which are the hallmark of classical comedy. Yet again the whole scheme is successfully transplanted to an English site, where it retains the attraction of a complex dance sequence in which, after a series of intricate figures, each of the company arrives in the correct position. *Mother Bombie* is Lyly's least idiosyncratic play, yet it could scarcely have been evolved by anyone else, so perfectly is the playfulness of its patterned plot married to the carefully contrived elegant toughness of its playful language.

VI

The revolution in staging practice taking place in Western Europe during the Renaissance is too extensive to be summarized here, but some understanding of the manner in which these plays were presented must obviously enhance their appreciation on the printed page. Implied or overt references to the presence of spectators make it clear that players in the sixteenth century still enjoyed a far more intimate relationship with their audiences than they expect today. This was inevitable when plays were performed in settings which brought actors and auditors into close contact – the halls of

Oxford and Cambridge colleges, the assembly areas of Tudor schools, the halls or presence-chambers of royal palaces or noble houses, the guildhalls of towns and cities, were all pressed into service in Tudor times. Only Lyly's comedies were presented in anything resembling a regular playhouse, and they too were adapted on occasion to fit auditoria designed for other ends.

This tradition established the custom of players addressing spectators directly, apologizing to them, requesting them to make room for entries or action to take place, appealing to them for advice or for their collusion in some piece of knavery. Hodge can thus appeal to the crowd to 'stand out ones way' before he strikes out at Dame Chat; Jenkin Careaway can pass among the audience looking for Jack Juggler, complaining that 'Many here smell strong but none so ranke as he'. This easy familiarity with which he and Jack himself, Diccon and Merrygreek, acknowledge the assembled company may spring from the example supplied by the morality Vice or the characters of the cycle plays, or those accustomed to the proximity of the audience at banquet-hall interludes, but it is worth recalling that 'direct address' is a feature of many plays in the Plautine canon too. Indeed, it is common to any form of theatre which makes no attempt to pretend that the spectacle which is being presented on stage is likely to be mistaken for reality.

Nonetheless, as Professor A. M. Nagler has stressed, sixteenth-century stage conventions represent a blend of competing influences, and something of the hybrid nature of English Renaissance presentations is reflected in the staging of these comedies. In some perhaps no attempt at dramatic illusion would be made at all. It would have been impossible where methods such as those employed at Lambeth Palace in 1497 for staging Medwall's *Fulgens and Lucres* were adopted. Here the acting area consisted of the space before the High Table, the areas between the tables at floor-level and in front of the openings in the wooden screen which separated dining-hall from buttery and kitchen. This mode of staging with its accent on close audience-contact and the imaginative use of unpretentious facilities would certainly suit *Jacke Jugeler* with its interlude-like economies of plot and character, and its relatively simple scenic requirements, namely a practicable entrance door for Bongrace's house and an open platform or floor area. Yet the other comedies printed here need rather more elaborate settings, and all four may have utilized the conventions believed to have pertained in the theatres of ancient Rome.

On this topic the observations of Vitruvius, the Roman writer on architecture, were central; his lengthy and influential treatise, *De architectura*, published in 1486, helped reinforce the trend towards unity of artistic effect and scenic illusion in the theatre towards which Italian stage-designers were striving under the impact of the rediscovery of perspective. As George R. Kernodle points out:

> Where the Middle Ages had been content with many disparate units or details which were only loosely bound together, the new age felt that these units or details must be organized into some kind of unity ...
>
> (*From Art to Theatre*, Chicago, 1944, p. 14)

We have already seen this principle at work in the field of dramatic construction, and it also affected the manner in which Renaissance plays were staged. Vitruvius' description of a typical Roman theatre setting, in which a scenic façade at the rear of the stage offered players exit and entrance arches as well as access at the sides of the platform, was highly influential, encouraging neoclassical playwrights to organize their action so that only a single permanent location was needed. This, coupled with the desire to adhere to the so-called Aristotelian 'unities' of time, place, and action, led eventually to the establishment of the conventions of dramatic realism which sought to secure an impression of actuality on stage. While English playwrights, especially those writing for the Elizabethan popular playhouse, did not adhere to these conventions as many Italian and French dramatists chose to do, it is significant that all the comedies in the present volume assume the creation of the conventional classical stage-setting, namely a street-scene consisting of an open space backed by one or more 'citizens' houses'.

These scenic units could be suggested by the openings in the hall-screens, or by building actual settings either on the dais at one end of the hall, or on a low temporary platform erected against the screens at the other end. The screen openings could easily be employed as doorways, provided these were all the dramatic action required. On the other hand, as T. W. Craik suggests, mere openings would prove inadequate for Custance's house in *Roister Doister* or the two cottages in *Gammer Gurton*. Probably for these plays a street setting was constructed on semi-representational lines, the 'houses' being simple but solid structures, especially if Hodge had to appear at an upstairs window when searching for the cat. *Mother Bombie* also requires practicable 'houses'; even if the tavern were suggested by a mere doorway, the houses of Memphio and Sperantus would need to be constructed, as both require upper storeys, unless galleries after the manner of the Elizabethan public playhouses were available for use. The visual comedy of Dr Rat's intrusion into Dame Chat's residence would obviously be more effective if there were actually a practicable entry 'on the backside' by which he could creep in. But it is unlikely that anything very complex was envisaged, and certainly no effort was expended to achieve total scenic illusion.

Indeed, there is little doubt that the original staging of these comedies would have been unambitious by twentieth-century standards. Yet one may guarantee that the finished production did not suffer by it, since the accent could the more readily be placed on the performances and not the *mise-en-scène*. The relatively plentiful acting resources of schools and colleges would enable playwrights to provide a generous range of parts to suit individual talents, and to develop character roles without that concern for doubling which preoccupied the small professional troupes. The verve and exuberance of the writing triumphed over anything remotely elementary about the plays' mounting, a testimony to the writers' confidence in their casts. The prominence given to the virtuoso and demanding roles of Jenkin and Jack, Merrygreek and Roister Doister, Diccon, Hodge, and the two 'gammers', the quartets of precocious pages and crafty old men in *Mother Bombie*, leaves one in little doubt that their original performers needed few lessons in 'good behaviour and audacitye'.

A GUIDE TO FURTHER READING

The bibliography which follows is far from exhaustive; I have simply listed those works which I have found of most value while editing the texts and writing the Introduction. Fuller details may be sought in the *New Cambridge Bibliography*, in Stratman's *Bibliography of Mediaeval Drama*, in the *Revels History of Drama in English*, and in the *Oxford History of English Literature*, all cited below. Data concerning other editions of the plays reprinted in *Four Tudor Comedies* are given in the introduction to each separate work. Place of publication is London unless otherwise indicated.

Bibliographies and Reference Works

W. W. Greg, ed., *A Bibliography of English Printed Drama to the Restoration*, 4 vols., 1939–59.

A. Harbage, ed., *Annals of English Drama, 975–1700*, Philadelphia, 1940; revised S. Schoenbaum, 1964.

Carl J. Stratman, ed., *A Bibliography of Mediaeval Drama*, Berkeley, 1954; rev. ed., 2 vols., New York, 1972.

George Watson, ed., *The New Cambridge Bibliography of English Literature: I, 600–1660*, Cambridge, 1974.

M. P. Tilley, *A Dictionary of the Proverbs in England in the Sixteenth and Seventeenth Centuries*, Ann Arbor, 1950.

B. J. Whiting, *Proverbs in the Earlier English Drama*, Cambridge, Mass., 1938.

B. J. and H. W. Whiting, *Proverbs, Sentences, and Proverbial Phrases from English Writings Mainly before 1500*, Cambridge, Mass., 1968.

F. P. Wilson, *The Oxford Dictionary of English Proverbs*, rev. ed., 1970.

General Works on Comedy

R. W. Corrigan, ed., *Comedy: Meaning and Form*, San Francisco, 1965.

Northrop Frye, *The Anatomy of Criticism*, Princeton, 1957.

W. D. Howarth ed., *Comic Drama: The European Heritage*, 1978.

P. Lauter, ed., *Theories of Comedy*, New York, 1964.

W. M. Merchant, *Comedy*, 1972.

Elder Olsen, *The Theory of Comedy*, Bloomington, 1968.

Classical Comedy

Michael Anderson, 'The comedy of Greece and Rome', in Howarth, ed., *Comic Drama: The European Heritage*, 1978, pp. 22–39.

W. Beare, *The Roman Stage*, 1950; rev. ed., 1964 (esp. chapters 5–8, 11–12).

T. A. Dorey and Donald R. Dudley, eds., *Roman Drama*, 1965 (esp. chapters 2–4).

G. E. Duckworth, *The Nature of Roman Comedy*, Princeton, 1952.

G. Norwood, *The Art of Terence*, Oxford, 1923.

E. Segal, *Roman Laughter: The Comedy of Plautus*, Cambridge, Mass., 1968.

Early Tudor Comedy

Joel B. Altman, *The Tudor Play of Mind*, Berkeley, 1978.

David M. Bevington, *From 'Mankind' to Marlowe: Growth and Structure in the Popular Drama of Tudor England*, Cambridge, Mass., 1962.

Tudor Drama and Politics: A Critical Approach to Topical Meaning, Cambridge, Mass., 1968.

F. S. Boas, *An Introduction to Tudor Drama*, Oxford, 1933.

J. V. Curry, *Deception in Elizabethan Comedy*, Chicago, 1955.

William G. McCollom, 'From dissonance to harmony: the

evolution of early English comedy', *Theatre Annual* 21 (1964), pp. 69–96.

A. P. Rossiter, *English Drama from Early Times to the Elizabethans*, 1950.

Norman Sanders and others, *The Revels History of Drama in English*: II, *1500–76*, 1980.

F. P. Wilson, *The English Drama 1485–1585* (*Oxford History of English Literature*, IV, 1), Oxford, 1969.

The Classical Heritage

T. W. Baldwin, *William Shakspere's Five-Act Structure*, Urbana, 1947. *William Shakspere's Small Latine and Lesse Greeke*, 2 vols., Urbana, 1944.

D. G. Boughner, *The Braggart in Renaissance Comedy*, Minneapolis, 1954.

Laurence Bradner, 'The Latin drama of the Renaissance (1340–1640)', *Studies in the Renaissance* 4 (1957), pp. 31–54. 'The rise of secular drama in the Renaissance', *Studies in the Renaissance* 3 (1956), pp. 7–22.

C. C. Coulter, 'The Plautine tradition in Shakespeare', *Journal of English and Germanic Philology* 19 (1920), pp. 60–83.

Richard Hosley, 'The formal influence of Plautus and Terence', in J. R. Brown and Bernard Harris, eds., *Elizabethan Theatre*, Stratford-on-Avon Studies 9 (1966), pp. 130–45.

L. G. Salingar, *Shakespeare and the Traditions of Comedy*, Cambridge, 1974.

B. R. Smith, 'Sir Amorous Knight and the indecorous Romans; or, Plautus and Terence in the Renaissance', *Renaissance Drama*, n.s. 6 (1973), pp. 3–27.

J. A. K. Thomson, *Shakespeare and the Classics*, 1952.

John W. Velz, *Shakespeare and the Classical Tradition: A Critical Guide to Commentary*, Minneapolis, 1968.

General Background

M. C. Bradbrook, *The Growth and Structure of Elizabethan Comedy*, Cambridge, 1955.

Madeleine Doran, *Endeavors of Art: A Study of Form in Elizabethan Drama*, Madison, 1963.

Marvin T. Herrick, *Comic Theory in the Sixteenth Century*, Urbana, 1950.

Italian Comedy in the Renaissance, Urbana, 1969.

B. K. Jeffery, *French Renaissance Comedy 1552–1630*, Oxford, 1969.

Individual Plays

JACKE JUGELER

G. Dudok, 'Has *Jack Juggler* been written by the same author as *Ralph Roister Doister?*', *Neophilologus* 1 (1916), pp. 50–62.

R. Marienstras, '*Jack Juggler*: aspects de la conscience individuelle dans une farce du 16e siècle', *Études anglaises* 16 (1963), pp. 321–32.

Jacques Voisine, 'A propos de *Jack Juggler*', *Études anglaises* 18 (1965), p. 166 (see also Marienstras's reply, pp. 167–8).

W. H. Williams, 'The date and authorship of *Jacke Jugeler*', *Modern Language Review* 7 (1912), pp. 289–95.

ROISTER DOISTER

W. L. Edgerton, 'The date of *Roister Doister*', *Philological Quarterly* 44 (1965), pp. 555–60.

Nicholas Udall, New York, 1966.

D. L. Maulsby, 'The relation between Udall's *Roister Doister* and the comedies of Plautus and Terence', *Englische Studien* 38 (1907), pp. 251–77.

Edwin S. Miller, 'Roister Doister's "Funeralls"', *Studies in Philology* 43 (1946), pp. 42–58.

A. R. Moon, 'Was Nicholas Udall the author of *Thersites?*', *The Library*, 4th series, 7 (1926), pp. 184–93.

T. H. V. Motter, *The School Drama in England*, 1929; reprinted New York, 1968.

William Peery, 'The prayer for the Queen in *Roister Doister*', *University of Texas Studies in English* 27 (1948), pp. 222–3.

A. W. Plumstead,' Satirical parody in *Roister Doister*: a reinterpretation', *Studies in Philology* 60 (1963), pp. 141–54.

A. W. Reed, 'Udall and Thomas Wilson', *Review of English Studies* 1 (1925), pp. 275–83.

GAMMER GURTON'S NEDLE

F. S. Boas, *University Drama in the Tudor Age*, Oxford, 1914.

Anthony Graham-White, 'Elizabethan punctuation and the actor: *Gammer Gurton's Needle* as a case study', *Theatre Journal* 34 (1982), pp. 96–106.

R. W. Ingram, '*Gammer Gurton's Needle*: comedy not quite of the lowest order?' *Studies in English Literature 1500–1900* 8 (1968), pp. 257–68.

William B. Toole, 'The aesthetics of scatology in *Gammer Gurton's Needle*', *English Language Notes* 11 (1973), pp. 252–8.

H. A. Watt, 'The staging of *Gammer Gurton's Nedle*', in *Elizabethan Studies in Honour of G. F. Reynolds*, Boulder, 1945.

THE PLAYS OF JOHN LYLY

Jonas A. Barish, 'The prose style of John Lyly', *English Literary History* 23 (1956), pp. 14–35.

Michael R. Best, 'The staging and production of the plays of John Lyly', *Theatre Research* 9 (1968), pp. 104–17.

R. Warwick Bond, Introduction to *The Complete Works of John Lyly*, 3 vols., Oxford, 1902; reprinted 1967.

Joseph Houppert, *John Lyly*, New York, 1975.

G. K. Hunter, *John Lyly: the Humanist as Courtier*, 1962.

Walter N. King, 'John Lyly and Elizabethan rhetoric', *Studies in Philology* 52 (1955), pp. 149–61.

Marco Mincoff, 'Shakespeare and Lyly', *Shakespeare Survey* 14 (1961), pp. 15–24.

Jocelyn Powell, 'Lyly and the language of play', in J. R. Brown and Bernard Harris, eds., *Elizabethan Theatre*, *Stratford-on-Avon Studies* 9 (1966), pp. 146–67.

Peter Saccio, *The Court Comedies of Lyly: a Study in Allegorical Dramaturgy*, Princeton, 1969 (chiefly devoted to *Campaspe* and *Gallathea*).

General Works on Staging

T. W. Craik, *The Tudor Interlude*, Leicester, 1958.

A. M. Nagler, 'Sixteenth-century Continental stages', *Shakespeare Quarterly* 5 (1954), pp. 359–70.

Richard Southern, *The Staging of Plays before Shakespeare*, London, 1973.

William Tydeman, *The Theatre in the Middle Ages*, Cambridge, 1978.

Translations

Plautus, *The Rope and Other Plays*, translated by E. F. Watling, Harmondsworth, 1964 (contains the *Amphitruo*).
The Pot of Gold and Other Plays, translated by E. F. Watling, Harmondsworth, 1965 (contains the *Miles gloriosus*).

Terence, *The Brothers and Other Plays*, translated by Betty Radice, Harmondsworth, 1965 (contains the *Eunuchus*).
Phormio and Other Plays, translated by Betty Radice, Harmondsworth, 1967.

A NOTE ON THE TEXTS

In preparing these comedies for publication I have steered a course between supplying the general reader (or performer) with a readable (or actable) play, and offering the student of literature (or drama) a completely accurate picture of the earliest texts as they appear on the page. My solution has been to retain as much of the original versions as possible, but to add to or subtract from them where they are obviously in error or where they seem likely to cause difficulty or uncertainty to those not trained to cope with sixteenth-century publications in the raw. I have not felt it sensible, for example, to retain the original punctuation, since without modern pointing Tudor English can become a jungle of ambiguities; yet even here I have tried to practise restraint. Some still argue that the original punctuation offers an essential clue to the way the lines were delivered, and should therefore be retained, but I am far from convinced that Tudor printing practice reflects playhouse technique. At all events, to reproduce the punctuation of the originals would only alarm or irritate the average reader.

Since Tudor dramatists were never concerned to supply stage-directions in the quantity or detail that modern readers of plays are accustomed to, I have added supplementary rubrics of my own in order to clarify situations which might prove potentially puzzling, and I have on occasion repositioned an original direction such as an entrance or exit cue where it affects the stage situation. These, and all other textual adjustments of an editorial nature, are placed within the customary square brackets to distinguish them, but what appear to me to be obvious errors I have corrected silently.

The typeface used for the original texts (black-letter or Gothic in the case of all but *Mother Bombie*) has been replaced by modern roman or italic as appropriate; proper names printed in italic have been converted to roman type and to capitals in stage-directions as is the modern custom. 'Old spelling' has, however, been retained for the texts except for a few conventional alterations, and the Glossary has been expanded accordingly. It may be of general assistance to remember that Tudor spelling, although inconsistent, was basically phonetic, and that a word which looks odd is frequently a familiar term in a strange disguise. Exceptions to the 'old spelling' rule are those generally accepted: 'u' and 'j' are substituted for 'v' and 'i' and *vice versa* to comply with modern practice; 'ff' for 'f' and 'vv' for 'w' disappear, as does long 's'. Abbreviations and numerals both roman and arabic are spelt out in full without comment; the use of capital letters (both in stage-directions and generally) and the divisions of words follow the present-day pattern.

Unfamiliar words and phrases are glossed at the foot of each page, and are usually repeated unless they recur within a brief interval of their most recent appearance; a complete glossary is included at the end of the book. More complex explanations and additional commentary are provided in the Notes, which are organized by reference to the line numbering of each text. Notes on points of purely textual interest have been provided only sparingly.

ACKNOWLEDGEMENTS

I should like to thank the General Editor of the Penguin English Library, Donald McFarlan, for his interest and encouragement; my former colleague Vivien Thomas with whom I discussed the contents of this collection, and above all, my wife, who not only sacrificed my company for almost a whole summer, but also cheerfully compiled the Glossary.

*

The title-page of the First Quarto edition of *Jacke Jugeler* is reproduced by permission of the Rosenbach Museum and Library, Philadelphia, USA; the title-page of the Second Quarto edition is reproduced by permission of the Henry E. Huntington Library and Art Gallery, San Marino, California, USA. The title-pages of *Gammer Gurton's Nedle* and *Mother Bombie* are reproduced by permission of the Bodleian Library, Oxford.

Jacke Jugeler

A new Enterlued for
Chyldren to playe, named Iacke Iugeler, both
wytte, very playsent and merye, Neuer
before Imprentede.

The Players names.
Maysters. Boungrace.   A galant
Dame coye.   A Gentelwoman
Iacke Iugler.   the vyce.
Ienkin careaway   A Lackey.
Ales trype and go   A mayd.

Iak iugler   M. boûgrace   Dame coye.

Facsimile of the title-page to the First Quarto edition of *c.* 1562

Facsimile of the title-page to the Second Quarto edition of *c.* 1565–9

Evidence exists for believing that at least two editions of *Jacke Jugeler* were printed during the 1560s, each in all probability from the press of William Copland, who died in 1568–9. The first seems to have appeared in November 1562, for an entry in the Stationers' Company Register for around that date reads:

Recevyd of William Coplande for his lycense for pryntinge of an interlude intituled Iack Iuggeler & m[rs.] boundgrace   iiij[d.]

That this entry refers to the first edition appears likely, since the same mistake of putting 'Maysters Boungrace' for 'Mayster Boungrace' occurs both in the Register entry and on the title-page, where the 'new Enterlued' is said to be one 'Never before Imprented'. This version of the text remained unknown until the sale of the Mostyn Library in March 1919; it later formed the basis for the Malone Society reprint of 1933 and is now in the library of the Rosenbach Foundation, Philadelphia.

Another edition, announced as 'Newly Imprented', came from Copland's press, probably between 1565 and his death; it is closely based on the first edition, and is now in the Henry E. Huntington Library at San Marino, California. In the same library is a two-leaf fragment, evidently detached from a further edition, published around 1570 by John Allde, of which a complete copy is now housed in the Folger Shakespeare Library, Washington. It has been suggested that this probably represents a revised version of the second surviving edition.

Several previous editions of *Jacke Jugeler* have been published during this century; the chief are:

J. S. Farmer, ed., *Anonymous Plays*, Early English Dramatists, 1907

Jack Juggler, Tudor Facsimile Texts, 1912

W. H. Williams, ed., *Jack Juggler*, Cambridge, 1914

Eunice Lilian Smart and W. W. Greg, *Jack Juggler*, Malone Society Reprints, 1933 (text taken from the First Quarto). The present edition is based on that of Smart and Greg, with some use made of Farmer's edition of 1907 and 1912 and of readings from the quarto of 1565–9.

A new Enterlued for
Chyldren to playe named Jacke Jugeler, both
wytte, very playsent and merye, Never
before Imprented.

The Players names.

MAYSTERS BOUNGRACE	*A Galant*
DAME COYE	*A Gentelwoman*
JACKE JUGLER	*The Vyce*
JENKIN CAREAWAY	*A Lackey*
ALES TRYPE AND GO	*A Mayd*

Maysters: Mistress (an obvious error, corrected to 'Mayster' in the second edition) *The Vyce*: see Introduction, pp. 9–35 above   *A Lackey*: a servant or footman, employed chiefly to run errands

51

JACKE JUGELER

The Prologue

[*Enter the* PROLOGUE.]
[PROLOGUE:] *Interpone tuis interdum gaudia curis,*
  Ut possis animo quemvis sufferre laborem.
Doo any of you knowe what Latyne is this,
Or ells wold you have an *expositorem*
To declare it in Englyshe *per sensum planiorem*?
It is best I speak Englyshe or ells within a whylle
I may percace myne own selfe with my Latin begile.

The two verses which I rehersid before
I finde writen in the boke of Cato the wyse
Emongs good precepts of lyving a thousand more,   *10*
Which to folowe there he doth all men avise,
And they may be Englyshed breflie in this wise:
Emongs thy carfull busines use sumetime mirth
    and joye
That no bodilye worke thy wytts breke or noye.

For the mynd (saith he), in serius matters
    occupied,
If it have not sum quiet mirthe and recreacion
Interchaungeablie admixed, must niddes be sone
    weried,
And (as who should saye) tried through continual
    operacion
Of labour and busines without relaxacion:
Therfor intermix honest mirthe in suche wise   *20*
That your strength may be refreshid, and to
    labours suffise.

1–2 *Interpone tuis*, etc: see note   7 *percace*: perhaps   8 *rehersid*: quoted   11 *avise*: advise
14 *noye*: harm   17 *niddes*: needs, necessarily

For as meat and drinke, naturall rest and slype
For the conservacion and helth of the bodye
Must niddes be had, soo the mynd and wittes to kype
Pregnant, freshe, industrius, quike and lustie,
Honest mirthe and pastime is requisite and necessarie,
For *Quod caret alterna requie durabile non est*:
Nothyng may endure (saith Ovyd) without sum rest.

Example proufe herof in erth is well founde
30   Manifest, open, and verie evident;
For except the husbandman suffer his ground
Sumtymes to rest, it woll bere no frute verament:
Therfore they lcat the filde lye everie second yere
To the end that aftir rest it may the better corne
    beare.

Thus than (as I have sayed) it is a thing naturall
And naturallie belonging to all living creatures
And unto man especiallie above others all,
To have at tymes convenient, pastaunce, mirthe
    and pleasurs,
So they be joynid with honestie and keape within
    due mesars,
40   And the same well allowen not onlye the said Cato,
But also the Philosophers, Plutarke, Socrates and
    Plato.

And Cicero Tullius, a man sapient and wyse,
Willeth the same in that his first boke
Which he wrot and entytelid Of an Honest Man's
    Office,
(Whoso is disposid therupon to looke)
Wher to define and affirme he boldlie on him tooke,
That to heare Enterluds is pastime convenient
For all maner men, and a thing congruent.

---

22 *slype*: sleep 24 *kype*: keep 25 *Pregnant*: fertile *lustie*: vigorous 27 *Quod caret* etc: see
note 32 *verament*: truly 35 *than*: then 39 *mesars*: measure, bounds 40 *allowen*: allow

He rekeneth that namelie as a verie honest disport,
And above all other thinges commendeth the old
    commedie,   *50*
The hearing of which may doo the mynd cumfort,
For they be replenished with precepts of
    Philosophie,
They conteine mutch wisdome and teache prudent
    pollecie
And though thei be al writen of mattiers of non
    importaunce
Yet they shew great wite and mutch pretie
    conveiaunce.

And in this maner of making Plautus did excell
As recordeth the same Tullius commending him bi
    name;
Wherfore this maker deliteth passinglie well
Too folow his arguments and to draw out the same
For to make at seasuns convenient pastims mirth and
    game,   *60*
As now he hath don this matter not worthe an oyster
    shel
Except percace it shall fortune too make you laugh
    well.

And for that purpose oonlye this maker did it write
Taking the ground therof out of Plautus' first
    commedie,
And the first scentence of the same for higher
    things endite
In no wise he wold, for yet the tyme is so quesie
That he that speakith best is lest thankeworthie;
Therfore sithe nothing but trifles may be had
You shall heare a thing that onlie shal make you
    merie and glad,

49 *namelie*: especially, particularly   55 *wite*: wit *pretie conveiaunce*: felicity of expression
56 *making*: literary composition   58 *this maker*: the present author   62 *percace*: perhaps
64 *ground*: basis   66 *quesie*: unsettled   68 *sithe*: since, seeing that

70   And suche a trifling matter as when it shalbe done
You may report and saye ye have hearde nothing
    at all:
Therfore I tell you all before it bee begone
That no man looke to heare of mattiers
    substancyall
Nor mattiers of any gravitee either great or small,
For this maker shewed us that such maner things
Doo never well besime litle boyes' handelings.

Wherfore yf ye wyl not sowrelie your broues bend
At suche a fantasticall conceite as this
But can be content to heare and see the ende,
80   I woll goo shew the actours what your pleasure is,
Which to wait upoon you I know bee redie or this:
I woll goo send them hither intoo your presens
Desiryng that they may have quiet audience.

    [*Exit the* PROLOGUE. *Enter* JACK JUGGLER.]
JAKE JUGLER: Our lord of hevene and swite Saint
    Jhone
Rest you merye my maistirs everychone,
And I praie too Christ and swete Saint Steven
Send you all many a good evine!
And you to, syr, and you, and you also,
Good evine to you an hunderid times and a
    thousand mo!
90   Now by all thes crosses of fleshe, bone, and blod,
I rekine my chaunce right marvylus good
Here now to find all this cumpanie
Which in my mynd I wyshed for hartylie,
For I have labored all daye tyll I am werie
And now am disposed too passe the tyme and be
    merie.
And I thinke noon of you but he wold doo the
    same,

---

76 *besime*: beseem, suit   81 *or*: ere, before   84 *swite*: sweet   85 *everychone*: everyone   88 *to*:
too, also   91 *rekine*: reckon

For who wol be sad, and nedithe not, is foull to
    blame!
And as for me, of my mother I have byn tought
To bee merie when I may, and take no thought,
Which leasune I bare so well awaye   *100*
That I use to make merie oons a daie.
And now if all things happin ryght
You shall see as mad a pastime this night
As you saw this seven yers – and as propre a toye
As ever you saw played of a boye!
I am called Jake Jugler of many an oon
And in fayth I woll playe a jugling cast anon;
I woll cungere the moull and God before
Or elles leat me lese my name for ever more!
I have it devised and compacced hou   *110*
And what wayes I woll tell and shew to you.
You all know well Maister Baungrace,
The gentilman that dwellith here in this place,
And Jenkine Carreawaie his page, as cursed a lad
And as ungracious as ever man had,
An unhappy wage, and as folishe a knave withall
As any is now within London Wall.
This Jenkine and I been fallen at great debate
For a mattier that fell betwine us a late,
And hitherto of him I could never revengid bee   *120*
For his maister mentainyth him and lovethe not mee.
(Albeit the very truth to tell
Nother of them both knoweth me verie well)
But against all other boyes the said gentleman
Mayntenyth him all that he can.
But I shall set litle by my wyte
If I do not Jenkine this night requite;
Ere I slepe Jenkine shall here bee mete

---

97 *sad*: possibly 'solemn', rather than 'sorrowful'   100 *leasune*: lesson   104 *as propre a toye*:
as perfect a trick   107 *a jugling cast*: a deceptive contrivance   108 *cungere*: bewitch, baffle
108 *moull*: mole (which is of course blind)   109 *lese*: lose   116 *An unhappy wage*:
mischievous lad (wag)   119 *a late*: of late, recently   121 *mentainyth*: defends, supports

And I trust to cume partlye out of his dete
130 And whan we mete againe, if this do not suffise
I shall paie Jenkine the residue, in my best wyse.
It chaunced me right now in the other end of the
next stret
Withe Jenkine and his maistire in the face to met;
I abod ther awhille plaing for to see
At the buklers, as wel becommed mee –
It was not long tyme, but at the last
Bake cumithe my cosune Careawaye homward ful
fast,
Pricking, praunsing, and springing in his short cote,
And pleasauntlie synging with a mery note.
140 'Whyther awaye so fast? tary a while,' sayed oon;
'I cannot now,' sayd Jenkine, 'I must nides been
goon;
My maister suppeth herbie at a gentylman's place
And I must thither feache my dame, Maistres
Boundgrace,
But yet er I go I care not motche
At the bukelers to playe with the oon faire toche.'
To it they went and plaied so long
Tyll Jenkine thought he had wrong:
'By Coke's precious potstike, I wyll not home this
nyght!'
Quod he, 'but as good a stripe oon thie hed light!'
150 Within halfe an houre or sumewhat lese
Jenkine lefte playng, and went to feache his
maisteris,
But by the waie he met with a freuter's wife;
Ther Jenkine and she fell at suche strife
For snatching of an apple, that doune he cast
Her basket, and gatherid up the apples fast

134–5 *plaing . . . At the buklers*: fencing (sword-play) 137 *cosune*: 'friend' 138 *Pricking*:
pressing forward 141 *nides*: needs 144 *I care not motche*: I don't mind if 148 *Coke's*:
God's *potstike*: a stick for stirring with (but see note) 152 *freuter*: fruiterer

And put them in his sleve, then came he his waye
By another lane as fast as he maye,
Tyll he came at a corner by a shoop's stall
Wher boies were at dice, faryng at all.
When Careawaye with that good cumpany met,   *160*
He fell to faring withouten let,
Forgettyng his message, and so well dyd he fare
That whan I came bye, he gan swere and stare
And ful bitterly began to curse
As oone that had lost almost all in his porse.
For I knowe his olde gise and condicyon
Never to leave tyll all his mony bee goon,
For he hath noo mony but what he doth stell
And that woll he plaie awaie every dell.
I passed by, and then called unto my mynd   *170*
Sertayne old rekeaninges that were behind
Bitwene Jenkine and me, whom partelie to
    recompense
I trust by God's grace, ere I goo hens.
This garments – cape, and all other geare
That now you see apon me here –
I have doon oon all like unto his
For the nons, and my purpose is
To make Jenkine bylive if I can
That he is not himselfe but another man!
For except he hath better loke then he had   *180*
He woll cum hyther starke staryng mad;
When he shall cum I woll handle my captine soo
That he shal not well wott whether too goo.
His maisteris I know she woll him blame
And his maistir also wyll doo the same,
Bycause that she of her supper deceivid is –
For I am sure they have all supped by thys!

159 *faryng*: playing at fare (see note)   161 *withouten let*: without restraint   168 *stell*: steal
169 *dell*: deal, bit, piece   174 *cape*: cap   176 *doon oon*: put on, dressed myself   177 *For the
nons*: for the time being, for the purpose   180 *loke*: luck   182 *captine*: captain (ironic)

But and if Jenkyne wold hither resort,
I trust he and I should make sum sport –
Yf I had sooner spokine he wold have sooner been
190 here
For mysimithe I doo his voice heare.
 [JACK JUGGLER *retires. Enter* JENKIN
 CAREAWAY.]

CAREAWAYE: A syr, I may saie I have been at a fest!
I have lost two shillings and syxpence at the lest!
Mary syr, of this gaynes I nyd make no bost,
But the dyvell goo with all, more have I lost!
My name is Careawaie – let all sorow passe –
I woll ere toomorow night be as rich as ever I was
Or at the forthest within a day or twaine:
Me mayster's purse shall paye me agayne.
200 Therfor hogh, Careawaie, now wol I sing, hei hey!
But bi the Lorde, now I remembre another thing –
By my fayth, Jenkine, my maisteris and thou
Ar lyke too agree God knowith hou,
That thou comest not for her incontinent
To bryng hir too supper when thou wer sent!
And now they have all supped thou wolt shurlie abye
Except thou imagine sum pretie and craftye lye,
For she is as all other weomen bee,
A verie cursed shrew, by the blessid Trinitie,
210 And a verye divell, for yf she oons begine
To fight or chyd in a weke she wol not lyne;
And a great pleasure she hath specyally now of late
To gette poore me now and then by the pate,
For she is an angrie pece of fleshe and sone
  displeasyd,
Quikely moved but not lyghtlye appesed;
We use to call hir at home Dame Coye;
A cresie gingerlie pice, God save hir and Saint Loy!

---

191 *mysimithe*: meseemeth, it seems to me 204 *incontinent*: immediately 206 *abye*: pay for it
211 *lyne*: cease 217 *cresie*: unstable *Saint Loy*: St Eloi or Eligius

As denty and nice as an halpeny worthe of sylver
   spoons
But vengable melancolie in the aftirnoons:
She useth for hir bodylie helth and safegard   *220*
To chid daylie oone fite too supperward,
And my mayster hymselfe is worse then she
If he ons throughlye angeryd bee.
And a mayd we have at hom Aulsoon
   Tripe-and-Goo –
Not all London can shewe suche other twoo –
She simperith, she prankith and getteth without faille
As a pecocke that hath spred and sheweth hir gaye
   taylle;
She mynceth, she bridelethe, she swimmith to and
   fro,
She tredith not one here awrye, she tryppeth like a
   do;
Abrod in the stret going or cumming homward   *230*
She quaverith and warbelith like one in a galiard,
Everie joint in her bodie and everie part –
Oh it is a joylie wenche to myns and devyd a fart!
She talketh, she chatteth like a pye all daye,
And speaketh like a paratt Poppagaye,
And that as fine as a small silken threede –
Yea, and as high as an eagle can fle for a neade!
But it is a spitfull lying girle and never well
But whan she may sum yll tale by me tell:
She woll, I warrant you, anon at the first   *240*
Of me imagine and saye the worst,
And whatsoever she too my maisteris doth saye
It is writen in the gospell of the same daye.
Therfore I woll here with myselfe devise
What I may best say, and in what wise
I may excuse this my long taryeng

219 *vengable*: dreadfully   226 *getteth*: jets, struts   231 *warbelith*: wobbles   237 *for a neade*: if
it has to

That she of my negligence may suspect nothyng;
For if the fault of this be found in mee,
I may give me life for halpenis three!
　　Hic cogitabundo similis sedeat.
250　Let me stodie this moneth and I shall not fiend
A better devise then now is cume to my mynd:
'Maistries,' woll I saye, 'I am bound by my dutie
Too see that your womanhod have noo injurie,
For I heare and see more then you now and then
And yourselfe partlie know the wantin wyles of men.
When wee came yender, there dyd I see
My mayster kisse gentilwomen tow or three
And to come emongs others mythought bysye;
He had a myrvayllus great phantasye!
260　Anon he commaundyd me to run thens for you
To cume supe ther if you wold but I wot not how;
My hart grudgid mistrusting lest that I being awai
My maister wold sum light cast playe.
Wherupon, maistries, to see the ende
I tarried halfe supper time so God me mend!
And besyds that ther was such other compainye
As I know your maistriship settith nothyng by:
Gorges dames of the corte and galaunts also,
With doctours, and other rufflers mo.
270　At last when I thought it tyme and seasune,
I cam too certifie you as it was reasune,
And by the way whome should I mete
But that most honest gentilman in the stret
Which the last wike was with you here
And made you a banket, and bouncing cheare!
'Ah Jenkine,' quoth he, 'Good spid! How farest thou?'
'Mary wel, God yld it you, maister,' quoth I, 'How
　　do you?'

249 *me life*: my life　*Hic cogitabundo* etc: here he remains as if pondering　259 *phantasye*:
ingenious notion　263 *sum light cast*: some wanton trick　265 *mend*: amend
269 *other rufflers mo*: more braggarts besides　274 *wike*: week　275 *banket*: banquet
bouncing: thumping good　277 *God yld it you*: God recompense you

'How dothe thy maisteris? Is she at home?'
'Ye, syr,' quoth I, 'and suppith all alone,
And but that she hath noo maner good chere   *280*
I am sure she wold gladlye have you there!'
'I cannot cum now,' sayd he, 'I have busines
But thou shalt carie a tokine from me to thy
     maisteris;
Goo with me too my chaumbre at yone lane end
And I woll a dishe of costerds unto hyr send.'
I folowid him, and was bolde by your leave
To receive and bring them here in my sleve;
But I wold not for all Englond, by Jhesu Chryst,
That my maister Boungrace herof wyst
Or knew that I should any such geare to you
     bring,   *290*
Lest he misdime us both in sum worse thyng
Nor shew him nothing of that I before saied,
For then indyd, syr, I am araied;
Yf you doo I may nothing heraftir unto you tell
Whether I se my maister doo ill or well;
But yf you now this counsaile kepe
I wol ease you parchaunce twise in a wike.
You may saye you wer sike and your hed did ake,
That you lusted not this night any supper make
Speciallye without the dores, but thought it best   *300*
Too abyde at home and take your rest;
And I woll to my mayster too bryng hym home,
For you know he wol be angrie if he come alone.'
This woll I saye and face it so well
That she shall belyve it everie dell:
Hou saie you, frinds, by the armes of Robyn Hood?
Wol not this excuse be resonable good?
To muse for any better great foly it is,

---

285 *costerds*: large apples   291 *misdime*: misjudge   293 *araied*: in trouble, put on the spot
304 *face it*: brazen it out   305 *everie dell*: every detail

For I may make sure rekenning of this,
310   That and if I wold sit stoding this seven yere
I shall not ells find how to save me all clere;
And as you see, for the most part our witts be best
When wee be takine most unrediest.
But I wol not give for that boie a flye
That hathe not al tymes in store one good lye
And cannot set a good face upon the same;
Therfore Saint Gorge the boroue, as it wol let him
    frame!
I woll jeoperd a joint, bee as bee may,
I have had many like chauncis before this daye,
320   But I promise you I do curstlie feare
For I fell a vengeable burning in my lift ere,
And it hath byn a saying of tyme long
That swete mete woll have source sauce among,
And surelie I shall have sum ill hape
For my here standith up under my cape:
I would knocke, but I dare not, by Our Ladye!
I feare hanging wherunto no man is hastie:
But seing there is non other remedie,
Thus too stand any longer it is but folye –
    Hic pulset ostium.
330   They bee soo fare within they cannot heare –
    [JACK JUGGLER *advances.*]
JAKE JUGLER: Soft thy knoking, saucie knave; what
    makest thou there?
JENKINE CAREAWAIE: What knave is that? He
    speaketh not too me, I trowe;
And we mete the one of us is lyke too have a
    blowe!
For now that I am wel chafed, and sumwhat hote,

---

310 *stoding*: reflecting 317 *the boroue*: be your surety 318 *jeoperd a joint*: hazard a finger
321 *fell*. feel *vengeable*: dreadful *lift*: left 325 *here*: hair 329 *Hic pulset ostium*: Here he
knocks at the door 330 *fare*: far off 334 *chafed*: glowing with anger

Twentye suche could I hewe as small as fleshe too
   pote,
And surelie if I had a knyfe
This knave should escape hardelye with his lyfe,
Too teache hym to aske of me any more
What I make at my owne maistir's doore!

JACKE JUGLER: But if thou cum from that gate, thou
   knave,   *340*
I woll fett thee by the swet lookes, so God me save!

JENKINE CAREAWAIE: Woll the horesoon fight
   indede, by myn honestie?
I know noo quarell he hath too me –
But I wold I were within the house
And then I wold not set by hym a louse,
For I feare and mistrust suche quareling thives –
See how he beginnith to strike up his sleves!

JAKE JUGLER: His arse makith buttens now, and
   who lustith to feale
Shall find his hart creping out at his heelle,
Or ells lying hiden in sum corner of his hose   *350*
(Yf ıt be not alredie dropped out of his nose)
For, as I doubt not but you have hard beforne,
A more dastard couerd knave was never borne.

JENKINE CAREAWAIE: The divell set the house afier,
   I trowe it is acurste!
When a man hath most hast he spedith worst:
Yf I bee robed, or slane, or any harme geate,
The fault is in them that dothe not me in lete.
And I durst jeoper an hunderid pounde
That sum bauderie might now within be founde;
But except sum of them come the soner   *360*
I shall knocke suche a peale that all Englond shall
   wonder!

---

340 *But if*: unless   341 *fett*: fetch, seize   *lookes*: locks   342 *horesoon*: rogue   353 *dastard*:
sneaky   358 *jeoper*: hazard   359 *bauderie*: hanky-panky (but see note)

JAKE JUGLER: Knoke at the gate hardelye againe if
    thou dare –
    And seing thou wolt not bie faire words beware –
    Now fistes, methinkithe yesterdaie seven yers past
    That four men asleepe at my fete you cast
    And this same daye you did noo manar good
    Nor were not washed in warme blod!

JENKINE CAREAWAIE: What whoreson is this that
    washith in warme blod?
    Sum divell broken loose, out of hell for wood!
370   Four hath he slayne, and now well I see
    That it must be my chaunce the fift to bee!
    But rather then thus shamefullie too be slayne,
    Wold Chryst mi frinds had hanged me being but
      yers [twain]!
    And yet yf I take good harte and be bolde
    Percace he wolbe the more sobre and coulde.

JAKE JUGLER: Now handes, bestur you about his
    lyppes and face
    And streake out all his teth without any grace!
    Gentelman, are you disposed to eate any fist met?

JENKIN CAREAWAYE: I have supped, I thanke you,
    syr, and lyst not to ete:
380   Geve it to them that are hungrie if you be wyse.

JACKE JUGLER: Yt shall do a man of your dyet no
    harme to suppe twise –
    This shalbe youre chise to make your met digest,
    For I tell you thes handes weighith of the best!

JENKIN CAREAWAYE: I shall never escape – see how
    he waghith his handes!

JAKE JUGLER: With a stroke they wyll lay a knave in
    Our Ladye boons,
    And this day yet they have done no good at all.

---

362 *hardelye*: boldly   369 *for wood*: madly, in a fury   377 *streake*: strike   378 *met*: meat
381 *dyet*: feeding habits   382 *chise*: cheese   384 *waghith*: wags, spars   385 *Our Ladye boons*:
Our Lady's grace (see note)

JENKIN CAREAWAYE: Ere thou assaye them on mee
    I praie thee lame them on the wal –
  But speake you all this in earnest, or in game?
  Yf you be angrie with me trulee you are to blam
  For have you any just quarell to mee?   *390*
JAKE JUGLER: Ere thou and I parte that wol I shew
    thee.
JENKINE CAREAWAYE: Or have I doone you any
    maner displeasure?
JAKE JUGLER: Ere thou and I parte thou shalt know,
    thou maist be sure.
JENKIN CAREAWAYE: By my fayth, yf thou be angrie
    without a cause,
  You shall have amendes made with a cople of straus:
  By the I sete whatsoever thou arte,
  But for thy displeasure I care not a farte.
  May a man demaund whose servant you bee?
JAKE JUGLER: My maister's servaunt I am for veritie.
JENKIN CAREAWAYE: What busynes have you at
    thys place now?   *400*
JAKE JUGLER: Nay, mary tell me, what busynes hast
    thou?
  For I am commaunded for to watche and give
    diligence
  That in me good maister Boungrace's absence
  Noo misfortune may happen to his house sertayne.
JENKIN CAREAWAYE: Well now I am cume you may
    go hens agine
  And thanke them that so much for my maister
    have doone,
  Shewing them that the servants of the house be
    cume home –
  For I am of the house, and now in woll I goo.
JAKE JUGLER: I canot tell whether thou be of the
    house or noo.

402 *give diligence*: take care

67

410 But goo no nere, lest I handle thee like a strainger:
Thanke no man but thyselfe yf thou be in any
daunger.

JENKINE CAREAWAIE: Marye, I defye the and
planly unto the tell
That I am a servaunt of this house, and her I
dwel!

JAKE JUGLER: Now soo God me snache but thou goo
the waies
Whille thou maiest, for this fortie dayes
I shall make the not able to goo nor ryde,
But in a dungcart or a whilberow liyng on on[e] syd.

JENKEN CAREAWAIE: I am a servaunt of this house,
by thes ten bons!

JAKE JUGLER: Noo more prating but geat the hens
at towns!

JENKIN CAREAWAYE: Why, my maistir hath sent me
420 home in his message —

JAKE JUGLER: Pike and walke a knave, here a waye
is no passage!

JENKIN CAREAWAYE: What, wilt thou let me from
my nowne maistir's house?

JAKE JUGLER: Be tredging, or i'faith you bere me a
souse!
Here my maistier and I have our habitacion
And hath continuallye dwelling in this mansyon
At the least this doosen yers and od,
And here wol we end our lyves by the grace of God.

JENKIN CAREAWAIE: Why then, where shall my
maistier and I dwell?

JAKE JUGLER: At the dyvell yf you lust; I cannot tell.

JENKEN CAREAWAYE: *In nomine patris*, now this geare
430 doth passe!
For a litel before supper here our house was

412 *planly*: plainly 414 *God me snache*: God seize me! *but*: unless 416 *goo*: walk 419 *at
towns*: at once 421 *Pike*: clear off 422 *let*: prevent, hinder 423 *tredging*: trudging *souse*:
thump 430 *In nomine patris*: in the name of the Father

And this daye in the mornyng I woll on a booke
   swere
That my maister and I both dwellid here.

JAKE JUGLER: Who is thy maister? tell me without lye,
   And thine owne name also let me knowe shortlye,
   For my maisters all, let me have the blame
   Yf this knave know his master or his owne name!

CAREAWAYE: My maister's name is Maister
   Boungrace;
   I have dwelled with him a longe space,
   And I am Jenkin Careawaye his page.   *440*

JAKE JUGLER: What, ye drunkin knave, begine you to
   rage?
   Take that – [*Strikes him.*] Art thou Maister
   Boungracis page?

CAREAWAYE: Yf I be not I have made a verye good
   viage!

JAKE JUGLER: Darest thou too my face saie thou art
   I? [*Strikes him again.*]

CAREAWAIE: I wolde it were true and no lye –
   For then thou sholdest smart and I should bet,
   Whereas now I do all the blowes get!

JACK JUGLER: And is Maister Boungrace thy
   mayster, doest thou then saye?

CAREAWAIE: I woll swere on a booke he was ons this
   daye!

JAKE JUGLER: And for that thou shalt sumwhat have   *450*
   Because thou presumest like a [saucye] lying
   knave
   To saye my maister is thyne? [*Strikes him.*] Who is
   thy maister now?

CAREAWAYE: By my trouthe, syr, whosoever please you:
   I am your owne, for you bete me soo
   As no man but my mayster sholde doo!

---

441 *rage*: rave, lose your wits 443 *viage*: journey, undertaking 446 *bet*: beat 449 *ons*: at one period

JAKE JUGLER: I woll handle thee better if faut be not
    in fyst. [*Strikes him.*]

CAREAWAIE: Helpe! Save my life, maisters, for the
    passion of Christ!

JAKE JUGLER: Why, thou lowsy thefe, doest thou
    crye and rore?

CAREAWAYE: No fayth, I woll not crye one whit more;
    [JACK *hits him again.*]

460   Save my lyfe, helpe or I am slaine!

JACKE JUGLER: Ye, doest thou make a roweringe yet
    againe?

Dyd not I byde the holde thy peace?

CAREAWAYE: In faith now I leave crying, now I
    sease —
    [JACK *strikes him.*]
            Helpe, helpe, help!

JAKE JUGLER: Who is thy maister?

CAREAWAYE: Maister Boungrace.

JAKE JUGLER: I woll make the chaung that song ere
    wee pas this place,

For he is my maister, and againe too [thee] I saye

That I am his Jenkin Careawaye.
    [*Hits* CAREAWAY *again.*]

Who art thou? Now tell me plaine —

CAREAWAY: Noobodye, but whom please you
    sertayne!

JAKE JUGLER: Thou saydest even now thy name was

470   Careaw[a]ie.

CARAWAYE: I crye yow marcye, syr, and forgivenes
    praie;

I sayd amysse, because it was soo toodaye

[I] thought it should have continuede alwaies;

Like a fole as I am and a drunken knave.

But in faith, syr, ye see all the wytte I have,

Therfore I beseche you do me no more blame

---

456 *faut*: fault   461 *roweringe*: roaring   471 *marcye*: mercy   474 *fole*: fool

But give me a new maister, and another name,
For it wold greve my hart, soo helpe me God,
To runne about the stretes like a maisterlis doge.

JAKE JUGLER: I am he that thou saidest thou were,   *480*
    And Maister Boungrace is my maister that
      dwelleth hear:
    Thou art noo poynte Careawaye; thy witts do the
      faylle.

CAREAWAYE: Ye, mary syr, ye have bette them
    doune into my taille!
    But, syr, myght I be bolde too saye on thinge,
    Without any bloues, and without any beatynge?

JAKE JUGLER: Truce for a whyle; say one what
    [thee] lust.

CAREAWAYE: May a man too your honeste by your
    woord trust?
    I praye you, swere by the masse youe woll do me
    no yll.

JAKE JUGLER: By my faithe I promise, pardone thee
    I woll.

CAREAWAYE: What and you keape not
    promise?

JA[CK] JUGLER: Then upon Ca[reawaye]   *490*
    I praie God may light as much mor as hath on
    thee this dai!

CAREAWAYE: Now dare I speake – soo mote I thee –
    Maister Boungrace is my maister, and the name of
    mee
    Is Jenkine Careaway.

JACKE JUGLER [*threatening him again*]: What, saiest
    thou soo?

CAREAWAYE: And yf thou woll strike me, and breake
    thy promise, doo,
    And beate on me tyll I stinke and tyll I dye,
    And yet woll I stiell saye that I am I!

479 *doge*: dog   482 *noo poynte*: in no respect   484 *on*: one   486 *one*: on   *lust*: wish, desire
492 *soo mote I thee*: as I may thrive

JAKE JUGLER: This bedelem knave without dought is
    mad!

CAREAWAYE: No, by God! for all that I am a wyse lad
500   And can cale to rememberaunce everythyng
    That I dyd this daye, sithe my uperysinge:
    For went not I with my mayster todaye
    Erelie in the mornyng to the tenis playe?
    At noone whyle my maister at his dynner sate
    Played not I at dice at the gentylman's gate?
    Did not I wayte on my maister too supperward?
    And I thinke I was not chaunged the way
      homward!
    Or ells yf you thynke I lye,
    Aske in the stret of them that I came bye,
510   And sith that I came hether into your presens,
    What man lyving could carye me hens?
    I remembre I was sent to feache my maisteris
    And what I devised to save me harmeles.
    Doo not I speake now? Is not this my hande?
    Be not these my feet that on this ground stande?
    Did not this other knave her knoke me about the
      hede?
    And beat me tyll I was almost dede?
    How may it then bee, that he should bee I?
    Or I not myselfe? – it is a shamfull lye!
520   I woll home to our house whosoever say naye,
    For surelye my name is Jenkin Careawaye.

JAKE JUGLER: I woll make thee say otherwise ere we
    depart if I can.

CAREAWAYE: Nay that woll I not, in faith, for no man,
    Except thou tell me what thou hast doone
    Ever sythe five of the cloke this afternoone:
    Reherse me all that without anye lye,
    And then I wol confese that thou art I.

---

498 *bedelem*: bedlam, mad (see note) 506 *too supperward*: on his way to supper
512 *feache*: fetch, collect 513 *save me harmeles*: save myself from harm 516 *her*: here
525 *sythe*: since

JAKE JUGLER: When my maister came to the
    gentylman's place,
He commaundid me too rune home a great pace
Too fet thither my maisteris, and by the waye   *530*
I dyd a good whill at the bukelers playe;
Then came I by a wife that did costerds sell
And cast downe hir basket fayre and well,
And gatherid as many as I could gete,
And put theim in my sleve – here they bee yet!
CAREWAIE [*to audience*]: How the divell should thei
    cume there? –
For I dyd them all in my owne sleve bere!
He lyeth not a worde in all this
Nor dothe in any one poynt myse,
For ought I se yet betwene erneste and game   *540*
I must go sike me another name –
[*to* JACK] But thou mightest see all this; tell the
    rest that is behind,
And there I know I shall thee a lyer fynd!
JAKE JUGLER: I ran thens homewarde a contrarye
    waye
And whether I stoped there or naye,
I could tell if me lusteth a good token,
But it may not here very well be spoken.
CAREAWAIE: Noo, may I praye thee let no man that
    here,
But tell it me pryvelye in myne ere.
JAKE JUGLER [*aside*]: I, thou lost all thy mony at
    dice, Christ geve it his curse!   *550*
Wel and truelye pycked before out of another
    man's porse!
CAREAWAYE: Gode's bodye, horeson thife, who told
    thee that same?
Sum counnyng divell is within the, payne of
    shame!

530 *fet*: fetch, bring 532 *costerds*: large apples 540 *ought*: aught 541 *sike*: seek 546 *if me lusteth*: if I wanted to 550 *I*: aye

In nomine patris, God and Our Blessed Ladye
Now and evermore save me from thy cumpanie!

JAKE JUGLER: How now, art thou Careawaye or not?

CAREAWAYE: By the Lorde I doubte, but sayest thou
    nay to that?

JAKE JUGLER: Ye mary, I tell the, Careawaye is my
    name!

CAREAWAYE: And by these tene bones, myne is the
    same!

560   Or ells tell me yf I be not hee,
What my name frome hensforth shall bee?

JAKE JUGLER: By my faith, the same that it was
    before
Whan I lust too be Careawaye no more!
Looke well upon me and thou shalt see as now
That I am Jenkyne Careawaye and not thou;
Looke well apon me, and by everye thyng
Thou shalt well know that I make no leasing!

CAREAWAYE: I se it is soo without any doubte —
But how the dyvell came it aboute? —

570   Whosoo in England lokethe on hym stedelye
Sall perceive plainelye that he is I:
I have sene myselfe a thousand times in a glasse
But soo lyke myselfe as he is never was:
He hath in everye poynt my clothing and my
    geare —
My hed, my cape, my shirt and notted heare,
And of the same coloure, my yes, nose, and lypps,
My chekes, chyne, neake, fyte, leges, and hyppes;
Of the same stature, and hyght and age,
And is in every poynt Maister Boungrace page

580   That if he have a hole in his tayle,
He is even I myne owne selfe without any faile!
And yet when I remembre I wot not how —

---

554 *In nomine patris*: in the name of the Father   567 *leasing*: lie   575 *heare*: hair   576 *yes*:
eyes

The same man that I have ever byne methinkith I
    am now:
I know my maister, and this house, and my five
    witts I have,
Why then should I give credence to this folishe
    knave
That nothing entendith but me delude and
    mooke –
For whome should I feare at my maister's gate to
    knoke?

JAKE JUGLER: Thinkest thou I have sayd all thys in
    game?
Goo or I shall send the hens in the dyvill's name!
Avoyde, thou lousye lurden and precious stinking
    slave,   *590*
That nether thi name knowest nor canst ani
    master have;
Thou wine shakine pylorye picpours, of lice not
    without a pecke,
Hens, or by God's precious I shal breake thy
    necke!

CAREAWAIE: Then maister, I besiche you hartylye,
    take the paine
Yf I be found in any place too bringe me to me
    againe!
Now is not this a wonderfull case
That a man should lease himselfe soo in ony place?
Have any of you harde of such a thyng heretofore?
No, nor never shall I dare saye from hensforth any
    more!

JAKE JUGLER [*to audience*]: Whyle he museth and
    judgeth hymselfe apon,   *600*
I woll stele awaye for a whyle and let hym aloon.
    [*Exit.*]

---

590 *lurden*: rascal, beggar   592 *wine shakine*: drunken (see note)   *pylorye*: i.e. fit for the
pillory   593 *by God's precious*: i.e. by God's precious blood or bones   597 *lease*: lose

CAREAWAIE: Good lorde of hevyne, wher dyd I
    myselfe leave
Or who dyd me of my name by the waye bereve?
For I am sure of this in my mynde,
That I dyd in no place leve myselfe byhynde.
Yf I had my name played awaye at dyce,
Or had sold myselfe too any man at a pryce,
Or had made a fray and had lost it in fightyng,
Or it had byne stolne from me sleapyng,
It had byne a matter and I wold have kept
610   pacience –
But it spiteth my hart to have lost it by suche open
    negligence!
Ah, thou horesone drousie drunken sote,
It were an almes dyde too walke thy cote!
And I shrew him that wold for thee be sorye
Too see thee well curryed by and by,
And by Chryst, if any man wold it doo,
I myselfe wold helpe theretoo –
For a man may see, thou horesone goose,
Thou woldest lysse thyne arse yf it were loose!
620   Albeit I wold never the dyde beleve
But that the thyng itselfe dothe shewe and prive;
There was never ape so lyke unto an ape
As he is to me in feature and shape,
But what woll my maister saye, trow ye,
When he shall this geare here and see?
[Wyl] he know me, thinke you, when he shall see
    mee?
Yf he do not another woll as good as he!
[*Looking round*] But wher is that other I? Whether is
    he gon? –
Too my maister, by Cocke's precius passion!
630   Eyther too put me out of my place

608 *fray*: disturbance, scrap 610 *It had byne a matter*: it would have been something
611 *spiteth*: offends 612 *sote*: sot 613 *too walke thy cote*: to beat you 615 *curryed*: thrashed
619 *lysse*: lose 621 *prive*: prove 629 *Cocke's*: God's

Or too accuse me too my maister Boungrace:
But I woll after as fast as I can flee –
I trust to be there as soone as hee –
That if my maister be not redye home to come,
I woll bee here agayne as fast as I cane rune
In any wyse to speake with my maysteris,
Or ells I shall never escape hanging dubtles!

   [*Exit* JENKIN CAREAWAY. *Enter from the house*
   DAME COYE, *attended by* ALICE TRIP-AND-GO.]

DAME COYE: I shall not suppe this night full well I see,
For as yet noobodie cumithe for to fet mee;
But good ynough, let me alone –   *640*
I woll bee even with theim everychone!
I saye nothyng, but I thinke sumwhat I wis;
Sum ther bee that shall here of this!
Of al unkind and churlishe husbands this is the cast
To let ther wives set at home and fast
While they bee forthe and make good cheare,
Pastime and sporte, as now he doth there;
But yf I wer a wise woman as I am a mome,
I shold make myselfe as good chere at home!
But if he have thus unkindlye servyde mee,   *650*
I wol not forget it this monethis three;
And if I weste the fault were in him, I praie God I
   be dede
But he should have suche a *Kyrie* ere he went too
   bede,
As he never had before in all his lyfe
Nor any man ells have had of his wife!
I wolde rate him and shake him after such a sorte
As sholde be to him a corrasive full lytle to his
   cumforte!

ALLS TRIPPE AND GOO: Yf I may be so bolde by
   your maisteriship's lycens
As too speake and shew my mynde and sentence,

---

639 *fet*: fetch 644 *cast*: characteristic style 648 *mome*: fool 652 *weste*: wist 653 *Kyrie*:
Kyrie eleison (Christ, have mercy) i.e. a hiding 657 *corrasive*: caustic medicine

660   I thinke of this you may the boye thanke –
For I know that he playeth you many a lyke pranke;
And that wolde you saye yf you knew as mutch as
    wee
That his daylye conversacion and byhaviore see,
For if you commaund him to goo speake with
    sumone
Yt is an houre ere he wol be gone,
Then woll he rune forth and plaie in the strete
And cume againe and say that he cannot with him
    mete!

DAME COYE: Naye, naye, it is his maister's playe;
He servithe me soo almost everye third daye

670   But I wol be even with him as God geve me joy! –
And yet the faulte may bee in the boye,
As ungracious a graft, so mot I thrive,
As any goeth on Godde's ground alyve.

    [*They draw aside. Re-enter* JENKIN CAREAWAY.]

CAREAWAYE: My witte is breched in suche a brake
That I cannot devise what way is best to take:
I was almost as fare as my maister is
But then I begane to remember this,
And to cast the worst as on in fere –
Yf he chaunce to see mee and kepe me there

680   Tyl he cum himselfe, and speake with mi maisteris
Then am I lyke to bee in shrewd dystres.
Yet were I better, thought I, to rune hom again
And fyrst speake with her certayne –
Cocke's bodie, yonder she standeth at the dore!
Now is it wourse then it was before!
Wold Christ I could get againe out of hir syght
For I see be her looke she is disposid to fyght –
By the Lord, she hath ther an angrie shrewe's
    looke!

---

668 *playe*: trick, way of going on   672 *graft*: scion, sprig   674 *breched in suche a brake*:
?broken on the rack (see note)   678 *on*: one   684 *Cocke's*: God's

DAME COYE: Loe, yender cumithe that unhappie
    hooke!

CAREAWAYE: God save you maysteris! Doo you
    know me well?   *690*

DAME COYE: Cume ner hyther unto mee, and I shall
    the tell –

Why, thou noughtie vyllan, is that thy gyce

To gest with thy maisteris in suche wise?   [*Strikes
    him.*]

Take that to begyne with, and God before,

When thy maister cumith home thou shalt have
    more!

For he told me when he forth wente

That thou shouldest cume bake againe
    incontynente

To brynge me to supper where he now is,

And thou has plaid by the waye, and they have
    don by this:

But no force, I shall (thou maiest trust mee)   *700*

Teache all naughtie knaves to beware by thee!

CAREAWAYE: Forsothe maisteris, yf you knew as
    much as I,

Ye wolde not be with me halfe so angrie,

For the faulte is neither in mi maister nor in me
    nor you,

But in another knave that was here even now –

And his name was Jenkin Careawaie!

DAME COYE: What, I see my man is disposid to playe!

I wine he be dronken or mad, I make God a vou!

CAREAWAYE: Nay, I have byn made sobre and tame
    inow –

I was never so handelid before in all my lyfe –   *710*

I would every man in Englond had so beat me hys
    wyfe!

689 *hooke*: fellow   692 *gyce*: guise, habit   697 *incontynente*: straightaway   700 *no force*: no
matter   708 *wine*: ween, believe *vou*: vow   709 *tame*: meek, docile *inow*: enow, enough
711 *beat me*: beat for my benefit

[*Aside*] (I have forgotten withe tousing by the here
What I devysed to say a lytle ere!)

DAME COYE: Have I lost my supper this nyght
through thy negligence?

CAREAWAYE: Nay, then were I a knave, misteris,
saving your revirence.

DAME COYE: Why, I am sure that by this tyme it is
doone.

CAREAWAYE: Ye that it is, more then an our agone.

DAME COYE: And was not thou sent to feache mee
theyther?

CAREAWAYE: Yes, and had cume right quiklie hither
720   But that by the waye I had a gret fall,
And my name, body shape, legges and all,
And meat with one that from me did it stelle –
But be God, he and I sum bloues dyd deale!
I wold he were now before your gate
For you wold poumile him joylile about the pate!

DAME COYE: Truelie, this wagepastie is either
drunken or mad!

CAREAWAYE: Never man sofred so mutch wrong as I
had –
But maisteris, I should saye a thinge to you –
Tary, it wol cum to my remembrence even now –
[*Aside*] (I must niddes use a substancyal
730   premeditacon
For the matter lyeth gretylie mee apon)
I besiche your maisterishipe of pardon and
forgivenes,
Desyering you to impute it to my simple and rude
dullness –
I have forgotten what I have thought to have
sayed
And am therof full ill apaied,
But whan I lost my selfe I knew verie well,

717 *our*: hour   722 *meat*: met   *stelle*: steal   725 *poumile*: pummel   726 *wagepastie*: rogue
733 *dullness*: stupidity (see note)   735 *apaied*: repaid

I lost also that I should you tell!

DAME COYE: Why, thou wrechid villen, doest thou
   me scorne and moke
  To make me to thes folkes a laufyng stoke?
  Ere thou go out of my handes thou shalt have
   sumthynge   740
  And I woll rekine better in the mornynge!

CAREAWAYE: And yf you bete me, maisteris, avise you,
  For I am none of your servaunts now –
  That other I is now your page
  And I am no longer in your bondage!

DAME COYE: Now walke, precious thife; get the out
   of my syght!
  And I charge thee cum in my presens no more this
   night –
  Get thee hens and wayte on thy maister at ons!

    [*Exit* DAME COYE *and* ALICE TRIP-AND-GO.]

CAREAWAYE: Mary syr, this is handeling for the noons!
  I wold I had byn hanged before that I was lost,   750
  I was never this canvased and tost;
  That if my maister on his part also
  Handle me as my maisteris and the other I do,
  I shall surelie be killed bytwine theim thre,
  And all the divels in hell shal not save me!
  And yet if the other I might have with me parte,
  All this wold never greve my harte.   [*Exit.*]

    [*Re-enter* JACK JUGGLER.]

JAKE JUGLER: Hou saye you maisters, I pray you tell,
  Have not I requited my marchent well?
  Have not I handelyd hym after a good sort?   760
  Had it not byne pytie to have lost this sporte?
  Anone his maister on his behalphe
  You shall see how he woll handle the calphe;
  Yf he throughlye angered bee,

742 *avise you*: consider, think it over 749 *for the noons*: a tag – 'if you like' 751 *this*: thus
canvased: tossed about (see note) 759 *marchent*: merchant; here 'chap' 763 *calphe*: calf,
dolt

He wol make hym smart, so mot I thee!
I wold not for the price of a new payre of shoone
That any parte of this had byne undune;
But now I have partelye revenged my quarell,
I woll go do of this myne apparell,
770 And now let Careawaye be Careawaye agayne –
I have done with that name now certayne –
Except peraventure I shal take the selfesam wede
Sum other tyme agayne for a like cause and nide!
    [*Exit* JACK JUGGLER. *Enter from the other side of
    the stage* BONGRACE *and* CAREAWAY.]
BOUNGRACE: Why then, daryst thou to presume too
        tell mee
    That I know is no wyse possible for to bee?
CAREAWAYE: Now by my truth maister, I have told
        you no lie
    And all these folkes knowith as well as I –
    I had no sooner knoked at the gate
    But straightwayes he had me by the pate!
780 Therfore yf you bet me tyll I fart and shyt agayne,
    You shall not cause me for any payne
    But I wol affirme, as I said before,
    That when I came nere another stode at the dore!
BOUNGRACE: Why, thou naughtye vyllayne, darest
        thou affirme to me
    That which was never syne nor hereafter shal be –
    That on man may have too bodies and two faces,
    And that one man at one time may be in two
        placys?
    Tell me, drankest thou anywhere by the waye?
CAREAWAIE: I shreue me yf I dranke any more then
        twise today
790 Tyll I met even now with that other I –
    And withe him I supped and dranke truelye!

769 *do of*: take off 772 *wede*: clothing 780 *bet*: beat 785 *syne*: seen 786 *on*: one 789 *I
shreue me*: a curse on me 791 *supped and dranke*: got soundly beaten (ironic)

82

But as for you, yf you gave me drinke and meate
As oftentymes as you do me bete,
I were the best fed page in all this cytie;
But as touchyng that, you have on me no pitye,
And not onlye I but all that do you sarve
For meat and drynke maye rather starve!

BOUNGRACE: What, you saucye malypert knave,
 Begine you with your maister to prate and rave?
 Your tonge is lyberall ar.J all out of frame   *800*
 I must niddes counger it and make it tame!
 Where is that other Careaway that thou said was
  here?

CAREAWAYE: Now by my chrystendome, syr, I wot
 nere!

BOUNGRACE: Why, canst thou fynde no man to moke
 but mee?

CAREAWAYE: I moke you not, maister, soo mot I thee;
 Everye word was trew that I you tolde.

BOUNGRACE: Nay, I know toyes and prankes of olde,
 And now thou art not satisfied nor content
 Without regarde of my biddings and
  commaundement
 To have played by the waye as a leude knave and
  negligent   *810*
 When I thee on my message home sent,
 But also woldest willinglie me delude and moke
 And make me too all wise men a laughing stoke;
 Shewing me suche thinges as in no wise be maye
 To the intent that thi leudnes mai turne to jest and
  play;
 Therfore if thou speake any such thing to me
  againe
 I promyse it shal be unto thy payne.

CAREAWAYE: Loo, is not he in myserable case

---

796 *sarve*: serve 798 *malypert*: malapert, impudent 801 *niddes*: needs *counger*: constrain
803 *wot*: know 804 *moke*: mock 813 *stoke*: stock

That sarveth suche a maister in any place,
820   That with force woll compel him the thing to denye
That he knoweth true, and hath syne with his ye?

BOUNGRACE: Was it not, troiest thou, thyne owne
  shadoo?

CAREAWAYE: My shadoo could never have beten me
  soo!

BOUNGRACE: Why, by what reason possyble may
  suche a thyng bee?

CAREAWAYE: Nay I marvael and wonder at it more
  than ye,
And at the fyrst it dyd me curstelye meave
Nor I wold myne owne yes in no wyse belyve
Untyll that other I beate me soo
That he made me belive it whither I wold or no,
830   And if he had yourselfe now within his reache
He wold make you say so too or ells beshite your
  breach!

MAISTER BOUNGRACE: I durst a good mede and a
  wager laye
That thou laiest doune and slepest by the waye,
And dremist all this that thou haste me tolde.

JENKYNE CAREAWAYE: Naye, there you lye,
  maister, if I might be so bold –
But we ryse so erlye that yf I hadde
I hadde doone well and a wyse ladde;
Yet, mayster, I wolde you underestoode
That I have allwayes byn trusty and good
840   And flye as fast as a bere in a cage
Whensooever you sende me in your message.
In faythe, as for thys that I have tolde you,
I sawe and felte it as waking as I am nowe
For I had noo soner knocked at the gate
But the other I knave had mee by the pate,

---

821 *syne*: seen   *ye*: eye   826 *meave*: move   831 *breach*: breeches   832 *mede*: reward
839 *byn*: been

And I durst to you one a boke swere
That he had byn wachyng for mee there
Longe ere I came, hyden in sum pryvye place,
Even for the nons too have me by the face.

MAISTER BOUNGRACE: Why then, thou speakest not
    with my wyfe?   *850*

CAREAWAYE: No, that I dyd not, maister, by my lyfe,
Untyll that other I was gone,
And then my maisteris sent me after anone
To waight on you home in the dyvelle's name –
I wene the dyvell never so beate his dame!

MAISTER BOUNDGRACE: And where became that
    other Careawaye?

CAREAWAYE: By myne honestie, syr, I cannot saye –
But I warrant he is now not far hens:
He is here amonge this cumpany for forty pens!

MAISTER BOUNGRACE: Hence at tonce, sike and
    smell hym out!   *860*
I shall rape thee one the lying knave's snought;
I woll not bee deludyd with such a glosing lye
Nor give credens tyll I see it with my oune iye!

CAREAWAIE: Trulye, good syr, by your
    maistershipp's favoure,
I cannot well fynd a knave by the savoure;
Many here smell strong but none so ranke as he –
A stronger sented knave then he was cannot bee –
But, syr, yf he be happelye founde anone,
What amends shal I have for that you have me done?

MASTER BOUNGRACE: If he may be found I shal
    walke his cote.   *870*

CAREAWAIE: Ye, for Our Lady sake, syr, I bisiche
    you spare him not;
For it is sum false knave witheouten doubt:

---

846 *one*: on   849 *for the nons*: for the purpose   855 *wene*: ween, reckon   860 *sike*: seek
861 *rape*: rap   862 *glosing*: specious, deceitful   868 *happelye*: luckily   870 *walke his cote*:
beat him

I had rather then forty pens wee could find him out,
For if a man maye belive a glase
Evin my verie oune selfe it was,
And here he was but evyn right now
And steped awaye sodenlie, I wat not how;
Of such another thing I have nether hard ne sene
By Our Blyssyd Lady, heaven quene!

MAISTER BOUNGRACE: Plainelye it was thy shadow
880   that thou didest see,
For in fayth, the other thyng is not possible to be.

CAREAWAYE: Yes in good faith, syr, by youre leave;
I know it was I by my apples in my sleve –
And speakith as like me as ever you harde –
Suche here, such a cape, suche hose and cote,
And in everything as just as four pens to a grote
That if he were here you should well see
That you could not discerne nor know him from me –
For thinke you that I do not myselfe knowe?
890   I am not so folishe a knave, I trowe!
Let who woll looke him by and by
And he woll depose upon a boke that he is I;
And I dare well say you woll saye the same,
For he called hymselfe by my owne name,
And tolde me all that I have done
Syth five of the cloke this afternone:
He could tell when you were to supper sete,
You send me home my maisteris to fete
And shewed me all thinges that I dyd by the
    waie –

BOUNGRACE: What was that?

CAREAWAYE: How I dyd at the
900   bukelers playe,
And whan I scaterid a basket of apples from a stall
And gethered them into my sleve all

873 *then*: than 874 *glase*: glass, mirror 878 *hard*: heard 885 *here*: hair *cape*: cap
891 *who woll looke him*: whoever wants to inspect or examine him 896 *Syth*: since
897 *sete*: set, sat down 898 *fete*: fetch

And how I played after that also –

BOUNGRACE: Thou shalt [aby] therfore, so mote I go!
Is that the guise of a trustie page
To plaie when he is sent on his master's message?
[*As* BONGRACE *strikes* CAREAWAY, DAME COYE
enters from the house.]

DAME COYE: Laye on and spare not, for the love of
Chryst!
Joll his hed to a post and favoure your fyste!
Now for my sake, swetehart, spare and favoure
your hand
And lay hym about the rybbes with this wande!   *910*

CAREAWAYE: Now marcy that I aske of you both
twaine!
Save my lyfe and let me not be slayne!
I have had beting ynough for one daye,
That a mischife take the other me, Careawaye,
That if ever he cume to my handes agayne
Iwis it shal be to his payne!
But I marvayll greatlye, by our Lorde Jhesus,
How he-I escapid I-me, beat me thus,
And is not he-I an unkind knave
That woll no more pytie on myselfe have?   *920*
Here may you see, evydentyle iwis,
That in hym-me no drope of honestie is!
Now a vengaunce light on suche a churle's knave
That no more love toward myselfe have!

DAME COYE: I knew verye well, switeharte, and saied
right now
That no fault therof should be in you.

MAISTER BOUNGRACE: No, trulye, good bedfelow, I
wer then mutch unkinde
Yf you at any tyme should be out of my mynde.

DAME COYE: Surelye I have of you a great treasure,

---

904 *aby*: pay for 908 *Joll*: bang, bash 910 *wande*: rod, cane 916 *Iwis*: truly, indeed
925 *switeharte*: sweetheart

For you do all thynges which may be to my
930   pleasure.

BOUNGRACE: I am sory that your chaunce hath now
    byne so yll;

I wolde gladely byne unsupped soo you had your fyll.

But goo we in, pigesnie, that you may suppe:

You have cause now to thanke this same hangeupe

For had not he byne, you had faryd very wel.

DAME COYE: I bequeth hym with a hott vengeaunce
    to the divell of Hell!

And hartelye I besiche him that hanged on the rode,

That he never eate ne drynke that may do hym good,

And that he dye a shamefull dethe, saving my
    cheryte!

[*Exit* BONGRACE *and* DAME COYE, *into the house.*]

CAREWAYE [*to the audience*]: I pray God send him
940   suche prosperitie

That hath caused me to have all this busines –

And yet, syrs, you see the charitye of my maistris?

She livethe after a wonderful charytable facion,

For I assure you she is alwayes in this passion

And scacelye on daye throughout the hole yere

She woll wishe any man better chere,

And sumtyme if she well angred bee

'I pray God' (woll she saye) 'the house may sinke
    under me!'

But, maisters, if you happen to see that other I –
950   As that you shal it is not verye likelye

Nor I wol not desyre you for him purposelye to
    looke

For it is an uncomparable unhappye hooke –

And if it be I you might happin to seeke

And not fynd me out in an hole weeke,

For when I was wonte to rune awaye

---

931 *byne*: been   933 *pigesnie*: darling (literally 'pig's eye')   934 *hangeupe*: one fit for the
gallows   937 *rode*: rood, cross   941 *busines*: distress, trouble   945 *scacelye*: scarcely
952 *hooke*: fellow, lout

I used not to cum againe in lesse than a moneth or
   twaye;
Houbeit for all this I thinke it be not I,
For to shew the matter indyde trulye,
I never use to rune awaye in wynter nor in vere
But allwayes in suche tyme and season of the yere   *960*
When honye lieth in the hives of bees,
And [all] maner frute falleth from the trees,
As apples, nuttes, peres, and plummes also,
Wherby a boie maie live abrod a moneth or two.
This cast do I use – I woll not with you fayne –
Therfore I wonder if he be I sertaine?
But and if he be, and you mete me abrod by
   chaunce,
Send me home to my maister with a vengaunce
And shew him if he cume not ere tomorowe nyght
I woll never receyve him agayne if I myght,   *970*
And in the meanetyme I woll give hym a grote
That woll well and thryftelye walke his cote!
For a more ungracious knave is not even now
Bytwene this place and Calycow,
[Nor] a more frantike mad knave in Bedelem,
Nor a more folle hence to Jherusalem,
That if to cume agayne parcace he shall refuse
I woll continew as I am and let hym choose;
And but he cum the soner, by Our Lady bright,
He shall lye without the dores all night,   *980*
For I wol shyte up the gate, and gete me to bede,
For I promisse you I have a verie gydie hede!
I nede no supper for this night
Nor wolde eate no meat though I myght,
And for you also, maister[s], I thinke it best
You go to bede, and take your rest,
For who of you had byn handelyd as I have ben

956 *twaye*: two   959 *vere*: spring   965 *cast*: tactic   967 *abrod*: at large, out of doors
972 *walke his cote*: make him sore   976 *folle*: fool   980 *without*: outside   981 *shyte*: shut
987 *who*: whoever

Wold not be long out of his bede I ween!
No more woll I, but stele out of syght;

990   I praye God geve you all good nyght,
And send you better hape and fortune,
Then to lesse yourselfe homward as I have don!

    [*Exit* CAREAWAY. *Enter the* EPILOGUE.]

[EPILOGUE:] Sumwhat it was, sayeth the proverbe olde,
That the catte winked when here ye was out;
That is to saye no tale can be tolde
But that sum Englyshe maye be piked therof out,
Yf to serche the Laten and ground of it men will go
    aboute;
As this trifling enterlud that before you hath bine
    rehersed
May sygnifye sum further meaning if it be well
    serched.

1000   Such is the fashyon of the worlde nowadayes
That the symple innosaïntes ar deluded
And an hundred thousand divers wayes
By suttle and craftye meanes shamefullie abused,
And by stren[g]th force, and vyolence oft tymes
    compelled
To belive and saye the moune is made of a grene
    chese,
Or ells have gret harme, and percace their life lese.

Ande an olde saying it is that most tymes might,
Force, strength, power, and colorable subtlete,
Dothe oppresse, debare, overcum and defeate ryght
Though the cause stand never so greatlye against
1010   equite,
And the truth therof be knowen for never so perfit
    certantye;

---

991 *hape*: luck, chance 992 *lesse*: lose 994 *ye*: eye 996 *piked*: picked 998 *bine*: been
rehersed: played, gone through 1001 *innosaintes*: innocents 1005 *moune*: moon 1006 *lese*:
lose 1008 *colorable*: plausible 1009 *debare*: strip, denude 1011 *perfit*: perfect

Ye, and the poore semple innocent that hath had
   wrong and injury
Must call the other his good maister for shewing
   hym such marcye.

And as it is daylie syne for fere of ferther disprofite
He must that man his best frende and maister call
Of whome he never received any maner benefite
And at whose hand he never had any good at all,
And must graunt, affirme, or denye, whatsoever he
   shall:
He must saye the croue is whight, yf he be so
   commaunded,
Ye, and that he himselfe is into another body
   chaunged.   *1020*

He must saye he dyd amysse though he never dyd
   offende;
He must aske forgivenes where he did no trespace,
Or ells be in troble, care, and meserye without ende
And be cast in sum arrierage without any grace;
And that thing he sawe done before his owne face
He must by compulsion stifelie denye,
And for feare whether he woll or not saye 'Tonge,
   you lye!'

And in everye faculte this thing is put in ure
And is so unyversall that I nede noone to name,
And as I fere is like evermore to endure   *1030*
For it is in all faculties a commyn sporte and game
The weker to saie as the stronger biddeth, or to
   have blam,
As a cunning sophist woll by argument bring to passe
That the rude shall confesse and graunt himselfe an
   ase.

1012 *semple*: simple   1014 *syne*: seen, observed   1019 *croue*: crow   1020 *Ye*: yea
1024 *arrierage*: a state of debt, in arrears   1026 *stifelie*: stoutly   1028 *put in ure*: put into
practice   1031 *commyn*: common   1034 *rude*: uneducated man

And this is the daylye exersise and practise of their
    scoles –
And not emongs them onlie but also emong all
    others –
The stronger to compell and make poore symple
    foles
To say as they commaund them in all maner
    matiers;
I woll name none particular but set them all
    togithers
1040   Without any exception, for I praye you shewe me
    one
Emonges all in the worlde that usethe not suche
    fasion.

He that is stronger, and more of power and might,
If he be disposed to revenge his cause
Woll sone pike a quarell, be it wrong or ryght,
To the inferior and weker for a cople of straues,
And woll agaynst him so extremelie lay the lawes
That he woll put hym to the worse, other by false
    injurie
Or by some crafte and subtelete, or ells by playne
    terani.

As you sawe ryght now by example playne,
1050   Another felowe being a counterfeat page
Brought the gentylman's servaunt out of his braine
And made hym graunt that himselfe was fallen in
    dotage,
Baryng hymselfe in hand that he dyd rage
And when he could not bryng that to passe by
    reason
He made him graunt it and saye so by
    compulsyon.

1036 *emongs*: amongst   1038 *matiers*: matters   1044 *sone pike*: soon pick   1047 *other*: either
1048 *terani*: tyranny   1052 *dotage*: madness, insanity   1053 *Baryng hymselfe in hand*:
deluding himself   *rage*: rave, run mad

Therfore happy are they that can beware
Into whose handes they fall by any suche chaunce,
Which if they do, they hardlye escape care,
Troble, miserie, and wofull grevaunce,
And thus I make an end, committing you to his
   gidaunce   *1060*
That made, and redemed us all, and to you that be
   now here,
I praye God graunt and send many a good newe
   yere.
   [*Exit the* EPILOGUE.]

Finis

Imprinted at London in Temes strete at the Vintre
unpon the thre Crayne wharfe by me
Wyllyam Copland

Roister Doister

NICHOLAS UDALL

The earliest known edition of *Roister Doister* survives in a single copy now preserved appropriately enough in the Library of Eton College. It is complete but for its first leaf, which no doubt carried the title-page which, had it been preserved, could have resolved the issue of the play's correct title: *Roister Doister* or *Ralph Roister Doister*. A key to its date of publication is provided by an entry in the accounts of the Stationers' Company for the year 1566–7:

R[cd] of Thomas hackett for his lycense for pryntinge of a play intituled Rauf Ruyster Duster &c' / iiij[d]

Its position in the Register suggests a date around October 1566 as the earliest possibility for the extant edition; however, the play was clearly written some years earlier, since the ambiguous letter read in Act III, scene 4, is quoted in the third edition of Thomas Wilson's *Rule of Reason*, which appeared, according to William L. Edgerton, in January 1553. Edgerton believes that the play was first presented before King Edward VI at Windsor in September 1552; if so, several references to the 'queen' in the present text suggest that it was revised during the reign of Mary I or Elizabeth I, either for publication or revival on stage. Indeed, there is reason to assume that at least one edition of the play was published prior to the extant version, which was printed by Henry Denham, and was presumably that licensed to Hackett by the Stationers' Company.

The play was not printed again until the nineteenth century; among the most useful modern editions are the following:

Joseph Quincy Adams, ed., *Chief Pre-Shakespearean Dramas*, Boston, 1924

F. S. Boas, ed., *Five Pre-Shakesperean Comedies*, Oxford, 1933

W. W. Greg, ed., *Roister Doister*, Malone Society Reprints, Oxford, 1934 (1935)

G. Scheurweghs, ed., *Nicholas Udall's Roister Doister* (Materials for the Study of Old English Drama, New Series 16), Louvain, 1939.

The present edition has been based primarily on that of Greg, with some use made of the others cited above; the cast-list has been adapted from that of Greg.

List of Characters

MATTHEW MERRYGREEK, *companion to Roister Doister*

RALPH ROISTER DOISTER, *a well-to-do braggart*

MADGE (OR MARGERY) MUMBLECRUST, *former nurse to Christian Custance*

TIBET TALKAPACE
ANNOT ALYFACE } *maids to Christian Custance*

DOBINET DOUGHTY
HARPAX } *servants to Roister Doister*

CHRISTIAN CUSTANCE, *a widow betrothed to Gawyn Goodluck*

TOM TRUEPENNY, *servant to Christian Custance*

A SCRIVENER

SYM SURESBY, *servant to Gawyn Goodluck*

GAWYN GOODLUCK, *a merchant*

TRISTRAM TRUSTY, *Gawyn Goodluck's friend*

Servants and Musicians in Roister Doister's household

Merrygreek: a merry mischief-maker   *Roister Doister*: a riotous blusterer   *Alyface*: ?'sour-face' (see note on line 280)   *Harpax*: a character of this name appears in Plautus' *Pseudolus*, the servant of an army officer   *Christian Custance*: for this name see note on line 172

ROISTER DOISTER

The Prologue

[*Enter the* PROLOGUE.]
[PROLOGUE:] What creature is in health, eyther
   yong or olde,
But som mirth with modestie wil be glad to use,
As we in thys Enterlude shall now unfolde,
Wherin all scurilitie we utterly refuse,
Avoiding such mirth wherin is abuse;
Knowing nothing more comendable for a man's
   recreation
Than Mirth which is used in an honest fashion:
For Myrth prolongeth lyfe, and causeth health.
Mirth recreates our spirites and voydeth
   pensivenesse,
Mirth increaseth amitie, not hindring our wealth,   *10*
Mirth is to be used both of more and lesse,
Being mixed with vertue in decent comlynesse,
As we trust no good nature can gainsay the same;
Which Mirth we intende to use, avoidyng all blame.
The wyse poets long time heretofore,
Under merrie Comedies secretes did declare,
Wherein was contained very vertuous lore,
With mysteries and forewarnings very rare.
Suche to write neither Plautus nor Terence dyd
   spare,
Whiche among the learned at this day beares the
   bell;   *20*
These with such other therein dyd excell.
Our Comedie or Enterlude which we intende to
   play

4 *refuse*: reject   9 *voydeth*: casts out   10 *amitie*: friendship   11 *both of more and lesse*: great
and lesser personages   20 *beares the bell*: takes the prize

Is named 'Royster Doyster' indeede,
Which against the vayneglorious doth invey,
Whose humour the roysting sort continually doth
    feede.
Thus by your pacience we intende to proceede
In this our Enterlude, by God's leave and grace,
And here I take my leave for a certaine space.

                                        [*Exit.*]

FINIS

Actus i   Scaena i.

Mathewe Merygreeke.   *He entreth singing.*
[MERRYGREEK:] As long lyveth the mery man (they
    say)
30   As doth the sory man, and longer by a day:
Yet the grassehopper for all his sommer pipyng,
Sterveth in winter wyth hungrie gripyng;
Therefore another sayd sawe doth men advise,
That they be together both mery and wise.
Thys lesson must I practise, or else ere long,
Wyth mee Mathew Merygreeke it will be wrong!
Indeede, men so call me, for by him that us bought,
Whatever chaunce betide, I can take no thought;
Yet wisedome woulde that I did myselfe bethinke
40   Where to be provided this day of meate and drinke:
For knowe ye, that for all this merie note of mine,
He might appose me now that should aske where I
    dine.
My lyving lieth heere and there, of God's grace,
Sometime wyth this good man, sometyme in that
    place,
Sometime Lewis Loytrer biddeth me come neere,
Somewhyles Watkin Waster maketh us good cheere,
Sometime Davy Diceplayer when he hath well cast

25 *roysting*: blustering, riotous 30 *sory*: solemn 33 *sawe*: saying, maxim. 42 *appose*:
baffle, perplex, put me to it

Keepeth revell route as long as it will last.
Sometime Tom Titivile maketh us a feast,
Sometime with Sir Hugh Pye I am a bidden gueast,   50
Sometime at Nichol Neverthrive's I get a soppe,
Sometime I am feasted with Bryan Blinkinsoppe,
Sometime I hang on Hankyn Hoddydodie's sleeve
But thys day on Ralph Royster Doyster's by hys
    leeve.
For truely of all men he is my chiefe banker
Both for meate and money, and my chiefe
    shootanker.
For, sooth Roister Doister in that he doth say,
And require what ye will ye shall have no nay.
But now of Roister Doister somewhat to expresse,
That ye may esteeme him after hys worthinesse;   60
In these twentie townes and seke them throughout,
Is not the like stocke, whereon to graffe a loute.
All the day long is he facing and craking
Of his great actes in fighting and fraymaking;
But when Roister Doister is put to his proofe,
To keepe the Queene's peace is more for his
    behoofe.
If any woman smyle or cast on hym an eye,
Up is he to the harde eares in love by and by,
And in all the hotte haste must she be hys wife,
Else farewell hys good days, and farewell his life!   70
Maister Raufe Royster Doister is but dead and gon
Excepte she on hym take some compassion;
Then chiefe of counsell must be Mathew
    Merygreeke –
'What if I for mariage to suche an one seeke?'
Then must I sooth it, whatever it is;
For what he sayth or doth cannot be amisse;

---

56 *shootanker*: sheet-anchor   57 *sooth*: flatter or humour by supporting   62 *graffe*: graft
63 *facing and craking*: bragging and boasting   66 *for his behoofe*: suits him better   68 *the
harde eares*: the very ears   75 *sooth*: support, encourage

Holde up his yea and nay, be his nowne white sonne,
Prayse and rouse him well, and ye have his heart
   wonne,
For so well liketh he his owne fonde fashions
80   That he taketh pride of false commendations.
But such sporte have I with him as I would not leese,
Though I should be bounde to lyve with bread and
   cheese.
For exalt hym, and have hym as ye lust indeede:
Yea, to hold his finger in a hole for a neede!
I can with a worde make him fayne or loth,
I can with as much make him pleased or wroth,
I can when I will make him mery and glad,
I can when me lust make him sory and sad,
I can set him in hope and eke in dispaire,
I can make him speake rough, and make him
90   speake faire.
But I marvell I see hym not all thys same day,
I wyll seeke him out – But loe, he commeth thys
   way!
I have yond espied hym sadly comming,
And in love for twentie pounde, by hys glommyng.

Actus i.   *Scaena ii.*

Rafe Roister Doister.   *Mathew Merygreeke.*
[*Enter* ROISTER DOISTER.]

R. ROYSTER: Come, death, when thou wilt, I am
   weary of my life!
M. MERY [*to audience*]: I tolde you, I, we should wowe
   another wife!
R. ROYSTER: Why did God make me suche a goodly
   person?
M. MERY [*to audience*]: He is in by the weke; we shall
   have sport anon.

77 *white sonne*: blue-eyed boy, favourite 78 *rouse*: encourage, stir up 81 *leese*: lose
89 *eke*: also 94 *glommyng*: sullen look 98 *in by the weke*: madly in love, over the moon

R. ROYSTER: And where is my trustie friende,
  Mathew Merygreeke?
M. MERY [*to audience*]: I wyll make as I sawe him not;
  he doth me seeke.   *100*
R. ROISTER: I have hym espyed methinketh, yond is
  hee,
  Hough Mathew Merygreeke, my friend, a worde
  with thee!
M. MERY [*to audience*]: I wyll not heare him, but make
  as I had haste –
  Farewell, all my good friendes, the tyme away
  dothe waste,
  And the tide they say tarrieth for no man!
R. ROISTER: Thou must with thy good counsell helpe
  me if thou can.
M. MERY: God keepe thee, worshypfull Maister
  Roister Doister –
  [*pretending to go*] And farewell, the lustie Maister
  Roister Doister!
R. ROYSTER: I muste needes speake with thee a
  worde or twaine –
M. MERY: Within a month or two I will be here
  againe;   *110*
  Negligence in greate affaires ye knowe may marre
  all.
R. ROISTER: Attende upon me now, and well
  rewarde thee I shall.
M. MERY: I have take my leave, and the tide is well
  spent.
R. ROISTER: I die except thou helpe; I pray thee be
  content;
  Doe thy parte wel nowe, and aske what thou wilt,
  For without thy aide my matter is all split!
M. MERY: Then to serve your turne I will some
  paines take,

108 *lustie*: brave, bold   116 *split*: ruined

And let all myne owne affaires alone for your sake.

R. ROYSTER: My whole hope and trust resteth onely
in thee.

120 M. MERY: Then can ye not doe amisse, whatever it bee!

R. ROYSTER: Gramercies, Merygreeke; most bounde
to thee I am.

M. MERY: But up with that heart, and speake out like
a ramme;

Ye speake like a capon that had the cough now:

Bee of good cheere; anon ye shall doe well ynow!

R. ROYSTER: Upon thy comforte, I will all things
well handle.

M. MERY: So loe, that is a breast to blowe out a
candle!

But what is this great matter I woulde faine
knowe?

We shall fynde remedie therefore, I trowe.

Doe ye lacke money? Yè knowe myne olde offers;

130 Ye have always a key to my purse and coffers.

R. ROYSTER: I thanke thee; had ever man suche a
frende?

M. MERY: Ye gyve unto me; I must needes to you lende.

R. ROYSTER: Nay, I have money plentie all things to
discharge.

M. MERY [aside]: That knewe I ryght well when I
made offer so large.

[R. ROISTER:] But it is no suche matter.

M. M[ERY:]   What is it than?

Are ye in daunger of debte to any man?

If ye be, take no thought nor be not afraide,

Let them hardly take thought how they shall be
paide.

R. ROYSTER: Tut, I owe nought.

M. M[ERY:]   What then? Fear ye
imprisonment?

123 *capon*: a cock castrated and fattened for table   124 *ynow*: enough   135 *than*: then
138 *hardly*: by all means, certainly

R. R[OISTER:] No.

M. M[ERY:]   No, I wist ye offende not, so to be
shent.   *140*

But if ye had, the Toure coulde not you so holde,

But to breake out at all times ye would be bolde.

What is it? hath any man threatned you to beate?

R. ROYSTER: What is he that durst have put me in
that heate?

He that beateth me, by his armes, shall well fynde

That I will not be farre from him nor runne
behinde!

M. MERY: That thing knowe all men ever since ye
overthrewe

The fellow of the lion which Hercules slewe.

But what is it than?

R. R[OISTER:]   Of love I make my mone.

M. MERY: Ah, this foolishe love, wilt neare let us
alone?   *150*

But bicause ye were refused the last day,

Ye sayd ye woulde nere more be intangled that way:

'I woulde medle no more, since I fynde all so unkinde.'

R. ROYSTER: Yea, but I cannot so put love out of my
minde!

MATH. MER: But is your love, tell me first, in any wise

In the way of mariage, or of merchandise?

If it may otherwise than lawfull be founde,

Ye get none of my helpe for an hundred pounde!

R. ROYSTER: No, by my trouth, I woulde have hir to
my wife.

M. MERY: Then are ye a good man, and God save
your life!   *160*

And what or who is she with whome ye are in love?

R. ROYSTER: A woman whome I knowe not by what
meanes to move.

M. MERY: Who is it?

---

140 *shent*: disgraced, ruined 149 *than*: then 151 *the last day*: yesterday

R. R[OISTER:]   A woman yond.

M. M[ERY:]   What is hir
name?

R. ROYSTER: Hir yonder.

M. M[ERY:]   Whom?

R. R[OISTER:]   Mistresse – ah –

M. M[ERY:]   Fy,
fy, for shame!

  Love ye, and know not whome but 'Hir yonde',
  'a woman'?

  We shall then get you a wife, I cannot tell whan!

R. ROYSTER: The faire woman that supped wyth us
yesternyght,

  And I harde hir name twice or thrice, and had it
ryght.

M. MERY: Yea, ye may see ye nere take me to good
cheere with you –

170   If ye had, I coulde have tolde you hir name now.

R. ROYSTER: I was to blame indeede, but the nexte
tyme perchaunce:

  And she dwelleth in this house –

M. M[ERY:]   What, Christian
Custance!

R. ROYSTER: Except I have hir to my wife, I shall
runne madde!

M. MERY: Nay, unwise perhaps, but I warrant you
for madde.

R. ROYSTER: I am utterly dead unlesse I have my
desire!

M. MERY: Where be the bellowes that blewe this
sodeine fire?

R. ROYSTER: I heare she is worthe a thousande
pounde and more –

M. MERY: Yea, but learne this one lesson of me afore:

  An hundred pounde of marriage money doubtlesse,

166 *whan*: when 168 *harde*: heard 169 *nere*: never 174 *for madde*: against madness

Is ever thirtie pounde sterlyng, or somewhat lesse,   *180*
So that hir thousande pounde yf she be thriftie
Is muche neere aboute two hundred and fiftie,
Howebeit wowers and widowes are never poore.

R. ROYSTER: Is she a widowe? I love hir better
    therefore!

M. MERY: But I heare she hath made promise to
    another –

R. ROYSTER: He shall goe without hir, and he were
    my brother!

M. MERY: I have hearde say – I am right well advised
    That she hath to Gawyn Goodlucke promised.

R. ROYSTER: What is that Gawyn Goodlucke?

M. M[ERY:]   A mer-
    chant man.

R. ROYSTER: Shall he speede afore me? Nay, sir, by
    sweete Sainct Anne!   *190*
    Ah, sir, 'Backare!' quod Mortimer to his sowe;
    I wyll have hir myne owne selfe, I make God a vow!
    For I tell thee she is worthe a thousande pounde.

M. MERY: Yet a fitter wife for your maship might be
    founde:
    Suche a goodly man as you might get one wyth lande,
    Besides poundes of golde a thousande and a
        thousande,
    And a thousande, and a thousande, and a
        thousande,
    And so to the summe of twentie hundred
        thousande;
    Your most goodly personage is worthie of no lesse.

R. ROYSTER: I am sorie God made me so comely
    doubtlesse,   *200*
    For that maketh me eche where so highly
    favoured,
    And all women on me so enamoured.

186 *and*: even if   191 *Backare*!: get back there!   *quod*: quoth   194 *maship*: mastership

M. MERY: 'Enamoured' quod you? Have ye spied out
 that?
Ah, sir, mary, nowe I see you know what is what!
'Enamoured' ka? Mary, sir, say that againe;
But I thought not ye had marked it so plaine!

R. ROYSTER: Yes, eche where they gaze all upon me
 and stare.

M. MERY: Yea, Malkyn, I warrant you as muche as
 they dare!
And ye will not beleve what they say in the streete,
210 When your mashyp passeth by all such as I meete,
That sometimes I can scarce finde what aunswere
 to make:
'Who is this?' (sayth one) 'Sir Launcelot du Lake?'
'Who is this, greate Guy of Warwike?' sayth
 another;
'No' (say I) 'it is the thirtenth Hercules' brother';
'Who is this? noble Hector of Troy?' sayth the
 thirde;
'No, but of the same nest' (say I) 'it is a birde.'
'Who is this? greate Goliah, Sampson, or
 Colbrande?'
'No' (say I) 'but it is a Brute of the Alie lande.'
'Who is this? greate Alexander? or Charle le
 Maigne?'
220 'No, it is the tenth worthie', say I to them agayne –
I knowe not if I sayd well?

R. R[OISTER:]   Yes, for so I am.

M. MERY: Yes, for there were but nine worthies
 before ye came.
To some others the thirde Cato I doe you call.
And so as well as I can I aunswere them all.
'Sir, I pray you, what lorde or great gentleman is
 this?'

---

205 *ka*: quotha, indeed, 'you don't say?' 208 *Malkyn*: a term of derision (see note)
217 *Goliah*: Goliath *Colbrande*: see note. 218 *Brute*, etc.: see note

'Maister Ralph Roister Doister, dame,' say I, ywis.
'O Lorde' (sayth she than) 'what a goodly man it
is;
Woulde Christ I had suche a husbande as he is!'
'O Lorde', (say some) 'that the sight of his face we
lacke!'
'It is inough for you' (say I) 'to see his backe;   *230*
His face is for ladies of high and noble parages,
With whome he hardly scapeth great mariages.'
With muche more than this, and much otherwise.

R. ROYSTER: I can thee thanke that thou canst suche
answeres devise:
But I perceyve thou doste me throughly knowe.

M. MERY: I marke your maners for myne owne
learnyng, I trowe;
But suche is your beautie, and suche are your
actes,
Suche is your personage, and suche are your
factes,
That all women faire and fowle, more and lesse,
They eye you, they lubbe you, they talke of you
doubtlesse.   *240*
Your pleasant looke maketh them all merie,
Ye passe not by, but they laugh till they be werie,
Yea and money coulde I have, the truth to tell,
Of many, to bryng you that way where they dwell.

R. ROYSTER: Merygreeke, for this thy reporting well
of mee –

M. MERY: What shoulde I else, sir? It is my duetie,
pardee!

R. ROYSTER: I promise thou shalt not lacke, while I
have a grote.

M. MERY: Faith, sir, and I nere had more nede of a
newe cote!

226 *ywis*: truly 231 *parages*: descent, rank 238 *factes*: feats 240 *lubbe*: love (cf. line
1189) 246 *pardee*: by God

R. ROYSTER: Thou shalte have one tomorowe, and
        golde for to spende.

M. MERY: Then I trust to bring the day to a good
250   ende!

    For as for mine owne parte, having money inowe,
    I coulde lyve onely with the remembrance of you —
    Bot nowe to your widowe whome you love so hotte.

R. ROYSTER: By Cocke, thou sayest truthe; I had
        almost forgotte!

M. MERY: What if Christian Custance will not have
        you? What?

R. ROISTER: Have me? yes, I warrant you, never
        doubt of that;

    I knowe she loveth me, but she dare not speake.

M. MERY: Indeede, meete it were somebody should it
        breake.

R. ROISTER: She looked one me twentie tymes
        yesternight,

    And laughed so —

M. M[ERY:]   That she coulde not sitte
260   upright —

R. ROISTER: No, faith, coulde she not.

                                No, even such
        a thing I cast!

R. ROYSTER: But for wowing thou knowest women
        are shamefast;

    But, and she knewe my minde, I knowe she would
        be glad,

    And thinke it the best chaunce that ever she had.

M. MERY: Too hir then like a man, and be bolde forth
        to starte;

    Wowers never speede well that have a false harte!

R. ROISTER: What may I best doe?

M. M[ERY:]   Sir, remaine ye a
        while [here]

251 *inowe*: enough   254 *Cocke*: God   261 *cast*: guessed   262 *shamefast*: bashful, modest

Ere long one or other of hir house will appere.
  Ye knowe my minde.
R. R[OISTER:]   Yea; now hardly lette me
  alone.
M. MERY: In the meanetime, sir, if you please, I wyll
  home,   *270*
  And call your musitians, for in this your case
  It would sette you forth, and all your wowyng
    grace;
  Ye may not lacke your instrumentes to play and
    sing.
R. ROYSTER: Thou knowest I can doe that.
M. M[ERY:]   As well as
  anything!
  Shall I go call your folkes, that ye may shewe a cast?
R. ROYSTER: Yea, runne, I beseeche thee, in all
  possible haste.
M. MERY: I goe.   *Exeat.*
R. R[OISTER:] Yea, for I love singyng out of
  measure;
  It comforteth my spirites and doth me great
  pleasure.
  [*Enter* MADGE MUMBLECRUST *and* TIBET
  TALKAPACE *from* DAME CUSTANCE*'s house.*]
  But who commeth forth yond from my swetehearte
  Custance?
  My matter frameth well; thys is a luckie chaunce!   *280*

Actus i.   *Scaena iii.*

MAGE MUMBLECRUST, *spinning on the distaffs.*
TIBET TALKAPACE, *sowyng.* ANNOT ALYFACE
knittyng. R. ROISTER.
M. MUMBL[ECRUST:] If thys distaffe were spoonne,
  Margerie Mumblecrust –

---

269 *hardly*: truly   275 *shewe a cast*: give a taste of your skill   277 *Exeat*: he goes out

TIB. TALK[APACE:] Where good stale ale is, will
    drinke no water I trust!

M. MUMBL: Dame Custance hath promised us good
    ale and white bread.

TIB. TALK: If she kepe not promise, I will beshrewe
    hir head!

    But it will be starke nyght before I shall have
    done.

R. ROYSTER [*to himself*]: I will stande here awhile,
    and talke with them anon;

    I heare them speake of Custance, which doth my
    heart good,

    To heare hir name spoken doth even comfort my
    blood.

M. MUMBL: Sit downe to your worke, Tibet, like a
    good girle.

TIB. TALK: Nourse, medle you with your spyndle
290   and your whirle!

    No haste but good, Madge Mumblecrust, for whip
    and whurre,

    The olde proverbe doth say, never made good furre.

M. MUMBL: Well, ye wyll sitte downe to your worke
    anon, I trust.

TIB. TALK: Soft fire maketh sweete malte, good
    Madge Mumblecrust.

M. MUMBL: And sweete malte maketh joly good ale
    for the nones –

TIB. TALK: Whiche will slide downe the lane without
    any bones!
    Cantet.

    'Olde browne bread crustes must have much good
    mumblyng,

    But good ale downe your throte hath good easie
    tumbling.'

284 *beshrewe*: curse   285 *starke nyght*: the dead of night   290 *whirle*: whorl, fly-wheel
291 *whurre*: haste, rushing about   292 *furre*: furrow   297 *Cantet*: she sings. *mumblyng*:
chewing

R. ROYSTER [*aside*]: The jolyest wenche that ere I
    hearde, little mouse;
  May I not rejoyce that she shall dwell in my
    house?   *300*

TIB. TALK: So, sirrha, nowe this geare beginneth for
    to frame.

M. MUMBL: Thanks to God, though your work stand
    still, your tong is not lame!

TIB. TALK: And though your teeth be gone, both so
    sharpe and so fine,
  Yet your tongue can renne on patins as well as
    mine!

M. MUMBL: Ye were not for nought named Tyb
    Talkeapace.

TIB. TALK: Doth my talke grieve you? Alack, God
    save your grace!

M. MUMBL: I holde a grote ye will drinke anon for
    this geare –

TIB. TALK: And I wyll not pray you the stripes for
    me to beare!

M. MUMBL: I holde a penny, ye will drinke without a
    cup.

TIB. TALK: Wherein so ere ye drinke, I wote ye
    drinke all up!   *310*

AN[NOT] ALYFACE [*entering*]: By Cock, and well
    sowed, my good Tibet Talkeapace!

TIB. TALK: And e'en as well knitte, my nowne Annot
    Alyface!

R. ROYSTER [*aside*]: See, what a sort she kepeth that
    must be my wife!
  Shall not I when I have hir leade a merrie life?

TIB. TALK: Welcome, my good wenche, and sitte
    here by me just.

AN. ALYFACE: And howe doth our olde beldame
    here, Mage Mumblecrust?

304 *patins*: clogs (which make a clatter)   307 *geare*: matter   309 *holde*: bet   311 *Cock*:
God   316 *beldame*: aged woman, 'granny'

TIB. TALK: Chyde, and finde faultes, and threaten to complaine.

AN. ALYFACE: To make us poore girles shent to hir is small gaine.

M. MUMBL: I dyd neyther chyde, nor complaine, nor threaten!

R. ROYSTER [*aside*]: It woulde grieve my heart to see
320   one of them beaten.

M. MUMBL: I dyd nothyng but byd hir worke and holde hir peace.

TIB. TALK: So would I, if you coulde your clattering ceasse;

But the devill cannot make Old Trotte holde hir tong!

AN. ALYFACE: Let all these matters passe, and we three sing a song;

So shall we pleasantly bothe the tyme beguile now,
And eke dispatche all our workes ere we can tell how.

TIB. TALK: I shrew them that say nay, and that shall not be I.

M. MUMBL: And I am well content.

TIB. TALK: Sing on then, by and by.

R. ROYSTER [*aside*]: And I will not away, but listen to their song,
330   Yet Merygreeke and my folkes tary very long!

     TIB, AN, *and* MARGERIE, *doe singe here.*

[ALL:] Pipe, mery Annot, etc.

Trilla, Trilla, Trillarie;
Worke, Tibet, worke, Annot, worke, Margerie.
Sewe, Tibet, knitte, Annot, spinne, Margerie.
Let us see who shall winne the victorie:

TIB. TALK: This sleve is not willyng to be sewed, I trowe;

A small thing might make me all in the grounde to throwe.

318 *shent*: blamed, scolded

Then they sing agayne.

[ALL:] Pipe, merrie Annot, etc.
  Trilla, Trilla, Trillarie;
  What, Tibet? What, Annot? What, Margerie?   *340*
  Ye sleepe, but we doe not; that shall we trie.
  Your fingers be nombde; our worke will not lie:

TIB. TALK: If ye doe so againe, well, I would advise
  you nay;
  In good sooth one stoppe more, and I make
  holyday!
    They sing the thirde tyme.

[ALL:] Pipe, mery Annot, etc.
  Trilla, Trilla, Trillarie;
  Nowe, Tibbet, now Annot, nowe Margerie,
  Nowe whippet apace for the maystrie,
  But it will not be, our mouth is so drie:

TIB. TALK: Ah, eche finger is a thombe today
  methinke;   *350*
  I care not to let all alone, choose it swimme or
  sinke!
    They sing the fourth tyme.

[ALL:] Pipe, mery Annot, etc.
  Trilla, Trilla, Trillarie;
  When, Tibet? When, Annot? When, Margerie?

[TIB. TALK:] I will not –

[AN. ALYFACE:]   I cannot –

[M. MUMBL:]   No more can I –

[ALL:] Then give we all over, and there let it lye!
    Lette hir [TIBET TALKAPACE] *caste down hir worke.*

TIB. TALK: There it lieth; the worst is but a curried
  cote;
  Tut, I am used therto; I care not a grote!

AN. ALYFACE: Have we done singyng since? Then
  will I in againe;

344 *stoppe:* check   348 *whippet:* bustle about   *for the maystrie:* to your utmost   357 *curried:*
beaten

Here I founde you, and here I leave both
360   twaine.   *Exeat.*

M. MUMBL: And I will not be long after – [*Sees*
RALPH ROISTER DOISTER.]

                                         Tib Talkeapace!

TIB TALK: What is the matter?

M. MUMB: Yond stode a man al
this space,

And hath hearde all that ever we spake togyther!

TIB. TALK: Mary, the more loute he for his comming
hither!

And the lesse good he can to listen maiden's talke;
I care not and I go byd him hence for to walke:
It were well done to knowe what he maketh here
away.

R. ROYSTER: Nowe myght I speak to them, if I wist
what to say.

M. MUMBL [*to* TIBET]: Nay, we will go both off, and
see what he is.

R. ROYSTER: One that hath hearde all your talke
370   and singyng ywis.

TIB. TALK: The more to blame you; a good thriftie
husbande

Woulde elsewhere have had some better matters in
hande.

R. ROYSTER: I dyd it for no harme, but for good love
I beare

To your dame, Mistresse Custance, I did your
talke heare.

And, Mistresse Nource, I will kisse you for
acquaintance.

M. MUMBL: I come anon, sir.

TIB. T[ALK:]   Faith, I would our Dame Custance
Sawe this geare!

M. M[UMBL] [*wiping her mouth eagerly*]: I must first
wipe al cleane; yea, I must.

360 *Exeat*: she goes out   366 *and*: if   370 *ywis*: certainly   375 *Nource*: nurse

TIB TALK: Ill chieve it, dotyng foole, but it must be
    cust!

    [ROISTER DOISTER *kisses* MADGE
    MUMBLECRUST.]

M. MUMBL: God yelde you, sir; chad not so much
    ichotte not whan,

  Nere since chwas bore chwine, of such a gay
    gentleman.   *380*

R. ROYSTER: I will kisse you too, mayden, for the
    good will I beare you.

TIB. TALK: No, forsoth; by your leave, ye shall not
    kisse me!

R. ROYSTER: Yes; be not afearde, I doe not disdayne
    you a whit.

TIB. TALK: Why shoulde I feare you? I have not so
    little wit;

  Ye are but a man, I knowe very well!

R. R[OISTER:]   Why then?

TIB. TALK: Forsooth, for I wyll not; I use not to kisse
    men.

R. ROYSTER: I would faine kisse you too, good
    maiden, if I myght.

TIB. TALK: What shold that neede?

R. R[OISTER:]   But to honor you
    by this light!

  I use to kisse all them that I love, to God I vowe.

TIB. TALK: Yea, sir? I pray you, when dyd you last
    kisse your cowe?   *390*

R. ROYSTER: Ye might be proude to kisse me, if ye
    were wise.

TIB. TALK: What promotion were therin?

R. R[OISTER:]   Nourse is
    not so nice.

TIB. TALK: Well, I have not bene taught to kissing
    and licking.

378 *Ill chieve it*: bad luck to her   *cust*: kissed   379 *chad* etc.: see Appendix   386 *I use not*: it
is not my habit   392 *nice*: reluctant, shy

R. ROYSTER: Yet I thanke you, Mistresse Nourse; ye
    made no sticking.

M. MUMBL: I will not sticke for a kosse with such a
    man as you!

TIB. TALK: They that lust: I will againe to my
    sewyng now.
    [*Enter* ANNOT ALYFACE.]

AN. ALYFAC[E:] Tidings, hough! Tidings! Dame
    Custance greeteth you well.

R. ROYSTER: Whome, me?

AN. AL[YFACE:]   You, sir? No, sir! I do no
    suche tale tell!

R. ROYSTER: But and she knewe me here!

AN. AL[YFACE:]   Tybet
    Talkeapace,
  Your mistresse Custance and mine must speake
400   with your grace.

TIB. TALK: With me?

AN. ALY[FACE:] Ye muste come in to hir out of all
    doutes.

TIB. TALK: And my work not half done? A mischief
    on all loutes!
    Ex[*eant*] *am*[*bae.*]

R. ROYSTER: Ah, good sweet nourse!

M. MUMB[L:]   A, good sweete
    gentleman!

  R. R[OISTER:]   [How now?]

M. MUMBL: Nay, I cannot tel, sir, but what thing
    would you?

R. ROYSTER: Howe dothe sweete Custance, my heart
    of gold, tell me how?

M. MUMBL: She dothe very well sir, and commaunde
    me to you.

R. ROYSTER: To me?

M. M[UMBL:]   Yea, to you, sir.

---

395 *kosse*: kiss 400 *your grace*: ironic 402 *Exeant ambae*: they both exit

R. R[OISTER:]   To me? Nurse,
  tel me plain –
  To me?
M. MUMB[L:] Ye.
R. R[OISTER:]   That word maketh me alive again.
M. MUMBL: She commaunde me to one last day,
  whoere it was.
R. ROYSTER: That was e'en to me and none other,
  by the Masse!   *410*
M. MUMBL: I cannot tell you surely, but one it was.
R. ROYSTER: It was I and none other: this commeth
  to good passe.
  I promise thee, nourse, I favour hir.
M. MUMB[L:]   E'en so sir.
R. ROYSTER: Bid her sue to me for mariage.
M. MUMB[L:]   E'en so sir.
R. ROYSTER: And surely for thy sake she shall speede.
M. MUMB[L:] E'en so sir.
R. ROYSTER: I shall be contented to take hir.
M. MUMB[L:]   E'en so sir.
R. ROYSTER: But at thy request and for thy sake.
M. MUMB[L:]   E'en so sir.
R. ROISTER: And come hearke in thine eare what to say.
M. MUMB[L:]   E'en so sir.
  Here lette him tell hir a great long tale in hir eare.

             Actus i.   Scaena iiii.

  Mathew Merygreeke.   Dobinet Doughtie.   Harpax.
       Ralph Royster.   Margerie Mumblecrust.
  [*Enter* MERRYGREEK, *followed by* DOBINET
  DOUGHTY, HARPAX *and another servant with their
  instruments.*]
M. MERY: Come on, sirs, apace, and quite yourselves
  like men;
  Your pains shal be rewarded.

409 *last day*: yesterday   415 *speede*: proceed successfully

121

420 D. DOU[GHTY:]   But I wot not when.

M. MERY: Do your maister worship as ye have done
    in time past.

D. DOUGH: Speake to them; of mine office he shall
    have a cast.

M. MERY: Harpax, looke that thou doe well too, and
    thy fellow.

HARPAX: I warrant, if he will myne example folowe.

M. MERY: Curtsie, whooresons; douke you and
    crouche at every worde!

D. DOUGH: Yes, whether our maister speake earnest
    or borde.

M. MERY: For this lieth upon his preferment indeede.

D. DOUGH: Oft is hee a wower, but never doth he
    speede.

M. MERY: But with whome is he nowe so sadly
    roundyng yond?

430 D. DOUGH: With *Nobs nicebecetur miserere* fonde.

[M.] MERY [*to* ROISTER DOISTER]: God be at your
    wedding, be ye spedde alredie?

I did not suppose that your love was so greedie;

I perceive nowe ye have chose of devotion,

And joy have ye, ladie, of your promotion!

R. ROYSTER: Tushe, foole, thou art deceived; this is
    not she!

M. MERY: Well mocke muche of hir, and keepe hir
    well, I vise ye:

I will take no charge of such a faire piece keeping.

M. MUMBL: What ayleth thys fellowe? He driveth me
    to weeping!

M. MERY: What weepe on the weddyng day? Be
    merrie, woman!

440   Though I say it, ye have chose a good gentlemen.

---

422 *a cast*: a sample 425 *whooresons*: term of abuse *douke*: duck 426 *borde*: jest 429 *sadly roundyng*: whispering earnestly 430 *Nobs nicebecetur miserere*: see note 436 *mocke*: see note 436 *vise*: advise

R. ROYSTER: Kock's nownes! What meanest thou,
   man? Tut, a whistle!

M. MERY: Ah, sir, be good to hir; she is but a gristle;
   Ah, sweete lambe and coney!

R. R[OISTER:]   Tut, thou art deceived.

M. MERY: Weepe no more, lady; ye shall be well
   received:
   Up wyth some mery noyse, sirs, to bring home the
   bride!

R. ROYSTER: Gog's armes, knave, art thou madde? I
   tel thee thou art wide!

M. MERY: Then ye entende by nyght to have hir
   home brought?

R. ROYSTER: I tel thee no.

M. M[ERY:]   How then?

R. R[OISTER:]   'Tis neither
   ment ne thought.

M. MERY: What shall we then doe with hir?

R. R[OISTER:]   Ah, foolish harebraine!
   This is not she!

M. M[ERY:]   No is? Why then, unsayde againe,   *450*
   And what yong girle is this with your mashyp so
   bolde?

R. ROYSTER: A girle?

M. M[ERY:]   Yea. I daresay, scarce yet three
   score yere old!

R. ROYSTER: This same is the faire widowe's nourse
   of whome ye wotte.

M. MERY: Is she but a nourse of a house? Hence,
   home, olde trotte;
   Hence at once!

R. R[OISTER:]   No, no!

M. M[ERY:]   What, an please your maship,
   A nourse talke so homely with one of your worship?

---

441 *Kocks nownes*: God's wounds   *a whistle*: (she is only) a mouthpiece (for Dame
Custance)   442 *a gristle*: a tender or feeble person   443 *coney*: a rabbit (term of
endearment)

R. ROYSTER: I will have it so: it is my pleasure and will.

M. MERY: Then I am content. Nourse, come againe,
tarry still.

R. ROYSTER: What, she will helpe forward this my
sute for hir part.

M. MERY: Then ist mine owne pygsnie, and blessing
460   on [her] hart!

R. ROYSTER: This is our best frend, man.

M. M[ERY:]   Then teach
hir what to say.

M. MUMBL: I am taught alreadie.

M. M[ERY:]   Then go, make no delay.

R. ROYSTER [*to* MADGE MUMBLECRUST]: Yet hark
one word in thine eare.

M. M[ERY] [*to the* SERVANTS]: Back, sirs, from his taile!

R. ROYSTER: Backe, vilaynes, will ye be privie of my
counsaile?

M. MERY: Backe, sirs, so; I tolde you afore ye woulde
be shent.

R. ROYSTER [*to* MADGE MUMBLECRUST]: She shall
have the first day a whole pecke of argent.

M. MUMBL: A pecke? *Nomine patris*, have ye so much
spare?

R. ROYSTER: Yea, and a cartelode therto, or else
were it bare;

Besides other movables, housholde stuffe, and lande.

M. MUMBL: Have ye lands too?

R. R[OISTER:]   An hundred marks.

470 M. M[ERY:]   Yea, a thousand!

M. MUMBL: And have ye cattell too? and sheepe too?

R. R[OISTER:]   Yea, a fewe.

M. MERY: He is ashamed the number of them to shewe.
E'en rounde about him as many thousande sheepe
goes,

460 *pygsnie*: darling (see note) 465 *shent*: blamed, scolded 466 *argent*: silver 467 *Nomine patris*: in the name of the Father

124

As he and thou and I too have fingers and toes.

M. MUMBL: And how many yeares olde be you?

R. R[OISTER:]   Fortie
at lest.

M. MERY: Yea, and thrice fortie to them!

R. R[OISTER:]   Nay, now thou dost jest!
I am not so olde; thou misreckonest my yeares!

M. MERY: I know that; but my minde was on
bullockes and steeres.

M. MUMBL: And what shall I shewe hir your
maistership's name is?

R. ROYSTER: Nay; she shall make sute ere she know
that ywis.   480

M. MUMBL: Yet let me somewhat knowe.

M. M[ERY:]   This is hee understand,
That killed the blewe spider in Blanchepouderlande.

M. MUMBL: Yea, Jesus; William, zee law, dyd he zo, law?

M. MERY: Yea, and the last elephant that ever he sawe,
As the beast passed by, he start out of a buske,
And e'en with pure strength of armes pluckt out
his great tuske!

M. MUMBL: Jesus, *nomine patris*, what a thing was that?

R. ROISTER: Yea but, Merygreke, one thing thou
hast forgot.

M. M[ERY:]   What?

R. ROYSTER: Of thother elephant —

M. M[ERY:]   Oh, hym that
fledde away?

R. ROYSTER: Yea.

M. M[ERY:]   Yea, he knew that his match was   490
in place that day;
Tut, he bet the King of Crickets on Christmasse day
That he crept in a hole, and not a worde to say.

---

483 *zee law*, etc.: see Appendix 485 *buske*: bush 491 *bet*: beat

M. MUMBL: A sore man, by zembletee.

M. M[ERY:]   Why, he wrong
    a club

Once in a fray out of the hande of Belzebub!

R. ROYSTER: And how when Mumfision – ?

M. M[ERY:]   Oh, your
    coustrelyng

Bore the lanterne afielde so before the gozelyng –

Nay, that is to long a matter now to be tolde:

Never aske his name, Nurse, I warrant thee, be bolde!

He conquered in one day from Rome to Naples

And woonne townes, Nourse, as fast as thou canst

500   make apples!

M. MUMBL: O Lorde, my heart quaketh for feare! He
    is to sore!

R. ROYSTER: Thou makest hir to much afearde; Mery-
    greeke, no more!

This tale would feare my sweetheart Custance
    right evill.

M. MERY: Nay, let hir take him, Nurse, and feare not
    the devill.

But thus is our song dasht. Sirs, ye may home
    againe –

    [DOBINET DOUGHTY, HARPAX, *etc. start to leave.*]

R. ROYSTER: No, shall they not! I charge you all
    here to remaine –

The villaine slaves! A whole day ere they can be
    founde!

M. MERY: Couche on your marybones, whooresons,
    down to the ground!

Was it meete he should tarie so long in one place

510   Without harmonie of musike, or some solace?

Whoso hath suche bees as your maister in hys
    head

---

493 *sore*: fierce   *by zembletee*: apparently   *wrong*: wrung   495 *coustrelyng*: lad, attendant
496 *gozelyng*: gosling   501 *to sore*: too fierce   503 *feare*: scare   508 *marybones*: knees

Had neede to have his spirites with musike to be fed!
[*Strikes* ROISTER DOISTER's *shoulder*.]
By your maistership's licence –
R. R[OISTER:]   What is that? a moate?
M. MERY: No, it was a foole's feather had light on
your coate.
R. ROISTER: I was nigh no feathers since I came
from my bed!
M. MERY: No, sir, it was a haire that was fall from
your hed.
R. ROISTER: My men com when it plese them.
M. M[ERY] [*striking him again*]:   By your leve –
R. R[OISTER:]   What is that?
M. MERY: Your gown was foule spotted with the foot
of a gnat.
R. ROISTER: Their maister to offende they are
nothing afearde.
[MERRYGREEK *hits him again*.]
What now?
M. M[ERY:]   A lousy haire from your maistership's
beard.   *520*
And, sir, for Nurse's sake, pardon this one offence.
OMNES[FAMULI:] We shall not after this shew the
like negligence.
R. ROYSTER: I pardon you this once, and come sing
nere the wurse.
M. MERY: How like you the goodnesse of this
gentleman, Nurse?
M. MUMBL: God save his maistership that so can his
men forgeve,
And I wyll heare them sing ere I go, by his leave.
R. ROYSTER: Mary, and thou shalt, wenche; come,
we two will daunce.
M. MUMBL: Nay, I will by myne owne selfe foote the
song perchaunce.

514 *foole's*: a pun on 'fool's' and 'fowl's' 522 *Omnes famuli*: all the servants

127

R. ROYSTER: Go to it, sirs, lustily.

M. MUMBL: Pipe up a mery note;

530   Let me heare it playde, I will foote it for a grote.

Cantent

[DOBINET, HARPAX, *etc.*:] Whoso to marry a minion
    wyfe
    Hath hadde good chaunce and happe,
    Must love hir and cherishe hir all this life,
    And dandle hir in his lappe.

    If she will fare well, yf she yll go gay,
    A good husbande ever styll,
    Whatever she lust to doe or to say,
    Must lette hir have hir owne will.

    About what affaires soever he goe,
540   He must shewe hir all his mynde,
    None of hys counsell she may be kept froe,
    Else is he a man unkynde.

R. ROYSTER: Now, Nurse, take thys same letter here
    to thy mistresse,
    And as my trust is in thee, plie my businesse.

M. MUMBL: It shal be done.

M. M[ERY:]   Who made it?

R. R[OISTER:]   I wrote it ech whit.

M. MERY: Then nedes it no mending.

R. R[OISTER:]   No, no!

M. M[ERY:]   No, I
    know your wit.

R. ROYSTER: I warrant it wel.

                  It shal be delivered.
    But if ye speede, shall I be considered?

M. MERY: Whough! Dost thou doubt of that?

MADGE: What
    shal I have?

---

530 *Cantent*: they sing   531 *minion*: dainty, pretty   537 *lust*: wishes   541 *froe*: from
548 *speede*: succeed

M. MERY: An hundred times more than thou canst
    devise to crave.   *550*
M. MUMBL: Shall I have some newe geare? for my
    olde is all spent.
M. MERY: The worst kitchen wench shall goe in
    ladie's rayment.
M. MUMBL: Yea?
M. M[ERY:]   And the worst drudge in the house
    shal go better
Than your mistresse doth now.
MAR[GERY:] Then I trudge with your letter. [*Exit
into house.*]
R. ROYSTER: Now may I repose me; Custance is
    mine owne.
Let us sing and play homeward that it may be knowne.
M. MERY: But are you sure that your letter [shall win her?]
R. ROYSTER: I wrote it myselfe.
M. MERY: Then sing we to dinner!
    Here they sing, and go out singing.

Actus i.   *Scaena v.*

   Christian Custance.   *Margerie Mumblecrust.*
[*Enter* CHRISTIAN CUSTANCE *from the house,
carrying the letter, followed by* MARGERY
MUMBLECRUST.]

C[HRISTIAN] CUSTANCE: Who tooke thee thys letter,
    Margerie Mumblecrust?
M. MUMBL: A lustie gay bacheler tooke it me of trust,   *560*
And if ye seeke to him he will lowe your doing.
C. CUSTANCE: Yea, but where learned he that
    manner of wowing?
M. MUMBL: If to sue to hym you will any paines take,
He will have you to his wife (he sayth) for my sake.

---

559 *tooke*: brought 560 *lustie*: pleasant, cheerful 561 *lowe your doing*: approve of your
doing so

C. CUSTANCE: Some wise gentleman belike! I am
    bespoken;
  And I thought verily thys had bene some token
  From my dear spouse Gawin Goodluck, whom
    when him please
  God luckily sende home to both our heartes' ease.

M. MUMBL: A joyly man it is, I wote well by report,
570   And would have you to him for marriage resort:
  Best open the writing, and see what it doth speake.

C. CUSTANCE: At thys time, Nourse, I will neither
    reade ne breake.

M. MUMBL: He promised to give you a whole pecke of
    golde –

C. CUSTANCE: Perchaunce lacke of a pynte when it
    shall be all tolde!

M. MUMBL: I would take a gay riche husbande, and I
    were you.

C. CUSTANCE: In good sooth, Madge, e'en so would I
    if I were thou!
  But no more of this fond talke now, let us go in,
  And see thou no more move me folly to begin,
  Nor bring mee no mo letters for no man's pleasure,
  But thou know from whom.

580 M. M[UMBL:]   I warrant, ye shall be sure.
  [*They go back into the house.*]

Actus ii.   Scaena i.

Dobinet Doughtie.

[*The following morning. Enter* DOBINET DOUGHTY
with a package.]

D. DOUGH: Where is the house I goe to, before or
    behinde?
  I know not where nor when how I shal it finde:
  If I had ten men's bodies and legs and strength,

572 *breake*: nor tear it up 577 *fond*: foolish 579 *mo*: more 580 *But*: unless

This trotting that I have must needes lame me at
    length.
And nowe that my maister is new set on wowyng,
I trust there shall none of us finde lacke of doyng:
Two paire of shoes a day will nowe be too litle
To serve me, I must trotte to and fro so mickle!
'Go beare me thys token!' 'Carrie me this letter!'
Nowe this is the best way, nowe that way is better;   *590*
Up before day, sirs, I charge you, an houre or twaine,
'Trudge, do me thys message, and bring worde
    quicke againe',
If one misse but a minute, then 'His armes and
    woundes!
I woulde not have slacked for ten thousand poundes!'
'Nay, see, I beseeche you, if my most trustie page
Goe not nowe aboute to hinder my mariage!'
So fervent hotte wowyng, and so farre from wiving,
I trowe never was any creature livyng!
With every woman is he in some love's pang,
Then up to our lute at midnight, 'twangledome
    twang',   *600*
Then 'twang' with our sonets, and 'twang' with
    our dumps,
And 'heyhough' from our heart, as heavie as lead
    lumpes:
Then to our recorder with 'toodleloodle poope'
As the howlet out of an yvie bushe should hoope.
Anon to our gitterne, 'Thrumpledum,
    thrumpledum thrum,
Thrumpledum, thrumpledum, thrumpledum,
    thrumpledum thrum'.
Of songs and balades also he is a maker,
And that can he as finely doe as Jacke Raker;
Yea, and *extempore* will he dities compose,
Foolishe Marsias nere made the like, I suppose;   *610*

588 *mickle*: much 601 *sonets*: songs *dumps*: mournful tunes 604 *howlet*: owl 605 *gitterne*:
an early form of guitar 608 *Jacke Raker*: see notes 610 *Marsias*: see note

Yet must we sing them, as good stuffe I undertake,
As for such a penman is well fittyng to make:
'Ah, for these long nights, heyhow, when will it be
    day?
I feare ere I come she will be wowed away.'
Then when aunswere is made that it may not bee,
'O death, why commest thou not by and by?'
    (sayth he).
But then from his heart to put away sorowe,
He is as farre in with some newe love next morowe.
But in the meane season we trudge and we trot,
620   From dayspring to midnyght I sit not nor rest not.
And now am I sent to Dame Christian Custance:
But I feare it will endé with a mocke for pastance!
I bring hir a ring, with a token in a cloute,
And by all gesse, this same is hir house out of
    doute.
I knowe it nowe perfect; I am in my right way:
    [*Enter* MADGE MUMBLECRUST.]
And loe, yond the olde nourse that was wyth us
    last day!

Actus ii.   *Scaena ii.*

Mage Mumblecrust.   *Dobinet Doughtie.*

M. MUMBL [*to herself*]: I was nere so shoke up afore
    since I was borne,
    That our mistresse coulde not have chid, I wold
     have sworne:
    And I pray God I die if I ment any harme,
630   But for my lifetime this shall be to me a charme.
D. DOUGH: God you save and see, Nurse, and howe
    is it with you?
M. MUMBL: Mary, a great deale the worse it is for
    suche as thou!

616 *by and by*: straightaway   622 *a mocke for pastance*: something derisory only providing
amusement   623 *cloute*: a piece of cloth

D. DOUGH: For me? Why so?

M. MUMB: Why wer not thou one
   of them, say,
  That song and playde here with the gentleman last
   day?

D. DOUGH: Yes, and he would know if you have for
   him spoken,
  And prayes you to deliver this ring and token.

M. MUMBL: Nowe, by the token that God tokened,
   brother,
  I will deliver no token one nor other!
  I have once ben so shent for your maister's pleasure,
  As I will not be agayne for all hys treasure.   640

D. DOUGH: He will thank you, woman.

M. M[UMBL:]   I will none of
  his thanke.   *Ex[it.]*

D. DOUGH: I weene I am a prophete, this geare will
   prove blanke:
  But what? should I home againe without answere go?
  It were better go to Rome on my head than so.
  I will tary here this moneth, but some of the house
  Shall take it of me, and then I care not a louse.

    [*Enter* TRUEPENNY *from the house.*]

  But yonder commeth forth a wenche or a ladde;
  If he have not one Lumbarde's touche, my lucke is
   bad.

    [*Stands aside.*]

     Actus ii.   *Scaena iii.*

   Truepenie.   *D. Dough.*   *Tibet T.*   *Anot Al.*

TRUPENY: I am cleane lost for lacke of mery companie;
  We gree not halfe well within, our wenches and I;   650
  They will commaunde like mistresses, they will
   forbyd:

---

637 *token … tokened*: sign … signified   645 *moneth*: month   648 *Lumbarde's touche*: see
note   650 *gree*: agree, accord

If they be not served, Trupeny must be chyd.
Let them be as mery nowe as ye can desire;
With turnyng of a hande, our mirth lieth in the mire:
I cannot skill of such chaungeable mettle,
There is nothing with them but 'In docke, out nettle!'

D. DOUGH [*aside*]: Whether is it better that I speake
to him furst,
Or he first to me; it is good to cast the wurst.
If I beginne first, he will smell all my purpose,

660 Otherwise I shall not neede anything to disclose.

TRUPENY: What boy have we yonder? I will see what
he is.

D. DOUGH: He commeth to me. It is hereabout ywis.

TRUPENY: Wouldest thou ought, friende, that thou
lookest so about?

D. DOUGH: Yea, but whether ye can help me or no,
I dout.
I seeke to one mistresse Custance house here
dwellyng.

TRUPENIE: It is my mistresse ye seeke too by your
telling.

D. DOUGH: Is there any of that name heere but shee?

TRUPENIE: Not one in all the whole towne that I
knowe, pardee.

D. DOUGH: A widowe she is, I trow —

TRUP[ENY:]   And what and she be?

D. DOUGH: But ensured to an husbande —

670 TRUP[ENY:]   Yea, so thinke we.

D. DOUGH: And I dwell with hir husbande that
trusteth to be.

TRUPENIE: In faith, then must thou needes be
welcome to me;
Let us for acquaintance shake handes togither,
And whatere thou be, heartily welcome hither!

---

655 *skill of*: understand, cope with   658 *cast*: calculate, assess   668 *pardee*: truly
670 *ensured*: engaged, pledged to

[*They shake hands. Enter* TIBET TALKAPACE *and*
ANNOT ALYFACE.]

TIB. TALK: Well, Trupenie, never but flinging?

AN. AL[YFACE:]   And frisking?

TRUPENIE: Well, Tibet and Annot, still swingyng
    and whiskyng?

TIB. TALK: But ye roile abroade!

AN. AL[YFACE:]   In the streete everewhere.

TRUPENIE: Where are ye twaine? In chambers, when
    ye mete me there?

But come hither, fooles, I have one nowe by the
    hande,

Servant to hym that must be our mistresse
    husbande,   *680*

Byd him welcome.

AN. ALYFACE: To me truly is he welcome.

TIB. TALK: Forsooth, and as I may say, heartily
    welcome.

D. DOUGH: I thank you, mistresse maides.

AN. AL[YFACE:]   I hope we
    shal better know.

TIB. TALK: And when wil our new master come?

D. DOU[GH:]   Shortly, I trow.

TIB. TALK: I would it were tomorrow; for till he resorte,

Our mistresse being a widow hath small comforte,

And I hearde our nourse speake for an husbande today

Ready for our mistresse, a riche man and a gay,

And we shall go in our Frenche hoodes every day,

In our silke cassocks (I warrant you) freshe and gay,   *690*

In our tricke ferdegews and billiments of golde,

Brave in our sutes of chaunge seven double folde,

Then shall ye see Tibet, sirs, treade the mosse so
    trimme —

Nay, why sayd I treade? Ye shall see hir glide and swimme,

675 *flinging*: dashing about   676 *whiskyng*: whirling around   677 *roile*: roam, rampage
everewhere: everywhere   690 *cassocks*: long gowns   691 *tricke ferdegews*: smart farthingales
billiments: ornamental head-dresses   692 *Brave*: fine

Not lumperdee clumperdee like our spaniell Rig!

TRUPENY: Mary then, prickmedaintie, come toste
me a fig;

Who shall then know our Tib Talkeapace, trow ye?

AN. ALYFACE: And why not Annot Alyface as fyne as
she?

TRUPENY: And what, had Tom Trupeny a father or
none?

AN. ALYFACE: Then our prety newecome man will
700   looke to be one.

TRUPENY: We foure, I trust, shall be a joily mery knot:
Shall we sing a fitte to welcome our friende,
Annot?

AN. ALYFACE: Perchaunce he cannot sing.

D. DOUGH: I am at all assayes.

TIB. TALK: By Cocke, and the better welcome to us
alwayes!

Here they sing.

[ALL:] A thing very fitte
        For them that have witte,
        And are felowes knitte
        Servants in one house to bee,
        Is fast, fast for to sitte,
710   And not oft to flitte,
        Nor varie a whitte,
        But lovingly to agree.

        No man complainyng,
        Nor other disdayning,
        For losse or for gainyng,
        But felowes or friends to bee:
        No grudge remainyng,
        No worke refrainyng,
        Nor helpe restrainyng,
720   But lovingly to agree.

---

696 *prickmedaintie*: 'Miss Fancy-pants' (see note) *toste*: toast 700 *prety*: pleasant, clever
702 *fitte*: song 703 *at all assayes*: ready for anything 704 *Cocke*: God

No man for despite,
By worde or by write
His felowe to twite,
But further in honestie;
No good turnes entwite,
Nor olde sores recite,
But let all goe quite,
And lovingly to agree.

After drudgerie,
When they be werie,   730
Then to be merie,
To laugh and sing they be free;
With chip and cherie,
Heigh derie derie,
Trill on the berie,
And lovingly to agree.

Finis.

TIB. TALK: Wyll you now in with us unto our
   mistresse go?
D. DOUGH: I have first for my maister an errand or
   two.
   But I have here from him a taken and a ring,
   They shall have moste thanke of hir that first doth
   it bring.   740
TIB. TALK [*taking the package*]: Mary, that will I!
TRUPEN[Y:]   See
   and Tibet snatch not now!
TIB. TALK: And why may not I, sir, get thanks as
   well as you?   *Exeat.*
AN. ALYFACE [*calling after her*]: Yet get ye not all; we
   will go with you both,
   And have part of your thanks, be ye never so loth!
   Exeant omnes.

---

723 *twite*: taunt   725 *entwite*: rebuke   735 *Trill on the berie*: ? pass round the wine (see
note)   739 *taken*: i.e. token   742 *Exeat*: she exits (cf. line 746)   744 *Exeant omnes*: they all
exit

D. DOUGH: So my handes are ridde of it; I care for no
    more:
I may now returne home: so durst I not afore.

Exeat.

Actus ii   Scaena iiii.

C. Custance.   Tibet.   Annot Alyface.   Trupeny.
[*Enter* CHRISTIAN CUSTANCE *in a rage, followed
by* TIBET, ANNOT, *and* TRUEPENNY.]
C. CUSTANCE: Nay, come forth all three; and come
    hither, pretie mayde:
    [TIBET *steps forward*]
Will not so many forewarnings make you afrayde?
TIB. TALK: Yes, forsoth.
C. CUSTANCE: But stil be a runner up and
    downe,
750   Still be a bringer of tidings and tokens to towne?
TIB. TALK: No, forsooth, mistresse.
C. CUSTANCE: Is all your delite and joy
    In whiskyng and ramping abroade like a tomboy?
TIB. TALK: Forsoth, these were there too, Annot and
    Trupenie.
TRUPENIE: Yea, but ye alone tooke it, ye cannot
    denie.
ANNOT ALY[FACE:] Yea, that ye did!
TIBET: But if I had
    not, ye twaine would.
C. CUSTANCE [*to* TIBET]: You great calfe, ye should
    have more witte, so ye should;
    [*To the others*] But why shoulde any of you take
    such things in hande?
TIBET: Bicause it came from him that must be your
    husbande.
C. CUSTANCE: How do ye know that?

752 *whiskyng and ramping*: charging about, on the rampage

138

TIBET: Forsoth, the
  boy did say so.
C. CUSTANCE: What was his name?
AN. AL[YFACE:] We asked not.
C. CUST[ANCE:] [Why did ye no?] *760*
AN. ALIFACE: He is not farre gone of likelyhod.
TRUPENY: I will
  see.
C. CUSTANCE: If thou canst finde him in the streete,
  bring him to me.
TRUPENIE: Yes. *Exeat.*
C. CUST[ANCE:] Well ye naughty girles, if ever I
  perceive
  That henceforth you do letters or tokens receive,
  To bring unto me from any person or place,
  Except ye first shewe me the partie face to face,
  Eyther thou or thou, full truly abye thou shalt.
TIBET: Pardon this, and the next tyme pouder me in
  salt!
C. CUSTANCE: I shall make all girles by you twaine
  to beware.
TIBET: If I ever offende againe, do not me spare! *770*
  But if ever I see that false boy any more,
  By your mistreshyp's licence, I tell you afore:
  I will rather have my cote twentie times swinged,
  Than on the naughtie wag not to be avenged.
C. CUSTANCE: Good wenches would not so rampe
  abrode ydelly,
  But keepe within doores, and plie their worke
  earnestly;
  If one would speake with me that is a man likely,
  Ye shall have right good thanke to bring me worde
  quickly.
  But otherwyse with messages to come in post,

---

763 *Exeat*: he goes out *naughty*: wayward (see note – also for line 774) 767 *abye*: pay for
it 768 *pouder*: preserve, pickle 773 *swinged*: thrashed

780 From henceforth I promise you, shall be to your
cost.

Get you in to your work!

TIB [*and*] AN[NOT:]   Yes, forsoth.

C. C[USTANCE:]   Hence both
twaine!

And let me see you play me such a part againe!

> [TIBET *and* ANNOT *exit into the house. Re-enter*
> TRUEPENNY *from the street.*]

TRUPENY: Maistresse, I have runne past the farre
ende of the streete,

Yet can I not yonder craftie boy see nor meete.

C. CUSTANCE: No?

TRUPENY: Yet I looked as farre beyonde the
people,

As one may see out of the toppe of Paule's steeple.

C. CUSTANCE: Hence in at doores, and let me no
more be vext!

TRUPENY: Forgeve me this one fault, and lay on for
the next.   [*Exit.*]

C. CUSTANCE: Now will I in too, for I thinke, so God
me mende,

790 This will prove some foolishe matter in the ende.

                                        Exeat.

Actus iii.   Scaena i.

Mathewe   Merygreeke.

[*Enter* MERRYGREEK.]

M. MERY: Nowe say thys againe: he hath somewhat
to dooing

Which followeth the trace of one that is wowyng,

Specially that hath no more wit in his hedde

Than my cousin Roister Doister withall is ledde.

I am sent in all haste to espie and to marke

---

792 *Which*: who   794 *my cousin*: 'our friend'

How our letters and tokens are likely to warke:
Maister Roister Doister must have aunswere in
   haste,
For he loveth not to spende much labour in waste.
Nowe as for Christian Custance, by this light,
Though she had not hir trouth to Gawin Goodluck
   plight,   800
Yet rather than with such a loutishe dolte to marie,
I daresay would lyve a poore lyfe solitarie;
But fayne would I speake with Custance, if I wist
   how,
To laugh at the matter –
[*Enter* TIBET *from the house.*]
                    yond commeth one forth now.

Actus iii.   *Scaena ii.*

    Tibet.   *M. Merygreeke.*   *Christian Custance.*
TIB. TALK: Ah, that I might but once in my life have
   a sight
Of him that made us all so yll shent, by this light;
He should never escape if I had him by the eare,
But even from his head I would it bite or teare!
Yea, and if one of them were not inowe,
I would bite them both off, I make God avow!   810
M. MERY: What is he whome this little mouse doth so
   threaten?
TIB. TALK: I woulde teache him, I trow, to make
   girles shent or beaten.
M. MERY: I will call hir – Maide, with whome are ye
   so hastie?
TIB. TALK: Not with you, sir, but with a little
   wagpastie,
  A deceiver of folkes, by subtill craft and guile.

796 *warke*: work   806 *yll shent*: severely scolded or punished   809 *inowe*: enough
814 *wagpastie*: mischievous rogue

M. MERY [*aside*]: I knowe where she is: Dobinet hath
    wrought some wile.

TIB. TALK: He brought a ring and token which he
    sayd was sent

From our dame's husbande, but I wot well I was
    shent:

For it liked hir as well, to tell you no lies,

820   As water in hir shyppe, or salt cast in hir eies:

And yet whence it came neyther we nor she can tell.

M. MERY [*aside*]: We shall have sporte anone: I like
    this very well.

    [*Aloud*] And dwell ye here with Mistresse
    Custance, faire maide?

TIB. TALK: Yea, mary, doe I, sir: what would ye
    have sayd?

M. MERY: A little message unto hir by worde of mouth.

TIB. TALK: No messages, by your leave, nor tokens
    forsoth!

M. MERY: Then help me to speke with hir.

TIBET: With a
    good wil that.

    [*Enter* CHRISTIAN CUSTANCE *from the house.*]

Here she commeth forth. Now speake ye know best
    what.

C. CUSTANCE: None other life with you, maide, but
    abrode to skip?

TIB. TALK: Forsoth, here is one would speake with

830   your mistresship.

C. CUSTANCE: Ah, have ye ben learning of mo
    messages now?

TIB. TALK: I would not heare his minde, but bad
    him shewe it to you.

C. CUSTANCE: In at dores!

TI[BET:]   I am gon!   *Ex*[*it.*]

M. M[ERY:]   Dame Custance, God ye save!

816 *where she is*: what she refers to   831 *mo*: more

C. CUSTANCE: Welcome, friend Merygreeke! And
 what thing wold ye have?

M. MERY: I am come to you a little matter to breake.

C. CUSTANCE: But see it be honest, else better not to
 speake.

M. MERY: Howe feele ye yourselfe affected here of late?

C. CUSTANCE: I feele no maner chaunge but after the
 olde rate.

But wherby do ye meane?

M. M[ERY:]   Concerning mariage.

Doth not love lade you?

C. CUST[ANCE:]   I feele no such cariage. *840*

M. MERY: Doe ye feele no pangues of dotage?
 Aunswere me right.

C. CUSTANCE: I dote so that I make but one sleepe
 all the night.

But what neede all these wordes?

M. M[ERY:]   Oh Jesus, will ye see

What dissemblyng creatures these same women be?

The gentleman ye wote of, whome ye doe so love,

That ye woulde fayne marrie him, yf ye durst it move –

Emong other riche widowes, which are of him glad,

Lest ye for lesing of him perchaunce might runne mad,

Is nowe contented that upon your sute making,

Ye be as one in election of taking. *850*

C. CUSTANCE: What a tale is this? 'That I wote of'?
 'Whome I love'?

M. MERY: Yea, and he is as loving a worme againe as
 a dove;

E'en of very pitie he is willyng you to take,

Bicause ye shall not destroy yourselfe for his sake.

C. CUSTANCE: Mary, God yelde his mashyp
 whatever he be,

It is gentmanly spoken.

---

835 *breake*: broach 840 *lade you*: load you down *cariage*: burden 841 *pangues*: pangs
dotage: infatuation 848 *lesing*: losing 850 *election of taking*: chosen to be his wife
855 *yelde*: reward

M. M[ERY:]   Is it not, trowe ye?
If ye have the grace now to offer yourself, ye
    speede.

C. CUSTANCE: As muche as though I did, this time it
    shall not neede;
But what gentman is it, I pray you tell me plaine,
That woweth so finely?

860   M. M[ERY:]   Lo, where ye be againe;
As though ye knewe him not!

C. CUSTANCE: Tush, ye speake in
    jest!

M. MERY: Nay, sure the partie is in good knacking
    earnest,
And have you he will (he sayth), and have you he
    must.

C. CUSTANCE: I am promised duryng my life, that is
    just.

M. MERY: Mary, so thinketh he – unto him alone.

C. CUSTANCE: No creature hath my faith and trouth
    but one,
That is Gawin Goodlucke: and if it be not hee,
He hath no title this way. whatever he be,
Nor I know none to whome I have such worde
    spoken.

M. MERY: Ye knowe him not, you, by his letter and
870   token?

C. CUSTANCE: Indede true it is, that a letter I have,
But I never reade it yet, as God me save.

M. MERY: Ye a woman, and your letter so long
    unredde?

C. CUSTANCE: Ye may therby know what hast I have
    to wedde.
But now who it is, for my hande, I knowe by gesse.

M. MERY: Ah well I say –

---

862 *good knacking earnest*: utterly sincere   874 *hast*: haste

C. CUSTANCE: It is Roister Doister
   doubtlesse!
M. MERY: Will ye never leave this dissimulation?
   Ye know hym not?
C. CUSTANCE: But by imagination,
   For no man there is but a very dolt and loute
   That to wowe a widowe woulde so go about.   *880*
   He shall never have me hys wife while he doe live.
M. MERY: Then will he have you if he may, so mote I
    thrive;
   And he biddeth you sende him worde by me,
   That ye humbly beseech him ye may his wife be,
   And that there shall be no let in you nor mistrust,
   But to be wedded on Sunday next if he lust,
   And biddeth you to looke for him.
C. CUSTANCE: Doth he byd so?
M. MERY: When he commeth, aske hym whether he
    did or no!
C. CUSTANCE: Goe say that I byd him keepe him
    warme at home,
   For if he come abroade he shall cough me a mome!   *890*
   My mynde was vexed, I shrew his head, sottish dolt!
M. MERY: He hath in his head –
C. CUST[ANCE:]   As much braine as a burbolt.
M. MERY: Well, Dame Custance, if he heare you thus
    play choploge –
C. CUSTANCE: What will he?
M. M[ERY:]   Play the devill in the horologe!
C. CUSTANCE: I defye him, loute!
M. M[ERY:]   Shal I tell hym what ye say?
C. CUSTANCE: Yea, and adde whatsoever thou canst,
    I thee pray,
   And I will avouche it whatsoever it bee.

---

882 *so mote I*: as I may   885 *let*: obstruction   886 *lust*: desires it   890 *cough me a mome*: prove himself a fool   892 *burbolt*: blunt-headed arrow   893 *choploge*: chop-logic (see note)   894 *horologe*: clock (see note)

M. MERY: Then let me alone; we will laugh well, ye
    shall see;
It will not be long ere he will hither resorte.

C. CUSTANCE: Let hym come when hym lust, I wishe
900   no better sport.
Fare you well, I will in, and read my great letter;
I shall to my wower make answere the better.   *Exeat.*

Actus iii.   *Scaena iii.*

Mathew Merygreeke.   *Roister Doister.*

M. MERY: Nowe that the whole answere in my devise
    doth rest,
I shall paint out our wower in colours of the best,
And all that I say shall be on Custance's mouth;
She is author of all that I shall speake, forsoth.
    [*Enter* ROISTER DOISTER.]
But yond commeth Roister Doister nowe in a traunce.

R. ROYSTER: Juno sende me this day good lucke and
    good chaunce!
I cannot but come see how Merygreeke doth
    speede.

M. MERY [*aside*]: I will not see him, but give him a
910   jutte indeede.
    [*Runs into* ROISTER DOISTER.] I crie your
    mastershyp mercie!

R. R[OISTER:]   And whither now?

M. MERY: As fast as I could runne, sir, in poste
    against you.
But why speake ye so faintly, or why are ye so sad?

R. ROYSTER: Thou knowest the proverbe: bycause I
    cannot be had.
Hast thou spoken with this woman?

M. M[ERY:]   Yea, that I have.

R. ROYSTER: And what, will this geare be?

910 *jutte*: shove 916 *geare*: business

M. M[ERY:]   No, so God me save.

R. ROISTER: Hast thou a flat answer?

M. M[ERY:]   Nay, a sharp answer.

R. R[OISTER:]   What?

M. MERY: Ye shall not (she sayth) by hir will marry
 hir cat!

 Ye are such a calfe, such an asse, such a blocke,

 Such a lilburne, such a hoball, such a lobcocke,   *920*

 And bicause ye shoulde come to hir at no season,

 She despised your maship out of all reason.

 'Bawawe what ye say' (ko I) 'of such a jentman!'

 'Nay, I feare him not' (ko she), 'doe the best he can;

 He vaunteth himselfe for a man of prowesse greate,

 Whereas a good gander I daresay may him beate.

 And where he is louted and laughed to skorne,

 For the veriest dolte that ever was borne,

 And veriest lubber, sloven, and beast,

 Living in this worlde from the west to the east;   *930*

 Yet of himselfe hath he suche opinion,

 That in all the worlde is not the like minion.

 He thinketh eche woman to be brought in dotage

 With the onely sight of his goodly personage:

 Yet none that will have hym: we do hym loute and
  flocke,

 And make him among us our common sporting stocke,

 And so would I now' (ko she) 'save onely bicause –'

 'Better nay' (ko I) – 'I lust not medle with dawes.'

 'Ye are happy' (ko I) 'that ye are a woman,

 This would cost you your life in case ye were a man.' *940*

R. ROYSTER: Yea, an hundred thousand pound
 should not save hir life!

M. MERY: No, but that ye wowe hir to have hir to
 your wife;

 But I coulde not stoppe hir mouth –

920 *lilburne ... hoball ... lobcocke*: lubber ... fool ... clown 923 *Bawawe*: beware *ko*:
quoth 927 *louted*: mocked 932 *minion*: gallant, dandy 935 *flocke*: despise 938 *dawes*:
fools

R. R[OISTER:]   Heigh how, alas!

M. MERY: Be of good cheere, man, and let the worlde
    passe.

R. ROYSTER: What shall I doe or say, nowe that it
    will not bee?

M. MERY: Ye shall have choise of a thousande as
    good as shee,

And ye must pardon hir, it is for lacke of witte.

R. ROYSTER: Yea, for were not I an husbande for hir
    fitte?

Well, what should I now doe?

M. M[ERY:]   In faith, I cannot tell.

R. ROYSTER: I will go home and die.

M. M[ERY:]   Then shall I
950   bidde toll the bell?

R. ROYSTER: No.

M. M[ERY:]   God have mercie on your soule! Ah,
    good gentleman,

That er ye shuld thus dye for an unkinde woman!

Will ye drinke once ere ye goe?

R. R[OISTER:]   No, no, I will none.

M. MERY: How feeles your soule to God?

R. R[OISTER:]   I am nigh
    gone.

M. MERY: And shall we hence streight?

R. R[OISTER:]   Yea.

M. M[ERY:]   Placebo
    dilexi.

Maister Roister Doister will streight go home and
    die,

Our Lorde Jesus Christ his soule have mercie
    upon:

Thus you see today a man, tomorow John.

Yet saving for a woman's extreeme crueltie,

960   He might have lyved yet a moneth or two or three,

---

955 *Placebo dilexi*: part of Latin funeral services (see note)   958 *John*: see note

But in spite of Custance which hath him weried,
His mashyp shall be worshipfully buried;
And while some piece of his soule is yet hym
    within,
Some parte of his funeralls let us here beginne.

R. ROYSTER: Heigh how, alas, the pangs of death my
    hearte do breake.

M. MERY: Holde your peace for shame, sir; a dead
    man may not speake.

Nequando: What mourners and what torches shall
    we have?

R. ROYSTER: None.

M. M[ERY:]   *Dirige.* He will go darklyng to his
    grave;

Neque lux, neque crux, neque mourners, *neque* clinke,
He will steale to heaven, unknowing to God, I
    thinke.   *970*

A porta inferi. Who shall your goodes possesse?

R. ROYSTER: Thou shalt be my sectour, and have all
    more and lesse.

M. MERY: *Requiem aeternam.* Now God reward your
    mastershyp.

And I will crie halfepenie doale for your worshyp.
    Evocat servos militis.

Come forth, sirs; heare the dolefull newes I shall
    you tell.

    [*Enter* DOBINET DOUGHTY, HARPAX, *and two
    others.*]

Our good maister here will no longer with us
    dwell,
Yet, sirs, as ye wyll the blisse of heaven win,
When he commeth to the grave lay hym softly in.

---

967 *Nequando*: see note to line 955 above (cf. *Dirige* at line 968)   969 *Neque lux, neque crux*:
neither light nor a cross   *clinke*: the sound of a bell   971 *A porta inferi*: see note to line
955 above (also for 972 *Requiem aeternam*, 979 *Audivi vocem*, and 989)   972 *sectour*: executor
974 *halfepenie doale*: a halfpenny worth of charity   975 *Evocat servos militis*: he calls the
soldier's servants

Audivi vocem. All men take heede by this one
    gentleman,
Howe your sette your love upon an unkinde
980   woman;
For these women be all such madde pievishe elves,
They will not be wonne except it please
    themselves.
But, in fayth, Custance, if ever ye come in hell,
Maister Roister Doister shall serve you as well –
[*Breaking off*] And will ye needes go from us thus
    in very deede?
R. ROYSTER: Yea, in good sadnesse!
M. M[ERY:]   Now Jesus
    Christ be your speede –
Good night, Roger, olde knave; farewell, Roger,
    olde knave;
Good night, Roger, olde knave; knave, knap.
Nequando. Audivi vocem. Requiem aeternam.
990 Pray for the late maister Roister Doister's soule,
And come forth, parishe clarke; let the passing bell
    toll.
    Ad servos militis.
Pray for your mayster, sirs, and for hym ring a
    peale:
He was your right good maister while he was in
    heale.
[*Enter the* PARISH CLERK.]
*The Peale of belles rong by the parish clark, and Roister
Doister's foure men.*

                The first Bell a Triple
           When dyed he? When dyed he?
                 The seconde.
           We have hym, we have hym.
                 The thirde.

---

986 *in good sadnesse*: in all seriousness 988 *knap*: see note 992 *Ad servos militis*: to the
soldier's servants 994 *a Triple*: a treble

    Royster Doyster, Royster Doyster.
        The fourth Bell.
    He commeth, he commeth.
        The greate Bell.
    Our owne, our owne.
  [*Exit the* PARISH CLERK *and the four servants.*]

M. MERY: *Qui Lazarum.*
R. R[OISTER:]   Heigh how!
M. M[ERY:]   Dead men go not so fast.
  In Paradisum.
R. R[OISTER:] Heihow!
M. M[ERY:]   Soft, heare what I have cast.   *1000*
R. ROYSTER: I will heare nothing, I am past.
M. M[ERY:]   Whough, wellaway!
  Ye may tarie one houre, and heare what I shall say;
  Ye were best, sir, for a while to revive againe,
  And quite them er ye go.
R. R[OISTER:]   Trowest thou so?
M. M[ERY:]   Ye, plain.
R. ROYSTER: How may I revive, being nowe so farre
    past?
M. MERY: I will rubbe your temples, and fette you
    againe at last.
R. ROYSTER: It will not be possible.
M. M[ERY:]   Yes, for twentie
    pounde! [*Slaps him.*]
R. ROYSTER: Armes! What dost thou?
M. M[ERY:]   Fet you again
    out of your sound;
  By this crosse, ye were nigh gone indeede; I might
    feele
  Your soule departing within an inche of your
    heele!   *1010*
  Now folow my counsell.

999 *Qui Lazarum*: see note to line 955 above (cf. *In Paradisum* at line 1000) 1000 *cast*: thought of 1004 *quite*: pay them back *Ye*: yea 1006: *fette*: fetch, restore 1008 *Armes*!: i.e. God's arms! *sound*: swoon

R. R[OISTER:]   What is it?

M. M[ERY:]   If I wer you,
Custance should eft seeke to me, ere I woulde bowe.

R. ROYSTER: Well, as thou wilt have me, even so will
I doe.

M. MERY: Then shall ye revive againe for an houre or
two.

R. ROYSTER: As thou wilt I am content for a little
space.

M. MERY: Good happe is not hastie: yet in space
comth grace;
To speake with Custance yourselfe shoulde be very
well,
What good therof may come, nor I, nor you can tell.
But now the matter standeth upon your mariage,

1020   Ye must now take unto you a lustie courage;
Ye may not speake with a faint heart to Custance,
But with a lusty breast and countenance,
That she may knowe she hath to answere to a man.

R. ROYSTER: Yes, I can do that as well as any can.

M. MERY: Then bicause ye must Custance face to
face wowe,
Let us see how to behave yourselfe ye can doe:
Ye must have a portely bragge after your estate.

R. ROISTER: Tushe, I can handle that after the best
rate. [*Struts about.*]

M. MERY: Well done, so loe; up, man, with your head
and chin!

1030   Up with that snoute, man! So loe, nowe ye begin;
So, that is somewhat like, but prankiecote – nay
whan –
That is a lustie brute; handes under your side, man:
So loe, now is it even as it shoulde bee,

1012 *eft*: again   1020 *lustie*: vigorous   1022 *lusty*: valiant   1027 *portely bragge*: imposing
demeanour   *after your estate*: befitting your position   1031 *prankiecote*: ?show yourself off,
swagger about   *whan*: when   1032 *brute*: 'devil'

That is somewhat like, for a man of your degree!
Then must ye stately goe, jetting up and downe;
Tut, can ye no better shake the taile of your
    gowne?
There; loe, suche a lustie bragge it is ye must make.

R. ROYSTER: To come behind, and make curtsie,
    thou must som pains take.

M. MERY: Else were I much to blame; I thanke your
    mastershyp.

The lorde one day all to begrime you with worshyp,   *1040*
Backe, Sir Sauce, let gentlefolkes have elbowe
    roome!
Voyde, sirs, see ye not Maister Roister Doister
    come?
Make place, my maisters!

R. R[OISTER:]   Thou justlest nowe to nigh!

M. MERY: Back, al rude loutes!

R. R[OISTER:]   Tush!

M. M[ERY:]   I crie your
    maship mercy!

Hoighdagh, if faire fine mistresse Custance sawe
    you now,
Ralph Royster Doister were hir owne, I warrant you.

R. ROYSTER: Neare an 'M' by your girdle?

M. M[ERY:]   Your good
    mastershyp's
Maistershyp were hir owne mistreshyp's
    mistreshyps;
Ye were take up for haukes, ye were gone, ye were
    gone!
But now one other thing more yet I thinke upon.   *1050*

R. ROYSTER: Shewe what it is.

M. M[ERY:]   A wower, be he never so poore,

1035 *jetting*: strutting   1040 *all to begrime*: completely smear you all over   1047 *Neare an*
'M': i.e. the proverbial 'don't you address me as "Master"?'   1049 *take up for haukes*: see
note

153

Must play and sing before his best belove's doore;
How much more than you?

R. R[OISTER:]   Thou speakest wel out
of dout.

M. MERY: And perchaunce that woulde make hir the
sooner come out.

R. ROYSTER: Goe call my musitians, bydde them
high apace.

M. MERY: I wyll be here with them ere ye can say
trey ace!   *Exeat.*

R. ROYSTER: This was well sayde of Merygreeke; I
lowe hys wit:

Before my sweeteheart's dore we will have a fit,
That if my love come forth, that I may with hir
talke,

1060   I doubt not but this geare shall on my side walke.

[*Re-enter* MERRYGREEK *with* DOBINET DOUGHTY
and HARPAX *and other servants with their instruments*.]

But lo, how well Merygreeke is returned sence!

M. MERY: There hath grown no grasse on my heele
since I went hence;

Lo, here have I brought that shall make you pastance.

R. ROYSTER: Come, sirs, let us sing to winne my
deare love Custance.

Cantent.

[ALL:]   I mun be maried a Sunday,
             I mun be maried a Sunday,
             Whosoever shall come that way,
             I mun be maried a Sunday.

             Royster Doyster is my name,
1070   Royster Doyster is my name,
             A lustie brute I am the same,
             I mun be maried a Sunday.

1053 *than*: then 1056 *trey ace*: a three and a one at dice *Exeat*: he exits 1057 *lowe*:
admit 1058 *fit*: song 1060 *on my side walke*: benefit my cause 1061 *sence*: already
1063 *pastance*: pastime, sport 1065 *mun*: must

Christian Custance have I founde,
Christian Custance have I founde,
A wydowe worthe a thousande pounde,
I mun be maried a Sunday.

Custance is as sweete as honey,
Custance is as sweete as honey,
I hir lambe and she my coney,
I mun be maried a Sunday.   *1080*

When we shall make our weddyng feast,
When we shall make oure weddyng feast,
There shall bee cheere for man and beast,
I mun be married a Sunday.

I mun be maried a Sunday,
I mun be maried a Sunday,
Whosoever shall come that way,
I mun be maried a Sunday.

[*Enter* CHRISTIAN CUSTANCE *from the house. Exit
the* SERVANTS.]

M. MERY: Lo where she commeth, some
countenaunce to hir make,
  And ye shall heare me be plaine with hir for your
  sake.   *1090*

Actus iii.   Scaena iiii.
Custance.   Merygreeke.   Roister Doister.

C. CUSTANCE: What gaudyng and foolyng is this
afore my doore?

M. MERY: May not folks be honest, pray you, though
they be pore?

C. CUSTANCE: As that thing may be true, so rich folks
may be fooles.

R. ROYSTER [*aside*]: Hir talke is as fine as she had
learned in schooles!

1079 *coney*: darling, 'bunny'   1089 *countenaunce*: show of regard   1901 *gaudyng*: frivolous
nonsense

M. MERY [*to* ROISTER DOISTER]: Looke partly
    towarde hir, and drawe a little nere.

C. CUSTANCE: Get ye home, idle folkes!

M. M[ERY:]   Why, may
    not we be here?

  Nay and ye will haze, haze: otherwise, I tell you
    plaine,

  And ye will not haze, then give us our geare againe.

C. CUSTANCE: Indeede I have of yours much gay
    things, God save all!

R. ROYSTER [*to* MERRYGREEK]: Speake gently unto

1100   hir, and let hir take all.

M. MERY [*to* ROISTER DOISTER]: Ye are to
    tenderhearted: shall she make us dawes?

  [*To* CHRISTIAN CUSTANCE] Nay, dame, I will be
    plaine with you in my friend's cause –

R. ROYSTER [*coming forward*]: Let all this passe,
    sweeteheart, and accept my service.

C. CUSTANCE: I will not be served with a foole in no
    wise;

  When I choose an husbande I hope to take a man!

M. MERY: And where will ye finde one which can doe
    that he can?

  Now thys man towarde you being so kinde,

  You not to make him an answere somewhat to his
    minde!

C. CUSTANCE: I sent him a full answere by you, dyd
    I not?

M. MERY: And I reported it.

1110   Nay, I must speake it againe!

R. ROYSTER: No, no, he tolde it all.

M. M[ERY:]   Was I not metely plaine?

R. ROYSTER: Yes.

M. M[ERY:] But I would not tell all, for, faith, if I had,

1097 *haze*: scold   1101 *to*: too   *dawes*: fools   1111 *metely*: sufficiently

With you, Dame Custance, ere this houre it had
    ben bad,
And not without cause: for this goodly personage
Ment no lesse than to joyne with you in mariage.

C. CUSTANCE: Let him wast no more labour nor sute
    about me.

M. MERY: Ye know not where your preferment lieth,
    I see;
He sending you such a token, ring and letter.

C. CUSTANCE: Mary, here it is; ye never sawe a
    better!

M. MERY: Let us see your letter.

C. CUSTANCE: Holde, reade it if ye
    can,   *1120*
And see what letter it is to winne a woman!

M. MERY: 'To mine owne deare coney birde,
    sweteheart, and pigsny,
Good Mistresse Custance, present these by and
    by' –
Of this superscription do ye blame the stile?

C. CUSTANCE: With the rest as good stuffe as ye
    redde a great while!

M. MERY: 'Sweete mistresse, whereas I love you
    nothing at all,
Regarding your substance and richesse chiefe of all,
For your personage, beautie, demeanour and wit
I commende me unto you never a whit,
Sorie to heare report of your good welfare.   *1130*
For (as I heare say) suche your conditions are,
That ye be worthie favour of no living man,
To be abhorred of every honest man.
To be taken for a woman enclined to vice.
Nothing at all to verture gyving hir due price,
Wherfore concerning mariage, ye are thought
Suche a fine paragon, as nere honest man bought.

1122 *coney*: term of endearment *pigsny*: sweetheart 1127 *richesse*: wealth

And nowe by these presentes I do you advertise
That I am minded to marrie you in no wise.
For your goodes and substance, I coulde bee
1140   content
To take you as ye are. If ye mynde to bee my wyfe,
Ye shall be assured for the tyme of my lyfe,
I will keepe ye ryght well from good rayment and
     fare;
Ye shall not be kepte but in sorowe and care.
Ye shall in no wyse lyve at your owne libertie;
Doe and say what ye lust, ye shall never please me,
But when ye are mery I will be all sadde;
When ye are sory I will be very gladde.
When ye seeke your hearte's ease I will be
     unkinde,
1150   At no tyme in me shall ye muche gentlenesse finde.
But all things contrary to your will and minde
Shall be done: otherwise I wyll not be behinde
To speake. And as for all them that woulde do you
     wrong,
I will so helpe and mainteyne, ye shall not lyve
     long;
Nor any foolishe dolte shall cumbre you but I:
I, whoere say nay, wyll sticke by you tyll I die.
Thus, good Mistresse Custance, the Lorde you save
     and kepe
From me, Roister Doister, whether I wake or
     slepe;
Who favoureth you no lesse (ye may be bolde)
1160   Than this letter purporteth, which ye have unfolde.'
    C. CUSTANCE: Howe by this letter of love? Is it not
       fine?
    R. ROYSTER: By the armes of Caleys, it is none of
       myne!

1146 *lust*: wish, desire   1147 *sadde*: serious, solemn   1155 *cumbre*: distress, perplex
1162 *Caleys*: Calais

M. MERY [*to* ROISTER DOISTER]: Fie, you are fowle
to blame; this is your owne hand!

C. CUSTANCE: Might not a woman be proude of such
an husbande?

M. MERY [*to* ROISTER DOISTER]: Ah, that ye would in
a letter shew such despite!

R. ROYSTER: Oh, I would I had hym here, the which
did it endite!

M. MERY: Why, ye made it yourselfe, ye tolde me by
this light!

R. ROYSTER: Yea, I ment I wrote it myne owne selfe
yesternight.

C. CUSTANCE: Ywis, sir, I would not have sent you
such a mocke!

R. ROYSTER: Ye may so take it, but I ment it not.so,
by Cocke!   *1170*

M. MERY: Who can blame this woman to fume and
frette and rage?

[*To* ROISTER DOISTER] Tut, tut, yourselfe nowe
have marde your owne marriage!

[*To* CHRISTIAN CUSTANCE] Well, yet, Mistresse
Custance, if ye can this remitte,

This gentleman otherwise may your love requitte.

C. CUSTANCE: No, God be with you both, and seeke
no more to me!   *Exeat*.

R. ROYSTER: Wough, she is gone for ever; I shall hir
no more see!

[ROISTER DOISTER *bursts into tears*.]

M. MERY: What, weepe? Fye, for shame! And
blubber? For manhod's sake,

Never lette your foe so muche pleasure of you take!

Rather play the man's parte, and doe love refraine:

If she despise you, e'en despise ye hir againe!   *1180*

R. ROYSTER: By Gosse and for thy sake, I defye hir
indeede!

1166 *endite*: compose, set down   1170 *Cocke*: God   1173 *remitte*: pardon   1181 *Gosse*: God

M. MERY: Yea, and perchaunce that way ye shall
    much sooner speede,
For one madde propretie these woman have, in fey,
When ye will, they will not: will not ye, then will
    they!
Ah, foolishe woman, ah, moste unluckie Custance;
Ah, unfortunate woman, ah, pievishe Custance;
Art thou to thine harmes so obstinately bent,
That thou canst not see where lieth thine high
    preferment?
Canst thou not lub dis man, which coulde lub dee
    so well?
Art thou so much thine own foe? –

1190 R. R[OISTER:]   Thou dost the truth tell.
M. MERY: Wel, I lament.
R. R[OISTER:]   So do I.
M. M[ERY:]   Wherfor?
R. R[OISTER:]   For this thing:
Bicause she is gone.
M. M[ERY:]   I mourne for another thing.
R. ROYSTER: What is it, Merygreeke? Wherfore thou
    dost griefe take?
M. MERY: That I am not a woman myselfe for your
    sake;
I would have you myselfe, and a strawe for yond Gill,
And mocke much of you, though it were against
    my will.
I would not, I warrant you, fall in such a rage
As so to refuse suche a goodly personage!
R. ROYSTER: In faith, I heartily thanke thee,
    Merygreeke.
M. MERY: And I were a woman –
R. R[OISTER:]   Thou wouldest to
1200   me seeke.

1183 *in fey*: in faith   1189 *lub*: love (see note)   1195 *Gill*: wench   1196 *mocke*: ? make (see
note to line 436)   1197 *rage*: state of madness

M. MERY: For, though I say it, a goodly person ye bee.

R. ROYSTER: No, no!

M. M[ERY:]   Yes; a goodly man as ere I dyd see!

R. ROYSTER: No, I am a poore homely man as God
    made mee.

M. MERY: By the faith that I owe to God, sir, but ye bee.
    Woulde I might for your sake, spende a thousande
        pound land.

R. ROYSTER: I daresay thou wouldest have me to thy
    husbande.

M. MERY: Yea! And I were the fairest lady in the shiere,
    And knewe you as I know you, and see you nowe
        here —
    Well, I say no more.

R. R[OISTER:]   Gramercies, with all my hart!

M. MERY: But since that cannot be, will ye play a
    wise parte?   *1210*

R. ROYSTER: How should I?

M. M[ERY:]   Refraine from Custance a
        while now,
    And I warrant hir soone right glad to seeke to you;
    Ye shall see hir anon come on hir knees creeping,
    And pray you to be good to hir, salte teares weeping.

R. ROYSTER: But what and she come not?

M. M[ERY:]   In faith
        then, farewel she!
    Or else if ye be wroth, ye may avenged be.

R. ROYSTER: By Cock's precious potsticke, and e'en
        so I shall!
    I wyll utterly destroy hir, and house and all!
    But I woulde be avenged, in the meane space,
    On that vile scribler that did my wowyng disgrace.   *1220*

M. MERY: 'Scribler' (ko you)? Indeede, he is worthy
        no lesse;
    I will call hym to you, and ye bidde me doubtlesse.

1207 *shiere*: shire 1221 *ko*: quoth

R. ROYSTER: Yes, for although he had as many lives
 As a thousande widowes, and a thousande wives,
 As a thousande lyons, and a thousand rattes,
 A thousande wolves, and a thousande cattes,
 A thousande bulles, and a thousande calves,
 And a thousande legions divided in halves,
 He shall never scape death on my sworde's point,
1230 Though I shoulde be torne therfore joynt by joynt.
M. MERY: Nay, if ye will kyll him, I will not fette
  him;
 I will not in so muche extremitie sette him;
 He may yet amende, sir, and be an honest man;
 Therfore pardon him, good soule, as muche as ye
  can.
R. ROYSTER: Well, for thy sake, this once with his
  lyfe he shall passe, –
 But I wyll hewe hym all to pieces, by the Masse!
M. MERY: Nay, fayth, ye shall promise that he shall
  no harme have,
 Else I will not fet him.
R. R[OISTER:]   I shall, so God me save! –
 But I may chide him a good.
M. M[ERY:]   Yea, that do hardely.
R. ROYSTER: Go then.
M. M[ERY:]   I returne, and bring him to
1240 you by and by.   Ex[eat.]

    Actus iii. *Scaena v.*

Roister Doister. *Mathewe Merygreeke.* *Scrivener.*
R. ROYSTER: What is a gentleman but his worde and
  his promise?
 I must nowe save this vilaine's lyfe in any wise,
 And yet at hym already my handes doe tickle;
 I shall uneth holde them, they wyll be so fickle!

1231 *fette*: fetch 1239 *a good*: thoroughly *hardely*: boldly 1240 *by and by*: immediately
1244 *uneth*: scarcely

[MERRYGREEK *enters with the* SCRIVENER; *they stand apart, talking together.*]

But lo, and Merygreeke have not brought him sens!

M. MERY [*to* SCRIVENER]: Nay, I woulde I had of my
    purse payde fortie pens.

SCRIVENER: So woulde I too: but it needed not that
    stounde!

M. MERY: But the jentman had rather spent five
    thousande pounde,

For it disgraced him at least five tymes so muche.

SCRIVENER: He disgraced hymselfe; his loutishnesse
    is suche.   *1250*

R. ROYSTER: Howe long they stande prating! [*To*
    MERRYGREEK] Why comst thou not away?

M. MERY [*to* SCRIVENER]: Come nowe to hymselfe,
    and hearke what he will say.

SCRIVENER: I am not afrayde in his presence to
    appeere.

    [MERRYGREEK *and the* SCRIVENER *cross to*
    ROISTER DOISTER.]

R. ROYSTER: Arte thou come, felow?

SCRI[VENER:]   How thinke
    you? Am I not here?

R. ROYSTER: What hindrance hast thou done me,
    and what villanie?

SCRIVENER: It hath come of thyselfe, if thou hast
    had any.

R. ROYSTER: All the stocke thou comest of later or
    rather,

From thy fyrst father's grandfather's father's
    father,

Nor all that shall come of thee to the worlde's ende,

Though to three score generations they descende,   *1260*

Can be able to make me a just recompense

For this trespasse of thine and this one offense.

1245 *sens*: already   1247 *stounde*: ? attack   1257 *rather*: earlier

SCRIVENER: Wherin?

R. R[OISTER:]   Did not you make me a letter,
    brother?

SCRIVENER: Pay the like hire, I will make you suche
    another.

R. ROYSTER: Nay, see and these whooreson
    Phariseys and Scribes
    Doe not get their livyng by polling and bribes!
    If it were not, for shame –
    [*Goes to hit the* SCRIVENER.]

SCRIVENER: Nay, holde thy hands still!
    [*He hits* ROISTER DOISTER.]

M. MERY [*to* ROISTER DOISTER]: Why, did ye not
    promise that ye would not him spill?

SCRIVENER: Let him not spare me! [*Threatens*
    ROISTER DOISTER.]

R. R[OISTER:]   Why, wilt thou strike me again?

SCRIVENER: Ye shall have as good as ye bring of me,
1270   that is plaine.

M. MERY: I cannot blame him, sir, though your
    blowes wold him greve,
    For he knoweth present death to ensue of all ye geve.

R. ROYSTER [*to* SCRIVENER]: Well, this man for
    once hath purchased thy pardon.

SCRIVENER: And what say ye to me? Or else I will be
    gon.

R. ROYSTER: I say the letter thou madest me was not
    good.

SCRIVENER: Then did ye wrong copy it of likelyhood.

R. ROYSTER: Yes, out of thy copy worde for worde I
    it wrote.

SCRIVENER: Then was it as ye prayed to have it, I wote,
    But in reading and pointyng there was made some
    faulte.

1266 *polling*: extortion   1278 *wote*: know

R. ROYSTER: I wote not, but it made all my matter
  to haulte.   *1280*

SCRIVENER [*producing paper*]: Howe say you, is this
  mine originall or no?

R. ROYSTER: The selfe same that I wrote out of, so
  mote I go.

SCRIVENER: Loke you on your owne fist, and I will
  looke on this,

And let this man be judge whether I reade amisse.

'To myne owne dere coney birde, sweeteheart, and
  pigsny,

Good Mistresse Custance, present these by and
  by.'

How now? Doth not this superscription agree?

R. ROYSTER: Reade that is within, and there ye shall
  the fault see.

SCRIVENER: 'Sweete mistresse, whereas I love you,
  nothing at all

Regarding your richesse and substance; chiefe of all   *1290*

For your personage, beautie, demeanour and witte

I commende me unto you; never a whitte

Sory to heare reporte of your good welfare.

For (as I heare say) suche your conditions are,

That ye be worthie favour: of no living man

To be abhorred; of every honest man

To be taken for a woman enclined to vice

Nothing at all; to vertue giving hir due price.

Wherfore concerning mariage, ye are thought

Suche a fine paragon, as nere honest man bought.   *1300*

And nowe by these presents I doe you advertise,

That I am minded to marrie you; in no wyse

For your goodes and substance; I can be content

To take you as you are; yf ye will be my wife,

1283 *fist*: handwriting

Ye shall be assured for the time of my life
I wyll keepe you right well; from good raiment and
    fare,
Ye shall not be kept; but in sorowe and care
Ye shall in no wyse lyve; at your owne libertie,
Doe and say what ye lust; ye shall never please me
1310   But when ye are merrie; I will bee all sadde
When ye are sorie; I wyll be very gladde
When ye seeke your hearte's ease; I wyll be
    unkinde
At no time; in me shall ye muche gentlenesse finde.
But all things contrary to your will and minde
Shall be done otherwise; I wyll not be behynde
To speake. And as for all they that woulde do you
    wrong,
(I wyll so helpe and maintayne ye) shall not lyve
    long;
Nor any foolishe dolte shall cumber you; but I,
I, who ere say nay, wyll sticke by you tyll I die.
Thus, good Mistresse Custance, the Lorde you save
1320   and kepe.
From me, Roister Doister, whether I wake or slepe,
Who favoureth you no lesse, (ye may be bolde),
Than this letter purporteth, which ye have unfolde.'
Now, sir, what default can ye finde in this letter?
R. ROYSTER: Of truth in my mynde there cannot be
    a better.
SCRIVENER: Then was the fault in readyng, and not
    in writyng,
No, nor I dare say in the fourme of endityng,
But who read this letter, that it sounded so nought?
M. MERY: I redde it, indeede.
SCRI[VENER:]   Ye red it not as ye ought.
R. ROYSTER [to MERRYGREEK]: Why, thou wretched
1330   villaine, was all this same fault in thee?

1327 *endityng*: writing out

166

M. MERY: I knocke your costarde if ye offer to strike
 me!   [*Hits him.*]

R. ROYSTER: Strikest thou in deede, and I offer but
 in jest?

M. MERY: Yea, and rappe you againe except ye can
 sit in rest.

And I will no longer tarie here, me beleve.

R. ROYSTER: What, wilt thou be angry, and I do
 thee forgeve?

Fare thou well, scribler, I crie thee mercie
 indeede!

SCRIVENER: Fare ye well, bibbler, and worthily may
 ye speede!   [*Exit.*]

R. ROYSTER: [*to* MERRYGREEK]: If it were another
 but thou, it were a knave.

M. MERY: Ye are another yourselfe, sir, the Lorde us
 both save,

Albeit in this matter I must your pardon crave.   *1340*

Alas, woulde ye wyshe in me the witte that ye
 have?

But as for my fault I can quickely amende,

I will shewe Custance it was I that did offende.

R. ROYSTER: By so doing hir anger may be reformed.

M. MERY: But if by no entreatie she will be turned,

Then sette lyght by hir and bee as testie as shee,

And doe your force upon hir with extremitie.

R. ROISTER: Come on, therefore; lette us go home in
 sadnesse.

M. MERY: That if force shall neede all may be in a
 readinesse,

And as for thys letter, hardely let all go;   *1350*

We wyll know where she refuse you for that or no.

 Exeant am[*bo.*]

1331 *costarde*: head (literally 'apple') 1344 *reformed*: assuaged 1348 *in sadnesse*: solemnly
1350 *hardely*: boldly 1351 *where*: whether *Exeant ambo*: they both go out

Actus iiii.   *Scaena i.*

Sym Suresby.

[*Enter* SYM SURESBY.]

SIM SURE [SBY:] Is there any man but I, Sym
    Suresby alone,
That would have taken such an enterprise him upon,
In suche an outragious tempest as this was,
Suche a daungerous gulfe of the sea to passe?
I thinke verily Neptune's mightie godshyp
Was angry with some that was in our shyp,
And but for the honestie whiche in me he founde,
I thinke for the others' sake we had bene drownde.
But fye on that servant which for his maister's
1360   wealth
Will sticke for to hazarde both his lyfe and his
    health!
My maister, Gawyn Goodlucke, after me a day
Bicause of the weather, thought best hys shyppe to
    stay,
And now that I have the rough sourges so well past,
God graunt I may finde all things safe here at last —
Then will I thinke all my travaile well spent!
Nowe the first poynt wherfore my maister hath me
    sent
Is to salute Dame Christian Custance, his wife
Espoused, whome he tendreth no lesse than his life;
1370 I must see how it is with hir, well or wrong,
And whether for him she doth not now thinke long:
Then to other friendes I have a message or tway,
And then so to returne and mete him on the way.
Now wyll I goe knocke that I may dispatche with
    speede —
    [*Enter* CHRISTIAN CUSTANCE.]
But loe, forth commeth hirselfe happily indeede!

1360 *wealth*: well-being, prosperity   1361 *sticke*: hesitate, scruple   1364 *sourges*: surges
1369 *tendreth*: cherishes   1375 *happily*: fortunately

Actus iiii.   Scaena ii.

Christian Custance.   Sim Suresby.

C. CUSTANCE: I come to see if any more stirryng be here —
But what straunger is this, which doth to me appere?

SYM SURE: I will speake to hir. Dame, the Lorde you
save and see!

C. CUSTANCE: What, friende Sym Suresby? Forsoth,
right welcome ye be!
Howe doth mine owne Gawyn Goodlucke, I pray
the tell?   *1380*

SYM SURE: When he knoweth of your health he will
be perfect well.

C. CUSTANCE: If he have perfect helth, I am as I
would be.

SIM SURE: Such newes will please him well; this is as
it should be.

C. CUSTANCE: I thinke now long for him.

SYM S[URE:]   And he as
long for you.

C. CUSTANCE: When wil he be at home?

SYM S[URE:]   His heart is
here e'en now;
His body commeth after.

C. CUSTANCE: I woulde see that faine.

SIM SURE: As fast as wynde and sayle can cary it
amaine.
[*Looking offstage*] But what two men are yonde
comming hitherwarde?

C. CUSTANCE: Now I shrew their best Christmasse
chekes both togetherward!

─────────────────────────

1389 *shrew*: curse   *Christmasse chekes*: see note

169

Actus iiii.   Scaena iii.

*Christian Custance.   Sym Suresby.   Ralph
Roister.   Mathew Merygreke.   Trupeny.*
[*Enter* ROISTER DOISTER *and* MERRYGREEK.]

C. CUSTANCE [*aside*]: What meane these lewde
1390   felowes thus to trouble me stil?
Sym Suresby here perchance shal therof deme som yll,
And shall suspect in me some point of naughtinesse,
And they come hitherward.

SYM S[URE:]   What is their businesse?

C. CUSTANCE: I have nought to them, nor they to me
     in sadnesse,

SIM SURE: Let us hearken them; somewhat there is, I
     feare it.

R. ROYSTER [*to* MERRYGREEK]: I will speake out
     aloude best, that she may heare it.

M. MERY: Nay, alas, ye may so feare hir out of hir wit!

R. ROYSTER: By the crosse of my sworde, I will hurt
     hir no whit!

M. MERY: Will ye doe no harme indeede? Shall I
     trust your worde?

R. ROYSTER: By Roister Doister's fayth I will speake
1400   but in borde.

SIM SURE [*to* CHRISTIAN CUSTANCE]: Let us hearken
     them; somwhat there is, I feare it.

R. ROYSTER: I will speake out aloude, I care not who
     heare it!
[*Calling off*] Sirs, see that my harnesse, my tergat,
     and my shield,
Be made as bright now as when I was last in fielde,
As white as I shoulde to warre againe tomorrowe:
For sicke shall I be, but I worke some folke sorow!
Therfore see that all shine as bright as Sainct George,

1392 *naughtinesse*: wickedness, untoward conduct   1393 *And*: if   1394 *sadnesse*: in all
honesty   1400 *in borde*: lightly, jestingly   1403 *harnesse*: armour   *tergat*: small shield,
buckler   1405 *white*: spotless   1406 *but*: unless

Or as doth a key newly come from the smith's forge.
I woulde have my sworde and harnesse to shine so
  bright,
That I might therwith dimme mine enimies' sight;   *1410*
I would have it cast beames as fast, I tell you
  playne,
As doth the glittryng grasse after a showre of raine.
And see that in case I shoulde neede to come to
  arming,
All things may be ready at a minute's warning,
For such chaunce may chaunce in an houre, do ye
  heare —?

M. MERY: As perchance shall not chaunce againe in
  seven yeare.

R. ROYSTER: Now draw we neare to hir, and here
  what shall be sayde.

M. MERY: But I woulde not have you make hir too
  muche afrayde.

R. ROYSTER [*approaching* CHRISTIAN CUSTANCE]:
  Well founde, sweete wife (I trust), for al this your
  soure looke.

C. CUSTANCE: Wife? Why cal ye me wife?

SIM S[URE:]   Wife? This
  gear goth acrook!   *1420*

M. MERY: Nay, Mistresse Custance, I warrant you,
  our letter
Is not as we redde e'en nowe, but much better,
And where ye halfe stomaked this gentleman afore,
For this same letter, ye wyll love hym nowe therefore,
Nor it is not this letter, though ye were a queene,
That shoulde breake marriage betweene you
  twaine, I weene.

C. CUSTANCE: I did not refuse hym for the letter's sake.

R. ROYSTER: Then ye are content me for your
  husbande to take!

1419 *founde*: met with, encountered   1420 *acrook*: awry   1423 *stomaked*: resented, were
offended by   1426 *breake*: impair

C. CUSTANCE: You for my husbande to take? Nothing
    lesse truely!

R. ROYSTER: Yea, say so, sweete spouse, afore
1430   straungers hardly!

M. MERY: And though I have here his letter of love
    with me,

Yet his ryng and tokens he sent, keepe safe with ye.

C. CUSTANCE: A mischief take his tokens, and him
    and thee too!

But what prate I with fooles? Have I nought else
    to doo?

Come in with me, Sym Suresby, to take some repast.

SIM SURE: I must, ere I drinke, by your leave, goe in
    all hast,

To a place or two, with earnest letters of his.

C. CUSTANCE: Then come drinke here with me.

S. S[URE:]   I thank you.

C. C[USTANCE:]   Do not misse:

You shall have a token to your maister with
    you.

SYM SURE: No tokens this time, gramercies! God be
1440   with you!   *Exeat.*

C. CUSTANCE: Surely this fellowe misdeemeth some
    yll in me,

Which thing, but God helpe, will go neere to
    spill me.

R. ROYSTER: Yea, farewell, fellow, and tell thy
    maister Goodlucke

That he commeth to late of thys blossome to
    plucke!

Let him keepe him there still, or at leastwise make
    no hast,

As for his labour hither he shall spende in wast:

His betters be in place nowe.

M. M[ERY:]   As long as it will hold.

1430 *hardly*: bravely   1437 *earnest*: important   1441 *misdeemeth*: misjudges   1442 *spill*:
destroy, damage

C. CUSTANCE: I will be even with thee, thou beast,
    thou mayst be bolde!

R. ROYSTER: Will ye have us then?

C. CUSTANCE: I will never
    have thee.

R. ROYSTER: Then will I have you?

C. CUST[ANCE:]   No, the devill
    shal have thee!   *1450*
  I have gotten this houre more shame and harme
    by thee,
  Than all thy life-days thou canst do me honestie.

M. MERY: Why nowe may ye see what it comth too in
    the ende,
  To make a deadly foe of your most loving frende:
  And ywis this letter if ye woulde heare it now –

C. CUSTANCE: I will heare none of it.

M. M[ERY:]   In faith, would
    ravishe you.

C. CUSTANCE: He hath stained my name for ever;
    this is cleare.

R. ROYSTER: I can make all as well in an houre –

M. M[ERY:]   As
    ten yeare.
  How say ye, wil ye have him?

C. C[USTANCE:]   No.

M. M[ERY:]   Wil ye take him?

C. CUSTANCE: I defie him!

M. M[ERY:]   At my word?

C. CUST[ANCE:]   A shame take him!   *1460*
  Waste no more wynde, for it will never bee.

M. MERY: This one faulte with twaine shall be
    mended, ye shall see.
  Gentle Mistresse Custance now, good Mistresse
    Custance,
  Honey Mistresse Custance now, sweete Mistresse
    Custance,

1455 *ywis*: indeed

Golden Mistresse Custance now, white Mistresse
Custance,
Silken Mistresse Custance now, faire Mistresse
Custance.

C. CUSTANCE: Faith, rather than to mary with suche
a doltishe loute,
I woulde matche myselfe with a begger out of
doute.

M. MERY [*to* ROISTER DOISTER]: Then I can say no
more, to speede we are not like,

1470   Except ye rappe out a ragge of your Rhetorike.

C. CUSTANCE: Speake not of winnyng me: for it shall
never be so.

R. ROYSTER: Yes, dame, I will have you whether ye
will or no;
I commaunde you to love me, wherfore shoulde ye
not?
Is not my love to you chafing and burning hot?

M. MERY [*aside*]: Too hir; that is well sayd!

R. R[OISTER:]   Shall I so
breake my braine
To dote upon you, and ye not love us againe?

M. MERY [*aside*]: Wel sayd yet!

C. CUST[ANCE:]   Go to, thou goose!

R. R[OISTER:]   I say, Kit Custance,
In case ye will not haze, well, better yes
perchaunce.

C. CUSTANCE: Avaunt, lozell, picke thee hence!

M. M[ERY:]   Wel,
sir, ye perceive,

1480   For all your kinde offer, she will not you receive.

R. ROYSTER: Then a strawe for hir, and a strawe for
hir againe,
She shall not be my wife, woulde she never so faine,

1465 *white*: dearest   1467 *mary*: marry   1470 *rappe out a ragge of your Rhetorike*: let fly with
a sample of your eloquence, give her an ear-full of fancy talk   1475 *breake my braine*: wear
out my wits   1478 *haze*: scold   *better yes perchaunce*: perhaps it would be better to say
'Yes'   1479 *lozell*: scoundrel   *picke*: clear off

No, and though she would be at ten thousand
    pounde cost!

M. MERY: Lo, dame, ye may see what an husbande
    ye have lost!

C. CUSTANCE: Yea, no force; a jewell muche better
    lost than founde.

M. MERY: Ah, ye will not beleve how this doth my
    heart wounde!
How shoulde a mariage betwene you be towarde,
If both parties drawe backe, and become so
    frowarde?

R. ROYSTER: Nay, dame, I will fire thee out of thy [sty],
And destroy thee and all thine, and that by and by!   *1490*

M. MERY: Nay, for the passion of God, sir, do not so!

R. ROYSTER: Yes, except she will say 'yea' to that
    she sayde 'no'.

C. CUSTANCE: And what, be there no officers, trow
    we, in towne
To checke idle loytrers braggyng up and downe?
Where be they by whome vacabunds shoulde be
    represt,
That poore sillie widowes might live in peace and
    rest?
Shall I never ridde thee out of my companie?
I will call for helpe. What hough? Come forth,
    Trupenie!

TRUPENIE [*within*]: Anon. [*Entering.*] What is your
    will, mistresse? Dyd ye call me?

C. CUSTANCE: Yea, go runne apace, and as fast as
    may be;   *1500*
Pray Tristram Trusty, my moste assured frende,
To be here by and by, that he may me defende.

TRUPENIE: That message so quickly shall be done,
    by God's grace,
That at my returne ye shall say I went apace.

Exeat.

1485 *no force*: who cares about that?   1490 *by and by*: here and now   1496 *sillie*: helpless
1504 *Exeat*: he goes out

C. CUSTANCE [*to* ROISTER DOISTER]: Then shall we
    see, I trowe, whether ye shall do me harme.
R. ROYSTER: Yes, in faith, Kitte, I shall thee and
    thine so charme,
  That all women incarnate by thee may beware.
C. CUSTANCE: Nay, as for charming me, come hither
    if thou dare;
  I shall cloute thee tyll thou stinke, both thee and
    thy traine,
  And coyle thee [with] mine owne handes, and
1510   sende thee home againe!
R. ROYSTER: Yea, sayst thou me that, dame? Dost
    thou me threaten?
  Goe we, I will see whether I shall be beaten.
M. MERY: Nay, for the paishe of God, let me now
    treate peace,
  For bloudshed will there be in case this strife
    increace.
  Ah, good Dame Custance, take better way with you.
C. CUSTANCE: Let him do his worst.
M. M[ERY:]   Yeld in time.
R. R[OISTER:] Come hence, thou!
  Exeant ROISTER *and* MERY[GREEK].

Actus iiii.   *Scaena iiii.*

Christian Custance.   *Anot Alyface.*   *Tibet T.*
          M. Mumblecrust.

C. CUSTANCE: So, sirra, if I should not with hym
    take this way,
  I should not be ridde of him I thinke till
    doomesday!
  I will call forth my folkes, that without any mockes,
  If he come agayne we may give him rappes and
1520   knockes.

1506 *charme*: subdue 1510 *coyle*: thrash 1513 *paishe*: ? Passover (see note) 1514 *in case*:
if 1519 *without any mockes*: without being derided

[*Calling*] Mage Mumblecrust, come forth, and
    Tibet Talkeapace!
  Yea, and come forth too, Mistresse Annot Alyface!
ANNOT ALY[FACE] [*entering*]: I come!
TIBET [*entering*]:   And I am here!
M. MUMB [*entering*]: And I am here too at length!
C. CUSTANCE: Like warriers, if nede bee, ye must
    shew your strength:
  The man that this day hath thus begiled you
  Is Ralph Roister Doister, whome ye know well inowe,
  The moste loute and dastarde that ever on grounde
    trode.
TIB. TALK: I see all folke mocke hym when he goth
    abrode.
C. CUSTANCE: What, pretie maide? Will ye talke
    when I speake?
TIB. TALK: No, forsooth, good mistresse.
C. CUST[ANCE:]   Will ye my
  tale breake?   *1530*
  He threatneth to come hither with all his force to
    fight;
  I charge you, if he come, on him with all your
    might!
M. MUMBL: I with my distaffe will reache hym one
    rappe!
TIB. TALK: And I with my newe broome will sweepe
    hym one swappe,
  And then with our greate clubbe I will reache hym
    one rappe!
AN. ALIFACE: And I with our skimmer will fling him
    one flappe!
TIB. TALK: Then Trupenie's fireforke will him
    shrewdly fray,
  And you with the spitte may drive him quite away.
C. CUSTANCE: Go make all ready, that it may be e'en so.

1527 *The moste*: the greatest   1530 *breake*: interrupt

TIB. TALK: For my parte I shrewe them that last
1540   about it go!
     Exeant [all but CUSTANCE.]

     Actus iiii.   *Scaena v.*
  Christian Custance.   *Trupenie.*   *Tristram Trusty.*
C. CUSTANCE: Trupenie dyd promise me to runne a
     great pace,
  My friend Tristram Trusty to fet into this place;
  Indeede, he dwelleth hence a good stert, I confesse:
  But yet a quicke messanger might twice since, as I
     gesse,
  Have gone and come againe –
     [*Enter* TRUEPENNY *leading* TRISTRAM TRUSTY.]
                      Ah, yond I spie him now!
TRUPENY: Ye are a slow goer, sir, I make God avow!
  My mistresse Custance will in me put all the
     blame;
  Your leggs be longer than myne: come apace, for
     shame!
C. CUSTANCE: I can thee thanke, Trupenie; thou hast
     done right wele.
TRUPENY: Maistresse, since I went no grasse hath
1550   growne on my hele,
  But Maister Tristram Trustie here maketh no
     speede.
C. CUSTANCE: That he came at all I thanke him in
     very deede,
  For now have I neede of the helpe of some wise
     man.
T[RISTRAM] TRUSTY: Then may I be gone againe,
     for none such I am.
TRUPENIE: Ye may bee by your going: for no
     Alderman
  Can goe, I dare say, a sadder pace than ye can!

1542 *fet*: fetch   1543 *stert*: distance   1556 *sadder*: more sober

C. CUSTANCE: Trupenie, get thee in; thou shalt
    among them knowe
How to use thyselfe like a propre man I trowe!

TRUPENY: I go.   *Ex[eat.]*

C. C[USTANCE:] Now, Tristram Trusty, I thank you
    right much,
For at my first sending to come ye never grutch.   *1560*

T. TRUSTY: Dame Custance, God ye save, and while
    my life shall last,
For my friende Goodluck's sake ye shall not sende
    in wast.

C. CUSTANCE: He shal give you thanks.

T. TRUSTY: I wil do much
    for his sake.

C. CUSTANCE: But alack, I feare great displeasure
    shall be take.

T. TRUSTY: Wherfore?

C. C[USTANCE:]   For a foolish matter.

T. T[RUSTY:]   What is
    your cause?

C. CUSTANCE: I am yll accombred with a couple of
    dawes. [*She starts to cry.*]

T. TRUSTY: Nay, weepe not, woman: but tell me
    what your cause is
As concerning my friende; is anything amisse?

C. CUSTANCE: No, not on my part: but here was Sym
    Suresby —

T. TRUSTIE: He was with me and tolde me so.

C. C[USTANCE:]   And he
    stoode by   *1570*
While Ralph Roister Doister, with helpe of
    Merygreeke,
For promise of mariage dyd unto me seeke.

T. TRUSTY: And had ye made any promise before
    them twaine?

1560 *grutch*: complain, grumble   1564 *take*: taken   1566 *accombred*: oppressed
dawes: oafs

C. CUSTANCE: No; I had rather be torne in pieces
and flaine;
No man hath my faith and trouth, but Gawyn
Goodlucke,
And that before Suresby dyd I say, and there
stucke,
But of certaine letters there were suche words
spoken –
T. TRUSTIE: He tolde me that too.
C. CUST[ANCE:]   And of a ring and token;
That Suresby I spied dyd more than halfe suspect,
1580   That I my faith to Gawyn Goodlucke dyd reject.
T.TRUSTY: But there was no such matter, Dame
Custance, indeede?
C. CUSTANCE: If ever my head thought it, God sende
me yll speede!
Wherfore I beseech you with me to be a witnesse,
That in all my lyfe I never intended thing lesse;
And what a brainsicke foole Ralph Roister Doister is,
Yourselfe know.well enough!
T. TRUST[Y:]   Ye say full true, ywis.
C. CUSTANCE: Bicause to bee his wife I ne graunt nor
apply,
Hither will he com, he sweareth, by and by,
To kill both me and myne, and beate downe my
house flat.
Therfore I pray your aide.
1590 T. T[RUSTY:]   I warrant you that!
C. CUSTANCE: Have I so many yeres lived a sobre
life,
And shewed myselfe honest, mayde, widowe, and
wyfe,
And nowe to be abused in such a vile sorte?
Ye see howe poore widowes lyve all voyde of
comfort!

1574 *flaine*: flayed   1587 *apply*: agree to

T. TRUSTY: I warrant hym do you no harme nor
    wrong at all.

C. CUSTANCE: No, but Mathew Merygreeke doth me
    most appall,

That he woulde joyne hymselfe with suche a
    wretched loute!

T. TRUSTY: He doth it for a jest; I knowe hym out of
    doubte —

    [*Enter* MERRYGREEK.]

And here cometh Merygreke.

C. C[USTANCE:]   Then shal we here his mind.

Actus iiii.   *Scaena vi.*

  Merygreeke.   *Christian Custance.*   *Trist. Trusty.*

M. MERY: Custance and Trustie both, I doe you here
    well finde.   *1600*

C. CUSTANCE: Ah, Mathew Merygreeke, ye have
    used me well!

M. MERY: Nowe for altogether ye must your answere
    tell:

Will ye have this man, woman, or else will ye not?

Else will he come, never bore so brymme nor tost
    so hot.

TRIS. & CU[STANCE:] But why joyne ye with him?

T. TR[USTY:]   For mirth?

C. C[USTANCE:]   Or else in sadnesse?

M. MERY: The more fond of you both hardly the
    mater gesse.

TRISTRAM: Lo, how say ye, dame?

M. M[ERY:]   Why, do ye thinke,
    Dame Custance,

That in this wowyng I have ment ought but
    pastance?

1604 *brymme*: fierce   1605 *in sadnesse*: for a serious reason   1606 *fond*: stupid
1608 *pastance*: amusement

C. CUSTANCE: Much things ye spake, I wote, to
    maintaine his dotage.

M. MERY: But well might ye judge I spake it all in
1610   mockage,
  For why, is Roister Doister a fitte husbande for you?

T. TRUSTY: I daresay ye never thought it.

M. M[ERY:]   No, to God
    I vow!
  And dyd not I knowe afore of the insurance
  Betweene Gawyn Goodlucke and Christian
    Custance?
  And dyd not I for the nonce, by my conveyance,
  Reade his letter in a wrong sense for daliance?
  That if you coulde have take it up at the first
    bounde,
  We should therat such a sporte and pastime have
    founde,
  That all the whole towne should have ben the
    merier!

C. CUSTANCE: Ill ake your heades bothe, I was never
1620   werier,
  Nor never more vexte since the first day I was
    borne!

T. TRUSTY: But very well I wist he here did all in
    scorne.

C. CUSTANCE: But I feared therof to take dishonestie.

M. MERY: This should both have made sport, and
    shewed your honestie,
  And Goodlucke, I dare sweare, your witte therin
    would low.

T. TRUSTY: Yea, being no worse than we know it to
    be now!

M. MERY: And nothing yet to late, for when I come to
    him,

1609 *dotage*: infatuation   1613 *insurance*: engagement   1615 *conveyance*: manner of
delivery, or perhaps cunning   1617 *take it up*: grasped it, realized what was going on
1625 *low*: approve

Hither will he repaire with a sheepe's looke full
   grim,
By plaine force and violence to drive you to yelde.

C. CUSTANCE: If ye two bidde me, we will with him
   pitche a fielde,   *1630*
I and my maides together.

M. M[ERY:]   Let us see, be bolde!

C. CUSTANCE: Ye shal see women's warre.

T. TRUSTY: That fight
   wil I behold.

M. MERY: If occasion serve, takyng his parte full
   brim,
I will strike at you, but the rappe shall light on
   him.
When we first appeare –

C. CUST[ANCE:]   Then will I runne away
As though I were afeard.

T. TRUSTY: Do you that part wel play,
And I will sue for peace.

M. MERY: And I will set him on;
Then will he looke as fierce as a Cotssold lyon.

T. TRUSTY: But when gost thou for him?

M. M[ERY:]   That do I
   very nowe.

C. CUSTANCE: Ye shal find us here.

M. M[ERY:]   Wel, God have
   mercy on you!   *Ex[eat.]*   *1640*

T. TRUSTY: There is no cause of feare, the least boy
   in the streete –

C. CUSTANCE: Nay, the least girle I have will make
   him take his feete!
   [ROISTER DOISTER *and his men are heard offstage.*]
But hearke, methinke they make preparation!

T. TRUSTIE: No force; it will be a good recreation.

1633 *brim*: furiously   1638 *Cotssold lyon*: Cotswold lion, i.e. a sheep   1644 *No force*: no
matter

C. CUSTANCE: I will stande within, and steppe forth speedily,
And so make as though I ranne away dreadfully.
[CHRISTIAN CUSTANCE *enters the house*;
TRISTRAM TRUSTY *stands aside.*]

Actus iiii.   *Scaena vii.*

R. Royster.   *M. Merygreeke.*
C. Custance.   *D. Doughtie.*   *Harpax.*
Tristram Trusty.   *Two drummes with their Ensignes.*
[*Enter* ROISTER DOISTER, MERRYGREEK,
DOBINET DOUGHTY, HARPAX, (*and other
servants?*) *dressed for battle, together with two drummers.*]

R. ROYSTER: Nowe, sirs, keepe your ray, and see
your heartes be stoute –
But where be these caitives? Methink they dare not
route!
How sayst thou, Merygreeke? What doth Kit
Custance say?

M. MERY: I am loth to tell you.

R. R[OISTER:]   Tushe, speake, man;
1650   yea or nay?

M. MERY: Forsooth, sir, I have spoken for you all that
I can;
But if ye winne hir, ye must e'en play the man;
E'en to fight it out, ye must a man's heart take.

R. ROYSTER: Yea, they shall know, and thou
knowest, I have a stomacke.

M. MERY: 'A stomacke' (quod you?) yea, as good as
ere man had!

R. ROYSTER: I trowe they shall finde and feele that I
am a lad!

M. MERY: By this crosse, I have seene you eate your
meate as well
As any that ere I have seene of or heard tell;

1646 *dreadfully*: full of dread   1647 *ray*: martial order, line of battle   1648 *route*: assemble
1652 *e'en*: truly   1654 *I have a stomacke*: I am valiant (deliberately misunderstood by
Merrygreek)

'A stomacke' quod you? he that will that denie,
I know was never at dynner in your companie!   *1660*

R. ROYSTER: Nay, the stomacke of a man it is that I
    meane.

M. MERY: Nay, the stomacke of an horse or a dogge I
    weene!

R. ROYSTER: Nay, a man's stomacke with a weapon
    meane I.

M. MERY: Ten men can scarce match you with a
    spoone in a pie!

R. ROYSTER: Nay, the stomake of a man to trie in
    strife!

M. MERY: I never sawe your stomake cloyed yet in
    my lyfe.

R. ROYSTER: Tushe, I meane in strife or fighting to
    trie!

M. MERY: We shall see how ye will strike nowe, being
    angry!

R. ROYSTER [*lashing out*]: Have at thy pate then, and
    save thy head if thou may!

M. MERY: Nay then, have at your pate agayne by this
    day! [*Hits him.*]   *1670*

R. ROYSTER: Nay, thou mayst not strike at me
    againe in no wise!

M. MERY: I cannot in fight make to you suche
    warrantise:
    But as for your foes here, let them the bargaine bie.

R. ROYSTER: Nay, as for them, shall every mother's
    childe die!
    And in this my fume a little thing might make me
    To beate downe house and all, and else the devill
    take me!

M. MERY: If I were as ye be, by Gog's deare mother,
    I woulde not leave one stone upon another,
    Though she woulde redeeme it with twentie
    thousand poundes.

1666 *cloyed*: filled to bursting 1672 *warrantise*: guarantee 1675 *fume*: angry mood

1680   R. ROYSTER: It shall be even so, by his lily woundes!

    M. MERY: Bee not at one with hir upon any amendes.

    R. ROYSTER: No, though she make to me never so
        many frendes;

      Not if all the worlde for hir woulde undertake;

      No, not God hymselve neither shal not hir peace make.

      [*To his men*] On therfore, marche forwarde! – Soft,
        stay a while yet.

    M. MERY: On!

    R. R[OISTER:]Tary!

    M. M[ERY:]   Forth!

    R. R[OISTER:]   Back!

    M. M[ERY:]   On!

    R. R[OISTER:]   Soft! Now
      forward set!

      [*Enter* DAME CUSTANCE.]

    C. CUSTANCE: What businesse have we here? Out,
      alas, alas!   [*Exit.*]

    R. ROISTER: Ha, ha, ha, ha, ha! Dydst thou see that,
      Merygreeke? How afrayde she was!

    Dydst thou see how she fledde apace out of my sight?

1690   Ah, good sweete Custance, I pitie hir by this light!

    M. MERY: That tender heart of yours wyll marre
      altogether;

    Thus will ye be turned with waggyng of a fether.

    R. ROYSTER [*to his men*]: On, sirs! Keepe your ray!

    M. M[ERY:] On, forth, while this geare is hot.

    R. ROYSTER: Soft, the armes of Caleys! I have one
      thing forgot.

    M. MERY: What lacke we now?

    R. R[OISTER:]   Retire, or else we be
      all slain!

    M. MERY: Backe for the pashe of God! Backe, sirs,
      backe againe!

    What is the great mater?

1680 *his lily*: (Christ's) lovely   1693 *ray*: battle order   1695 *Caleys*: Calais   1696 *pashe*: ?
Passover; see note to line 1513

R. R[OISTER:]   This hastie forthgoyng
Had almost brought us all to utter undoing;
It made me forget a thing most necessarie.

M. MERY: Well remembred of a captaine, by Sainct
 Marie!   *1700*

R. ROYSTER: It is a thing must be had.

M. M[ERY:]   Let us have it then.

R. ROYSTER: But I wote not where nor how.

M. M[ERY:]   Then
 wote not I when.
But what is it?

R. R[OISTER:] Of a chiefe thing I am to seeke.

M. MERY: Tut, so will ye be when ye have studied a
 weke!
But tell me what it is.

R. R[OISTER:]   I lacke yet an hedpiece!

M. MERY: The kitchen *collocavit* – the best hennes to
 Grece!
Runne, fet it, Dobinet, and come at once withall,
And bryng with thee my potgunne, hangyng by
 the wall.
 [*Exit* DOBINET DOUGHTY.]
I have seene your head with it, full many a tyme,
Covered as safe as it had bene with a skrine: *1710*
And I warrant it save your head from any stroke,
Except perchaunce to be amased with the smoke:
I warrant your head therwith, except for the mist,
As safe as if it were fast locked up in a chist!
 [*Re-enter* DOBINET.]
And loe, here our Dobinet commeth with it nowe!

D. DOUGH: It will cover me to the shoulders well
 inow.

M. MERY: Let me see it on.
 [ROISTER DOISTER *puts the pail on his head.*]

R. R[OISTER:] In fayth, it doth metely well.

1706 *collocavit*: kitchen pail or tub (see note) *hennes*: from here 1708 *potgunne*: a short
gun, but more probably a pop-gun 1710 *skrine*: screen 1714 *chist*: chest

M. MERY: There can be no fitter thing. Now ye must
    us tell
  What to do.

R. R[OISTER:] Now forth in ray, sirs, and stoppe no
    more.

M. MERY: Now Sainct George to borow! Drum,
1720   dubbe a dubbe afore!

T. TRUSTY [*stepping forward*]: What meane you to do,
    sir, committe manslaughter?

R. ROYSTER: To kyll fortie such is a matter of laughter.

T. TRUSTY: And who is it, sir, whome ye intende
    thus to spill?

R. ROYSTER: Foolishe Custance here forceth me
    against my will.

T. TRUSTY: And is there no meane your extreme
    wrath to slake?
  She shall some amendes unto your good mashyp
    make.

R. ROYSTER: I will none amendes.

T. TR[USTY:]   Is hir offence so sore?

M. MERY: And he were a loute she coulde have done
    no more!
  She hath calde him foole, and dressed him like a
    foole,
1730   Mocked him lyke a foole, used him like a foole.

T. TRUSTY: Well, yet the Sheriffe, the Justice, or
    Constable,
  Hir misdemeanour to punishe might be able.

R. ROYSTER: No, sir, I mine owne selfe will in this
    present cause,
  Be Sheriffe, and Justice, and whole Judge of the
    lawes;
  This matter to amende, all officers be I shall,
  Constable, Bailiffe, Sergeant –

1720 *to borow*: be our surety   1723 *spill*: destroy   1729 *dressed*: scolded, dressed him down

M. M[ERY:]   And hangman and all.

T. TRUSTY: Yet a noble courage, and the hearte of a
    man,
    Should more honour winne by bearyng with a
      woman:
    Therfore take the lawe, and lette hir aunswere
      therto.

R. ROYSTER: Merygreeke, the best way were even so
    to do: *1740*
    What honour should it be with a woman to fight?

M. MERY: And what then, will ye thus forgo and lese
    your right?

R. ROYSTER: Nay, I will take the lawe on hir
    withouten grace!

T. TRUSTY: Or yf your mashyp coulde pardon this
    one trespace, –
    I pray you forgive hir.

R. R[OISTER:]   Hoh?

M. M[ERY:]   Tushe, tushe, sir, do
    not!

[T. TRUSTY:] Be good maister to hir.

R. R[OISTER:]   Hoh?

M. M[ERY:]   Tush, I
    say, do not!
    And what, shall your people here returne streight
      home?

T. TRUSTIE: Yea, levie the campe, sirs, and hence
    againe eche one.

R. ROISTER: But be still in readinesse if I happe to call;
    I cannot tell what sodaine chaunce may befall.   *1750*

M. MERY: Do not off your harnesse, sirs, I you advise,
    At the least for this fortnight in no maner wise;
    Perchaunce in an houre when all ye thinke least,
    Our maister's appetite to fight will be best.
    But soft, ere ye go, have once at Custance house!

1742 *lese*: lose   1748 *levie*: break up

R. ROYSTER: Soft, what wilt thou do?

M. M[ERY:]   Once discharge
   my harquebouse,
  And for my hearte's ease, have once more with my
     potgoon.

R. ROYSTER: Holde thy handes, else is all our
   purpose cleane fordoone!

M. MERY: And it cost me my life –!

R. R[OISTER:]   I say thou shalt not!

M. MERY: By the matte, but I will! Have once more
1760   with haile shot!
       [Fires his gun.]
     I will have some penyworth, I will not leese all!

             Actus iiii.   Scaena viii.

          M. Merygreeke.   C. Custance.
        R. Roister.   Tib. T.   An. Alyface.
       M. Mumblecrust.   Trupenie.   Dobinet
              Doughtie.   Harpax.
          Two drummes with their Ensignes.
       [*Enter* CHRISTIAN CUSTANCE *from the house.*]

C. CUSTANCE: What caitifes are those that so shake
   my house wall?

M. MERY: Ah, sirrha! Now Custance, if ye had so
   muche wit,
  I would see you aske pardon, and yourselves
     submit.

C. CUSTANCE: Have I still this adoe with a couple of
   fooles?

M.MERY [*to* ROISTER DOISTER]: Here ye what she
   saith?

C. C[USTANCE *calling*]: Maidens, come forth with your tooles!

R. ROYSTER: In a ray!
       [*Enter* CUSTANCE'S MAIDS, *armed with domestic tools*].

_____

1760 *the matte*: ? the Mass   1761 *leese*: lose

190

M. M[ERY *to a* DRUMMER]: Dubba dub, sirrha!

R. R[OISTER:]   In a
   ray!

They come sodainly on us!

M. M[ERY:]   Dubbadub!

R. R[OISTER:]   In a ray!

That ever I was borne! We are taken tardie!

M. MERY: Now, sirs, quite ourselves like tall men and
   hardie!   *1770*

C. CUSTANCE: On afore, Trupenie; holde thyne
   owne, Annot;

On towarde them, Tibet, for scape us they cannot!

Come forth, Madge Mumblecrust; so stande fast
   togither!

M. MERY: God sende us a faire day!

R. R[OISTER:]   See, they marche
   on hither!

TIB. TALK.: But mistresse –

C. C[USTANCE:]   What sayst thou?

TIB.:   Shal I
   go fet our goose?

C. CUSTANCE: What to do?

TIB.:   To yonder captain I will
   turne hir loose;

And she gape and hisse at him, as she doth at me,

I durst jeoparde my hande she wyll make him flee!

C. CUSTANCE: On, forward!

R. R[OISTER:]   They com!

M. M[ERY:]   Stand!

R. R[OISTER:] Hold!

M. M[ERY:]   Kepe!

R. R[OISTER:]   There!

M. M[ERY:]   Strike!

R. R[OISTER:]   Take heede!

C. CUSTANCE: Wel sayd, Trupeny!

1775 *fet*: fetch   1778 *jeoparde*: hazard

TRUP[ENNY:]   Ah, whooresons!
[*He strikes out.*]

1780 C. C[USTANCE:]   Wel don indeede!
[*General fighting breaks out.*]

M. MERY: Holde thine owne, Harpax! Downe with
them, Dobinet!

C. CUSTANCE: Now, Madge; there, Annot! Now
sticke them, Tibet!

TIB. TALK: All my chiefe quarell is to this same little
knave,
That begyled me last day; nothyng shall him save!
[TIBET *beats* DOBINET DOUGHTY.]

D. DOUGH: Downe with this litle queane that hath at
me such spite;
Save you from hir, maister; it is a very sprite!

C. CUSTANCE: I myselfe will Mounsire Graunde
Captaine undertake.
[*She attacks* ROISTER DOISTER.]

R. ROYSTER: They win grounde!

M. M[ERY:]   Save yourselfe, sir,
for God's sake!
[CHRISTIAN CUSTANCE *knocks* ROISTER
DOISTER *down.*]

R. ROYSTER: Out! Alas, I am slaine! Helpe!

M. M[ERY:]   Save yourself!

R. R[OISTER:]   Alas!

M. MERY [*to* CUSTANCE]: Nay then, have at you,
mistresse! [*Strikes* ROISTER DOISTER.]

1790 R. R[OISTER:]   Thou hittest *me*, alas!

M. MERY: I wil strike at Custance here!

R. R[OISTER:]   Thou hittest *me*!

M. M[ERY:]   So I wil!
Nay, Mistresse Custance!

R. R[OISTER:]   Alas, thou hittest me still!
Hold!

1780 *whooresons*: rascals   1785 *queane*: hussy, 'little cat' (see note)

M. M[ERY *still hitting him*]: Save yourself, sir!

R. R[OISTER:]   Help!
    Out, alas, I am slain!

M. MERY: Truce! Hold your hands! Truce for a
    pissing while or twaine!
  Now, how say you, Custance, for saving of your life,
  Will ye yelde and graunt to be this gentman's wife?

C. CUSTANCE: Ye told me he loved me; call ye this
    love?

M. MERY: He loved a while even like a turtle dove.

C. CUSTANCE: Gay love, God save it; so soone hotte,
    so soone colde!

M. MERY: I am sory for you; he could love you yet so
    he coulde.   *1800*

R. ROYSTER: Nay, by Cock's precious, she shall be
    none of mine.

M. MERY: Why so?

R. R[OISTER:]   Come away; by the matte, she is
    mankine:
  I durst adventure the losse of my right hande,
  If she dyd not slee hir other husbande!
  And see if she prepare not againe to fight!

M. MERY: What then? Sainct George to borow, Our
    Ladie's knight!

R. ROYSTER [*backing away*]: Slee else whom she will,
    by Gog, she shall not slee mee!

M. MERY: How then?

R. R[OISTER:]   Rather than to be slaine, I will flee!

C. CUSTANCE: Too it againe, my knightesses, downe
    with them all!

R. ROYSTER: Away, away, away, she will else kyll us
    all!   *1810*

M. MERY: Nay, sticke to it, like a hardie man and a
    tall! [*Hits him.*]

1794 *pissing while*: a brief space   1801 *by Cock's precious*: by God's precious blood or bones
1802 *by the matte*: ? by the Mass   *mankine*: furious, insane   1806 *Our Ladie's*: the Virgin
Mary's

R. ROYSTER: Oh bones, thou hittest me! Away, or
  else die we shall!

M. MERY: Away, for the pashe of our sweete Lord
  Jesus Christ!

C. CUSTANCE: Away, loute and lubber, or I shall be
  thy priest!
  Exeant om[*nes.*]
 So this fielde is ours; we have driven them all
  away.

TIB. TALK.: Thankes to God, mistresse, ye have had
  a faire day!

C. CUSTANCE: Well nowe goe ye in, and make
  yourselfe some good cheere.

OMNES PARITER: We goe. [*They go into the house.*]

T. TRUST: Ah, sir, what a field we have had heere!

C. CUSTANCE: Friend Tristram, I pray you be a
  witnesse with me.

T. TRUSTY: Dame Custance, I shall depose for your
1820 honestie;
 And nowe fare ye well, except something else ye
  wolde.

C. CUSTANCE: Not now, but when I nede to sende I
  will be bolde.
 I thanke you for these paines.
  Exeat [TRISTRAM TRUSTY.]
       And now I wyll get me in;
 Now Roister Doister will no more wowyng begin!
          Ex[*eat.*]

Actus v. Scaena i.

Gawyn Goodlucke. *Sym Suresby.*
[*Enter* GAWYN GOODLUCK *and* SYM SURESBY.]
[GAWYN GOODLUCK:] Sym Suresby, my trustie man,
  nowe advise thee well,

1814 *be thy priest*: i.e. dispatch you *Exeant omnes*: they all go out (i.e. Roister Doister
and his party) 1818 *Omnes pariter*: all together

And see that no false surmises thou me tell:
Was there such adoe about Custance, of a truth?

SIM SURE: To reporte that I hearde and sawe to me is
  ruth,
  But both my duetie and name and propretie
  Warneth me to you to shewe fidelitie.   *1830*
  It may be well enough, and I wyshe it so to be;
  She may hirselfe discharge and trie hir honestie,
  Yet their clayme to hir methought was very large,
  For with letters, rings, and tokens they dyd hir
  charge.
  Which when I hearde and sawe I would none to
  you bring.

G. GOODL.: No, by Sainct Marie, I allowe thee in
  that thing;
  Ah, sirra, nowe I see truthe in the proverbe olde:
  All things that shineth is not by and by pure golde!
  If any doe lyve a woman of honestie,
  I would have sworne Christian Custance had bene
  shee.   *1840*

SIM SURE: Sir, though I to you be a servant true and
  just,
  Yet doe not ye therfore your faithfull spouse mystrust,
  But examine the matter, and if ye shall it finde
  To be all well, be not ye for my wordes unkinde.

G. GOODL.: I shall do that is right, and as I see cause why.
  [*Enter* CUSTANCE *from the house.*]
  But here commeth Custance forth; we shal know
  by and by.

Actus v.   Scaena ii.

C. Custance.   Gawyn Goodlucke.   Sym Suresby.

C. CUSTANCE: I come forth to see and hearken for
  newes good,

1828 *ruth*: sadness   1829 *propretie*: character, good name   1832 *trie*: demonstrate, prove
1836 *allowe*: sanction, commend   1846 *by and by*: very shortly

For about this houre is the tyme, of likelyhood,
That Gawyn Goodlucke by the sayings of Suresby
1850   Woulde be at home, and lo! yond I see hym, I.
[*Approaching*] What, Gawyn Goodluck, the onely
    hope of my life,
Welcome home, and kysse me, your true espoused
    wife!
GA. GOOD.: Nay, soft, Dame Custance, I must first
    by your licence
See whether all things be cleere in your conscience;
I heare of your doings to me very straunge.
C. CUSTANCE: What feare ye? That my faith
    towardes you should chaunge?
GA. GOOD.: I must needes mistrust ye be elsewhere
    entangled,
For I heare that certaine men with you have
    wrangled
About the promise of mariage by you to them
    made.
C. CUSTANCE: Coulde any man's reporte your minde
1860   therein persuade?
GA. GOOD.: Well, ye must therin declare yourselfe to
    stande cleere,
Else I and you, Dame Custance, may not joyne
    this yere.
C. CUSTANCE: Then woulde I were dead, and faire
    layd in my grave!
Ah, Suresby, is this the honestie that ye have,
To hurt me with your report, not knowyng the
    thing?
SIM SURE: If ye be honest my wordes can hurte you
    nothing:
But what I hearde and sawe I might not but report.
C. CUSTANCE: Ah, Lorde, helpe poore widowes,
    destitute of comfort!

1865 *the thing*: the facts of the matter

Truly, most deare spouse, nought was done but for
    pastance.

G. GOOD.: But such kynde of sporting is homely
    daliance.   *1870*

C. CUSTANCE: If ye knewe the truthe, ye would take
    all in good parte.

GA. GOOD.: By your leave, I am not halfe well skilled
    in that arte.

C. CUSTANCE: It was none but Roister Doister, that
    foolishe mome.

GA. GOOD.: Yea, Custance; better (they say) a badde
    scuse than none.

C. CUSTANCE: Why, Tristram Trusty, sir, your true
    and faithfull frende,
Was privie bothe to the beginning and the ende:
Let him be the Judge, and for me testifie.

GA. GOOD.: I will the more credite that he shall verifie,
And bicause I will the truthe know e'en as it is,
I will to him myselfe, and know all without misse.   *1880*
Come on, Sym Suresby, that before my friend thou
    may
Avouch the same wordes which thou dydst to me
    say.
    Exeant. [GAWYN GOODLUCK *and* SYM SURESBY.]

Actus v.   *Scaena iii.*

Christian   *Custance.*

C. CUSTANCE: O Lorde, howe necessarie it is nowe of
    dayes,
That eche bodie live uprightly all maner wayes,
For lette never so little a gappe be open,
And be sure of this, the worst shall be spoken.
Howe innocent stande I in this, for deede or
    thought,

1869 *pastance*: amusement, pastime   1870 *homely*: intimate   1873 *mome*: clown
1874 *scuse*: excuse   1880 *misse*: uncertainty

And yet see what mistrust towardes me it hath
   wrought!
But thou, Lorde, knowest all folkes' thoughts and eke
   intents,
1890   And thou arte the deliverer of all innocentes;
Thou didst helpe the advoutresse that she might
   be amended,
Much more [them] helpe, Lorde, that never yll
   intended!
Thou didst helpe Susanna, wrongfully accused,
And no lesse dost thou see, Lorde, how I am now
   abused;
Thou didst helpe Hester, when she should have died;
Helpe also, good Lorde, that my truth may be tried!
Yet if Gawin Goodlucke with Tristram Trusty
   speake,
I trust of yll report the force shall be but weake.
   [*Enter* GAWYN GOODLUCK, TRISTRAM TRUSTY,
   and SYM SURESBY, *and stand a little apart.*]
And loe, yond they come, sadly talking togither;
I wyll abyde, and not shrinke for their comming
1900   hither.

Actus v.   *Scaena iiii.*

Gawyn Goodlucke.   *Tristram Trustie.*   *C. Custance.*
      Sym Suresby.

GA. GOOD.: And was it none other than ye to me
   reporte?
TRISTRAM: No, and here were ye wished to have
   seene the sporte.
GA. GOOD.: Woulde I had, rather than halfe of that
   in my purse!
SIM SURE: And I doe muche rejoyce the matter was
   no wurse,

1889 *eke*: also *intents*: intentions 1891 *advoutresse*: adulteress, i.e. Mary Magdalene or
'the woman taken in adultery' (see note) 1896 *tried*: proved 1899 *sadly*: seriously

198

And like as to open it I was to you faithfull,
So of Dame Custance honest truth I am joyfull:
For God forfende that I shoulde hurt hir by false
    reporte!

GA. GOOD.: Well, I will no longer holde hir in
    discomforte.

C. CUSTANCE: Nowe come they hitherwarde; I trust
    all shall be well.

G. GOOD.: Sweete Custance, neither heart can thinke
    nor tongue tell,   *1910*

Howe much I joy in your constant fidelitie!
Come nowe, kisse me, the pearle of perfect
    honestie!

C. CUSTANCE: God lette me no longer to continue in
    lyfe
Than I shall towardes you continue a true wyfe!
    [*They embrace.*]

G. GOODL.: Well, now, to make you for this some
    parte of amendes,
I shall desire first you, and then suche of our
    frendes
As shall to you seeme best, to suppe at home with me,
Where at your fought fielde we shall laugh and
    mery be.

SIM SURE: And, mistresse, I beseech you, take with
    me no greefe;
I did a true man's part, not wishyng your repreefe.   *1920*

C. CUSTANCE: Though hastie reportes through
    surmises growyng,
May of poore innocentes be utter overthrowyng,
Yet bicause to thy maister thou hast a true hart,
And I know mine owne truth, I forgive thee for my
    part.

G. GOODL.: Go we all to my house, and of this geare
    no more;

1905 *open*: reveal   1907 *forfende*: forbid   1919 *greefe*: grievance, anger   1920 *repreefe*:
reproof   1925 *geare*: matter

199

Goe prepare all things, Sym Suresby; hence, runne
afore!

SIM SURE: I goe. _Ex[eat.]_

G. GOOD [_looking off-stage_]: But who commeth yond,
M[atthew] Merygreeke?

C. CUSTANCE: Roister Doister's champion; I shrewe
his best cheeke!

T. TRUSTY: Roister Doister['s] selfe, your wower, is with
hym too;

1930   Surely something there is with us they have to doe.

Actus v.   Scaena v.

M. Merygreeke.   Ralph Roister.
Gawyn Goodlucke.   Tristram Trustie.   C. Custance.
[_Enter_ MERRYGREEK _and_ ROISTER DOISTER.]

M. MERY: Yond I see Gawyn Goodlucke, to whome
lyeth my message;

I wyll first salute him after his long voyage,

And then make all thing well concerning your
behalfe.

R. ROYSTER: Yea, for the pashe of God!

M. M[ERY:]   Hence, out of
sight, ye calfe,

Till I have spoke with them, and then I will you fet.

R. ROYSTER: In God's name.   [_He goes out._]

M. M[ERY:] What, Master Gawin Goodluck! Wel met!

And from your long voyage I bid you right
welcome home.

GA. GOOD.: I thanke you.

M. M[ERY:]   I come to you from an
honest mome.

GA. GOOD: Who is that?

M. M[ERY:]   Roister Doister, that
doughtie kite.

1928 _shrewe his best cheeke_: damn and blast him! (see note to line 1389 above)   1934 _calfe_:
twerp   1935 _fet_: fetch   1938 _mome_: dope   1939 _kite_: 'shark'

C. CUSTANCE: Fye, I can scarce abide ye shoulde his
  name recite.   *1940*

M. MERY: Ye must take him to favour, and pardon all
  past;

He heareth of your returne, and is full yll agast.

GA. GOOD.: I am ryght well content he have with us
  some chere.

C. CUSTANCE: Fye upon him, beast! Then wyll not I
  be there!

GA. GOOD.: Why, Custance, do ye hate hym more
  than ye love me?

C. CUSTANCE: But for your mynde, sir, where he
  were would I not be!

T. TRUSTY: He woulde make us al laugh!

M. M[ERY:]   Ye nere had
  better sport.

GA. GOOD.: I pray you, sweete Custance, let him to
  us resort.

C. CUSTANCE: To your will I assent.

M. M[ERY:]   Why, such a
  foole it is,

As no man for good pastime would forgoe or misse. *1950*

G. GOODL.: Fet him to go wyth us.

M. M[ERY:]   He will be a glad man.

Ex[eat]

T. TRUSTY: We must to make us mirth maintaine
  hym all we can.

[*Re-enter* ROISTER DOISTER *and* MERRYGREEK.]

And loe! yond he commeth, and Merygreeke with
  him.

C. CUSTANCE: At his first entrance ye shall see I wyll
  him trim;

But first let us hearken the gentleman's wise talke!

T. TRUSTY: I pray you marke if ever ye sawe crane
  so stalke!

1946 *mynde*: wish, intention   1952 *maintaine*: keep on good terms with   1954 *trim*:
reprimand, 'cut him down to size'

Actus v.   Scaena vi.

R. *Roister.*   M. *Merygreeke.*   C. *Custance.*

G. *Goodlucke.*   T. *Trustie.*   D. *Doughtie.*   *Harpax.*

R. ROYSTER [*to* MERRYGREEK]: May I then be bolde?

M. M[ERY:] I warrant you, on my worde,

They say they shall be sicke but ye be at theyr
      borde.

R. ROYSTER: Thei wer not angry then?

M. M[ERY:]   Yes, at first,
      and made strange,

But when I sayd your anger to favour shoulde
1960   change,

And therewith had commended you accordingly,

They were all in love with your mashyp by and by,

And cried you mercy that they had done you wrong.

R. ROYSTER: For why, no man, woman, nor childe
      can hate me long.

M. MERY: 'We feare' (quod they) 'he will be avenged
      one day;

Then for a peny give all our lives we may.'

R. ROYSTER: Sayd they so indeede?

M. M[ERY:]   Did they? Yea,
      even with one voice.

'He will forgive all' (quod I). Oh, how they did
      rejoyce!

R. ROYSTER: Ha, ha, ha!

M. M[ERY:]   'Goe fette hym' (say they)
      'while he is in good moode,

For have his anger who lust, we will not, by the
1970   Roode!'

R. ROYSTER: I pray God that it be all true that thou
      hast me tolde,

And that she fight no more.

M. M[ERY:]   I warrant you, be bolde!

Too them, and salute them.

1958 *borde*: meal-table   1959 *strange*: distant, unfriendly   1970 *the Roode*: the Cross

R. R[OISTER:]   Sirs, I greete you all well.

OMNES: Your maistership is welcom.

C. CUST[ANCE:]   Savyng my quarell!
 For sure I will put you up into the Eschequer.

M. MERY: Why so? Better nay. Wherfore?

C. CUST[ANCE:]   For an usurer.

R. ROYSTER: I am no usurer, good mistresse, by his
  armes!

M. MERY: When tooke he gaine of money to any
  man's harmes?

C. CUSTANCE: Yes, a fowle usurer he is, ye shall see els.

R. ROYSTER [*to* MERRYGREEK]: Didst not thou
  promise she would picke no mo quarels?   *1980*

C. CUSTANCE: He will lende no blowes, but he have
  in recompence
 Fiftene for one, whiche is to muche of conscience!

R. ROYSTER: Ah, dame, by the auncient lawe of
  armes, a man
 Hath no honour to foile his handes on a woman!

C. CUSTANCE: And where other usurers take their
  gaines yerely,
 This man is angry but he have his by and by!

GA. GOODL.: Sir, doe not, for hir sake, beare me your
  displeasure.

M. MERY: Well, he shall with you talke therof more at
  leasure;
 Upon your good usage, he will now shake your
  hande.

R. ROYSTER [*shaking hands with* GAWYN]: And much
  heartily welcome from a straunge lande!   *1990*

M. MERY: Be not afearde, Gawyn, to let him shake
  your fyst.

GA. GOODL.: Oh, the moste honest gentleman that
  ere I wist!

1974 *Omnes*: All 1975 *Eschequer*: the Court of Exchequer which dealt with financial matters 1980 *mo*: more 1984 *foile*: defile, soil 1986 *by and by*: immediately 1991 *fyst*: hand 1992 *wist*: knew

I beseeche your mashyp to take payne to suppe
with us.

M. MERY: He shall not say you nay – and I too, by
Jesus!

Bicause ye shall be friends, and let all quarels
passe.

R. ROYSTER: I wyll be as good friends with them as
ere I was.

M. MERY: Then let me fet your quier that we may
have a song.

R. ROYSTER: Goe.

[*Exit* MERRYGREEK.]

G. GOODLUCK: I have hearde no melodie all this
yeare long.

[*Re-enter* MERRYGREEK *with* DOBINET
DOUGHTY, HARPAX, *and the other servants.*]

M. MERY: Come on, sirs, quickly!

R. R[OISTER:]   Sing on, sirs, for my
frends' sake.

D. DOUGH: Cal ye these your frends?

R. R[OISTER:]   Sing on, and no
2000   mo words make!

Here they sing.

GA. GOOD: The Lord preserve our most noble
Queene of renowne,

And hir vertues rewarde with the heavenly crowne.

C. CUSTANCE: The Lord strengthen hir most
excellent Majestie,

Long to reigne over us in all prosperitie.

T. TRUSTY: That hir godly proceedings the faith to
defende,

He may stablishe and maintaine through to the
ende.

M. MERY: God graunt hir, as she doth, the Gospell to
protect,

1997 *fet your quier*: fetch your choir   2006 *He*: i.e. God

Learning and vertue to advaunce, and vice to
    correct.

R. ROYSTER: God graunt hir lovyng subjects both
    the minde and grace

Hir most godly procedyngs worthily to imbrace.   *2010*

HARPAX: Hir highnesse most worthy counsellers God
    prosper,

With honour and love of all men to minister.

OMNES: God graunt the nobilitie hir to serve and love,
    With all the whole commontie as doth them
    behove.

AMEN

2014 *commontie*: the common people, the commons

Gammer Gurton's Nedle

? WILLIAM STEVENSON

A Ryght
Pithy, Pleasaunt and me
rie Comedie: In-
tytuled Gammer gur
tons Nedle: Played on
Stage, not longe
ago in Chri-
stes
Colledge in Cambridge.

Made by Mr. S. Mr. of Art.

Imprynted at London in
Fletestreat beneth the Conduit at the signe of S. John
Evangelist by Tho-
mas Colwell.

1575.

Facsimile of the title-page to the Quarto edition of 1575

According to the colophon which concludes the text, it was in 1575 that Thomas Colwell, a Fleet Street printer, published his Quarto edition of this comedy, whose full title runs:

A Ryght Pithy, Pleasaunt and merie Comedie: Intytuled *Gammer gurtons Nedle*: Played on Stage, not longe ago in Christes *Colledge in Cambridge, Made by Mr. S. Mr.* [Master] *of Art.*

However, despite the phrase 'not longe ago', there is reason to assume that some version of *Gammer Gurton's Nedle* was in existence well before 1575, since the entry originally permitting Colwell to print what is probably this play, or something closely resembling it, appears in the Stationers' Company Register for 1562–3, and reads:

Recevyd of Thomas Colwell for his lycense for pryntinge of a playe intituled DYCCON of Bedlam &c.   iiij^d.

On the strength of this entry it has been variously argued that Colwell had his book set up in type in 1562–3 but did not actually issue it until 1575; that *Dyccon of Bedlam* represents the original version of a play later revised for publication in its present form; or that the 1575 publication was not the first edition, but that all copies of any earlier printing are now lost. There are also those who feel on the grounds of internal evidence that the composition of the work must date back to the reign of Edward VI (1547–53) or (less probably) that of Henry VIII (1509–47); much significance has been attached to line 1181 of the present edition, in which Dr Rat urges the Bailiff to arrest Diccon:

In the King's name, Master Bayly, I charge you set him fast!

but this may not be as vital a pointer to an early date as has often been argued. It could be a mere careless error, a deliberate comic device to suggest that Dr Rat prefers to live in the past, or one of several historical details which create a pre-Reformation setting for the play as a whole. However, when added to the evidence for William Stevenson as the play's author given below, the reference may support a date in the early 1550s for the composition of the piece.

Some eight copies of the 1575 Quarto seem to have survived, one the Bodleian copy, and two in the British Library. None of the volumes known to be extant in Britain is perfect, the pages of the Bodleian copy having suffered particularly from being clipped at the edge and foot. However, between them the available copies can supply almost all the text, although occasionally recourse has to be made to Thomas Johnson's reprint of 1661 to establish the correct reading of a line.

The debate over the true identity of 'Mr. S. Mr. of Art' is an academic one in both senses of the term, but the most probable candidate is now generally recognized as being a William Stevenson, Fellow of Christ's College from 1551 to 1554 and again from 1559 to 1561, whose participation in college dramatics is attested to in the college account-books which record that Stevenson presented a play or plays at the college on several occasions in the early fifties, possibly plays originating from his own pen. However, in 1588 'Martin Marprelate', the anonymous Puritan controversialist, in the course of satirizing the work of Dr John Bridges, Dean of Salisbury and a Fellow of Pembroke College, Cambridge, in two pamphlets known as *The Epistle* and *The Epitome*, alluded to Bridges as being the author of *Gammer Gurton's Nedle*, though there is little positive evidence to support the view. Some commentators have detected stylistic resemblances between the play and Bridges's polemical writings, and it is certainly true that Bridges, who eventually became Bishop of Oxford, never seems to have refuted the attribution. However, the notion that Colwell deliberately obscured Bridges's authorship by employing the fiction of 'Mr. S' as a 'blind' seems far-fetched; there is no denying that Stevenson is connected with Christ's College and with the staging of plays there in a relevant decade, and has an appropriate surname to qualify for Colwell's title-page.

The principal editions of the play are as follows:

Henry Bradley, ed., in *Representative English Comedies*, I, ed. C. M. Gayley, New York, 1903.

J. S. Farmer, ed., *Anonymous Plays*, Early English Dramatists, 1906; *Gammer Gurton's Needle*, Tudor Facsimile Texts, 1910

H. F. B. Brett-Smith, *Gammer Gvrtons Nedle*, Oxford, 1920

Joseph Quincy Adams, ed., *Chief Pre-Shakespearean Dramas*, Boston, 1924

F. S. Boas, ed., *Five Pre-Shakespearean Comedies*, World's Classics, Oxford, 1933.

The present edition is based on that of Brett-Smith, though I have frequently consulted that of Boas, as well as making extensive use of Farmer's facsimile.

The names of the Speakers in this Comedie.

DICCON THE BEDLEM

HODGE GAMMER GURTON'S SERVANTE

TYB GAMMER GURTON'S MAYDE

GAMMER GURTON

COCKE GAMMER GURTON'S BOYE

DAME CHATTE

DOCTOR RAT THE CURATE

MAYSTER BAYLYE

DOLL DAME CHATTE'S MAYDE

SCAPETHRYFT MAYST BEYLIE'S SERVANTE

MUTES

God Save the Queene

[To this list must be added the figure of The Prologue]

Bedlem: madman (see note) *Gammer*: literally 'grandmother', 'Granny'; old woman
Baylye: bailiff, law officer *Mayst*: Master

GAMMER GURTON'S NEDLE

The Prologue

[*Enter the* PROLOGUE.]

PROLOGUE: As Gammer Gurton, with manye a wyde
   styche,
  Sat pesynge and patching of Hodg her man's
   briche,
  By chance or misfortune as shee her geare tost
  In Hodge lether bryches her needle shee lost;
  When Diccon the Bedlem had hard by report
  That good Gammer Gurton was robde in thys
   sorte,
  He quyetly perswaded with her in that stound
  Dame Chat her deare gossyp this needle had
   found,
  Yet knew shee no more of this matter (alas)
  Then knoeth Tom our clarke what the Priest saith
   at Masse.   *10*
  Hereof there ensued so fearfull a fraye,
  Mas Doctor was sent for these gossyps to staye,
  Because he was Curate and estemed full wyse,
  Who found that he sought not, by Diccon's device.
  When all thinges were tombled and cleane out of
   fassion,
  (Whether it were by fortune, or some other
   constellacion)
  Sodenlye the neele Hodge found by the prickynge
  And drew it out of his bottocke where he felt it
   stickynge:
  Theyr hartes then at rest with perfect securytie,

---

2 *pesynge*: mending by adding a 'piece' 3 *geare*: 'tackle' *tost*: tossed aside 5 *hard*: heard
7 *in that stound*: in that time of trouble 8 *gossyp*: crony, friend (see note) 12 *Mas*:
Master 14 *device*: scheme 15 *tombled*: upset, mixed up *out of fassion*: disordered

With a pot of good nale they stroake up theyr
20   plauditie.   [*Exit.*]

The fyrst Acte.   *The fyrst Sceane.*

Diccon.

[*Enter* DICCON *from* GAMMER GURTON'*s house,
bearing a slice of bacon.*]

DICCON: Many a myle have I walked, divers and
    sundry waies,
And many a good man's house have I bin at in my
    daies;
Many a gossip's cup in my tyme have I tasted,
And many a broche and spyt have I both turned
    and basted;
Many a peece of bacon have I had out of thir balkes,
In ronnyng over the countrey, with long and were
    walkes;
Yet came my foote never within those doore
    cheekes,
To seeke flesh or fysh, garlyke, onyons or leekes,
That ever I saw a sorte in such a plyght,
30   As here within this house appereth to my syght.
There is howlynge and scowlyng, all cast in a
    dumpe,
With whewling and pewling, as though they had
    lost a trump:
Syghing and sobbing, they weepe and they wayle –
I marvell in my mynd, what the devill they ayle!
The olde trot syts groning, with 'alas and alas',
And Tib wringes her hands and takes on in worse
    case;

---

20 *nale*: ale *plauditie*: request for applause 23 *gossip's*: probably 'crony's', but see note
to line 8 24 *broche*: a pointed rod for roasting joints on at the fire 25 *thir balkes*: their
roof-beams 26 *were*: weary 27 *cheekes*: uprights, side-posts 29 *sorte*: company, crowd
31 *dumpe*: depressed mood 32 *a trump*: possibly a 'trumpery' article, but see note
35 *trot*: old woman, dame

With poore Cocke theyr boye, they be dryven in
   such fyts,
I feare mee the folkes be not well in theyr wyts!
Aske them what they ayle, or who brought them in
   this staye?
They aunswer not at all, but 'alacke and welaway!'   *40*
Whan I saw it booted not, out at doores I hyed mee
And caught a slyp of bacon, when I saw that none
   spyed mee,
Which I intend not far hence, unless my purpose
   fayle,
Shall serve for a shoinghorne to draw on two pots
   of ale.

The fyrst Acte.   *The second Sceane.*

Hodge.   *Diccon.*

[*Enter* HODGE *from the fields.*]

HODGE: See so cham arayed with dablynge in the
   durt –
She that set me to ditchinge ich wold she had the
   squrt!
Was never poore soule that such a life had?
Gog's bones, thys vylthy glaye hase drest mee to
   bad!
[*He rubs his breeches, and in doing so tears them.*]
God's soule, see how this stuffe teares!
Iche were better to bee a bearward and set to
   keepe beares!   *50*
By the Masse, here is a gasshe, a shamefull hole
   indeade,
And one stytch teare furder, a man may thruste in
   his heade!

---

39 *this staye*: this halt, standstill 41 *it booted not*: it was useless 42 *slyp*: sliver, long
narrow slice 44 *shoinghorne*: an appetizer, here one to provoke thirst 45 *so cham*: for this
and other dialect forms, see Appendix *durt*: mire 46 *the squrt*: 'the squitters',
diarrhoea 48 *Gog's*: God's *drest*: arrayed, covered 52 *And*: if *furder*: further

DICCON: By my father's soule, Hodge, if I shulde
now be sworne,
I cannot chuse but say thy breech is foule betorne,
But the next remedye in such a case and hap
Is to plaunche on a piece, as brode as thy cap.
HODGE: Gog's soule, man, 'tis not yet two dayes fully
ended
Synce my dame Gurton (chem sure) these breches
amended,
But cham made such a drudge to trudge at every
neede,
Chwold rend it though it were stitched wyth
60   sturdy pacthreede.
DICCON: Hoge, let thy breeches go, and speake and
tell mee soone –
What devill ayleth Gammer Gurton and Tib her
mayd to frowne?
HODGE: Tush, man, thart deceyved; 'tys theyr dayly
looke;
They coure so over the coles, theyr eyes be bleard
with smooke.
DICCON: Nay, by the Masse, I perfectly perceived as I
came hether
That eyther Tib and her dame hath ben by the
eares together,
Or els as great a matter as thou shalt shortly see.
HODGE: Now iche beseeche our Lord, they never
better agree!
DICCON: By Gog's soule, there they syt as still as
stones in the streite,
As though they had ben taken with fairies or els
70   with some il sprite.
HODGE: Gog's hart, I durst have layd my cap to a
crowne,

56 *plaunche*: clap on   64 *coure*: cower   *bleard*: dimmed, made bleary   66 *ben by the eares*:
quarrelled   70 *il*: evil

    Chwould lerne of some prancome as sone as ich
      came to town!
DICCON: Why, Hodge, art thou inspyred? Or dedst
    thou therof here?
HODGE: Nay, but ich saw such a wonder as ich saw
    nat this seven yere:
    Tome Tannkard's cow (be Gog's bones) she set me
      up her saile,
    And flynging about his halfe aker fysking with her
      taile,
    As though ther had ben in her ars a swarme of bees,
    And chad not cryed 'Tphrowh hoore!' shead lept
      out of his lees!
DICCON: Why, Hodg, lies the connyng in Tom
    Tankard's cowe's taile?
HODGE: Well, ich chave hard some say such tokens
    do not fayle,   *80*
    But [canst] thou not [tell], in faith Diccon, why she
      frownes or wherat?
    Hath no man stolne her ducks or henes, or gelded
      Gyb her cat?
DICCON: What devyll can I tell man? I cold not have
    one word –
    They gave no more hede to my talk then thou
      woldst to a lorde!
HODGE: Iche cannot styll but muse, what mervaylous
    thinge it is;
    Chyll in and know myselfe what matters are amys.
DICCON: Then farewell Hodge a while, synce thou
    doest inward hast,
    For I will into the good wyfe Chat's, to feele how
      the ale dooth taste.
    [DICCON *exits into the ale-house.* HODGE *stands
    musing.*]

---

72 *prancome*: trickery, peculiar happening   75 *be*: by   76 *fysking*: whisking   78 *lees*:
pastures   79 *connyng*: magic art or knowledge of the supernatural   80 *hard*: heard

The fyrst Acte.   *The thyrd Sceane.*

Hodge.   *Tyb.*

HODGE: Cham agast by the Masse, ich wot not what
to do –

90   Chad nede blesse me well before ich go them to:

Perchaunce some felon sprit may haunt our house
indeed,

And then chwere but a noddy to venter where cha
no neede.

[*Enter* TYB *from the house.*]

TIB: Cham worse then mad, by the Masse, to be at
this staye;

Cham chyd, cham blamd, and beaton all thoures
on the daye;

Lamed and hunger storved, prycked up all in jagges,

Havyng no patch to hyde my backe, save a few
rotten ragges!

HODGE: I say, Tyb, if thou be Tyb, as I trow sure
thou bee,

What devyll make adoe is this, betweene our dame
and thee?

TYB: Gog's breade, Hodg, thou had a good turne
thou warte not here this while:

It had ben better for some of us to have ben hence

100   a myle!

My Gammer is so out of course, and frantyke all at ones,

That Cocke our boy, and I, poore wench, have felt
it on our bones.

HODGE: What is the matter – say on, Tib – wherat
she taketh so on?

TYB: She is undone, she sayth (alas); her joye and life
is gone;

If shee here not of some comfort, she is sayth [she]
but dead;

---

92 *a noddy*: a fool   *venter*: venture   *cha*: i.e. I ha', I have (see Appendix)   93 *then*: than
staye: standstill   95 *prycked up*: tricked out, dressed up   *jagges*: tattered clothes   99 *warte*:
wert   101 *out of course*: abnormal

Shall never come within her lyps one inch of meate
ne bread!

HODGE: By'r Ladie, cham not very glad to see her in
this dumpe;

Cholde a noble her stole hath fallen, and shee hath
broke her rumpe!

TYB: Nay, and that were the worst, we wold not
greatly care

For bursting of her hucklebone, or breakyng of her
chaire,   *110*

But greatter, greater, is her grief, as, Hodge, we
shall all feele.

HODGE: Gog's woundes, Tyb, my Gammer has never
lost her neele?

TYB: Her neele.

HODGE: Her neele?

TIB: Her neele by him that made me; it is true,
Hodge, I tell thee!

HODGE: Gog's sacrament, I would she had lost tharte
out of her bellie!

The Devill, or els his dame, they ought her sure a
shame:

How a murryon came this chaunce, – say, Tib –
unto our dame?

TYB: My Gammer sat her downe on her pes, and bad
me reach thy breeches,

And by and by, a vengeance in it, or she had take
two stitches

To clap a clout upon thine ars, by chaunce asyde
she leares,

And Gyb our cat in the milke pan she spied over
head and eares!   *120*

'Ah hore! Out thefe!' she cryed aloud, and swapt
the breches downe;

---

106 *ne*: nor 107 *By'r*: By Our *dumpe*: depressed mood 108 *Cholde*: I wager *a noble*: see
note *stole*: stool *broke*: injured 110 *hucklebone*: haunch-bone 112 *neele*: needle
114 *tharte*: the heart 115 *ought*: owed, repaid her with 116 *murryon*: murrain, plague
117 *pes*: cushion, hassock 118 *by and by*: straightaway *or*: ere 119 *clout*: patch

Up went her staffe, and out leapt Gyb at doors
    into the towne;
And synce that time was never wyght cold set their
    eies upon it:
Gog's malison chave Cocke and I byd twenty
    times light on it!

HODGE: And is not then my breches sewid up,
    tomorow that I shuld were?

TYB: No, in faith Hodge, thy breeches lie for al this
    never the nere.

HODGE: Now a vengeance light on al the sort that
    better shold have kept it:
The cat, the house, and Tib our maid that better
    shold have swept it!

[*Enter* GAMMER GURTON *from the house.*]

Se where she commeth crawling; come on in
    twenty devils' way!
Ye have made a fayre daie's worke, have you not?
130   Pray you say.

The fyrste Acte.   The iiii Sceane.

Gammer.   Hodge.   Tyb.   Cocke.

GAMMER: Alas, Hoge, alas, I may well cursse and ban
This daie that ever I saw it, with Gyb and the
    milke pan!
For these and ill lucke togather, as knoweth Cocke
    my boye,
Have stacke away my deare neele, and robd me of
    my joye –
My fayre longe strayght neele, that was myne
    onely treasure –
The fyrst day of my sorow is, and last end of my
    pleasure!

122 *towne*: yard (see note) 123 *cold*: could 124 *malison*: curse 127 *sort*: crowd 131 *ban*:
swear 133 *togather*: together 134 *stacke*: stuck, stowed

HODGE: Might ha kept it when ye had it, but fooles
    will be fooles styll:
  Lose that is vast in your handes ye neede not but
    ye will.
GAMMER: Go hie thee, Tib, and run, thou hoore, to
    thend here of the towne –
  Didst cary out dust in thy lap, seeke wher thou
    porest it downe,   *140*
  And as thou sawest me roking in the asshes where
    I morned,
  So see in all the heape of dust thou leave no straw
    unturned.
TYB: That chal, Gammer, swythe and tyte, and sone
    be here agayne!
GAMMER: Tib, stoope and loke downe to the ground
    to it, and take some paine.
    [*Exit* TYB.]
HODGE: Here is a prety matter, to see this gere how
    it goes –
  By Gog's soule, I thenk you wold loes your ars,
    and it were loose!
  Your neele lost, it is pitie you shold lack care and
    endlesse sorow –
  Gog's deth, how shall my breches be sewid? shall I
    go thus tomorow?
GAMMER: Ah Hodg, Hodg, if that ich cold find my
    neele, by the reed,
  Chould sow thy breches, ich promise thee, with
    full good double threed,   *150*
  And set a patch on either knee, shuld last this
    monethes twaine –
  Now God and good Saint Sithe I praye, to send it
    home againe!
HODGE: Wherto served your hands and eies, but this
    your neele to kepe?

141 *roking*: ? raking (see note)   143 *swythe and tyte*: vigorously and quickly 145 *gere*:
business 146 *loes*: lose 149 *by the reed*: by the rood 152 *Saint Sithe*: St Osyth (see note)

What devill had you els to do? Ye kept ich wot no
    sheepe!
Cham faine abrode to dyg and delve in water,
    myre and claye;
Sossing and possing in the durte styll from day to
    daye;
A hundred thinges that be abrode cham set to see
    them weele,
And foure of you syt idle at home, and cannot
    keepe a neele!
GAMMER: My neele – alas ich lost it, Hodge, what
    time ich me up hasted
To save the milke set up for the, which Gib our cat
160   hath wasted.
HODGE: The Devill he burst both Gib, and Tib, with
    all the rest!
Cham alwayes sure of the worst end, whoever have
    the best;
Where ha you ben fidging abrode, since you your
    neele lost?
GAMMER: Within the house, and at the dore, sitting
    by this same post
Wher I was loking a long howre, before these folks
    came here;
But welaway, all was in vayne, my neele is never
    the nere!
HODGE: Set me a candle, let me seeke and grope
    where ever it bee –
Gog's hart, ye be so folish (ich thinke) you knowe
    it not when you it see!
GAMMER: Come hether Cocke! What, Cocke, I say!
    [*Enter* COCKE.]
COCKE: Howe, Gammer?
GAMMER: Goe hye thee soone,

156 *Sossing and possing*: splashing and tramping in mud   157 *abrode*: out of doors
163 *fidging abrode*: moving restlessly all over the place   166 *never the nere*: no nearer to
being found   167 *Set me*: provide me with

And grope behynd the old brasse pan, whych thing
  when thou hast done,   *170*

Ther shalt thou fynd an old shooe, wherin if thou
  looke well,

Thou shalt fynd lyeng an inche of a whyte tallow
  candell,

Lyght it, and brynge it tite awaye.

COCKE: That shalbe
  done anone.
  [COCKE *goes into the house.*]

GAMMER: Nay, tary, Hodg, til thou hast light, and
  then wee'le seke ech one.

HODGE: [*calling into the house*]: Cum away, ye horson
  boy, are ye aslepe? Ye must have a crier!

COCKE [*within*]: Ich cannot get the candel light; here
  is almost no fier.

HODGE: Chil hold the a peny, chil make thee come if
  that ich may catch thine eares!

  Art deffe, thou horson boy? Cocke, I say! Why
  canst thou not heare's?

GAMMER: Beate hym not, Hodge, but help the boy
  and come you two together.
  [HODGE *goes into the house.*]

The i. Acte.   *The v. Sceane*

Gammer.   *Tyb.*   *Cocke.*   *Hodge.*
[*Re-enter* TYB.]

GAMMER: How now, Tyb? Quycke, let's here what
  newes thou hast brought hether!   *180*

TYB: Chave tost and tumbled yender heap our and
  over againe,

  And winowed it through my fingers, as men wold
  winow grain;

---

173 *tite*: quickly 175 *horson*: whoreson, term of abuse 176 *light*: alight *fier*: fire
177 *hold*: bet, wager 181 *our*: over

Not so much as a hen's turd but in pieces I tare
    it,
Or whatsoever clod or clay I found, I did not spare
    it,
Lokyng within and eke without, to fynd your neele
    (alas),
But all in vaine and without help; your neele is
    where it was.

GAMMER: Alas, my neele, we shall never meete, adue,
    adue for aye!

TYB: Not so, Gammer, we myght it fynd if we knew
    where it laye.

[*Re-enter* COCKE *from the house.*]

COCKE: Gog's crosse, Gammer, if ye will laugh, looke
    in but at the doore.
And see how Hodg lieth tomblynge and tossing
190   amids the floure,
Rakyng there some fyre to find amonge the asshes
    dead,
Where there is not one sparke so byg as a pyn's
    head;
At last in a darke corner two sparkes he thought he
    sees,
Which where indede nought els but Gyb our cat's
    two eyes!
'Puffe' quod Hodg, thinking therby to have fyre
    without doubt;
With that Gyb shut her two eyes, and so the fyre
    was out,
And by and by them opened, even as they were
    before:
With that the sparkes appered even as they had
    done of yore,
And even as Hodge blew the fire as he did thincke,
200   Gyb as she felt the blast strayghtway began to wyncke,

186 *without help*: there's no help for it 190 *amids the floure*: in the middle of the floor
194 *where*: were 197 *by and by*: immediately

Tyll Hodge fell of swering, as came best to his turne,
The fier was sure bewicht and therfore wold not
   burne!
At last Gyb up the stayers, among the old postes
   and pinnes,
And Hodge he hied him after till broke were both
   his shinnes;
Cursynge and swering othes were never of his makyng,
That Gyb wold fyre the house, if that shee were
   not taken.
GAMMER: See, here is all the thought that the foolysh
   urchyn taketh,
And Tyb methinke at his elbowe almost as mery
   maketh!
This is all the wyt ye have when others make their
   mone, –
Come downe, Hodge, where art thou and let the
   cat alone!   *210*
HODGE [*appearing at the upstairs window*]: Gog's harte,
   help and come up, Gyb in her tayle hath fyre,
And is like to burne all if shee get a lytle hier!
'Cum downe,' quoth you? Nay then, you might
   count me a patch;
The house commeth downe on your heads if it take
   ons the thatch!
GAMMER: It is the cat's eyes, foole, that shineth in
   the darke!
HODGE: Hath the cat, do you thinke, in every eye a
   sparke?
GAMMER: No, but they shyne as lyke fyre as ever
   man see.
HODGE: By the masse, and she burne all, yoush
   beare the blame for mee!

---

201 *fell of*: fell to   *as came best*, etc.: as came most naturally to his nature   203 *Gyb up the stayers*: i.e. ran up the stairs   *pinnes*: wooden pegs holding the roof-timbers in position   209 *wyt*: intelligence, sense   213 *patch*: a fool (see note)   214 *ons*: once   218 *yoush*: i.e. you shall

GAMMER: Cum downe and help to seeke here our
    neele that it were found –
    Downe, Tyb, on the knees I say, downe Cocke to
220   the ground!
    [*All kneel.*]
    To God I make a vowe, and so to good Saint Anne,
    A candell shall they have apeece, get it where I can,
    If I may my neele find in one place or in other.
HODGE [*re-entering*]: Now a vengeaunce on Gib light,
    on Gyb and Gyb's mother,
    And all the generacyon of cats both far and nere!
    [*To* COCKE] Looke on the ground, horson; thinks
    thou the neele is here?
COCKE: By my trouth, Gammer, methought your
    neele here I saw,
    But when my fyngers toucht it, I felt it was a straw.
TYB: See, Hodge, what's thys? May it not be within it?
HODGE: Breake it, foole, with thy hand and see and
230   thou canst fynde it!
TYB: Nay, breake it you, Hodge, accordyng to your
    word.
HODGE: Gog's sydes, fye, it styncks; it is a cat's tourd!
    [*To* TYB] It were well done to make thee eate it, by
    the Masse!
GAMMER: This matter amendeth not; my neele is still
    where it wasse.
    Our candle is at an ende, let us all in quight
    And come another tyme, when we have more
    lyght.
    [*They all go wearily into the house.*]

The ii. Acte.   *Fyrste a Songe.*

[SINGERS *from the ale-house (off-stage)*]:
Backe and syde go bare, go bare;
Booth foote and hande go colde:

But bellye, God sende thee good ale ynoughe,
Whether it be newe or olde.   240

I cannot eate, but lytle meate,
My stomacke is not good:
But sure I thinke that I can drynke
With him that weares a hood.
Thoughe I go bare, take ye no care,
I am nothinge a-colde:
I stuffe my skyn so full within,
Of joly good ale and olde.
   Backe and syde go bare, go bare,
   Booth foote and hand go colde: 250
   But belly, God send the good ale inoughe,
   Whether it be new or olde.

I love no rost, but a nut browne toste
And a crab layde in the fyre,
A lytle bread shall do me stead,
Much breade I not desyre:
No froste nor snow, no winde I trowe
Can hurte mee if I wolde,
I am so wrapt and throwly lapt
Of joly good ale and old.   260
   Backe and syde go bare, &c.

And Tyb my wyfe, that as her lyfe
Loveth well good ale to seeke,
Full ofte drynkes shee, tyll ye may see
The teares run downe her cheekes:
Then dooth she trowle to mee the bowle,
Even as a mault worme shuld,
And sayth 'Sweetehart, I tooke my part
Of this joly good ale and olde.'
   Backe and syde go bare, &c.   270

244 *him that wears a hood*: ? any man (but see note)   253 *toste*: i.e. piece of toast   254 *crab*: crab-apple   255 *do me stead*: suffice me   259 *throwly*: totally, thoroughly   266 *trowle*: pass across or round   267 *a mault worme*: a lover of malt-drink, a boozer (see note)

Now let them drynke, tyll they nod and winke,
Even as good felowes shoulde doe;
They shall not mysse to have the blisse
Good ale doth bringe men to:
And all poore soules that have scowred boules
Or have them lustely trolde,
God save the lyves of them and theyr wyves,
Whether they be yonge or olde!

    Backe and syde go bare, &c.

The Second Act.   The fyrst Sceane.

Diccon.   Hodge.

[DICCON *appears at the ale-house door.*]

DICCON [*over his shoulder*]: Well done, be Gog's malt,
280   well songe and well sayde!
Come on, Mother Chat, as thou art true mayde,
One fresh pot of ale let's see to make an ende
Agaynst his colde wether my naked armes to
    defende;
This gere it warms the soule, now wind blow on
    the worst,
And let us drink and swill till that our bellies
    burste!
Now were he a wyse man by cunnynge colde defyne
Which way my journey lyeth or where Dyccon will
    dyne;
But one good turne I have, be it by nyght or daye,
South, East, North or West, I am never out of my
    waye.

    [*Enter* HODGE *from the house, with a piece of bread.*]

HODGE: Chym goodly rewarded, cham I not, do you
290   thyncke?
Chad a goodly dynner for all my sweate and
    swyncke;

280 *be*: by   284 *This gere*: 'this kind of thing'   *the worst*: ? thy worst   286 *Now were he*: now
he would be   *cunnynge*: skill, knowledge   291 *swyncke*: labour, toil

Neyther butter, cheese, mylke, onyons, fleshe nor
  fyshe
Save thys poor pece of barly bread, 'tis a pleasant
  costly dishe.

DICCON: Haile, fellow Hodge, and well to fare with
  thy meat, if thou have any?
But by thy words as I them smelled, thy daintrels
  be not manye.

HODGE: Daintrels, Diccon? – Gog's soule man! –
Save this pece of dry horsbred,
Cha byt no byt this lyvelonge daie, no crome come
  in my hed;
My gutts they yawle crawle and all my belly
  rumbleth;
The puddynges cannot lye still, ech one over other
  tumbleth!
By Gog's harte cham so vexte, and in my belly
  pende,   *300*
Chould one peece were at the spittlehouse, another
  at the castel's ende!

DICCON: Why, Hodge, was there none at home thy
  dinner for to set?

HODGE: Godg's bread, Diccon, ich came to late, was
  nothing ther to get;
Gib (a fowle feind might on her light!) lickt the
  milkepan so clene;
See, Diccon, 'twas not so well washt this seven
  yere as ich wene!
A pestilence lyght on all ill lucke! Chad thought
  yet for all thys
Of a morsell of bacon behynde the dore at worst
  shuld not misse,
But when ich sought a slyp to cut, as ich was wont
  to do,

295 *daintrels*: delicacies to eat   298 *yawle*: scream out   299 *puddynges*: entrails, guts
300 *pende*: griped, pained   301 *spittlehouse*: hospital   303 *Godg's*: i.e. Gog's, God's
304 *feind*: fiend   307 *shuld not misse*: would not fail me   308 *slyp*: slice

Gog's soule, Diccon, Gyb our cat had eate the bacon to!
Which bacon Diccon stole, as is declared before.

DICCON: Ill luck, quod he; mary, swere it, Hodg, this
310   day the trueth to tel,
Thou rose not on thy right syde, or els blest thee
    not wel:
Thy mylk slopt up, thy bacon filtched, that was to
    bad luck, Hodg!

HODGE: Nay, nay, ther was a fowler fault, my
    Gammer ga me the dodge –
Seest not how cham rent and torn, my heels, my
    knees and my breech?
Chad thought as ich sat by the fire, help here and
    there a stitch,
But there ich was powpte indeede.

DICCON: Why, Hodge?

HODGE: Bootes not man to tell;
Cham so drest amonst a sorte of fooles, chad better
    be in hell;
My Gammer (cham ashamed to say) by God,
    served me not weele!

DICCON: How so, Hodge?

HODGE: Hase she not gone trowest
    now and lost her neele?

DICCON: Her eele, Hodge, who fysht of late? That
320   was a dainty dysh!

HODGE: Tush tush, her neele, her neele, her neele,
    man; 'tys neyther flesh nor fysh!
A lytle thing with an hole in the end, as bright as
    any syller,
Small, longe, sharpe at the poynt, and straight as
    any pyller.

DICCON: I know not what a devill thou meenst; thou
    bringst me more in doubt.

312 *to*: too 313 *ga me the dodge*: gave me the slip, let me down 316 *powpte*: deceived, cheated *Bootes not*: it doesn't pay, it's not worth it 317 *so drest*: so placed, set 322 *syller*: silver

HODGE: Knowest not with what Tom Tailer's man
    sits broching throughe a clout?
  A neele, neele, a neele, my Gammer's neele is gone!

DICCON: Her neele, Hodge, now I smel thee, that
    was a chaunce alone:
  By the Masse, thou hadst a shamefull losse, and it
    wer but for thy breches –

HODGE: Gog's soule, man, should give a crown chad
    it but three stitches!

DICCON: How sayest thou, Hodge, what shuld he
    have again thy neele got?   *330*

HODGE: Be'm vather's soule, and chad it, should give
    him a new grot!

DICCON: Canst thou keepe counsaile in this case?

HODGE: Els
  chwold my tonge were out.

DICCON: Do thou but then by my advise, and I will
    fetch it without doubt.

HODGE: Chyll runne, chyll ryde, chyll dygge, chyl
    delve, chill toyle, chill trudge, shalt see;
  Chill hold, chil drawe, chil pull, chill pynche, chill
    kneele on my bare knee;
  Chill scrape, chill scratche, chill syfte, chyll seeke,
    chill bowe, chill bende, chill sweate,
  Chil stoop, chil stur, chil cap, chil knele, chil crepe
    on hands and feete;
  Chil be thy bondman, Diccon, ich sweare by sunne
    and moone,
  And channot sumwhat to stop this gap, cham
    utterly undone!
    Pointing behind to his torne breeches.

DICCON: Why, is ther any special cause thou takest
    hereat such sorow?   *340*

HODGE: Kirstian Clack, Tom Simson's maid, bi the
    Masse, coms hether tomorow;

325 *broching*: piercing   *clout*: garment   327 *smel thee*: get your drift   331 *Be'm*: by my
grot: groat   337 *chil cap*: I will doff my cap

Chamnot able to say betweene us what may hap;
She smyled on me the last Sonday when ich put of
my cap.
DICCON: Well, Hodge, this is a matter of weight, and
must be kept close;
It might els turne to both our costes as the world
now gose.
Shalt sware to be no blab, Hodge.
HODGE: Chyll, Diccon.
DICCON: Then go to,
Lay thine hand here, say after me as thou shalt
here me do —
Haste no booke?
HODGE: Cha no booke, I.
DICCON: Then needes
must force us both,
Upon my breech to lay thine hand, and thereto
take thine othe.
350 HODGE [*after* DICCON]: I Hodge breechelesse,
                          Sweare to Diccon rechlesse,
                          By the crosse that I shall kysse,
                          To kepe his counsaile close
                          And alwayes me to dispose
                          To worke that his pleasure is.

    Here he kysseth Diccon's breeche.
DICCON: Now, Hodge, see thou take heede
        And do as I thee byd,
        For so I judge it meete,
        This nedle againe to win;
360   There is no shift therin
        But conjure up a spreete.
HODGE: What the great devil Diccon, I saye?
DICCON: Yea, in good faith, that is the waye,
    Fet with some pretty charme.
HODGE: Softe, Diccon, be not to hasty yet,

By the Masse, for ich begyn to sweat!
Cham afrayde of some harme.

DICCON: Come hether then and sturre the nat
One inche out of this cyrcle plat,
But stande as I thee teache.   *370*

HODGE: And shall ich be here safe from theyr clawes?

DICCON: The mayster devill with his longe pawes
Here to thee cannot reache:
Now will I settle me to this geare.

HODGE: I saye, Diccon, heare me, heare:
Go softely to thys matter.

DICCON: What devyll, man, art afraide of nought?

HODGE: Canst not tarrye a lytle thought
Tyll ich make a curtesie of water?

DICCON: Stand still to it; why shuldest thou feare hym?   *380*

HODGE: Gog's sydes, Diccon, methinke ich heare him —
And tarrye — chal mare all!

DICCON: The matter is no worse then I tolde it!

HODGE: By the Masse, cham able no longer to holde it;
To bad iche must beraye the hall!

DICCON: Stand to it, Hodge; sture not, you horson!
[HODGE *fouls his breeches.*]
What Devyll, be thine ars strynges brusten?
Thyselfe awhile but staye,
The devill — I smell hym — wyll be here anone!

HODGE: Hold him fast, Diccon; cham gone, cham gone,   *390*
Chyll not be at that fraye!
[*Exit* HODGE *into the house.*]

The ii. Acte.   The ii. Sceane

Diccon.   Chat.

DICCON [*calling after* HODGE]: Fy, shytten knave, and
out upon thee!

---

369 *plat*: plot, patch of ground   374 *geare*: business   379 *make a curtesie of water*: relieve
myself   382 *mare*: mar   383 *then*: than   385 *beraye*: foul (see note)   387 *brusten*: burst,
broken   391 *fraye* disturbance, turmoil

Above all other loutes fye on thee!
Is not here a clenly prancke?
But thy matter was no better
Nor thy presence here no sweter,
To flye I can the thanke:
Here is a matter worthy glosynge
Of Gammer Gurton's nedle losynge

400 And a foule peece of warke;
A man I thyncke myght make a playe
And nede no worde to this they saye
Being but halfe a clarke.
Softe, let me alone, I will take the charge
This matter further to enlarge
Within a tyme shorte;
If ye will marke my toyes, and note,
I will geve ye leave to cut my throte
If I make not good sporte.

410 Dame Chat, I say, where be ye? Within?
CHAT [*within*]: Who have we there maketh such a din?
DICCON: Here is a good fellow maketh no great
daunger!
[DAME CHAT *appears at the ale-house door.*]
CHAT: What, Diccon? Come nere, ye be no straunger;
We be fast set at Trumpe, man, hard by the fyre;
Thou shalt set on the king, if thou come a litle nyer.
DICCON: Nay, nay, there is no tarying; I must be
gone againe,
But first for you in councel I have a word or
twaine.
CHAT [*calling*]: Come hether, Dol!
[DOLL *appears at the door.*]
Dol, sit downe and play this game,
And as thou sawest me do, see thou do even the same:

---

394 *prancke*: dirty trick (see note)   398 *worthy glosynge*: worth a bit of 'smooth talk'
404 *take the charge*: take the responsibility   407 *marke my toyes*: note my tricks – or
speeches (cf. line 398)   412 *daunger*: mischief, damage   414 *Trumpe*: a card-game (see
note)   417 *in councel*: in confidence

There is five trumps beside the Queene, the
    hindmost thou shalt finde her;   *420*
Take hede of Sim Glover's wife, she hath an eie
    behind her!
    [DOLL *goes inside.*]
Now, Diccon, say your will.
DICCON: Nay, softe a little yet.
    I wold not tel it my sister, the matter is so great.
    There I wil have you sweare by our dere Lady of
        Bullaine,
    S[aint] Dunstone, and S[aint] Donnyke, with the
        three Kinges of Kullaine,
    That ye shal keepe it secret.
CHAT: Gog's bread, that will
    I doo,
As secret as mine owne thought, by God and the
    devil two!
DICCON: Here is Gammer Gurton your neighbour, a
        sad and hevy wight,
Her goodly faire red cock at home was stole this
    last night.
CHAT: Gog's soule, her cock with the yelow legs, that
    nightly crowed so just?   *430*
DICCON: That cocke is stollen.
CHAT: What, was he fet out of
    the hens' ruste?
DICCON: I cannot tel where the devil he was kept,
        under key or locke,
But Tib hath tykled in Gammer's eare, that you
    shoulde steale the cocke.
CHAT: Have I, stronge hoore? By bread and salte –
DICCON: What, softe I say, be styl!
    Say not one word for all this geare.

---

421 *an eie behind her*: eyes in the back of her head 424 *Bullaine*: Boulogne (see note)
425 *Dunstone*, etc.: see note 427 *two*: too 430 *just*: regularly 431 *fet*: carried *ruste*: roost
433 *tykled*: whispered, tattled 434 *stronge*: arrant, brazen 435 *geare*: to-do

CHAT: By the Masse,
 that I wyl!
 I wyl have the yong hore by the head, and the old
  trot by the throte!
DICCON: Not one word, Dame Chat, I say, not one
  word for my cote!
CHAT: Shall such a begar's brawle as that, thinkest
  thou, make me a theefe?
 The pocks light on her hore's sydes, a pestlence
  and a mischeefe!
 Come out, thou hungry nedy bytche; o that my
440 nails be short!
DICCON: Gog's bred, woman, hold your peace, this
  gere wil els passe sport!
 I wold not for an hundred pound this matter shuld
  be knowen,
 That I am auctour of this tale, or have abrode it
  blowen.
 Did ye not sweare ye wold be ruled, before the tale
  I tolde?
 I said ye must all secret keepe, and ye said sure ye
  wolde.
CHAT: Wolde you suffer yourselfe, Diccon, such a
  sort to revile you,
 With slaunderous words to blot your name, and so
  to defile you?
DICCON: No, Goodwife Chat, I wold be loth such
  drabs shulde blot my name,
 But yet ye must so order all that Diccon beare no
  blame.
CHAT: Go to then, what is your rede? Say on your
450 minde; ye shall mee rule herein.
DICCON: Godamercye to Dame Chat; in faith thou
  must the gere begin:

438 *brawle*: brat 441 *this gere*, etc.: this business will otherwise get beyond a joke
443 *auctour*: author, inventor *abrode*: generally, at large 448 *drabs*: sluts 450 *rede*:
advice 451 *gere*: business, affair

It is twenty pound to a goose turd, my Gammer
    will not tary
But hetherward she comes as fast as her legs can
    her cary,
To brawle with you about her cocke, for well I
    hard Tib say
The cocke was rosted in your house, to breafast
    yesterday,
And when ye had the carcas eaten, the fethers ye
    out flunge,
And Doll your maid the legs she hid a foote depe
    in the dunge.

CHAT: Oh gracyous God, my harte it burstes!

DICCON: Well,
    rule yourselfe a space;
And Gammer Gurton when she commeth anon
    into thys place,
Then to the queane let's see; tell her your mynd
    and spare not,   *460*
So shall Diccon blamelesse bee, and then go to, I
    care not!

CHAT: Then, hoore, beware her throte, I can abide
    no longer;
In faith, old witch, it shal be seene, which of us
    two be stronger,
And, Diccon, but at your request, I wold not stay
    one howre.

DICCON: Well, keepe it in till she be here, and then
    out let it powre;
In the meanewhile get you in, and make no wordes
    of this;
More of this matter within this howre to here you
    shall not misse,
Because I know you are my freind, hide it I cold
    not doubtles:

454 *hard*: heard   455 *breafast*: breakfast   460 *queane*: whore   467 *here*: hear
468 *freind*: friend

Ye know your harm, see ye be wise about your
  owne busines.
So fare ye well.

CHAT: Nay, soft, Diccon, and drynke;
470   what, Doll, I say!
Bringe here a cup of the best ale, let's see, come
  quicly awaye!
  [*Exit* DAME CHAT. DOLL *brings* DICCON *a cup of
  ale, and exits.*]

The ii. Actt.   The iii. Sceane.

Hodge.   Diccon.

DICCON [*to audience*]: Ye see, masters, the one end
  tapt of this my short devise;
Now must we broche thoter to before the smoke arise,
And by the time they have awhile run, I trust ye
  need not crave it,
But loke what lieth in both their harts ye ar like
  sure to have it.
  [*Re-enter* HODGE.]

HODGE: Yea, Gog's soule, art alive yet? What,
  Diccon, dare ich come?

DICCON: A man is well hied to trust to thee, I will
  say nothing but mum,
But and ye come any nearer I pray you see all be
  sweete.

HODGE: Tush, man, is Gammer's neele found, that
  choulde gladly weete?

DICCON: She may thanke thee it is not found, for if
480   thou had kept thy standing,
The devil he wold have fet it out, even Hodg at thy
  commaunding.

HODGE: Gog's hart, and cold he tel nothing wher the
  neele might be found?

---

473 *broche thoter to*: start off the other   477 *well hied*: does well   479 *weete*: know, learn
481 *fet*: fetched

DICCON: Ye folysh dolt, ye were to seek ear we had
    got our ground;
  Therfore his tale so doubtfull was, that I cold not
    perceive it.

HODGE: Then ich se wel somthing was said; chope
    one day yet to have it,
  But Diccon, Diccon, did not the devill cry 'Ho, ho,
    ho'?

DICCON: If thou hadst taryed where thou stoodst,
    thou woldest have said so.

HODGE: Durst swere of a boke; chard him rore,
    streight after ich was gon,
  But tel me, Diccon, what said the knave? Let me
    here it anon.

DICCON: The horson talked to mee: I know not well
    of what –   *490*
  One whyle his tonge it ran and paltered of a cat,
  Another whyle he stamered styll uppon a rat,
  Last of all there was nothing but every word Chat,
    Chat;
  But this I well perceyved before I wolde him rid,
  Betweene Chat and the rat, and the cat, the nedle
    is hyd.
  Now wether Gyb our cat have eate it in her mawe,
  Or Doctor Rat our curat have found it in the straw,
  Or this Dame Chat your neighbour have stollen it,
    God hee knoweth,
  But by the morow at this time, we shal learn how
    the matter goeth.

HODGE: Canst not learn tonight, man, seest not what
    is here?   *500*
   Pointyng behind to his torne breeches.

DICCON: 'Tys not possyble to make it sooner appere.

---

483 *ye were to seek*: you had to be searched for *ear*: ere, before 484 *doubtfull*: ambiguous
490 *horson*: whoreson; term of abuse 491 *paltered*: mumbled, babbled 496 *mawe*:
stomach, gullet

HODGE: Alas, Diccon, then chave no shyft, but least
 ich tary to longe,
Hye me to Sym Glover's shop, theare to seeke for a
 thonge,
Therwith this breech to tatche and tye as ich may.
DICCON: Tomorow, Hodg, if we chaunce to meete,
 shalt see what I will say.
  [*Exit* HODGE.]

   The ii. Acte. The iiii. Sceane.

    Diccon. Gammer.
 [*Enter* GAMMER GURTON *from her house.*]
DICCON: Now this gere must forward goe, for here
 my Gammer commeth;
 [*To audience*] Be still awhile and say nothing, make
 here a litle romth.
GAMMER: Good lord, shall never be my lucke my
 neele agayne to spye?
Alas the whyle! 'tys past my helpe; where 'tis still
 it must lye.
DICCON: Now Jesus, Gammer Gurton, what driveth
510 you to this sadnes?
I feare me, by my conscience, you will sure fall to
 madnes.
GAMMER: Who is that? What, Diccon? Cham lost,
 man; fye, fye!
DICCON: Mary, fy on them that be worthy! But what
 shuld be your troble?
GAMMER: Alas, the more ich thinke on it, my sorow it
 waxeth doble:
My goodly tossing sporyar's neele, chave lost ich
 wot not where.
DICCON: Your neele? Whan?

---

502 *least*: lest 504 *tatche*: fasten 507 *romth*: room 515 *tossing*: 'dancing' *sporyar's*:
spur-maker's (see note)

GAMMER: My neele (alas) ich
     myght full ill it spare,
  As God himselfe he knoweth, nere one besyde
     chave.
DICCON: If this be all, good Gammer, I warrant you
     all is save.
GAMMER: Why, know you any tydings which way my
     neele is gone?
DICCON: Yea, that I do doubtlesse, as ye shall here
     anone: *520*
  A' see a thing this matter toucheth within these
     twenty howres,
  Even at this gate, before my face, by a neyghbour
     of yours;
  She stooped me downe, and up she toke a nedle or
     a pyn;
  I durst be sworne it was even yours, by all my
     mother's kyn.
GAMMER: It was my neele, Diccon, ich wot, for here
     even by this poste
  Ich sat, what time as ich up starte, and so my
     neele it loste:
  Who was it, leive son? Speke, ich pray the, and
     quickly tell me that!
DICCON: A suttle queane as any in thys towne, your
     neyghboure here, Dame Chat!
GAMMER: Dame Chat! Diccon, let me be gone; chil
     thyther in post haste!
DICCON: Take my councell yet or ye go, for feare ye
     walke in wast: *530*
  It is a murrion crafty drab, and froward to be pleased,
  And ye take not the better way, [your] nedle yet ye
     lose it:
  For when she tooke it up, even here before your
     doores,

---

520 *doubtlesse*: without doubt   521 *A' see*: I saw   527 *leive*: dear   531 *murrion*: plaguey,
infected

'What, soft, Dame Chat' (quoth I) 'that same is
    none of yours.'
'Avant!' (quoth she). 'Syr knave, what pratest
    thou of that I fynd?
I wold thou hadst kist me I wot whear'; (she ment,
    I know behind!)
And home she went as brag as it had ben a
    bodelouce,
And I after as bold as it had ben the goodman of
    the house.
But there an ye had hard her, how she began to
    scolde!
540   The tonge it went on patins, by hym that Judas solde!
Ech other worde I was a knave, and you a hore of
    hores,
Because I spake in your behalfe, and sayde the
    neele was yours.
GAMMER: Gog's bread, and thinks the callet thus to
    kepe my neele me fro?
DICCON: Let her alone, and she minds non other but
    even to dresse you so.
GAMMER: By the Masse, chil rather spend the cote
    that is on my backe!
Thinks the false quean by such a slyght that chill
    my neele lacke?
DICCON: Slepe not your gere I counsell you, but of
    this take good hede;
Let not be knowen I told you of it, how well soever
    ye spede.
GAMMER: Chil in, Diccon, a cleene aperne to take
    and set before me,
And ich may my neele once see, chil sure
550   remember the.

    [*Exit* GAMMER GURTON *into the house.*]

---

537 *brag*: lively, pleased with herself *bodelouce*: a louse on the body 539 *an*: if
540 *patins*: pattens, clogs (that clatter) 543 *callet*: whore 547 *Slepe not*: do not neglect
549 *aperne*: apron

The ii. Acte.   The v. Sceane.

Diccon.

DICCON [*to the audience*]: Here will the sporte begin, if
    these two once may meete;

Their chere (durst lay money) will prove scarsly
    sweete:

My Gammer sure entends to be uppon her bones,

With staves, or with clubs, or els with coble stones!

Dame Chat, on the other syde, if she be far behynde

I am right far deceived; she is geven to it of kynde.

He that may tarry by it a whyle, and that but shorte,

I warrant hym trust to it, he shall see all the sporte.

Into the towne will I, my frendes to vysit there,

And hether straight againe, to see thend of this gere.   *560*

[*To* MUSICIANS] In the meanetime, felowes, pype
    upp; your fiddles, I saie, take them,

And let your freyndes here such mirth as ye can
    make them.

[*Exit* DICCON. *The* MUSICIANS *play*.]

The iii. Acte   The i. Sceane.

Hodge.

[*Enter* HODGE *with a thong and an awl.*]

HODGE: Sym Glover, yet gramercy; cham meetlye
    well sped now,

Thart even as good a felow as ever kyste a cowe!

Here is a [thonge] indede, by the Masse, though
    ich speake it;

Tom Tankard's great bald curtal I thinke could
    not breake it,

And when he spyed my neede to be so straight and
    hard,

556 *of kynde*: 'it's in her nature'   560 *gere*: affair   562 *here*: hear   566 *bald curtal*: a horse
(see note)   567 *straight*: urgent   *hard*: essential

247

Hays lent me here his naull, to set the gyb
    forward.

As for my Gammer's neele, the flyenge feynd go
    weete,

Chill not now go to the doore againe with it to
570   meete!

Chould make shyfte good inough and chad a
    candel's ende;

The cheefe hole in my breeche with these two chil
    amende.

The iii. Acte.   *The ii. Sceane.*

Gammer.   *Hodge.*

[*Enter* GAMMER GURTON.]

GAMMER: How, Hodge mayst nowe be glade, cha
    newes to tell thee –

Ich knowe who hais my neele, ich trust soone shalt
    it see.

HODGE: The devyll thou does! Hast hard, Gammer,
    indeede, or doest but jest?

GAMMER: 'Tys as true as steele, Hodge.

HODGE: Why,
    knowest well where dydst leese it?

GAMMER: Ich know who found it, and tooke it up;
    shalt see or it be longe.

HODGE: God's mother dere, if that be true, farwel
    both naule an[d] thong!

But who hais it, Gammer, say on? Chould faine
    here it disclosed.

GAMMER: That false fixen, that same Dame Chat,
580   that counts herselfe so honest.

HODGE: Who tolde you so?

GAMMER: That same did Diccon the
    Bedlam, which saw it done.

568 *Hays*: he has *naull*: awl *gyb*: ? job (see note) 569 *weete*: know 576 *leese*: lose
577 *or*: ere 580 *fixen*: vixen

HODGE: Diccon? It is a vengeable knave, Gammer,
   'tis a bonable horson;
  Can do mo things then that, els cham deceyved evill;
  By the Masse, ich saw him of late cal up a great
   blacke devill;
  O, the knave cryed 'Ho, ho!' he roared and he
   thundred,
  And yead bene here, cham sure yould murrenly ha
   wondred.

GAMMER: Was not thou afraide, Hodge, to see him in
   this place?

HODGE: No, and chad come to me, chould have laid
   him on the face,
  Chould have promised him!

GAMMER: But, Hodge, had he no
   hornes to pushe?

HODGE: As long as your two armes – Saw ye never
   Fryer Rushe   *590*
  Painted on a cloth, with a sidelong cowe's tayle,
  And crooked cloven feete, and many a hoked nayle?
  For all the world (if I shuld judg) chould recken
   him his brother;
  Loke even what face Frier Rush had, the devil had
   such another.

GAMMER: Now, Jesus mercy, Hodg! Did Diccon in
   him bring?

HODGE: Nay, Gammer (heare me speke), chil tel you
   a greater thing:
  The devil (when Diccon had him, ich hard him
   wondrous weel)
  Sayd plainly (here before us), that Dame Chat had
   your neele!
  [DAME CHAT *appears at the door of the ale-house*.]

GAMMER: Then let us go, and aske her wherfore she
   minds to kepe it,

582 *vengeable*: revengeful *bonable*: abominable 583 *mo*: more 586 *yead...yould*: ye
had...you would *murrenly*: like the plague

Seing we know so much, 'tware a madnes now to
600   slepe it.

HODGE: Go to her, Gammer, see ye not where she
stands in her doores?

Byd her geve you the neele, 'tys none of hers but
yours!

The iii. Acte.   The iii. Sceane.

Gammer.   Chat.   Hodge.

GAMMER: Dame Chat, cholde praye the fair; let me
have that is mine:

Chil not this twenty yeres take one fart that is thyne;

Therfore give me mine owne and let me live
besyde the.

CHAT: Why, art thou crept from home hether to mine
own doores to chide me?

Hence, doting drab, avaunt, or I shall set the further!

Intends thou and that knave mee in my house to
murther?

GAMMER: Tush, gape not so on me, woman, shalt not
yet eate mee,

Nor all the frends thou hast in this shall not
610   intreate mee:

Mine owne goods I will have, and aske the no beleve;

What, woman? Pore folks must have right, though
the thing you agreve.

CHAT: Give thee thy right, and hang thee up, with al
thy bagger's broode!

What, wilt thou make me a theefe and say I stole
thy good?

GAMMER: Chil say nothing (ich warrant thee), but
that ich can prove it well;

Thou fet my good, even from my doore, cham able
this to tel!

600 *slepe it*: neglect it, let it slip   608 *murther*: murder   611 *beleve*: by-leave, permission
613 *bagger's*: beggar's   614 *good*: goods   616 *fet*: away

CHAT: Dyd I (olde witche) steale oft was thine? How
    should that thing be knowen?

GAMMER: Ich cannot tel, but up thou tokest it as
    though it had ben thine owne.

CHAT: Mary, fy on thee, thou old gyb, with al my
    very hart!

GAMMER: Nay, fy on thee, thou rampe, thou ryg,
    with al that take thy parte!   *620*

CHAT: A vengeaunce on those lips that laieth such
    things to my charge!

GAMMER: A vengeance on those callat's hips, whose
    conscience is so large!

CHAT: Come out, hogge!

GAMMER: Come out, hogge, and let me have right!

CHAT: Thou arrant witche!

GAMMER: Thou bawdie bitche, chil
    make thee cursse this night!

CHAT: A bag and a wallet!

GAMMER: A carte for a callet!

CHAT: Why,
    wenest thou thus to prevaile?
 I hold thee a grote, I shall patche thy coate –

GAMMER: Thou
    warte as good kysse my tayle!
 Thou slut, thou kut, thou rakes, thou jakes! Will
    not shame make thee hide the?

CHAT: Thou skald, thou bald, thou rotten, thou
    glotton! I will no longer chyd the.
 But I will teache the to kepe home –

GAMMER: Wylt thou,
    drunken beaste?

    [GAMMER GURTON *and* DAME CHAT *begin to fight.*]

---

617 *oft*: aught, anything 619 *gyb*: cat 620 *rampe*: fish-wife *ryg*: harlot 622 *callat's*:
whore's 625 *A bag and a wallet*: see note; *A carte*: see note 627 *kut*: bitch *rakes*: ?
dissipated women *jakes*: privy, or possibly excrement 628 *skald*: scurvy character
bald: hairless one

HODGE: Sticke to her, Gammer! Take her by the
630   head! Chil warrant you thys feast!

Smyte, I saye, Gammer! Byte, I say, Gammer! I
    trow ye wyll be keene;

Where be your nayls? Claw her by the jawes! Pull
    me out bothe her eyen!

Gog's bones, Gammer, holde up your head!

CHAT: I trow,
    drab, I shall dresse thee!

[GAMMER GURTON *falls*. HODGE *starts to retreat*.]

Tary, thou knave, I hold the a grote I shall make
    these hands blesse thee;

Take thou this old hore for amends, and lerne thy
    tonge well to tame,

And say thou met at this bickering, not thy fellow
    but thy dame!

HODGE: Where is the strong stued hore? Chill ge'are
    a hore's marke;

Stand out ones way, that ich kyll none in the darke!

Up, Gammer, and ye be alyve; chil feyght now for
    us bothe;

[*To* DAME CHAT] Come no nere me, thou scalde
640   callet; to kyll the ich wer loth!

CHAT: Art here agayne, thou hoddaypeke? [*Calling*]
    What, Doll? Bryng me out my spitte!

HODGE [*brandishing the awl*]: Chill broche thee wyth
    this; bi'm father soule, chyll conjure that foule sprete!

[DAME CHAT *advances on* HODGE; *he retreats to the
    house, and calls to* COCKE.]

Let dore stand, Cock! Why, coms indeede? Kepe
    dore, thou horson boy!

CHAT: Stand to it, thou dastard, for thine eares; ise
    teche thee a sluttish toye!

HODGE: Gog's woundes, hore, chil make the avaunte!

---

630 *Chil warrant*, etc.: 'I fancy your chances' 632 *eyen*: eyes 633 *dresse thee*: 'do you over'
634 *hold the*: bet you *blesse*: beat (ironic) 637 *strong stued*: brazenly unchaste (see note)
ge'are: give her 640 *scalde*: scabby 641 *hoddypeke*: blockhead 644 *dastard*: coward

Take heed! Cocke, pull in the latche!

[HODGE *dodges into the house.*]

CHAT: I' faith, Sir Loosebreche, had ye taried, ye
shold have found your match!

GAMMER [*rising*]: Now ware thy throte, losell, thouse
pay for al!

[*Attacks* CHAT *from behind.*]

HODGE [*reappearing with a stick*]: Well said, Gammer,
by my soule!

Hoyse her, souse her, bounce her, trounce her, pull
out her throte boule!

[DAME CHAT *falls.*]

CHAT: Comst behynd me, thou withered witch?
And I get once on foote,

Thouse pay for all, thou old tarlether, i'le teach the
what longs to it!   *650*

[*Rising*] Take thee this to make up thy mouth, til
time thou come by more!

[*Knocks* GAMMER GURTON *down, and exits.*]

HODGE [*emerging from the house*]: Up, Gammer, stand
on your feete; where is the olde hore?

Faith, woulde chad her by the face; choulde cracke
her callet crowne!

GAMMER [*rising*]: A, Hodg, Hodg, where was thy
help, when fixen had me downe?

HODGE: By the Masse, Gammer, but for my staffe
Chat had gone nye to spyl you!

Ich think the harlot had not cared, and chad not
com, to kill you!

But shall we loose our neele thus?

GAMMER: No, Hodge,
chwarde lothe doo soo;

Thinkest thou chill take that at her hand? No,
Hodg; ich tell the, no!

647 *ware*: beware *losell*: wretch 648 *Hoyse*: hoist *throte boule*: Adam's apple 650 *Thouse*:
thou shalt *tarlether*: 'skinny old bag' (see note) 655 *spyl*: destroy

253

HODGE: Chold yet this fray wer wel take up, and our
own neele at home;

'Twill be my chaunce els some to kil, wherever it
660 be or whome.

GAMMER: We have a parson – Hodge, thou knoes –
a man estemed wise;

Mast Doctor Rat, chil for hym send, and let me
here his advise;

He will her shrive for all this gere, and geve her
penaunce strait:

Wese have our neele, els Dame Chat comes nere
within heaven gate!

HODGE: Ye, mary, Gammer, that ich think best; wyll
you now for him send?

The sooner Doctor Rat be here, the soner wese ha
an ende.

And here, Gammer, Dyccon's devill (as iche
remember well)

Of cat, and Chat, and Doctor Rat a felloneus tale
dyd tell.

Chold you forty pound, that is the way your neele
to get againe.

GAMMER: Chil ha him strait; call out the boy, wese
670 make him take the payn.

HODGE: What, Coke, I saye! Come out! What devill,
canst not here?

COCKE [*entering*]: How now, Hodg? How does,
Gammer? Is yet the wether cleare?

What wold chave me to doo?

GAMMER: Come hether, Cocke, anon.

Hence swythe to Doctor Rat; hye the that thou
were gone!

And pray hym come speke with me; cham not well
at ease;

Shalt have him at his chamber, or els at Mother Bee's;

---

659 *Chold*: I would *wel take up*: made up, settled 662 *Mast*: Master 663 *shrive*: hear her
confession 664 *nere*: never 666 *Wese*: we shall 668 *felloneus*: atrocious 669 *Chold*: I
wager 674 *swythe*: swiftly

Els seeke him at Hob Fylcher's shop, for as charde
    it reported,
There is the best ale in al the towne, and now is
    most resorted.

COCKE: And shal ich brynge hym with me, Gammer?

GAMMER: Yea, by and by, good Cocke.

COCKE: Shalt see that shal be here anone, els let me
    have one the docke!   680
    [*Exit* COCKE.]

HODGE: Now, Gammer, shal we two go in, and tary
    for hys commynge.
What devill, woman, plucke up your hart, and leve
    of al this glomming!
Though she were stronger at the first, as ich thinke
    ye did find her,
Yet there ye drest the dronken sow, what time ye
    cam behind her!

GAMMER: Nay, nay, cham sure she lost not all, for set
    thend to the beginning,
And ich doubt not but she will make small bost of
    her winning.

The iii. Acte.   *The iiii. Sceane.*

Tyb.   *Hodge.*   *Gammer.*   *Cocke.*
[TYB *comes out of the house, carrying the cat.*]

TYB: Se, Gammer, Gammer, Gib our cat, cham
    afraid what she ayleth:
She standes me gasping behind the doore, as
    though her winde her faileth;
Now let ich doubt what Gib shuld mean that now
    she doth so dote.

HODGE: Hold hether; ichould twenty pound your
    neele is in her throte!   690

679 *by and by*: straightaway   680 *one*: on   *docke*: backside   682 *glomming*: frowning
689 *dote*: act-strangely

Grope her, ich say; methinkes ich feele it; does not
    pricke your hand?

GAMMER: Ich can feele nothing.

HODGE: No, ich know thar's
    not within this land

A muryner cat then Gyb is, betwixt the Tems and
    Tyne;

Shase as much wyt in her head almost as chave in
    mine.

TYB: Faith, shase eaten something that wil not
    easely downe;

Whether she gat it at home or abrode in the towne
Iche cannot tell.

GAMMER: Alas, ich feare it be some croked
    pyn!

And then farewell, Gyb, she is undone, and lost al
    save the skyn!

HODGE: 'Tys your neele, woman, I say! Gog's soule,
    geve me a knyfe,

And chil have it out of her mawe, or els chal lose
700   my lyfe!

GAMMER: What? Nay, Hodg, fy! Kil not our cat – 'tis
    al the cats we ha now!

HODGE: By the Masse, Dame Chat hase me so
    moved, iche care not what I kyll, ma God a
    vowe!

Go to, then, Tyb, to this geare; holde up her tayle
    and take her;

Chil see what devil is in her guts, chil take the
    paines to rake her!

GAMMER: Rake a cat, Hodge! What woldst thou do?

HODGE: What, thinckst that cham not able?

Did not Tom Tankard rake his curtal toore day,
    standing in the stable?

    [*Enter* COCKE.]

---

692 *thar's*: there's 693 *a muryner*: a plaguier 696 *abrode*: outside *towne*: yard 700 *mawe*:
gullet 702 *ma*: I make 704 *rake her*: scrape out her rear-end 706 *curtal*: horse with a
docked tail *toore*: the other

GAMMER: Soft, be content; let's here what newes
    Cocke bringeth from Maist Rat.
COCKE: Gammer, chave ben ther as you bad, you
    wot wel about what;
    'Twill not be long before he come, ich durst sweare
    of a booke;
    He byds you see ye be at home, and there for him
    to looke.   *710*
GAMMER: Where didst thou find him, boy? Was he
    not wher I told thee?
COCKE: Yes, yes, even at Hob Filcher's house, by
    him that bought and solde me!
    A cup of ale had in his hand, and a crab lay in the
    fyer;
    Chad much ado to go and come, al was so ful of myer.
    And, Gammer, one thing I can tel: Hob Filcher's
    naule was loste,
    And Doctor Rat found it againe, hard beside the
    dooreposte!
    I chould a penny can say something, your neele
    againe to fet.
GAMMER: Cham glad to heare so much, Cocke, then
    trust he wil not let
    To helpe us herein best he can; therfore tyl time he
    come,
    Let us go in; if there be ought to get, thou shalt
    have some.   *720*
    [*They all go into* GAMMER GURTON'S *house.*]

            The iiii. Acte.   The i. Sceane.

            Doctor Rat.   Gammer Gurton.
    [*Enter* DR RAT.]
D. RAT: A man were better twenty times be a bandog
    and barke,

---

713 *crab*: crab-apple   715 *naule*: awl   717 *chould*: wager   *fet*: bring back   718 *let*: hold
back, fail   720 *get*: be had   721 *bandog*: chained-up dog

Then here among such a sort be parish priest or
    clarke,
Where he shal never be at rest one pissing while a
    day,
But he must trudge about the towne, this way and
    that way;
Here to a drab, there to a theefe, his shoes to teare
    and rent,
And that which is worst of al, at every knave's
    commaundement!
I had not sit the space to drinke two pots of ale,
But Gammer Gurton's sory boy was straiteway at
    my taile:
And she was sicke, and I must come, to do I wot
    not what –
If once her finger's end but ake, trudge, call for
730   Doctor Rat!
And when I come not at their call, I only therby
    loose,
For I am sure to lacke therfore a tythe pyg or a
    goose.
I warrant you, when truth is knowen, and told
    they have their tale,
The matter whereabout I come is not worth a
    halfpenyworth of ale!
Yet must I talke so sage and smothe, as though I
    were a glosier,
Els or the yere come at an end, I shal be sure the
    loser.
    [*Enter* GAMMER GURTON.]
What worke ye, Gammer Gurton? Hoow? Here is
    your frend, M[aster] Rat.
GAMMER: A, good M[aster] Doctor, cha trobled, cha
    trobled you, chwot wel that.

722 *sort*: crowd, 'shower' 723 *pissing while*: short interval 728 *sory*: wretched
735 *glosier*: flatterer, sycophant

D. RAT: How do ye, woman? Be ye lustie, or be ye
    not wel at ease?

GAMMER: By Gys, master, cham not sick, but yet
    chave a disease!   *740*

  Chad a foule turne now of late; chill tell it you, by
    Gigs!

D. RAT: Hath your browne cow cast hir calfe, or your
    sandy sowe her pigs?

GAMMER: No, but chad ben as good they had, as this
    ich wot weel.

D. RAT: What is the matter?

GAMMER: Alas, alas, cha lost my
    good neele!

  My neele, I say, and wot ye what? A drab came by
    and spied it,

  And when I asked hir for the same, the filth flatly
    denied it!

D. RAT: What was she, that?

GAMMER: A dame, ich warrant
    you; she began to scold and brawle –
    [*Enter* HODGE.]

  Alas, alas, come hether, Hodge; this wretche can
    tell you all.

The iiii. Acte.   *The ii. Sceane.*

Hodge.   *Doctor Rat.*   *Gammer.*
Diccon.   *Chat.*

HODGE: God morow, gaffer Vicar.

D. RAT: Come on, fellow,
    let us heare.

  Thy dame hath sayd to me thou knowest of all this
    geare;   *750*

  Let's see what thou canst saie.

---

739 *lustie*: robust, vigorous   740 *Gys*: Jesus (cf. 'Gigs' in line 741)   742 *cast*: given birth
prematurely

HODGE: By'm fay, sir, that
    ye shall:
    What matter soever here was done, ich can tell
      your maship all.
    My Gammer Gurton heare, see now,
    Sat her downe at this doore, see now:
    And as she began to stirre her, see now,
    Her neele fell in the floore, see now,
    And while her staffe she tooke, see now,
    At Gyb her cat to flynge, see now,
    Her neele was lost in the floore, see now;
760   Is not this a wondrous thing, see now?
    Then came the queane Dame Chat, see now,
    To aske for hir blacke cup, see now:
    And even here at this gate, see now:
    She tooke that neele up, see now.
    My Gammer then she yeede, see now,
    Hir neele againe to bring, see now,
    And was caught by the head, see now;
    Is not this a wondrous thing, see now?
    She tare my Gammer's cote, see now,
770   And scratched hir by the face, see now,
    Chad thought shad stopt hir throte, see now;
    Is not this a wondrous case, see now?
    When ich saw this, ich was wrothe, see now,
    And start betwene them twaine, see now,
    Els ich durst take a booke othe, see now,
    My Gammer had bene slaine, see now.
GAMMER: This is even the whole matter, as Hodge
    has plainly tolde,
    And chould faine be quiet for my part, that chould!
    But helpe us, good master, beseech ye that ye doo!
780   Els shal we both be beaten and lose our neele too.
D. RAT: What wold ye have me to doo? Tel me that I
    were gone;

751 *By'm fay*: by my faith 752 *maship*: mastership 765 *yeede*: went 771 *stopt hir throte*: strangled her 775 *durst*: dare

I will do the best that I can, to set you both at one.
But be ye sure Dame Chat hath this your neele
    founde?
    [*Enter* DICCON.]

GAMMER: Here comes the man that see hir take it up
    of the ground;
Aske him yourselfe, Master Rat, if ye beleve not me,
And helpe me to my neele, for God's sake and
    Saint Charitie.

D. RAT: Come nere, Diccon, and let us heare what
    thou can expresse.
Wilt thou be sworne thou seest Dame Chat this
    woman's neele have?

DICCON: Nay, by S[aint] Benit wil I not, then might
    ye thinke me rave!

GAMMER: Why didst not thou tel me so even here?
    Canst thou for shame deny it?   *790*

DICCON: I, mary Gammer! But I said I wold not
    abide by it!

D. RAT: Will you say a thing, and not sticke to it to
    trie it?

DICCON: 'Stick to it' quoth you, Master Rat? Mary,
    sir, I defy it!
Nay, there is many an honest man, when he suche
    blastes hath blowne
In his freindes' eares, he woulde be loth the same
    by him were knowne:
If such a toy be used oft among the honestie,
It may beseme a simple man of your and my
    degree.

D. RAT: Then we be never the nearer, for all that you
    can tell!

DICCON: Yes, mary, sir, if ye will do by mine advise
    and counsaile.

---

789 *Saint Benit*: St Benedict   792 *trie*: test its veracity   796 *toy*: trick, device   *the honestie*:
honourable folk   797 *beseme*: become, suit

If Mother Chat se al us here, she knoweth how the
800   matter goes:

Therefore I red you three go hence, and within
keepe close,

And I will into Dame Chat's house, and so the
matter use,

That or you cold go twise to church, I warant you
here news.

She shal looke wel about hir, but I durst lay a
pledge,

Ye shal of Gammer's neele have shortly better
knowledge.

GAMMER: Now, gentle Diccon, do so, and good sir,
let us trudge.

D. RAT: By the Masse, I may not tarry so long to be
your judge.

DICCON: 'Tys but a litle while, man; what? take so
much paine;

If I here no newes of it, I will come sooner againe.

HODGE: Tary so much, good Master Doctor, of your
810   gentlenes.

D. RAT: Then let us hie us inward, and Diccon,
speede thy busines.

[*Exit all but* DICCON.]

DICCON [*to audience*]: Now, sirs, do you no more, but
kepe my counsaile juste,

And Doctor Rat shall thus catch some good, I
trust;

But Mother Chat, my gossop, talke first withall I
must:

[*He knocks at* DAME CHAT's *door.*]

For she must be chiefe captaine to lay the rat in
the dust.

[*Enter* DAME CHAT.]

---

801 *red*: advise   803 *or*: ere   804 *looke wel about hir*: be on her guard   811 *inward*: indoors
814 *gossop*: gossip, friend   815 *chiefe captaine*: leading figure

God deven, Dame Chat, in faith, and wel met in
  this place!
CHAT: God deven, my friend Diccon; whether walke
  ye this pace?
DICCON: By my truth, even to you, to learne how the
  world goeth!
Hard ye no more of the other matter? Say me now
  by your troth.
CHAT: O yes, Diccon, here the old hoore, and Hodge,
  that great knave –   *820*
But in faith, I would thou hadst sene – o Lord, I
  drest them brave!
She bare me two or three souses behind in the
  nape of the necke
Till I made hir olde wesen to answere againe
  'Kecke!'
And Hodge, that dirty dastard, that at hir elbow
  standes,
If one paire of legs had not bene worth two paire of
  hands,
He had had his bearde shaven, if my nayles wold
  have served,
And not without a cause, for the knave it well
  deserved!
DICCON: By the Masse, I can the thank, wench, thou
  didst so wel acquite the!
CHAT: And thadst seene him, Diccon, it wold have
  made thee beshite the
For laughter! The horsen dolt at last caught up a
  club,   *830*
As though he would have slaine the master devil
  Belsabub,
But I set him soone inwarde.
DICCON: O Lorde, there is the
  thing

817 *whether*: whither 822 *souses*: thumps 823 *wesen*: windpipe 824 *dastard*: coward

> That Hodge is so offended, that makes him starte
> and flyng!

CHAT: Why? Makes the knave any moyling, as ye
have sene or hard?

DICCON: Even now I sawe him last, like a madman
he farde,

And sware by heaven and hell, he would awreake
his sorowe,

And leve you never a hen on live, by eight of the
clock tomorow!

Therfore marke what I say, and my wordes see
that ye trust:

Your hens be as good as dead, if ye leave them on
the ruste!

CHAT: The knave dare as wel go hang himself, as go
840 upon my ground!

DICCON: Wel, yet take hede, I say; I must tel you my
tale round.

Have you not about your house, behind your
furnace or leade,

A hole where a crafty knave may crepe in for
neade?

CHAT: Yes, by the Masse, a hole broke down, even
within these two dayes.

DICCON: Hodge he intendes this same night to slip in
thereawayes.

CHAT: O Christ, that I were sure of it! In faith, he
shuld have his mede.

DICCON: Watch wel, for the knave wil be there as
sure as is your crede!

I wold spend myselfe a shilling to have him
swinged well.

CHAT: I am as glad as a woman can be, of this thing
to here tell:

833 *flyng*: dash about   834 *moyling*: agitation, fuss   835 *farde*: fared   836 *awreake*: avenge
837 *on live*: alive   839 *ruste*: roost   842 *leade*: cauldron   846 *mede*: reward   848 *swinged*:
thrashed

By Gog's bones, when he commeth, now that I
   know the matter,   *850*
He shal sure at the first skip to leape in scalding
   water,
With a worse turne besides! When he will, let him
   come!
DICCON: I tell you as my sister, you know what
   meaneth 'Mum'!
     [*Exit* DAME CHAT *into the ale-house.*]
Now lacke I but my doctor to play his part againe.
     [*Enter* DR RAT *from* GAMMER GURTON'*s house.*]
And lo, where he commeth towards, peradventure
   to his paine!
D. RAT: What, good newes, Diccon? Fellow, is
   Mother Chat at home?
DICCON: She is, syr, and she is not, but it please her
   to whome;
Yet did I take her tardy, as subtle as she was.
D. RAT: The thing that thou wentst for, hast thou
   brought it to passe?
DICCON: I have done that I have done, be it worse,
   be it better,   *860*
And Dame Chat at her wyt's ende I have almost
   set her.
D. RAT: Why, hast thou spied the neele? Quickly, I
   pray thee tell!
DICCON: I have spyed it, in faith, sir, I handled
   myselfe so well;
And yet the crafty queane had almost take my trumpe:
But or all came to an ende, I set her in a dumpe.
D. RAT: How so, I pray thee, Diccon?
DICCON: Mary, syr, will
   ye heare?
She was clapt downe on the backside, by Cock's
   mother dere,

855 *peradventure*: perhaps   865 *dumpe*: perplexity   867 *backside*: back of the house
Cock's: God's

And there she sat sewing a halter or a bande,
With no other thing save Gammer's nedle in her
    hande!
870   As soone as any knocke, if the filth be in doubte,
She needes but once puffe, and her candle is out:
Now I, sir, knowing of every doore the pin,
Came nycely, and said no worde, till time I was
    within,
And there I sawe the neele, even with these two
    eyes;
Whoever say the contrary, I will sweare he lyes!
D. RAT: O, Diccon, that I was not there then in thy
    steade!
DICCON: Well, if ye will be ordred, and do by my
    reade,
I will bring you to a place, as the house standes,
Where ye shall take the drab with the neele in her
    handes.
D. RAT: For God's sake, do so, Diccon, and I will
880   gage my gowne
To geve thee a full pot of the best ale in the towne.
DICCON: Follow me but a litle, and marke what I will
    say:
Lay downe your gown beside you; go to; come on
    your way:
Se ye not what is here? A hole wherin ye may creepe
Into the house, and sodenly unwares among them
    leape!
There shal ye finde the bitchfox and the neele
    together:
Do as I bid you, man! Come on your wayes hether.
D. RAT: Art thou sure, Diccon, the swil tub standes
    not here aboute?
DICCON: I was within myselfe, man, even now; ther
    is no doubt.

873 *nycely*: cautiously or pleasantly   877 *reade*: advice   886 *bitchfox*: vixen   888 *swil tub*: wash-tub, or tub of pig-swill

Go softly, make no noyse; give me your foote, Sir   *890*
     John;
Here will I waite upon you tyl you come out
     anone.
     [DR RAT *disappears into the ale-house; a splash,*
     blows, and cries are heard within.]
D. RAT [*within*]: Helpe, Diccon! Out alas! I shal be
     slaine among them!
DICCON: If they give you not the nedle, tel them that
     ye will hang them!
     [*More noise is heard.*]
Ware that! Hoow, my wenches? Have ye caught
     the foxe
That used to make revel among your hennes and
     cocks?
Save his life yet for his order, though he susteine
     some paine –
Gog's bread, I am afraide they wil beate out his
     braine!
     [*Exit* DICCON. *Re-enter* DR RAT *from the ale-house,*
     wet and limping.]
D. RAT: Wo worth the houre that I came heare!
And wo worth him that wrought this geare!
A sort of drabs and queanes have me blest;   *900*
Was ever creature halfe so evill drest?
Whoever it wrought, and first did invent it,
He shall, I warrant him, erre long repent it!
I will spend all I have without my skinne
But he shall be brought to the plight I am in!
Master Bayly, I trow, and he be worth his eares,
Will snaffle these murderers and all that them beares:
I will surely neither byte nor suppe,
Till I fetch him hether, this matter to take up.
                                        [*Exit.*]

890 *Sir John*: common name for a cleric (see note)   898 *Wo worth*: cursed be   900 *drabs*
and queanes: sluts and tarts   901 *drest*: treated   903 *erre*: ere   904 *without my skinne*: from
my skin outwards   907 *all that them beares*: those supporting them

The v. Acte.   The i. Sceane.

Master Bayly.   Doctor Rat.   [Scapethryft.]
[*Enter the* BAILEY, DR RAT, *and*
SCAPETHRYFT.]

BAILIE: I can perceive none other – I speke it from
910   my hart –
But either ye ar in al the fault or els in the greatest
      part.

D. RAT: If it be counted his fault, besides all his
      greeves,
When a poore man is spoyled and beaten among
      theeves,
Then I confesse my fault herein, at this season,
But I hope you wil not judge so much against
      reason.

BAILY: And methinkes, by your owne tale of all that
      ye name,
If any plaid the theefe, you were the very same:
The women they did nothing, as your words make
      probation,
But stoutly withstood your forcible invasion.
If that a theefe at your window to enter should
920   begin,
Wold you hold forth your hand and helpe to pull
      him in
Or [wold you] kepe him out? I pray you answere me.

D. RAT: Mary, kepe him out, and a good cause why:
But I am no theefe, sir, but an honest learned
      clarke.

BAILY: Yea, but who knoweth that, when he meets
      you in the darke?
I am sure your learning shines not out at your
      nose!
Was it any marvaile though, the poore woman
      arose

912 *greeves*: injuries, wrongs 913 *spoyled*: injured, robbed 918 *probation*: proof

And start up, being afraide of that was in hir
    purse?
Methinke you may be glad that your lueke was no
    worse.

D. RAT: Is not this evill ynough, I pray you as you
    thinke –?   *930*
    Showing his broken head.

BAILY: Yea, but a man in the darke, if chaunces do
    wincke,
As soone he smites his father as any other man,
Because for lacke of light discerne him he ne can.
Might it not have ben your lucke with a spit to
    have ben slaine?

D. RAT: I thinke I am little better, my scalpe is
    cloven to the braine;
If there be all the remedy, I know who beares the
    knockes!

BAILY: By my troth and well worthy besides to kisse
    the stockes!
To come in on the backe side, when ye might go
    about –
I know non such unles they long to have their
    braines knockt out!

D. RAT: Well, wil you be so good, sir, as talke with
    Dame Chat   *940*
And know what she intended? I aske no more but
    that.

BAYLY: Let her be called, fellow, because of Master
    Doctor –
    [SCAPETHRYFT *knocks at* DAME CHAT's *door.*]
I warrant in this case she wil be hir owne proctor;
She will tel hir owne tale in metter or in prose,
And byd you seeke your remedy, and so go wype
    your nose!

931 *if chaunces do wincke*: if he is out of luck   938 *on the backe side*: at the rear of the
premises   943 *proctor*: advocate, attorney   944 *metter*: metre

The v. Acte.   The ii. Sceane.

M. Bayly.   Chat.   D. Rat.
Gammer.   Hodge.   Diccon.

[*Enter* DAME CHAT.]

BAYLY: Dame Chat, Master Doctor upon you here
    complained
    That you and your maides shuld him much
      misorder,
    And taketh many an oth that no word he fained,
    Laying on your charge how you thought him to
      murder;
950   And on his part againe, that same man saith furder
    He never offended you in word nor intent;
    To heare you answer hereto, we have now for you
      sent.
CHAT: That I wold have murdered him, fye on him,
    wretch!
    And evil mought he thee for it, our Lord I besech!
    I will swere on al the bookes that opens and
      shuttes,
    He faineth this tale out of his owne guttes!
    For this seven weeks with me I am sure he sat not
      downe:
    [*To* DR RAT] Nay, ye have other minions in the
      other end of the towne,
    Where ye were liker to catch such a blow,
960   Then anywhere els, as farre as I know!
BAILY: Belike then, Master Doctor, yon stripe there
    ye got not?
D. RAT: Thinke you I am so mad that where I was
    bet I wot not?
    Will ye beleve this queane before she hath tryd it?

---

954 *mought he thee*: might he thrive   958 *minions*: darlings, girl-friends   961 *stripe*: wound
962 *bet*: beaten   963 *tryd it*: put it to the test

It is not the first dede she hath done and afterward
   denide it.

CHAT: What, man, will you say I broke your head?

D. RAT: How canst thou prove the contrary?

CHAT: Nay, how provest thou that I did the deade?

D. RAT: To plainly, by S[aint] Mary!

This profe I trow may serve, though I no word
   spoke.
   Showing his broken head.

CHAT: Bicause thy head is broken, was it I that it
   broke?   *970*

I saw thee, Rat, I tel thee, not once within this
   fortnight –

D. RAT: No, mary, thou sawest me not, for why, thou
   hadst no light!

But I felt thee for al the darke, beshrew thy smothe
   cheekes!

And thou groped me, this wil declare any day this
   six weekes.
   Showing his heade.

BAILY: Answere me to this, M[aster] Rat, when
   caught you this harme of yours?

D. RAT: A while ago, sir, God he knoweth; within les
   then these two houres.

BAILY: Dame Chat, was there none with you
   (confesse I'faith) about that season?

What, woman? Let it be what it wil; 'tis neither
   felony nor treason.

CHAT: Yes, by my faith, Master Bayly, there was a
   knave not farre

Who caught one good philup on the brow with a
   dore barre,   *980*

And well was he worthy, as it semed to mee:

---

974 *groped*: handled in the dark   975 *harme*: injury   977 *I'faith*: in good faith
980 *philup*: fillip, a sharp blow

But what is that to this man, since this was not
    hee?

BAILY: Who was it then? Let's here.

D. RAT: Alas, sir, aske
    you that?

Is it not made plain inough – by the owne mouth
    of Dame Chat –?

The time agreeth, my head is broken, her tong
    cannot lye,

Onely upon a bare 'Nay' she saith it was not I.

CHAT: No, mary, was it not indeede; ye shal here by
    this one thing:

This afternoone a frend of mine for good wil gave
    me warning,

And bad me wel loke to my ruste, and al my
    capons' pennes,

For if I toke not better heede, a knave wold have
990   my hennes.

Then I to save my goods toke so much pains as
    him to watch,

And as good fortune served me, it was my chaunce
    him for to catch:

What strokes he bare away or other what was his gaines

I wot not, but sure I am he had something for his
    paines!

BAILY: Yet telles thou not who it was.

CHAT: Who? It was a
    false theefe,

That came like a false foxe, my pullaine to kil and
    mischeefe.

BAILY: But knowest thou not his name?

CHAT: I know it, but
    what than?

It was that crafty cullyon Hodge, my Gammer
    Gurton's man.

---

993 *other what*: what else 996 *pullaine*: poultry 998 *cullyon*: term of abuse: 'sod'

BAILIE: Cal me the knave hether; he shal sure kysse
    the stockes:

I shall teach him a lesson, for filching hens or
    cocks.   *1000*

    [SCAPETHRYFT *knocks at* GAMMER GURTON's *door.*]

D. RAT: I marvaile, Master Bayly, so bleared be your
    eyes!

An egge is not so ful of meate as she is ful of lyes:

When she hath playd this pranke to excuse al this
    geare,

She layeth the fault in such a one as I know was
    not there.

CHAT: Was he not thear? Loke on his pate; that shal
    be his witnes!

D. RAT: I wold my head were half so hole; I wold
    seeke no redresse.

    [GAMMER GURTON *appears at her door.*]

BAILY: God bless you, Gammer Gurton.

GAMMER: God dylde
    you, master mine.

BAILY: Thou hast a knave within thy house, Hodge,
    a servant of thine.

They tel me that busy knave is such a filching one,

That hen, pig, goose or capon, thy neighbour can
    have none.   *1010*

GAMMER: By God, cham much ameved to heare any
    such reporte:

Hodge was not wont, ich trow, to bave him in that sort.

CHAT: A theevisher knave is not on live, more
    filching, nor more false;

Many a truer man then he hase hanged up by the
    halse:

And thou, his dame, of al his theft thou art the sole
    receaver;

1001 *bleared*: dimmed, blinded (see note)   1003 *geare*: business   1007 *God dylde you*: God
yield you, i.e. God repay you   1011 *ameved*: aroused, angered   1012 *bave*: behave
1013 *on live*: alive   1014 *halse*: neck

For Hodge to catch, and thou to kepe, I never
    knew none better!

GAMMER: Sir, reverence of your masterdome, and
    you were out adoore,

Chold be so bolde for al hir brags to cal her arrant
    whoore!

And ich knew Hodge so bad as tow, ich wish me
    endlesse sorow,

And chould not take the pains to hang him up

1020   before tomorow!

CHAT: What have I stolne from the or thine, thou
    ilfavored olde trot?

GAMMER: A great deale more (by God's blest) than
    chever by the got!

That thou knowest wel, I neade not say it —

BAILY: Stoppe
    there, I say!

And tel me here, I pray you, this matter by the
    way:

How chaunce Hodge is not here? Him wold I faine
    have had.

GAMMER: Alas, sir, hee'l be here anon; ha be handled
    to bad.

CHAT: Master Bayly, sir, ye be not such a foole, wel I
    know,

But ye perceive by this lingring there is a pad in
    the straw.
    Thinking that Hodg his head was broke, and that
    Gammer wold not let him come before them.

GAMMER: Chil shew you his face, ich warrant the —
    [*Enter* HODGE.]
    lo, now where he is!

BAILIE: Come on, fellow; it is tolde me thou art a

1030   shrew iwysse;

1017 *reverence of your masterdome*: with due respect to your status   *and*: if   1019 *as tow*: as
thou (sayest he is)   1022 *by God's blest*: i.e. God's blessed son   1028 *a pad in the straw*: a
toad in the straw, a hidden danger (see note)   1030 *shrew*: villain   *iwysse*: truly

Thy neighbour's hens thou takest, and playes the
  two-legged foxe,
Their chikens and their capons to, and now and
  then their cocks.
HODGE: Ich defy them al that dare it say; cham true
  as the best!
BAILY: Wart not thou take within this houre in
  Dame Chat's hens' nest?
HODGE: Take there? No, master, chold not do't for a
  houseful of gold!
CHAT: Thou or the devil in thy cote – sweare this I
  dare be bold!
D. RAT: Sweare me no swearing, queaṅ, the devill he
  geve the sorow!
  Al is not worth a gnat thou canst sweare till
  tomorow.
  Where is the harme he hath? Shew it, by God's
  bread!
  Ye beat him with a witnes, but the stripes light on
  my head!   *1040*
HODGE: Bet me? Gog's blessed body, chold first, ich
  trow, have burst the!
  Ich thinke and chad my hands loose, callet, chould
  have crust the!
CHAT: Thou shitten knave, I trow thou knowest the
  ful weight of my fist:
  I am fowly deceived onles thy head and my doore
  bar kyste!
HODGE: Hold thy chat, whore; thou criest so loude
  can no man els be hard!
CHAT: Well, knave, and I had the alone, I wold
  surely rap thy costard!
BAYLY: Sir, answer me to this: is thy head whole or
  broken?
CHAT: Yea, Master Bayly, blest be every good token!

1034 *take*: taken   1042 *crust*: ? beat to a crust   1046 *costard*: head (literally 'large apple')

HODGE: Is my head whole? Ich warrant you 'tis
neither scurvy nor scald;

[*To* DAME CHAT] What, you foule beast, does think
1050   'tis either pild or bald?

Nay, ich thanke God, chil not for al that thou
maist spend,

That chad one scab on myn arse as brode as thy
finger's end!

BAYLY: Come nearer heare.

HODGE: Yes, that ich dare.

[*The* BAILEY *inspects* HODGE's *head.*]

BAYLY: By Our Lady, here is no harme!

Hodge's head is hole ynough for al Dame Chat's
charme.

CHAT: By Gog's blest, however the thing he clockes
or smolders,

I know the blowes he bare away, either with head
or shoulders,

Camest thou not, knave, within this houre, creping
into my pens,

And there was caught within my hous, groping
among my hens?

HODGE: A plage both on thy hens and the; a carte,
whore, a carte!

Chould I were hanged as hie as a tree, and chware
1060   as false as thou art!

Geve my Gammer again her washical thou stole
away in thy lap!

GAMMER: Yea, Maister Bailey, there is a thing you
know not on mayhap;

This drab she kepes away my good, the devil he
might her snare!

Ich pray you that ich might have a right action on
her.

1049 *scald*: scabby 1050 *pild*: hairless 1054 *charme*: ? magic power 1055 *clockes or smolders*: cloaks or smothers 1059 *a carte*: see note on line 625 above 1060 *and*: if
1061 *washical*: 'what's-it-called?' 1063 *good*: goods

CHAT: Have I thy good, old filth, or any such old
    sowe's?
 I am as true, I wold thou knew, as skin betwene
    thy browes!
GAMMER: Many a truer hath ben hanged, though
    you escape the daunger!
CHAT: Thou shalt answer, by God's pity, for this thy
    foule slaunder!
BAILY [to GAMMER GURTON]: Why, what can ye
    charge hir withal? To say so ye do not well.
GAMMER: Mary, a vengeance to hir hart! That whore
    hase stoln my neele!   *1070*
CHAT: Thy nedle, old witch, how so? It were almes
    thy scul to knock;
 So didst thou say the other day that I had stolne thy cock,
 And rosted him to my breakfast, which shal not be
    forgotten:
 The devil pul out thy lying tong, and teeth that be so
    rotten!
GAMMER: Geve me my neele! As for my cocke,
    chould be very loth
 That chuld here tel he shuld hang on thy fals faith
    and troth.
BAILY: Your talke is such I can scarce learne who
    shuld be most in fault.
GAMMER: Yet shal ye find no other wight save she,
    by bred and salt!
BAILY: Kepe ye content awhile; se that your tonges
    ye holde;
 Methinkes you shuld remembre this is no place to
    scolde.   *1080*
 How knowest thou, Gammer Gurton, Dame Chat
    thy nedle had?
GAMMER: To name you, sir, the party, chould not be
    very glad.

1071 *almes*: a good deed

BAILY: Yea, but we must nedes heare it, and therfore
    say it boldly.

GAMMER: Such one as told the tale, full soberly and
    coldly;

Even he that loked on – wil sweare on a booke –

What time this drunken gossip my faire long neele
    up tooke:

Diccon, master, the Bedlam, cham very sure ye
    know him?

BAILIE: A false knave, by God's pitie! Ye were but a
    foole to trow him.

I durst aventure wel the price of my best cap

That when the end is knowen, all wil turne to a
1090   jape.

Tolde he not you that besides, she stole your cocke
    that tyde?

GAMMER: No, master, no indede, for then he shuld
    have lyed.

My cocke is, I thanke Christ, safe and wel afine.

CHAT: Yea, but that ragged colt, that whore, that
    Tyb of thine,

Said plainly thy cocke was stolne, and in my house
    was eaten;

That lying cut is lost that she is not swinged and
    beaten.

And yet for al my good name, it were a small
    amendes,

I picke not this geare (hearst thou?) out of my
    fingers' endes.

But he that hard it told me, who thou of late didst
    name,
1100   Diccon whom al men knowes, it was the very same.

BAILY: This is the case: you lost your nedle about the
    dores,

1086 *gossip*: female neighbour; see note to line 8   1088 *trow*: believe   1089 *aventure*: risk
1093 *afine*: completely   1094 *colt*: cheat   1096 *cut*: bitch   *swinged*: thrashed   1098 *I picke
not*, etc.: 'I'm not making this up out of my head'

And she answeres againe, she hase no cocke of
    your's;
Thus in your talke and action, from that you do
    intend
She is whole five mile wide, from that she doth
    defend.
Will you saie she hath your cocke?

GAMMER: No, mery, sir,
    that chil not.

BAYLY: Will you confesse hir neele?

CHAT: Will I? No, sir,
    will I not!

BAYLY: Then there lieth all the matter.

GAMMER: Soft, master,
    by the way,
Ye know she could do litle, and she cold not say
    nay.

BAYLY: Yea, but he that made one lie about your
    cock stealing,
Wil not sticke to make another what time lies be in
    dealing: *1110*
I weene the ende wil prove this brawle did first
    arise
Upon no other ground but only Diccon's lyes.

CHAT: Though some be lyes as you belike have
    espyed them,
Yet other some be true, by proof I have wel tryed
    them.

BAYLY: What other thing beside this, Dame Chat?

CHAT: Mary, syr, even this;
The tale I tolde before, the selfesame tale it was
    his:
He gave me like a frende warning against my losse;
Els had my hens be stolne, eche one, by God's
    crosse!

1105 *mery*: marry   1108 *and she cold not say nay*: if she couldn't deny it   1110 *in dealing*:
being doled out

He tolde me Hodge wold come, and in he came
    indeede,
But as the matter chaunsed, with greater hast then
1120   speede:
This truth was said, and true was found, as truly I
    report.

BAYLY: If Doctor Rat be not deceived, it was of
    another sort.

D. RAT [*to* DAME CHAT]: By God's mother, thou and
    he be a cople of suttle foxes!
Betweene you and Hodge I beare away the boxes:
Did not Diccon apoynt the place wher thou shuldst
    stand to mete him?

CHAT: Yes, by the Masse, and if he came, bad me
    not sticke to speet hym.

D. RAT: God's sacrament, the villain knave hath
    drest us round about:
He is the cause of all this brawle, that dyrty shitten
    loute!
When Gammer Gurton here complained and
    made a ruful mone,
I head him sweare that you had gotten hir nedle
1130   that was gone,
And this to try, he furder said, he was ful loth;
    howbeit
He was content with small adoe to bring me where
    to see it.
And where ye sat, he said ful certain, if I wold
    folow his read,
Into your house a privy way he wold me guide and
    leade,
And where ye had it in your hands, sewing about a
    clowte,
And set me in the backe hole, therby to finde you
    out.

1120 *speede*: success   1124 *boxes*: blows   1126 *speet*: spite, punish   1127 *drest us*: 'fixed us'
1133 *read*: advice   1135 *clowte*: garment

And whiles I sought a quietnes, creping upon my
    knees,
I found the weight of your dore bar for my reward
    and fees!
Such is the lucke that some men gets while they
    begin to mel
In setting at one such as were out, minding to
    make al wel.   *1140*

HODGE: Was not wel blest, Gammer, to scape that
    scoure? and chad ben there,
Then chad ben drest, belike, as ill by the Masse as
    gaffar Vicar!

BAYLY: Mary, sir, here is a sport alone; I loked for
    such an end:
If Diccon had not playd the knave, this had ben
    sone amend.
My Gammer here he made a foole, and drest hir as
    she was,
And Goodwife Chat he set to scole, till both partes
    cried 'Alas!'
And D[octor] Rat was not behind whiles Chat his
    crown did pare;
I wold the knave had ben starke blind, if Hodg
    had not his share!

HODGE: Cham meetly wel sped already amongs,
    cham drest like a coult,
And chad not had the better wit, chad bene made
    a doult.   *1150*

BAYLY [*to* SCAPETHRYFT]: Sir knave, make hast
    Diccon were here; fetch him wherever he bee.
    [*Exit* SCAPETHRYFT.]

CHAT: Fie on the villaine! Fie, fie! That makes us
    thus agree!

GAMMER: Fie on him, knave, with al my hart! Now
    fie and fie againe!

1137 *a quietnes*: ? peaceful settlement 1139 *mel*: occupy themselves 1141 *scoure*: score,
reckoning 1142 *drest*: treated 1144 *amend*: amended 1149 *amongs*: meanwhile *coult*:
cheater 1152 *thus agree*: i.e. agree so badly

D. RAT: Now fie on him may I best say, whom he
    hath almost slaine!

[DICCON enters, followed by SCAPETHRYFT.]

BAYLY: Lo, where he commeth at hand; belike he
    was not fare;

Diccon, heare be two or three thy company cannot
    spare.

DICCON: God blesse you, and you may be blest, so
    many al at once!

CHAT: Come, knave, it were a good deed to geld the,
    by Cocke's bones!

Seest not thy handiwarke? Sir Rat, can ye forbeare
    him?

DICCON: A vengeance on those hands lite, for my
1160   hands cam not nere hym!

The horsen priest hath lift the pot in some of these
    alewyves' chayres,

That his head wolde not serve him, belyke, to
    come downe the stayres.

BAILY: Nay, soft, thou maist not play the knave, and
    have this language to;

If thou thy tong bridle awhile, the better maist
    thou do.

Confesse the truth as I shall aske, and cease a
    while to fable,

And for thy fault, I promise the, thy handling shal
    be reasonable.

Hast thou not made a lie or two to set these two by
    the eares?

DICCON: What if I have? Five hundred such have I
    seene within these seven yeares.

I am sory for nothing else but that I see not the
    sport

Which was betwene them when they met, as they
1170   themselves report.

1155 *fare*: far 1158 *Cocke's*: God's 1161 *chayres*: seats 1167 *by the eares*: quarrelling

BAYLY: The greatest thing – Master Rat, ye se how
  he is drest?

DICCON: What devil nede he be groping so depe in
  Goodwife Chat's hens' nest?

BAYLY: Yea, but it was thy drift to bring him into
  the briars.

DICCON: God's bread, hath not such an old foole wit
  to save his eares?

  He showeth himselfe herein, ye see, so very a coxe;
  The cat was not so madly alured by the foxe,
  To run into the snares was set for him doubtlesse,
  For he leapt in for myce, and this Sir John for
  madnes.

D. RAT: Well, and ye shift no better, ye losel lyther
  and lasye,

  I will go neare for this to make ye leape at a dasye.   *1180*
  In the King's name, Master Bayly, I charge you
  set him fast!

DICCON: What? Fast at cardes or fast on slepe? It is
  the thing I did last.

D. RAT: Nay, fast in fetters, false varlet, according to
  thy deedes.

BAYLY: Master Doctor, ther is no remedy; I must
  intreat you needes

  Some other kinde of punishment –

D. RAT: Nay, by All
  Halowes!

  His punishment, if I may judg, shal be naught els
  but the gallous!

BAYLY: That were to sore; a spiritual man to be so
  extreame!

D. RAT: Is he worthy any better, sir? How do ye
  judge and deame?

BAYLY: I graunt him worthie punishment, but in
  no wise so great.

1173 *drift*: plan, intention *into the briars*: into 'hot water' 1175 *coxe*: cokes, a nitwit (see
note) 1179 *losel lyther and lasye*: wicked, lazy wretch 1180 *leape at a dasye*: be hanged (see
note) 1182 *fast at cards*: intent on a card-game

GAMMER: It is a shame, ich tel you plaine, for such
1190 false knaves intreat!

He has almost undone us al, this is as true as steele:

And yet for al this great ado cham never the nere
  my neele.

BAYLY: Canst thou not say anything to that, Diccon,
  with least or most?

DICCON: Yea, mary, sir, thus much I can say wel: the
  nedle is lost.

BAYLY: Nay, canst not thou tel which way that nedle
  may be found?

DICCON: No, by my fay, sir, though I might have an
  hundred pound.

HODGE: Thou lier lickdish, didst not say the neele
  wold be gitten?

DICCON: No, Hodge; by the same token you where
  that time beshitten

For feare of Hobgobling, you wot wel what I meane;

As long as it is sence, I feare me yet ye be scarce
1200 cleane.

BAYLY: Wel, Master Rat, you must both learne and
  teach us to forgeve:

Since Diccon hath confession made and is so
  cleane shreve.

If ye to me conscent to amend this heavie chaunce,

I wil injoyne him here with some open kind of
  penaunce:

Of this condition, where ye know my fee is twenty
  pence

For the bloodshed, I am agreed with you here to
  dispence.

Ye shal go quite, so that ye graunt the matter now
  to run,

To end with mirth emong us al, even as it was begun.

1197 *lickdish*: sponger (see note) 1198 *where*: were 1200 *sence*: since then 1202 *shreve*:
shriven, absolved 1207 *quite*: free, or completely *run*: lapse, ride

CHAT: Say yea, Master Vicar, and he shal sure
    confes to be your detter,
And al we that be heare present wil love you much
    the better.   *1210*

D. RAT: My part is the worst, but since you al hereon
    agree,
Go even to Master Bayly, let it be so for mee.

BAYLY: How saiest thou, Diccon? Art content this
    shal on me depend?

DICCON: Go to, M[aster] Bayly, say on your mind; I
    know ye are my frend.

BAYLY: Then marke ye wel; to recompence this thy
    former action,
Because thou hast offended al, to make them
    satisfaction
Before their faces, here kneele downe, and as I shal
    the teach,
For thou shalt take on othe of Hodge's leather
    breache:
First for Master Doctor, upon paine of his cursse,
Where he wil pay for al thou never draw thy
    pursse,   *1220*
And when ye meete at one pot, he shal have the
    first pull,
And thou shalt never offer him the cup, but it be full.
To Goodwife Chat thou shalt be sworne, even on
    the same wyse,
If she refuse thy money once, never to offer it twise;
Thou shalt be bound by the same, here as thou
    dost take it,
When thou maist drinke of free cost, thou never
    forsake it.
For Gammer Gurton's sake, againe sworne shalt
    thou bee
To helpe hir to hir nedle againe if it do lie in thee;
And likewise to be bound, by virtue of that,

1230   To be of good abering to Gib hir great cat.
       Last of al, for Hodge the othe to scanne,
       Thou shalt never take him for fine gentleman.
HODGE: Come on, fellow Diccon! Chal be even with
       thee now.
BAYLY: Thou wilt not sticke to do this, Diccon, I trow?
DICCON: No, by my father's skin, my hand downe I
       lay it:
       Loke, as I have promised, I wil not denay it.
       But, Hodge, take good heede now, thou do not
       beshite me!
       And gave him a good blow on the buttocke.
HODGE: Gog's hart, thou false villaine, dost thou bite
       me?
BAYLY: What, Hodge? Doth he hurt the or ever he
       begin?
HODGE: He thrust me into the buttocke with a
1240   bodkin or a pin!
       [*Feels his behind*] I saie, Gammer, Gammer!
GAMMER: How
       now, Hodge? How now?
HODGE: God's malt, Gammer Gurton!
GAMMER: Thou art mad,
       ich trow!
HODGE: Will you see? The devil, Gammer!
GAMMER: The devil,
       sonne, God blesse us!
HODGE: Chould iche were hanged, Gammer.
GAMMER: Mary, so
       ye might dresse us.
HODGE: Chave it, by the Masse, Gammer!
GAMMER: What, not
       my neele, Hodge?
HODGE: Your neele, Gammer, your neele!
GAMMER: No, fie,
       dost but dodge!

1230 *abering*: conduct 1239 *or*: ere 1244 *dresse us*: sort us all out 1246 *dodge*: prevaricate

HODGE: Cha found your neele, Gammer; here in my
    hand be it!

GAMMER: For al the loves on earth, Hodge, let me see
    it!

HODGE: Soft, Gammer.

GAMMER: Good Hodge –

HODGE: Soft, ich say;
    tarie a while.

GAMMER: Nay, sweete Hodge, say truth, and do not
    me begile.   *1250*

HODGE: Cham sure on it, ich warrant you; it goes no
    more astray.

GAMMER: Hodge, when I speake so faire, wilt stil say
    me nay?

HODGE: Go neare the light, Gammer; this – wel, in
    faith, good lucke –

  Chwas almost undone; 'twas so far in my buttocke!
  [HODGE *hands over the needle.*]

GAMMER: 'Tis min owne deare neele, Hodge; syklerly
    I wot!

HODGE: Cham I not a good sonne, Gammer? Cham I
    not?

GAMMER: Christ's blessing light on thee! Hast made
    me forever.

HODGE: Ich knew that ich must finde it, els choud a
    had it never.

CHAT: By my troth, Gossyp Gurton, I am even as
    glad

  As though I mine owne selfe as good a turne had!   *1260*

BAYLY: And I by concience, to see it so come forth,

  Rejoyce so much at it as three nedles be worth.

D. RAT: I am no whit sory to see you so rejoyce.

DICCON: Nor I much the gladder for al this noyce;

  Yet say 'Gramercy, Diccon', for springing of the
    game.

1255 *sykerly*: certainly   1256 *sonne*: suggesting Hodge is like a son to Gammer Gurton
1258 *choud a*: she would have   1264 *noyce*: noise

GAMMER: Grammercy, Diccon, twenty times! O how
　　glad cham!
　　[*To the* BAILEY] If that chould do so much your
　　　masterdome to come hether,
　　Master Rat, Goodwife Chat, and Diccon together;
　　Cha but one halfpeny, as far as iche know it,
1270　And chil not rest this night til ich bestow it.
　　If ever ye love me, let us go in and drinke.
BAYLY: I am content, if the rest thinke as I thinke?
　　Master Rat, it shal be best for you if we so doo,
　　Then shall you warme you and dresse yourself too.
DICCON: Soft, syrs, take us with you, the company
　　　shal be the more;
　　As proude coms behinde, they say, as any goes
　　　before.
　　[*To the audience*] But now, my good masters, since
　　　we must be gone
　　And leave you behinde us here all alone;
　　Since at our last ending thus mery we bee,
　　For Gammer Gurton's nedle ['s] sake, let us have a
1280　　plaudytie.
　　[*They all go into the ale-house.*]

1274 *dresse yourself*: have your wound attended to　1280 *plaudytie*: a round of applause

Finis

Imprinted at London
in Fleetestreate beneath the Conduite,
at the signe of S. John Evangelist, by
Thomas Colwell
1575

Mother Bombie

JOHN LYLY

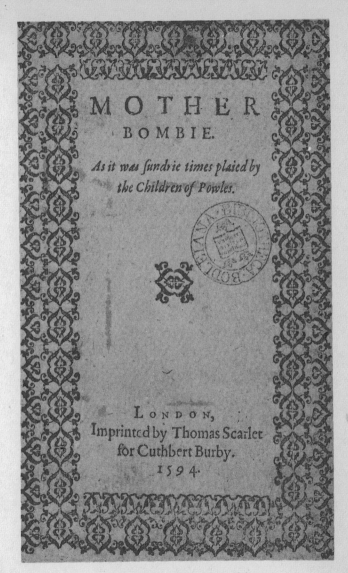

Facsimile of the title-page of the
First Quarto edition (1594)

Mother Bombie first appeared in quarto form, in an edition dated 1594 published by Cuthbert Burby who also published editions of *Romeo and Juliet* and *Love's Labour's Lost*. As with most of Lyly's plays, the text was attributed to no author; an entry in the Stationers' Company Register for 18 June 1594 reads:

Cuthbert Burby / Entred for his copie under thand [the hand] of m^r warden Cawood / a booke intituled Mother Bumbye beinge an enterlude / $\qquad$ vj^d C /

Only two copies of this edition, which was printed by Thomas Scarlet, are known to be in existence today, one in the Malone Collection at the Bodleian Library, Oxford, the other among a collection of plays once owned by David Garrick, now in the British Library. In 1598 Burby issued a second Quarto, printed by Thomas Creede (one of the best printers of his day who handled several Shakespearean quartos), in which errors in the 1594 edition were corrected but others perpetrated; some twelve copies of this edition survive in libraries in Britain and the United States of America. Like its predecessor, the second Quarto was anonymous, but when, in 1632, Edward Blount issued *Six Court Comedies* by 'Iohn Lilly, Master of Artes' in a single volume, 'Mother Bomby' formed the final play of the collection. Blount took as his text that printed in 1598, but supplied words for four out of the five songs apparently omitted in the two Quarto editions (see note on line 1819 below). Doubts have been expressed as to whether or not these songs are genuinely Lyly's work (see Appendix to G. K. Hunter, *Johy Lyly: The Humanist as Courtier*, 1962, pp. 367–72), but their presence in Blount's edition must be taken seriously.

Unlike some of Lyly's other comedies, *Mother Bombie* has been previously edited on only a handful of occasions; editions include:

C. W. Dilke, ed., *Old English Plays*, I, 1814

F. W. Fairholt, ed., *The Dramatic Works of John Lyly*, 2 vols., 1858 and 1892

R. Warwick Bond, ed., *The Complete Works of John Lyly*, 3 vols., Oxford, 1902; reprinted 1967

Kathleen M. Lea and D. Nichol Smith, eds., *Mother Bombie* (Malone Society Reprints), 1948 (based on the 1594 Quarto).

The present text derives initially from the Malone Society reprint, but with corrections and emendations adapted mainly from Bond's edition of 1902, including the songs printed by Blount in 1632. The cast-list is a simplified version of that given in the Malone Society's volume.

List of Characters

MEMPHIO, *presumed father of Accius, true father of Maestius*

DROMIO, *his servant*

MAESTIUS, *his son, presumed son of Vicinia*

ACCIUS, *his presumed son, true son of Vicinia*

STELLIO, *presumed father of Silena, true father of Serena*

RISIO, *his servant*

SERENA, *his daughter, presumed daughter of Vicinia*

SILENA, *his presumed daughter, true daughter of Vicinia*

PRISIUS, *father of Livia*

LIVIA, *in love with Candius*

LUCIO, *Prisius' servant*

RIXULA, *Livia's maid*

SPERANTUS, *father of Candius*

CANDIUS, *in love with Livia*

HALFPENNY, *Sperantus' servant*

VICINIA, *presumed mother to Maestius and Serena, true mother to Accius and Silena*

MOTHER BOMBIE, *a fortune-teller*

THREE MUSICIANS: SYNIS, NASUTUS, BEDUNEUS

A HACKNEYMAN

A SERGEANT

A SCRIVENER

Risio: also referred to as Riscio; I have eliminated the latter form as confusing. *Lucio*: sometimes called Luceo or Linceo; I have retained the form given above throughout. *A Hackneyman*: a man who hires out horses to ride.

A pleasant conceited Comoedie,
called MOTHER BOMBIE

Actus primus.   *Scena prima.*
Memphio.   *Dromio.*

[*Enter* MEMPHIO *and* DROMIO.]

MEMPHIO: Boy, there are three things that make my
life miserable: a threedbare purse, a curst wife, and
a foole to my heire.

DROMIO: Why then, sir, there are three medicines for
these three maladies: a pike-staffe to take a purse
on the highway, a holy wand to brush cholar from
my mistres' tong, and a young wench for my yong
master; so that as your worship being wise begot a
foole, so he, beeing a foole, may tread out a wise
man.   *10*

MEMP: I, but, Dromio, these medicines bite hot on
great mischiefs, for so might I have a rope about
my necke, hornes upon my head, and in my house
a litter of fooles.

DRO: Then, sir, you had best let some wise man sit
on your sonne, to hatch him a good wit; they saie,
if ravens sitte on hens' egs, the chickens will be
black, and so forth.

MEMP: Why, boy, my sonne is out of the shell, and
is growen a pretie cocke.   *20*

DROM: Carve him, master, and make him a capon,
els all your breed will prove cockescombes.

MEMPH: I marvell he is such an asse; hee takes it not
of his father.

Title: *conceited*: clever, witty   2 *curst*: shrewish   5 *pike-staffe*: a metal-pointed stick (see
note)   6 *a holy wand*: a holly switch   *cholar*: anger   9 *tread out*: beget   11 *I*: Aye   *bite hot*:
smart painfully   20 *cocke*: young blade   21 *capon*: castrated cockerel, fattened for table
22 *cockescombes*: i.e. fools (see note)

DRO: He may for anie thing you know.

MEM: Why, villain, dost thou think me a foole?

DRO: O no, sir; neither are you sure that you are his father.

MEMP: Rascall, doest thou imagine thy mistres
30 naught of her bodie?

DRO: No, but fantasticall of her mind; and it may be, when this boy was begotten, shee thought of a foole, and so conceived a foole, yourselfe beeing verie wise, and she surpassing honest.

MEM: It may be; for I have heard of an Aethiopian, that thinking of a faire picture, brought forth a faire [babie], and yet no bastard.

DROM: You are well read, sir; your sonne may be a bastard, and yet legitimate; yourselfe a cuckold,
40 and yet my mistres vertuous; all this in conceit.

MEM: Come, Dromio, it is my grief to have such a sonne that must inherit my lands.

DRO: He needs not, sir; I'le beg him for a foole.

MEM: Vile boy! Thy yong master?

DRO: Let me have in a device.

MEM: I'le have thy advice, and if it fadge, thou shalt eate [till thou] sweate, play till thou sleep, and sleepe till thy bones ake.

DRO: I, marie, now you tickle me, I am both hungrie,
50 gamesome, and sleepie, and all at once. I'le breake this head against the wal, but I'le make it bleed good matter.

MEM: Then this it is: thou knowest I have but one sonne, and he is a foole.

DRO: A monstrous foole!

MEMP: A wife, and she an arrand scold.

DRO: Ah, master, I smell your device; it will be excellent!

MEM: Thou canst not know it till I tell it!

30 *naught of her bodie*: a whore 40 *in conceit*: in fancy, with possible pun on 'conception'
43 *beg him for a foole*: see note 45 *have in a device*: come forward with a scheme 46 *fadge*:
comes off, works out 49 *I, marie*: Aye, marry 50 *gamesome*: playful 56 *arrand*: arrant
57 *smell*: detect, guess

300

DRO: I see it through your braines; your haire is so   *60*
  thin, and your scull so transparent, I may sooner
  see it than heare it.

MEM: Then, boy, hast thou a quicke wit, and I a slow
  tongue. But what is't?

DRO: Marie, either you would have your wive's tong
  in your son's head, that he might bee a prating
  foole; or his braines in hir brainpan that she might
  be a foolish scold.

MEM: Thou dreamst, Dromio; there is no such
  matter. Thou knowest I have kept [them] close, so   *70*
  that my neighbors thinke him to be wise, and her
  to be temperate, because they never heard them
  speake.

DRO: Well?

MEM: Thou knowest that Stellio hath a good farme
  and a faire daughter; yea, so faire that she is
  mewed up, and onely looketh out at the windows,
  least she should by some roisting courtier be
  stollen away.

DRO: So, sir?   *80*

MEM: Now if I could compasse a match between my
  sonne and Stellio's daughter, by conference of us
  parents, and without their's, I should be blessed,
  he coosned, and thou for ever set at libertie.

DRO: A singular conceit!

MEM: Thus much for my sonne. Nowe for my wife; I
  would have this kept from her, else shal I not be
  able to keepe my house from smoake; for let it
  come to one of her eares, and then wo to both
  mine! I would have her goe to my house into the   *90*
  countrie whilest we conclude this; and this once
  done, I care not if her tong never have done: these
  if thou canst effect, thou shalt make thy master
  happie.

DRO: Thinke it done: this noddle shall coin such new

67 *brainpan*: skull   77 *mewed up*: shut up (see note)   78 *roisting*: riotous   84 *coosned*:
cheated   95 *noddle*: head, brain

device as you shall have your sonne marryed by
tomorrow.

MEM: But take heed that neither the father nor the
maide speak to my sonne, for then his folly will
100   marre all.

DRO: Lay all the care on mee; *Sublevabo te onere*, I will
rid you of a foole.

MEM: Wilt thou rid me for a foole?

DRO: Tush, quarrell not!

MEM: Then for the dowrie, let it bee at least two
hundreth ducats, and after his death the farme.

DRO: What else?

MEM: Then let us in, that I may furnish thee with
some better counsell, and my sonne with better
110   apparell.

DRO: Let me alone. [*Aside*] I lacke but a wagge more
to make of my counsell, and then you shall see an
exquisite coosnage, and the father more foole than
the sonne. – But heare you, sir; I forgot one thing.

MEM: What's that?

DRO: Nay, *Expellas furca licet, usque recurret.*

MEM: What's the meaning?

DRO: Why, though your son's folly bee thrust up with
a paire of hornes on a forke, yet being naturall, it
120   will have his course.

MEM: I praie thee, no more, but about it!   *Exeunt.*

Act. I.   Sce. 2

Stellio.   Risio.

[*Enter* STELLIO *and* RISIO]

STEL[LIO:] Risio, my daughter is passing amiable,
but verie simple.

---

101 *Sublevabo te onere*: I shall lift a weight from you   103 *for a foole*: i.e. make a fool of me
112 *to make of my counsell*: to take into my confidence   116 *Expellas furca licet* etc.: You are
free to drive out [Nature] with a pitchfork; she will always rush back (see note)
118 *thrust up*, etc.: see note   119 *naturall*: also used in the punning sense of 'foolish'

RI[SIO:] You meane a foole, sir.

STEL: Faith, I implie so much.

RI: Then I apply it fit: the one shee takes of her
father, the other of her mother. Now you may bee
sure she is your owne.

STEL: I have penned her up in a chamber, having
onely a windowe to looke out, that youthes seeing   *130*
her fayre cheekes may be enamoured before they
heare her fond speech. How likest thou this head?

RI: There is verie good workmanship in it, but the
matter is but base; if the stuffe had bene as good as
the mold, your daughter had bene as wise as she is
beautifull.

STEL: Doest thou thinke she tooke her foolishnes of
mee?

RI [*aside*]: I, and so cunningly, that she toke it not
from you.   *140*

STEL: Well, *Quod natura dedit, tollere nemo potest.*

RI: A good evidence to prove the fee-simple of your
daughter's folly.

STEL: Why?

RI: It came by nature, and if none can take it awaie,
it is perpetuall.

STEL: Nay, Risio, she is no natural foole, but in this
consisteth her simplicitie, that she thinketh
herselfe subtile; in this her rudenesse, that she
imagines she is courtly; in this the overshooting of   *150*
herselfe, that she overweeneth of herselfe.

RI: Well, what followes?

STEL: Risio, this is my plot: Memphio hath a pretie
stripling to his sonne, whom with cockring he hath
made wanton: his girdle must be warmde, the ayre

---

132 *fond*: stupid *head*: ? main proposition (see note)   141 *Quod natura*, etc.: see note
142 *fee-simple*: absolute right of possession (see note)   149 *subtile*: shrewd *rudenesse*:
uncouthness   154 *cockring*: pampering   155 *girdle*: waist-belt

303

must not breath on him, he must lie a-bed til noon,
and yet in his bed breake his fast: that which I doe
to conceale the folly of my daughter, that doth hee
in too much cockering of his sonne. Now, Risio,

160 how shall I compasse a match betweene my girle
and his boy?

RI: Why, with a payre of compasses: and bring them
both into the circle, I'le warrant the 'il match
themselves.

STEL: Tush! plot it for me, that never speaking one to
another, they be in love one with another. I like
not solemne woing, it is for courtiers; let countrie
folkes beleeve others' reports as much as their own
opinions.

170 RI: O then, so it be a match you care not?

STEL: Not I, nor for a match neither, were it not I
thirst after my neighbor's farme.

RI: [aside]: A verie good nature. – Well, if by flat wit
I bring this to passe, what's my rewerd?

STEL: Whatsoever thou wilt aske.

RI: I'le aske no more than by my wit I can get in the
bargaine.

STEL: Then about it!   Exit.

RI: If I come not about you, never trust mee. I'le

180 seeke out Dromio, the counseller of my conceit. [Exit.]

Act. I.   Sce. 3.

Prisius.   Sperantus.

[Enter PRISIUS and SPERANTUS]

PRIS[IUS:] It is unneighbourly done to suffer your
son since hee came from schoole to spende his time
in love, and unwisely done to let him hover over
my daughter, who hath nothing to her dowrie but
her needle, and must prove a sempster; nor he

---

173 *flat wit*: sheer cleverness 174 *rewerd*: reward 179 *come not about you*: ? do not
out-manoeuvre you 180 *counseller of my conceit*: adviser in the notion I'm formulating

anything to take to but a Grammer, and cannot at
the best be but a schoolemaster.

SPE[RANTUS:] Prisius, you bite and whine, wring me
on the withers, and yet winch yourselfe; it is you
that goe about to match your girle with my boy,   *190*
shee beeing more fit for seames than for marriage,
and hee for a rod than a wife.

PRI: Her birth requires a better bridegrome than
such a groome!

SPE: And his bringing up another gate marriage than
such a minion!

PRI: Marie gup! I am sure he hath no better bread
than is made of wheat, nor worne finer cloth than
is made of woll, nor learned better manners than
are taught in schooles!   *200*

SPE: Nor your minxe had no better grandfather than
a tailer, who (as I have heard) was poore and
proud; nor a better father than yourselfe, unlesse
your wife borrowed a better to make her daughter
a gentlewoman.

PRI: Twit not me with my ancestors, nor my wive's
honestie; if thou doest –

SPE: Hold thy hands still, thou hadst best; and yet it
is impossible now I remember, for thou hast the
palsy.   *210*

PRI: My handes shake so, that wert thou in place
where, I would teach thee to cog!

SPE: Nay, if thou shake thy hands, I warrant thou
canst not teach anie to cog! But, neighbour, let not
two olde fooles fall out for two yong wantons.

PRI: Indeed, it becommeth men of our experience to
reason, not raile; to debate the matter, not to
combat it.

SPE: Wel then, this I'le tel thee friendly: I have

188–9 *wring me on the withers*: inflict pain on me (see note) *winch*: wince 195 *another gate*:
another kind of 197 *Marie gup!*: come off it! 199 *woll*: wool 206 *Twit*: taunt 211–12 *in
place where*: in a suitable place 212 *cog*: play on words, quibble 214 *cog*: cheat at dice
(see note) 218 *combat it*: fight over it

220   almost these two yeres cast in my head how I
might match my princockes with Stellio's
daughter, whom I have heard to be verie faire, and
know shal be verie rich: she is his heire; he doats,
he is stooping old, and shortly must die; yet by no
meanes, either by blessing or cursing, can I win
my sonne to be a woer, which I know proceeds not
of bashfulnesse but stubbornnesse; for hee knowes
his good, though I saie it; he hath wit at wil. As for
his personage, I care not who sees him, I can tell

230   you he is able to make a ladie's mouth water if she
winke not.

   PRI: Stay, Sperantus; this is like my case, for I have
bene tampering as long to have a marriage
committed betweene my wench and Memphio's
only son: they saie he is as goodly a youth as one
shall see in a summer's daie, and as neate a
stripling as ever went on neat's leather; his father
will not let him be forth of his sight, he is so tender
over him; he yet lies with his mother for catching

240   cold. Now my pretie elfe, as proud as the day is
long, she wil none of him, she forsooth wil choose
her owne husband! Made marriages prove mad
marriages; shee will choose with her eie, and like
with her heart, before she consent with her tong.
Neither father nor mother, kith nor kin, shal be her
carver in a husband, shee will fall too where she
likes best; and thus the chicke scarce out of the
shell, cackles as though she had bene troden with
an hundreth cockes, and mother of a thousand

250   egges!

   SPE: Well then, this is our best, seeing we knowe
each other's minde, to devise to governe our owne
children. For my boy, I'le keepe him to his bookes,

---

221 *princockes*: saucy youth   231 *winke not*: has her eyes open   239–40 *for catching cold*: so
he shan't catch cold   245–6 *be her carver* etc.: assign a husband to her   248 *bene troden
with*: copulated with

and studie shall make him leave to love: I'le break
him of his will, or his bones with a cudgell.

PRI: And I'le no more dandle my daughter; shee
shall prick on a clout till her fingers ake, or I'le
cause her leave to make my heart ake. [*Looking
offstage*] But in good time, though with ill lucke,
beholde if they be not both together! Let us stand   260
close and heare all, so shall we prevent all.

   [*They stand aside.*]
   Enter CANDIUS *and* LIVIA. [*He carries a book, she a
   sampler.*]

SPE [*aside*]: This happens pat, táke heed you cough
not, Prisius.

PRIS [*aside*]: Tush! spit not you, and I'le warrant, I,
my beard is as good as a handkerchiefe.

LIVIA: Sweet Candius, if thy father should see us
alone, would he not fret? The old man methinkes
should be full of fumes.

CAND[IUS:] Tush! let him fret one heartstring against
another, he shal never trouble the least vaine of my   270
little finger. The old churle thinkes none wise,
unles he have a beard hang dangling to his wast:
when my face is bedaubed with haire as his, then
perchance my conceit may stumble on his
staiednes.

PRI [*aside*]: I, in what booke read you that lesson?

SPE [*aside*]: I know not in what booke hee read it, but
I am sure he was a knave to learne it.

CAN: I beleeve, faire Livia, if your soure sire shuld
see you with your sweetheart, he would not be   280
verie patient.

LIV: The care is taken: I'le aske him blessing as a
father, but never take counsel for an husband;
there is as much oddes between my golden

256 *dandle*: pamper   257 *prick on a clout*: sew   268 *fumes*: irritability   270 *vaine*: vein
274 *my conceit may stumble*, etc.: my fancies may acquire his sobriety   282 *The care is
taken*: That's taken care of

thoughts and his leaden advice, as betweene his
silver haires and my amber lockes; I know hee will
cough for anger that I yeeld not, but he shall
cough mee a foole for his labour.

SPE [*aside to* PRISIUS]: Where pickt your daughter
290   that worke, out of broad-stitch?

PRI [*aside*]: Out of a flirt's sampler; but let us stay the
end. This is but the beginning; you shall heare two
children well brought up!

CAND: Parents in these daies are growen pievish; they
rocke their children in their cradles till they sleepe,
and crosse them about their bridals till their hearts
ake. Marriage among them is become a market:
'What will you give with your daughter?' 'What
joynter will you make for your sonne?' And many a
300   match is broken off for a penie more or lesse – as
though they could not afford their children at such
a price – when none should cheapen such ware but
affection, and none buy it but love!

SPE [*aside*]: Learnedly and scholerlike!

LIV: Indeed, our parents take great care to make us
aske blessing and say grace whenas we are lyttle
ones, and growing to yeeres of judgement, they
deprive us of the greatest blessing, and the most
gracious things to our mindes, the libertie of our
310   mindes: they give us pap with a spoon before we
can speak, and when wee speake for that wee love,
pap with a hatchet! Because their fansies beeing
growen musty with hoarie age, therefore nothing
can relish in their thoughtes that savours of sweet
youth: they studie twentie yeeres together to make
us grow as straight as a wande, and in the ende, by
bowing us, make us as crooked as a cammocke.

288 *cough mee a foole*: prove to me that he's a fool   290 *broad-stitch*: ? braid-stitch (see
note)   294 *pievish*: perverse (see note)   299 *joynter*: jointure, settlement (see note)
310 *pap*: pulpy food   312 *pap with a hatchet*: harsh treatment disguised as kindness
317 *cammocke*: a crocked stick

For mine owne part (sweet Candius), they shall
pardon me, for I will measure my love by min
owne judgement, not my father's purse or   *320*
peevishnes. Nature hath made me his child, not his
slave; I hate Memphio and his son deadly, if I wist
he would place his affection by his father's
appointment.

PRI [*aside*]: Wittily but uncivily!

CAN: Be of that minde still, my faire Livia; let our
fathers lay their purses together, we our harts: I
wil never woo where I cannot love. Let Stellio
injoy his daughter. [*Looking at her sampler*] But what
have you wrought here?   *330*

LIV: Flowers, fowles, beasts, fishes, trees, plants,
stones, and what not. Among flowers, cowslops
and lillyes, for our names Candius and Livia.
Among fowles, turtles and sparrowes, for our truth
and desires. Among beasts, the foxe and the ermin,
for beautie and policie, and among fishes, the
cockle and the tortuse, because of Venus. Among
trees, the vine wreathing about the elme, for our
embracings. Among stones, abeston, which being
hot will never be colde, for our constancies. Among   *340*
plants, time and harts-ease, to note that if we take
time, we shall ease our hearts.

PRI [*aside*]: There's a girle that knowes her
lerripoope!

SPE [*aside*]: Listen, and you shall heare my son's
learning.

LIV: What booke is that?

CAN: A fine pleasant poet, who entreateth of the Arte
of Love, and of the Remedie.

LIV: Is there arte in love?   *350*

CAN: A short art and a certain; three rules in three
lines.

324 *appointment*: dictation   332 *cowslops*: cowslips (see note)   334 *turtles*: i.e. turtle-doves
(see note)   339 *abeston*: asbestos   342 *time*: i.e. thyme   344 *lerripoope*: lesson (see note)
348 *A fine pleasant poet*: Ovid

LIV: I praie thee repeat them.

CAN: *Principio quod amare velis reperire labora,*
Proximus huic labor est placidam exorare puellam,
Tertius ut longo tempore duret amor.

LIV: I am no Latinist, Cand[ius]; you must conster
it.

CAN: So I will, and pace it too: thou shalt be
360   acquainted with case, gender, and number. First,
one must finde out a mistres whom before all
others he voweth to serve. Secondly, that he use al
the means that he may to obtaine her. And the
last, with deserts, faith, and secrecie, to studie to
keepe her.

LIV: What's the remedie?

CAN: Death.

LIV: What of all the booke is the conclusion?

CAN: This one verse, *Non caret effectu quod voluere duo*.

370 LIV: What's that?

CAN: Where two are agreed, it is impossible but they
must speed.

LIV: Then cannot we misse; therefore give mee thy
hand, Candius.

PRI [*advancing*]: Soft, Livia, take mee with you! It is
not good in lawe without witnes.

SPE [*advancing*]: And as I remember, there must be
two witnesses; God give you joy, Candius! I was
worth the bidding to dinner, though not worthy to
380   be of the counsell.

PRI: I thinke this hot love hath provided but cold
cheere.

SPE: Tush! in love is no lacke; but blush not,
Candius, you neede not bee ashamed of your
cunning: you have made love a booke case, and
spent your time well at schoole, learning to love by
arte, and hate against nature. But I perceive, the
worser childe, the better lover.

354 *Principio quod amare*, etc.: see note   357 *conster*: construe   359 *pace*: parse   369 *Non caret effectu*, etc.: where two desire a thing, the result is not in doubt   385 *cunning*: cleverness   *a booke case*: a matter of learning

PRI: And my minion hath wrought well, where every
stitch in her sampler is a pricking stitch at my   *390*
heart! You take your pleasure on parents; they are
peevish, fooles, churles, overgrowen with
ignorance because overworne with age: litle shalt
thou know the case of a father, before thyselfe be a
mother, when thou shalt breed thy childe with
continuall paines, and bringing it foorth with
deadly pangs, nurse it with thine owne paps, and
nourish it up with motherly tendernes; and then
finde them to curse thee with their hearts, when
they shoulde aske blessing on their knees, and the   *400*
collop of thine owne bowels to be the torture of
thine owne soul. With teares trickling downe thy
cheekes, and drops of bloud falling from thy heart,
thou wilt in uttering of thy minde wish them rather
unborne than unnatural, and to have had their
cradles their graves rather than thy death their
bridals. But I will not dispute what thou shouldst
have done, but correct what thou hast done: I
perceive sowing is an idle exercise, and that everie
daie there come more thoughtes into thine head   *410*
than stitches into thy worke; I'le see whether you
can spin a better mind than you have stitched, and
if I coope you not up, then let me be the capon.

SPE: As for you, sir boy, instead of poaring on a
booke, you shall holde the ploughe; I'le make
repentance reape what wantonnesse hath sowen.
But we are both well served: the sonnes must bee
masters, the fathers gaffers; what wee get together
with a rake, they cast abroade with a forke, and
wee must wearie our legges to purchase our   *420*
children armes. Well, seeing that booking is but

---

389 *minion*: 'precious'   397 *paps*: breasts   401 *collop*: literally 'slice'; piece   409 *sowing*:
sewing   413 *capon*: the fattened cock, i.e. 'the stupid one'   418 *gaffers*: 'old fellows', i.e.
of inferior rank to the masters   420–21 *purchase ... armes*: buy coats-of-arms, make
gentry of them   421 *booking*: studying

idlenesse, I'le see whether threshing be anie
occupation: thy minde shall stoope to my fortune,
or mine shall break the lawes of nature. How like a
micher he standes, as though he had trewanted
from honestie! Get thee in, and for the rest, let me
alone.

    [CANDIUS *hesitates*.] In, villaine!

PRI: And you, pretie minx, that must be fed with love
430   upon sops, I'le take an order to cram you with
sorrowes: get you in without looke or reply!

    Exeunt CANDIUS, [*and*] LIVIA.

SPE: Let us follow, and deale as rigorously with yours
as I will with mine, and you shall see that hot love
wil wax soone colde. I'le tame the proud boy, and
send him as far from his love as hee is from his
duetie.

PRI: Let us about it, and also go on with matching
them to our mindes: it was happie that we
prevented that by chance, which we could never
440   yet suspect by circumstance.

    Exeunt.

Act. 2.   Sce. I.

Dromio.   Risio.

[*Enter from different directions* DROMIO *and* RISIO.]

DRO: Now, if I could meete with Risio, it were a
world of waggery!

RI: Oh, that it were my chance, *Obviam dare Dromio*,
to stumble upon Dromio, on whome I doo nothing
but dreame!

DRO: His knaverie and my wit should make our
masters that are wise, fooles; their children that
are fooles, beggers; and us two that are bond, free.

425 *micher*: petty crook, truant   430 *sops*: food moistened with wine   438 *mindes*:
intentions, way of thinking   443 *Obviam dare Dromio*: Dromio to throw himself in my way
(see note)

RI: He to cosin, and I to conjure, would make such
alterations that our masters shuld serve   *450*
themselves; the ideots, their children, serve us; and
we to wake our wits betweene them all.

DR [*seeing* RISIO]: *Hem quam opportune*; looke if he drop
not ful in my dish!

RISIO [*seeing* DROMIO]: *Lupus in fabula*! Dromio,
imbrace me, hugge me, kisse my hand; I must
make thee fortunate!

DRO: Risio, honor me, kneele downe to mee, kisse my
feet; I must make thee blessed!

RI: My master, old Stellio, hath a foole to his   *460*
daughter.

DRO: Nay, my master, old Memphio, hath a foole to
his sonne.

RI: I must convey a contract.

DRO: And I must convey a contract.

RI: Betweene her and Memphio's sonne, without
speaking one to another.

DRO: Betweene him and Stellio's daughter, without
one speaking to the other.

RI: Doest thou mocke me, Dromio?   *470*

DRO: Thou doest me else.

RI: Not I, for all this is true.

DRO: And all this.

RI: Then are we both driven to our wits' endes, for if
either of them had bin wise, wee might have
tempered, if no marriage, yet a close marriage.

DRO: Well, let us sharpen our accounts; ther's no
better grindstone for a young man's head than to
have it whet uppon an olde man's purse. Oh, thou
shalt see my knaverie shave lyke a rasor!   *480*

RIS: Thou for the edge, and I the point, wil make the
foole bestride our mistres' backs, and then have at

---

449 *cosin*: cheat   *conjure*: deceive   453 *Hem quam opportune*: see note   455 *Lupus in fabula*:
talk of the devil! (see note)   464 *convey*: make over by law, possibly with the sense
'secretly' attached   476 *close*: secret 481–2 *the foole*: i.e. Accius

the bagge with the dudgin hafte – that is, at the
dudgen dagger, by which hanges his tantonie
pouch!

DRO: These old huddles have such strong purses with
locks; when they shut them, they go off like a
snaphance!

RIS: The old fashion is best, a purse with a ring
490   round about it, as a circle to course a knave's
hande from it. But, Dromio, two they saie may
keep counsell if one be awaie; but to convey
knaverie, two are too few, and foure too many.

DRO [*looking offstage*]: And in good time, looke where
Halfepenie, Sperantus' boy, commeth; though
bound up in *decimo sexto* for carriage, yet a wit in
folio for coosnage.

    Enter HALFEPENIE.

Single Halfepenie, what newes are now currant?

HALFEPENIE: Nothing, but that such double
500   coystrels as you be are counterfeit.

RIS: Are you so dapper? Wee'le sende you for an
halfepenie loafe.

HALFEPEN: I shall goe for silver though, when you
shall bee nailed up for slips.

DRO: Thou art a slipstring, I'le warrant.

HALF: I hope you shall never slip string, but hang
steddie.

    [RISIO *grabs* HALFPENNY.]

RI: Dromio, looke heere, now is my hand on my
halfepenie!

510 HALF: Thou lyest; thou hast not a farthing to laie thy
hands on, I am none of thine! But let mee bee
wagging; my head is full of hammers, and they

483 *the bagge*: purse   *the dudgin hafte ... pouch* etc.: see note   486 *huddles*: miserly old men
488 *snaphance*: flintlock on a musket (see note)   490 *course*: curse   496–7 *decimo
sexto ... folio*: see note   498 *currant*: in general circulation (see note)   500 *coystrels*: rogues
counterfeit: fraudulent   501 *dapper*: smart, 'sharp'   504 *slips*: spurious coins (see note)
505 *slipstring*: one fit for the gallows   508–9 *my hand on my halfepenie*: see note
512 *wagging*: chattering

have so maletted my wit that I am almost a
malcontent.

DRO: Why, what's the matter?

HALF: My master hath a fine scholer to his sonne,
Prisius a fayre lasse to his daughter.

DRO: Well?

HALF: They two love one another deadly.

RIS: In good time. 520

HALF: The fathers have put them up, utterly
disliking the match, and have appointed the one
shall have Memphio's sonne, the other Stellio's
daughter; this workes lyke wax, but how it will
fadge in the end, the hen that sits next the cocke
cannot tell.

RIS: If thou have but anie spice of knavery, we'le
make thee happie.

HALF: Tush! doubt not of mine, I am as full for my
pitch as you are for your's; a wren's egge is as ful 530
of meat as a goose eg, though there be not so much
in it: you shal find this head wel stuft, though there
went little stuffe to it.

DRO: *Laudo ingenium*, I lyke thy sconce; then harken:
Memphio made me of his counsell about marriage
of his sonne to Stellio's daughter; Stellio made
Risio acquainted to plot a match with Memphio's
sonne. To be short, they be both fooles.

HALF: But they are not fooles that bee short; if I
thought thou meantst so, *Senties qui vir sim*. Thou 540
shouldst have a crow to pull.

RI: Be not angrie, Halfepenie; for fellowship we will
be all fooles, and for gaine all knaves.

[HALFPENNY *laughs*.]

But why doest thou laugh?

514 *malcontent*: a discontented man 519 *deadly*: excessively 521 *put them up*: locked them
up 525 *fadge*: work out 534 *Laudo ingenium*: I praise your cleverness *sconce*: 'head' in
the sense of 'brains' 540 *Senties qui vir sim*: you shall learn what sort of a man I am
541 *a crow to pull*: dispute to sort out

HALF: At mine owne conceit and quicke censure.

RI: What's the matter?

HALF: Sodainly methought you two were asses, and
that the least asse was the more asse.

RI: Thou art a foole; that cannot be!

550 HALF: Yea, my yong master taught me to prove it by
learning, and so I can out of Ovid by a verse.

RI: Prethee how?

HALF: You must first, for fashion sake, confes
yourselves to be asses.

DRO: Well?

HALF: Then stand you here, and you there.

RE: Go to.

HALF: Then this is the verse as I point it: *Cum mala
per longas invaluere moras*. So you see the least asse is
560 the more asse!

RIS: Wee'le bite thee for an ape, if thou bob us lyke
asses! But to end all, if thou wilt joyne with us, we
will make a match betweene the two fooles, for
that must be our tasks; and thou shalt devise to
couple Candius and Livia, by over-reaching their
fathers.

HALF: Let me alone; *Non enim mea pigra juventus*,
there's matter in this noddle.

Enter LUCIO.

But looke where Prisius' boy comes, as fit as a
570 pudding for a dog's mouth.

[LUCIO:] Pop three knaves in a sheath, I'le make it a
right Tunbridge case, and be the bodkin.

RI: Nay, the bodkin is heere alreadie; you must be
the knife.

HALF: I am the bodkin; looke well to your eares, I
must boare them.

558–9 *Cum mala*, etc.: see note 561 *bite thee for an ape*: see note 565 *over-reaching*: getting
the better of 567 *Non enim mea*, etc.: for my youth is not lacking in resource (see note)
570 *pudding*: haggis-style food (see note) 572 *right*: proper *Tunbridge case*: see note
576 *boare*: bore (see note) 577 *Mew*: imprison (see note)

DRO: Mew thy tongue, or wee'le cut it out; this I
speake representing the person of a knife, as thou
didst that in shadow of a bodkin.

LUCIO: I must be gone: *Taedet*, it irketh; *Oportet*, it   *580*
behoveth: my wits worke like barme, alias yest,
alias sizing, alias rising, alias God's good.

HALF: The new wine is in thine head, yet was hee
faine to take this metaphor from ale – and now you
talke of ale, let us all to the wine.

DRO: Foure makes a messe, and wee have a messe of
masters that must be cosned: let us lay our heads
together; they are married and cannot.

HALF: Let us consult at the taverne, where, after to
the health of Memphio, drinke we to the life of   *590*
Stellio, I carouse to Prisius, and brinch you Mas
Sperantus; we shall cast [up] our accounts, and
discharge our stomackes, like men that can disgest
anything.

LU: I see not yet what you go about.

DRO: Lucio, that can pearce a mud wall of twentie
foot thicke, would make us beleeve he cannot see a
candle through a paper lanthorne; his knaverie is
beyond *Ela*, and yet he sayes he knowes not *Gam
ut*.   *600*

LU: I am readie: if anie cosnage be ripe, I'le shake
the tree.

HALF: Nay, I hope to see thee so strong, to shake
three trees at once.

DRO: Wee burne time, for I must give a reckning of
my daye's worke; let us close to the bush *ad
deliberandum*.

HALF: Indeede, *Inter pocula philosophandum*; it is good
to plea among pots.

580 *it irketh*: annoys me, 'I'm fed up'   581 *alias*: in other words   582 *sizing*: sizzling, yeast
God's good: another nickname for yeast   586 *messe*: a group eating together (see note)
591 *brinch*: drink to   *Mas*: Master   593 *disgest*: digest   599 *Ela ... Gam ut*: musical terms
(see note)   606 *close to the bush*: enter the tavern   606–7 *ad deliberandum*: in order to
consult   608 *Inter pocula*, etc.: see note

610 RI: Thine will be the worst; I feare we shall leave a
    halfepenie in hand.
  HALF: Why sayest thou that? Thou hast left a print
    deeper in thy hand alreadie than a halfepenie canne
    leave, unles it should sing worse than an hot yron.
  LU: All friendes, and so let us sing: 'tis a pleasant
    thing to goe into the taverne cleering the throate.

Song

OMNES: *Iô Bacchus!* To thy Table
            Thou call'st every drunken Rabble;
            We already are stiffe Drinkers,
620   Then seale us for thy jolly Skinckers.
  DRO: Wine, O Wine!
            O Juyce Divine!
            How do'st thou the Nowle refine!
  RIS: Plump thou mak'st men's Rubie faces,
            And from Girles canst fetch embraces.
  HALF: By thee our Noses swell,
            With sparkling Carbuncle:
  LUC: O the deare bloud of Grapes
            Turnes us to Anticke shapes,
630   Now to shew trickes like Apes,
  DRO: Now Lion-like to rore,
  RIS: Now Goatishly to whore,
  HALF: Now Hoggishly ith' mire,
  LUC: Now flinging Hats ith' fire.
  OMNES: *Iô Bacchus!* at Thy Table,
            Make us of thy Reeling Rabble.

Exeunt [into tavern.]

Act. 2.   Sce. 2.

Enter MEMPHIO alone.

MEM: I marvell I heare no newes of Dromio; either he
    slackes the matter, or betrayes his master. I dare

---

612 *thou hast left a print*, etc.: implying that Risio has been branded in the palm as a felon
617 *Iô Bacchus!*: hail to the god of wine!   620 *Skinckers*: drawers and servers of wine
623 *Nowle*: originally the 'noll' or head; 'drunkard'   629 *Anticke*: grotesque

not motion anie thing to Stellio, till I knowe what
my boy hath don. I'le hunt him out: if the   *640*
loitersacke be gone springing into a taverne, I'le
fetch him reeling out.   *Exit* [*into tavern*].
    Enter STELLIO *alone.*

STEL: Without doubt Risio hath gone beyond
himselfe, in casting beyond the moone; I feare the
boy be runne mad with studying, for I know hee
[loveth] me so well, that for my favour hee will
venture to runne out of his wits; and it may be, to
quicken his invention, hee is gone into this
ivy-bush, a notable neast for a grape owle. I'le
firret him out, yet in the end use him friendly: I   *650*
cannot be merrie till I heare what's done in the
marriages.   *Exit* [*into tavern*].
    Enter PRISIUS *alone.*

PRI: I thinke Lucio be gone a-squirelling, but I'le
squirell him for it: I sent him on my arrande, but I
must goe for an answere myselfe! I have tied up
the loving worme my daughter, and will see
whether fansie can worme fansie out of her head.
This green nosegaie I feare my boy hath smelt to,
for if he get but a penny in his purse, he turnes it
sodainly into *Argentum potabile*: I must search every   *660*
place for him, for I stand on thornes till I heare
what he hath done.   *Exit* [*into tavern*].
    Enter SPERANTUS *alone.*

SPE: Well, be as bee may is no banning; I thinke I
have charmde my yong master: a hungry meale,
a ragged coate, and a drie cudgell, have put him
quite beside his love and his logick to; besides, his
pigsnie is put up, and therefore now I'le let him
take the aire, and follow Stellio's daughter with all

---

639 *motion*: propose   641 *loitersacke*: idle rogue   649 *ivy-bush*: tavern   *neast*: nest
650 *firret*: ferret   654 *arrande*: errand   656 *worme*: 'poor thing'   658 *This green nosegaie*: the
bush hanging before the tavern   660 *Argentum potabile*: drinkable silver (see note)   663 *be
as bee may*, etc.: see note   666 *to*: too   667 *pigsnie*: darling (see note)

his learning, if he meane to be my heire. The boye
670 hath wit sance measure, more than needs; cats'
meat and dogs' meate inough for the vantage.
Well, without Halfepenie all my witte is not
woorth a dodkin: that mite is miching in this
grove, for as long as his name is Halfepenie, he will
be banquetting for thether Halfepenie.

Exit [*into tavern*],

Act. 2.   Sce. 3.

Candius.   Silena.

[*Enter* CANDIUS.]

CAND: He must needs goe that the devill drives! A
father? a fiend! that seekes to place affection by
appointment, and to force love by compulsion! I
have sworne to woo Sylena, but it shall be so
680 coldly, that she shall take as small delight in my
wordes, as I do contentment in his
commandement. I'le teach him one schoole tricke
in love!

Enter SILENA.

But behold, who is that that commeth out of
Stellio's house? it should seem to be Silena by
her attire! By her face I am sure it is she! Oh
faire face! oh lovely countenance! How now,
Candius, if thou begin to slip at beautie on a
sodaine, thou wilt surfet with carousing it at the
690 last! Remember that Livia is faithful; I, and let
thine eyes witnesse Silena is amiable! Heere
shall I please my father and myselfe; I wyll
learne to be obedient, and come what will, I'le
make a way; if shee seeme coy, I'le practise all

670 *sance*: sans, without   673 *dodkin*: a doit, small coin of small value   *miching*: playing
truant   674 *grove*: i.e. the ivy-bush   675 *thether*: the other   688 *slip at*: slip the leash at
689 *carousing*: toasting   690 *I*: aye

the arte of love, if I [find] her [coming], all the
pleasures of love.

SILE[NA:] My name is Silena, I care not who knowe
it, so I doo not: my father keeps me close, so he
does; and now I have stolne out, so I have, to goe
to olde Mother Bombie to know my fortune, so I   *700*
wil; for I have as fayre a face as ever trode on shoo
sole, and as free a foote as ever lookt with two eyes.

CAND [*aside*]: What? I thinke she is lunatike or
foolish! Thou art a foole, Candius; so faire a face
cannot bee the scabbard of a foolish minde! Mad
she may bee, for commonly in beautie so rare,
there fals passion's extreame. Love and beautie
disdaine a meane, not therefore because beautie is
no vertue, but because it is happines; and we
schollers know that vertue is not to be praised, but   *710*
honored. I wil put on my best grace. [*To* SILENA]
Sweete wench, thy face is lovely, thy bodie comely,
and all that the eyes can see inchanting! – You see
how, unacquainted, I am bold to boord you.

SIL: My father boordes mee alreadie; therefore I care
not if your name were Geoffrey.

CAND [*aside*]: Shee raves, or over-reaches. – I am one,
sweet soule, that loves you, brought hether by
reporte of your beautie, and here languisheth with
your rarenesse.   *720*

SIL: I thanke you that you would call.

CAND: I will alwaies call on such a saint that hath
power to release my sorrowes; yeeld, fayre creature,
to love.

SIL: I am none of that sect.

CAN: The loving sect is an auncient sect and an
honorable, and therefore [love] should bee in a
person so perfect.

---

695 *coming*: eager, forward, willing   707 *fals*: occurs   708 *a meane*: a middle course
714 *boord you*: make advances to you (taken in another sense by Silena)   716 *your name
were Geoffrey*: see note   717 *over-reaches*: is pulling a fast one   718 *hether*: hither

SIL: Much!

730 CAN: I love thee much; give mee one worde of comfort.

SIL: I' faith, sir, no! And so tell your master.

CAN: I have no master, but come to make choise of a mistress.

SI: Aha, are you there with your beares?

CAND [*aside*]: Doubtles she is an idiot of the newest cut. I'le once more trye hir. – I have loved thee long, Silena.

SI: In your tother hose.

740 CAND [*aside*]: Too simple to be naturall: too senslesse to be arteficiall. – You sayd you went to know your fortune: I am a scholler and am cunning in palmistry.

SIL: The better for you, sir; here's my hand. What's a clocke?

CAN: The line of life is good, Venus' mount very perfect; you shall have a scholler to your first husband.

SI: You are well seene in crane's durt, your father
750 was a poulter. Ha, ha, ha!

CAND: Why laugh you?

SIL: Because you should see my teeth.

CAND [*aside*]: Alas, poore wench, I see now also thy folly; a fayre foole is lyke a fresh weed, pleasing leaves and soure juyce. I will not yet leave her; shee may dissemble. – [*Aloud*] I cannot choose but love thee.

SIL: I had thought to aske you.

CAND: Nay then, farewell, either to proud to accept,
760 or too simple to understand.

SIL: You need not bee so crustie; you are not so hard backt.

---

735 *are you there with your beares?*: are you still on the same tack? (see note) 737 *cut*: style, fashion 741 *arteficiall*: artful 749 *well seene in*: an expert on *durt*: excrement 750 *poulter*: poulterer 762 *backt*: baked

CAND: Now I perceive thy folly, who hath rakt
together all the odde blinde phrases that helpe
them that knowe not howe to discourse, but when
they cannot aunswere wisely, eyther with gybing
cover theyr rudenesse, or by some newe-coyned
buy-worde bewraie theyr peevishnesse. I am glad
of this: nowe shall I have coulour to refuse the
match, and my father reason to accept of Livia: I   *770*
will home, and repeate to my father oure wise
incounter, and hee shall perceive there is nothing
so fulsome as a shee-foole.   *Exit.*

SIL: Good God, I thinke gentlemen had never lesse
wit in a yeere. Wee maides are madde wenches; we
gird them and flout them out of all scotch and
notch, and they cannot see it. I will knowe of the
olde woman whether I bee a maide or no, and
then, if I bee not, I must needes be a man. [*Knocks
at* MOTHER BOMBIE'S *door.*] God be heere!   *780*
    Enter MOTHER BOMBIE.

BOM[BIE:] Who'se there?

SIL: One that would be a maide.

BOM: If thou be not, it is impossible thou shuldst be,
and a shame thou art not.

SIL: They saie you are a witch.

BOMB: They lie; I am a cunning woman.

SIL: Then tell mee something.

BOMB: Holde up thy hande; [SILENA *holds it above her
head.*] not so high –
Thy father knowes thee not,   *790*
Thy mother bare thee not,
Falsely bred, truely begot:
Choise of two husbands, but never tyed in bandes,
Because of love and naturall bondes.

SILENA: I thanke you for nothing, because I

---

764 *blinde*: meaningless   768 *buy-worde*: by-word, pet phrase   *bewraie*: betray, reveal
769 *coulour*: colour, excuse   773 *fulsome*: cloying, loathsome   776 *gird*: mock   776–7 *scotch
and notch*: see note   778 *maide*: virgin   781 *Who'se*: who's   786 *cunning*: clever, skilful

understand nothing: though you bee as olde as you
are, yet am I as younge as I am, and because that
I am so fayre, therefore are you so fowle; and so
farewell frost, my fortune naught me cost.   *Ex*[*it.*]

800 BOM: Farewell, faire foole, little doest thou know thy
hard fortune, but in the end thou shalt, and that
must bewraie what none can discover: in the mean
season I wil professe cunning for all commers. *Exit.*

Act. 2.   Sce. 4.

Dromio.   Risio.   Lucio.   Halfepenie.
[*Enter* DROMIO, RISIO, LUCIO *and* HALFPENNY
from the tavern.]

DRO: Wє were all taken tardie.

RIS: Our masters will be overtaken if they tarry.

HALF: Now must everie one by wit make an excuse,
and everie excuse must bee coosnage.

LUC: Let us remember our complot.

DRO: We will all plod on that; oh, the wine hath
810   turnd my wit to vineger!

RI: You meane 'tis sharpe.

HALF: Sharpe? I'le warrant 'twill serve for as good
sauce to knaverie as –

LU: As what?

HALF: As thy knaverie meat for his wit.

DRO: We must all give a reckning for our daye's
travell.

RI: Tush! I am glad we scapt the reckning for our
liquor. If you be examined how we met, sweare by
820   chance; for so they met, and therefore will beleeve
it: if how much we drunke, let them answere
themselves; they know best because they paid it.

---

805 *overtaken*: overcome by drink   807 *coosnage*: deceitfulness   808 *complot*: combined
conspiracy   817 *travell*: travail, labour   818 *scapt*: escaped

HAL: We must not tarry; *abeundum est mihi*, I must go
and cast this matter in a corner.

DRO: *I prae, sequar*: a bowle and I'le come after with a
broome; everie one remember his que.

RIS: I, and his k, or else we shall thrive ill.

HALF: When shall we meete?

RI: Tomorrow, fresh and fasting.

DRO: Fast eating our meate, for we have drunke for   *830*
tomorow, and tomorow we must eat for today.

HALF: Away, away! If our masters take us here, the
matter is mard.

LU: Let us everie one to his taske.

    Exeunt.

        Act. 2.   Sce. 5.

   Memphio.   Stellio.   Prisius.   Sperantus.
[*Enter* MEMPHIO, STELLIO, PRISIUS, and
SPERANTUS *from the tavern.*]

MEM: How luckily we met on a sodaine in a taverne,
that drunke not together almost these thirtie
yeeres!

STEL: A taverne is the Randevous, the Exchange, the
staple for good fellowes: I have heard my
great-grandfather tell how his great-grandfather   *840*
shoulde saie, that it was an olde proverbe when his
greate-grandfather was a childe, that it was a good
winde that blew a man to the wine.

PRIS: The olde time was a good time! Ale was an
ancient drinke, and accounted of our ancestors
autentical; Gascone wine was liquor for a lord,
sack a medicine for the sicke; and I may tell you,
he that had a cup of red wine to his oysters, was
hoysted in the Queene's subsidie booke.

---

823 *abeundum est mihi*: I must go away 824 *cast this matter*: see note 825 *I prae, sequar*: go
ahead, I'll follow (see note) 826 *que*: cue 838 *Randevous*: rendezvous 846 *autentical*: the
genuine article, trustworthy 849 *hoysted*: elevated; see note

850   SPE: I, but now you see to what loosenes this age is
growen – our boies carouse sack like a double
beere, and saith that which doth an old man good
can do a yong man no harme: 'old men' (say
they) 'eat pap; why shoulde not children drinke
sacke? Their white heads have cosned time out of
mind our yong yeres.'

MEMPH: Well! the world is wanton since I knew it
first; our boyes put as much nowe in their bellies in
an houre, as would cloath theyr whole bodies in a

860   yeere. Wee have paide for their tipling eight
shillinges, and as I have hearde, it was as much as
bought Rufus, sometime king of this land, a paire
of hose.

PRI: Is't possible?

STEL: Nay, 'tis true; they saie ale is out of request,
'tis hogges' porredge, broth for beggers, a caudle
for cunstables, watchmen's mouth-glew; the better
it is, the more like bird lime it is, and never makes
one staid but in the stockes.

870   MEMPH: I'le teach my wag-halter to know grapes
from barley.

PRI: And I mine to discerne a spigot from a faucet.

SPE: And I mine to judge the difference between a
blacke boule and a silver goblet.

STEL: And mine shall learne the oddes betweene a
stand and a hogs-head – yet I cannot choose but
laugh to see how my wag aunswered mee, when I
stroke him for drinking sacke.

PRI: Why, what sayd he?

880   STEL: 'Master, it is the soveraigntest drinke in the
world, and the safest for all times and weathers; if
it thunder, though all the ale and beere in the
towne turne, it will be constant; if it lighten, and

---

850 *I*: aye   851 *carouse*: booze   854 *pap*: baby food   855 *cosned*: cheated, deceived
866 *caudle*: a warming drink (see note)   870 *wag-halter*: gallows-bird   872 *spigot* . . .
faucet: see note   876 *stand*: cask (see note)

that any fire come to it, it is the aptest wine to
burn, and the most wholesomest when it is burnt.
So much for summer. If it freeze, why, it is so hot
in operation that no ise can congeale it; if it rayne,
why, then he that cannot abide the heate of it may
put in water. So much for winter.' And so ranne
his way, but I'le overtake him.   *890*

SPE: Who woulde thinke that my
hoppe-on-my-thumbe, Halfpenie, scarse so high as
a pint pot, wold reason the matter? But hee
learnde his leere of my sonne, his young master,
whom I have brought up at Oxford, and I thinke
must learne heere in Kent at Ashford.

MEMPH: Why, what sayd he?

SPE: Hee boldly rapt it out: *Sine Cerere et Baccho friget
Venus*, without wine and sugar his veins wold waxe
colde.   *900*

MEMPH: They were all in a pleasant vaine! But I
must be gone, and take account of my boye's
businesse; farewell, neighbours, God knowes when
we shall meete again! – [*Aside*] Yet I have
discovered nothing: my wine hath been my wittes'
friende. I longe to heare what Dromio hath done!
                                                                   Exit.

STEL: I cannot staie, but this good fellowshippe shall
cost mee the setting-on at our next meeting. –
[*Aside*] I am gladde I blabd nothing of the
marriage; now I hope to compas it. I know my boy   *910*
hath bin bungling about it.   *Exit.*

PRIS: Let us all goe, for I must to my clothes that
hang on the tenters. – [*Aside*] My boy shall hang
with them, if hee aunswere mee not his daye's
worke!   *Exit.*

885 *burnt*: mulled 887 *ise*: ice 894 *leere*: lessons, learning 896 *learne*: teach (see note)
898–9 *Sine Cerere et Baccho friget Venus*: Venus grows cold without Ceres and Bacchus, i.e.
without food and drink love freezes up 905 *discovered*: let out 908 *setting-on*: standing
treat 909 *blabd*: revealed indiscreetly in talk 911 *bungling*: blundering 913 *tenters*:
frames for stretching cloth (see note)

SPE: If all bee gone, I'le not staie: Halfepenie I am
sure hath done mee a penniewoorth of good, else
I'le spend his bodie in buying a rod.   *Exit.*

Act. 3.   Sce. I.

Maestius.   Serena.
[*Enter* MAESTIUS *and* SERENA.]

MAEST[IUS:] Sweet sister, I know not how it

920   commeth to passe, but I finde in myselfe passions
more than brotherly.

SER[ENA:] And I, deare brother, finde my thoughts
intangled with affections beyonde nature, which so
flame into my distempered head, that I can neither
without danger smother the fire, nor without
modestie disclose my furie.

MAEST: Our parents are pore, our love unnaturall:
what can then happen to make us happie?

SER: Onely to be content with our father's mean

930   estate, to combat against our own intemperate
desires, and yeld to the succes of fortune, who,
though she hath framd us miserable, cannot make
us monstrous.

MAEST: It is good counsel, faire sister, if the
necessitie of love could be releeved by counsell. Yet
this is our comfort, that these unnaturall heates
have stretched themselves no further than
thoughts. Unhappie me, that they should stretch
so!

940   SER: That which nature warranteth, laws forbid.
Straunge it seemeth in sense, that because thou art
mine, therefore thou must not be mine.

MAEST: So it is, Serena; the neerer we are in bloud,
the further wee must be from love; and the greater
the kindred is, the lesse the kindnes must be; so
that between brothers and sisters superstition hath

---

918 *his bodie*: i.e. a halfpenny 924 *distempered*: disturbed, troubled 926 *modestie*: shame,
confusion 931 *succes*: upshot, outcome 933 *monstrous*: abnormal, unnatural

made affection cold; between strangers custome
hath bred love exquisite.

SER: They say there is hard by an old cunning
woman, who can tell fortunes, expound dreames,   *950*
tell of things that be lost, and devine of accidents
to come: she is called the good woman, who yet
never did hurt.

MAEST: Nor anie good, I thinke, Serena; yet to
satisfie thy minde we will see what she can saie.

SER: Good brother, let us.

    [MAESTIUS *knocks at* MOTHER BOMBIE'S *door.*]

MAEST: Who is within?

    Enter MOTHER BOMBIE.

BOM: The dame of the house!

MAEST [*aside*]: She might have said the beldam, for
her face, and yeeres, and attire.   *960*

SER: Good mother, tell us, if by your cunning you
can, what shall become of my brother and me.

BOM: Let me see your hands, and looke on me
stedfastly with your eyes:

You shall be married tomorow, hand in hand,
By the lawes of good Nature, and the land;
Your parents shall be glad, and give you their
   lande,
You shal each of you displace a foole,
And both together must releeve a foole.:
If this be not true, call me olde foole.   *970*

MAEST: This is my sister; marrie we cannot: our
parents are poore and have no land to give us:
each of us is a foole to come for counsell to such an
olde foole.

SER [*to* MAESTIUS]: These doggrell rimes and
obscure words, comming out of the mouth of such
a weather-beaten witch, are thought divinations of

---

949 *cunning*: skilful, knowledgeable   959 *beldam*: witch, hag

329

some holy spirite, being but dreames of decayed
braines: [*To* BOMBIE] for mine owne parte, I
980 would thou mightest sit on that stoole, till he and I
marrie by lawe!

BOM: I saie Mother Bombie never speakes but once,
and yet never spake untruth once.

SER: Come, brother, let us to our poore home; this is
our comfort, to bewraie our passions, since we
cannot injoy our love.

MAEST: Content, sweet sister; and learne of me
hereafter, that these old sawes of such olde hags
are but false fires to leade one out of a plaine path
990 into a deepe pit.

Exeunt.

Act. 3   Sce. 2.

Dromio.   Risio.   Halfepenie.   Lucio.
[*Enter* DROMIO *and* RISIO *from different directions.*]

DRO: *Ingenium quondam fuerat pretiosius auro*: the time
was wherein wit would work like waxe, and crock
up golde like honnie.

RI: *At nunc barbaries grandis habere nihil*, but nowe wit
and honestie buy nothing in the market.

DRO: What, Risio! How spedst thou after thy
potting?

RI: Nay, my master rong all [out] in the taverne, and
thrust all out in the house. But how spedst thou?

1000 DRO: I? It were a daye's worke to discourse it: he
spake nothing but sentences, but they were
vengible long ones, for when one word was out,
hee made pause of a quarter long till he spake
another.

985 *bewraie*: expose, reveal (see note)   988 *sawes*: sayings   991 *Ingenium*, etc.: wit was
once more precious than gold (see note)   994 *At nunc*, etc.: but now to have nothing is
the highest form of barbarity   998 *rong all out*: ? found out all   999 *thrust all out*: ? let
loose; let me have it   1002 *vengible*: extraordinarily, awful   1003 *a quarter long*: lasting a
quarter of an hour

RI: Why, what did he in all that time?

DRO: Breake interjections lyke winde, as 'eho!' 'ho!'
   'to!'

RI: And what thou?

DRO: Aunswere him in his owne language, as '*evax!*'
   '*vah!*' '*hui!*'   *1010*

RI: These were conjunctions rather than
   interjections. But what of the plot?

DRO: As we concluded, I tolde him, that I
   understood that Silena was verie wise, and could
   sing exceedingly; that my devise was, seeing
   Accius his sonne a proper youth, and could also
   sing sweetly, that he should come in the nicke
   when she was singing, and answere her.

RI: Excellent!

DRO: Then hee asked how it should be devised that   *1020*
   she might come abroade: I tolde [him] that was
   cast alreadie by my meanes: then the song beeing
   ended, and they seeing one another, noting the
   apparell, and marking the personages, he should
   call in his sonne for feare he should over-reach his
   speech.

RI: Very good.

DRO: Then that I had gotten a young gentleman,
   that resembled his sonne in yeeres and favour, that
   having Accius' apparell should court Silena;   *1030*
   whome shee, finding wise, would after that by
   small intreatie be won without mo wordes; and so
   the marriage clapt up by this cosnage, and his
   sonne never speake word for himselfe.

RI: Thou boy! so have I done in everie point, for the
   song, the calling her in, and the hoping that
   another shall woo Accius, and his daughter wed
   him. I told him this wooing should be tonight, and
   they early marryed in the morning, without anie
   wordes, saving to saie after the Priest.   *1040*

1009 '*evax!*', etc.: Latin ejaculations (see note)   1015 *exceedingly*: surpassing others

DRO: All this fodges well! now if Halfpenie and Lucio
have playde theyr partes, wee shall have excellent
sporte – and here they come.
Enter HALFPENIE [*and*] LUCIO.
Howe wrought the wine, my lads?

HALF: How? like wine, for my bodie, being the
rundlet, and my mouth the vent, it wrought two
daies over, till I had thought the hoopes of my
head woulde have flowen asunder.

LU: The best was, our masters were as well whitled
1050   as we, for yet they lie by it.

RI: The better for us! We dyd but a little parboile our
livers, they have sod theyrs in sacke these fortie
yeeres.

HAL: That makes them spit white broth as they doo.
But to the purpose. Candius and Livia will send
their attires; you must send the apparell of Accius
and Silena: they wonder wherefore, but commit
the matter to our quadrapertit wit.

LUC: If you keepe promise to marrie them by your
1060   device, and their parents consent, you shall have
tenne pounds apeece for your paines.

DRO: If wee doo it not, wee are undone for we have
broacht a cosnage alreadie, and my master hath
the tap in his hand, that it must needs runne out!
Let them be ruld, and bring hether their apparell,
and we wil determine; the rest commit to our
intricate considerations: depart!
Exeunt HALFPENIE [*and*] LUCIO. *Enter* ACCIUS
and SILENA [*separately.*]

DRO: Here comes Accius tuning his pipes; I perceive
my master keepes touch.

1041 *fodges*: comes off   1046 *rundlet*: runlet, a small cask   *wrought two daies over*: ?
fermented (see note)   1049 *whitled*: intoxicated   1050 *lie by it*: laid up as a result
1051 *parboile*: half boil   1052 *sod*: soaked   1054 *white broth*: phlegm   1057 *they*: i.e.
Candius and Livia   1058 *quadrapertit*: composed of four parts   1063 *broacht a cosnage*:
embarked on a piece of deception   1069 *keepes touch*: maintains the agreement

RI: And here comes Silena with her wit of proofe!   1070
    Marie, it will scarse holde out question shot! Let
    us in to instruct our masters in the que.
DRO: Come, let us be jogging: but wer't not a world
    to heare them woe one another?
RI: That shall be hereafter to make us sport, but our
    masters shall never know it.
    Exeunt.

Act. 3.   Sce. 3.

[ACCIUS *and* SILENA] *singing*
    Song
SIL: O Cupid! Monarch over Kings,
                    Wherefore hast thou feete and wings?
                    It is to shew how swift thou art,
                    When thou wound'st a tender heart: 1080
                Thy wings being clip'd, and feete held still,
                    Thy Bow so many could not kill.
ACC[IUS:]   It is all one in Venus' wanton schoole,
                Who highest sits, the wise man or the foole:
                        Fooles in love's colledge
                        Have farre more knowledge,
                    To reade a woman over,
                    Than a neate prating lover:
[? TOGETHER:]   Nay, 'tis confest,
                    That fooles please women best.   1090
    [*Enter*] MEMPHIO *and* STELLIO.
MEM: Accius, come in, and that quickly! what!
    walking without leave?
STEL: Silena, I praie you looke homeward, it is a
    colde aire, and you want your mufler.
    Exeunt ACCIUS *and* SILENA.
MEM [*aside*]: This is pat! if the rest proceed, Stellio is
    like to marrie his daughter to a foole; but a bargen
    is a bargen!

1070 *of proofe*: proven, tested   1072 *que*: cue   1073 *a world*: a marvellous experience
1074 *woe*: woo   1088 *neate*: smart

333

STEL [*aside*]: This frames to my wish! Memphio is like
to marrie a foole to his sonne; Accius' tongue shall
1100   tie all Memphio's land to Silena's dowrie, let his
father's teeth undoo them if he can – but heere I
see Memphio. I must seeme kind, for in kindnes
lies cosnage.

ME [*aside*]: Wel, here is Stellio; I'le talke of other
matters, and flie from the marke I shoot at,
lapwing-like flying far from the place where I
nestle. [*Aloud*] Stellio, what make you abroad? I
heard you were sicke since our last drinking.

STEL: You see reports are no truths: I heard the like
1110   of you, and we are both well. I perceive sober men
tel most lies, for *in vino veritas*. If they had drunke
wine, they would have tolde the truth.

MEM: Our boies will be sure then never to lie, for they
are ever swilling of wine – but, Stellio, I must
straine cursie with you; I have busines, I cannot
stay.

STEL: In good time, Memphio! for I was about to
crave your patience to departe; it stands me
uppon. – [*Aside*] Perhaps [I may] move his
1120   patience ere it be long.

MEM [*aside*]: Good silly Stellio, we must buckle
shortly.

     Exeunt.

Act. 3.   Sce. 4.

Halfepenie.   Lucio.   Rixula.
     Dromio.   Risio.

[*Enter* LUCIO, HALFPENNY *with clothes belonging to*
CANDIUS, *and* RIXULA *carrying clothes belonging to*
LIVIA.]

1111 *in vino veritas*: there is truth in wine, i.e. the truth emerges when people are drinking
1115 *straine cursie*: treat you with too little respect   1121 *silly*: foolish, simple   *buckle*:
encounter one another

LU: Come, Rixula, wee have made thee privie to the
whole packe; there laie downe the packe.

RIX[ULA:] I beleeve unlesse it be better handled, wee
shall out of doores.

HALF: I care not; *Omne solum forti patria*, I can live in
Christendom as well as in Kent.

LU: And I'le sing *Patria ubicunque bene*; everie house is
my home, where I may stanch hunger.   *1130*

RIX: Nay, if you set all on hazard, though I be a pore
wench I am as hardie as you both; I cannot speake
Latine, but in plaine English, if aniething fall out
crosse, I'le runne away.

HALF: He loves thee well that would runne after.

RIX: Why, Halfpenie, there's no goose so gray in the
lake, that cannot finde a gander for her make.

LU: I love a nutbrowne lasse; 'tis good to recreate.

HALF: Thou meanest a browne nut is good to crack.

LU: Why, wold it not do thee good to crack such a nut?   *1140*

HAL: I feare she is worm-eaten within, she is so
moth-eaten without.

RIX: If you take your pleasure of mee, I'le in and tell
your practises against your masters.

HALF: In faith, soure heart, hee that takes his pleasure
on thee is verie pleasurable.

RIX: You meane knavishly, and yet I hope foule water
will quench hot fire as soone as fayre.

HALF: Well then, let fayre wordes coole that cholar,
which foule speeches hath kindled; and because we   *1150*
are all in this case, and hope all to have good
fortune, sing a roundelay, and wee'le helpe, – such
as thou wast woont when thou [beatedst] hempe.

1124 *packe*: plot   *packe*: ? bundle   1126 *out of doores*: turned out, given the sack
1127 *Omnem solum*, etc.: to the brave man every land is his own country (see note)
1129 *Patria ubicunque*, etc.: wherever good is, is my native land   1130 *stanch*: staunch,
satisfy   1134 *crosse*: amiss   1138 *recreate*: refresh or amuse oneself   1143 *take your
pleasure*: laugh at, mock   1145 *takes his pleasure*: i.e. sexually   1146 *pleasurable*: ? easily
pleased (see note)   1149 *cholar*: anger

LU: It was crabbs she stampt, and stole away one to make her a face.

RIX: I agree, in hope that the hempe shall come to your wearing: a halfepenie halter may hang you both, that is, Halfepeny and you may hang in a halter.

1160 HALF: Well brought about!

RIX: 'Twill when 'tis about your necke.

LUCIO: Nay, now shee's in she will never out.

RIX: Nor when your heads are in, as it is lykely, they should not come out. But harken to my song.

    Cantant.

Song

RIX:
          Full hard I did sweate,
          When hempe I did beate,
    Then thought I of nothing but hanging;
          The hempe being spun,
          My beating was done;
1170   Then I wish'd for a noyse
          Of crack-halter Boyes,
   On those hempen strings to be twanging!
          Long lookt I about,
          The City throughout, –

[THE PAGES:]   And fownd no such fidling varlets.

RIX: Yes, at last comming hither,
          I saw foure together.

[THE PAGES:]May thy hempe choake such singing
          harlots!

RIX: 'To-whit to-whoo' the Owle does cry;
1180   'Phip, phip', the sparrowes as they fly;
         The goose does hisse; the duck cries 'Quack';
         'A Rope' the Parrot that holds tack;

[THE PAGES]:The parrat and the rope be thine:

RIX: The hanging yours, but the hempe mine.

1170 *noyse*: company of musicians, band   1171 *crack-halter*: gallows-bird, rogue-like
1175 *fidling*: fiddle-playing (see note)   1182 *holds tack*: holds its own

Enter DROMIO, [*carrying* ACCIUS' *clothes and*]
RISIO [*carrying* SILENA'S *clothes*].

DR: Yonder stands the wags; I am come in good time.

RI: All here before me! You make hast.

RIX: I beleeve, to hanging; for I thinke you have all
    robd your masters: here's every man his baggage!

HAL: That is, we are all with thee, for thou art a verie
    baggage!   *1190*

RIX: Hold thy peace, or of mine honesty I'le buy an
    halfpenie purse with thee!

DRO: Indeed, that's big inough to put thy honesty in!
    But come, shall we go about the matter?

LU: Now it is come to the pinch my heart pants.

HALF: I for my part am resolute, *in utrumque paratus*,
    redie to die or to runne away.

LU: But heare me! I was troubled with a vile dream,
    and therefore it is little time spent to let Mother
    Bomby expound it: she is cunning in all things.   *1200*

DRO: Then will I know my fortune.

RIX: And I'le ask for a silver spoone which was lost
    last daie, which I must pay for.

RI: And I'le know what wil become of our devices.

HALF: And I!

DRO: Then let us all go quickly; we must not sleep in
    this busines, our masters are so watchfull about it.

    [*They knock at* MOTHER BOMBIE'S *door. Enter*
    MOTHER BOMBIE.]

BOM: Why do you rap so hard at the doore?

DRO: Because we would come in.

BOMB: Nay, my house is no inne.   *1210*

HALF [*aside*]: Crosse your selves, looke how she lookes!

DRO [*aside*]: Marke her not; shee'le turne us all to
    apes!

BOM: What would you with me?

RI: They say you are cunning, and are called the good
    woman of Rochester.

1196 *in utrumque paratus*: prepared to go in either direction   1200 *cunning*: skilled, learned
1203 *last daie*: yesterday

BOM: If never to doo harme be to doo good, I dare
saie I am not ill. But what's the matter?

LU: I had an ill dream, and desire to know the
1220   signification.

BOM: Dreames, my sonne, have their weight; though
they be of a troubled minde, yet are they signes of
fortune. Say on.

LU: In the dawning of the day – for about that time by
my starting out of my sleepe, I found it to bee –
meethought I sawe a stately peece of beefe, with a
cape-cloke of cabidge, imbrodered with pepper;
having two honorable pages with hats of mustard
on their heades; himselfe in greate pompe sitting
1230   uppon a cushion of white brewish, linde with
browne breade; methought being poudred he was
much trobled with the salt rume; and therfore there
stood by him two great flagons of sacke and beere,
the one to drie up his rume, the other to quench his
cholar. I as one envying his ambition, hungring and
thirsting after his honor, began to pull his cushion
from under him, hoping by that means to give him
a fall; and with putting out my hand awakt, and
found nothing in all this dreame about me but the
1240   salt rume.

DRO: A dreame for a butcher!

LU: Soft, let me end it! – then I slumbred againe, and
methought there came in a leg of mutton.

DRO: What! all grosse meat? A racke had bene daintie.

LU: Thou foole! how could it come in, unlesse it had
bin a leg? Methought his hose were cut and drawen
out with parsly; I thrust my hand into my pocket
for a knife, thinking to hoxe him, and so awakt.

BOMB: Belyke thou wentst supperlesse to bed.

1227 *cape-cloke*: cloak with a cape attached   1230 *brewish*: bread soaked in broth
1231 *poudred*: salted   1232 *rume*: a cold   1244 *grosse meat*: flesh of large animals   *racke*: a
neck or fore-part of the spine, cut from pork or mutton   1246–7 *drawen out*: extended in
length   1248 *hoxe*: hamstring, cut off the knuckle

338

LU: So I doo everie night but Sundaies: Prisius hath a   *1250*
    weake stomacke, and therefore we must starve.

BOM: Well, take this for answere, though the dream be
    fantasticall –

    · They that in the morning-sleep dream of eating,
       Are in danger of sicknesse, or of beating,
       Or shall heare of a wedding fresh a-beating.

LU: This may be true.

HALF: Nay then, let me come in with a dreame, short
    but sweet, that my mouth waters ever since I wakt.
    Methought there sate upon a shelfe three damaske   *1260*
    prunes in velvet caps and prest satten gownes like
    judges; and that there were a whole handfull of
    curants to be araigned of a riot, because they
    clunged together in such clusters; twelve raisons of
    the sunne were impannelled in a Jewry, and, as a
    leafe of whole mase, which was bailief, was carrying
    the quest to consult, methoght ther came an angrie
    cooke, and gelded the Jewry of theyr̄ stones, and
    swept both judges, jurers, rebels, and bailiefe into a
    porredge pot; whereat I beeing melancholy, fetcht a   *1270*
    deepe sigh, that wakt myselfe and my bed-fellow.

DRO: This was devisd, not dreamt; and the more
    foolish being no dreame, for that dreames excuse
    the fantasticalnesse.

HALF: Then aske my bed-felow, you know him, who
    dremt that night that the King of Diamonds was
    sicke?

BOM: But thy yeeres and humours, pretie child, are
    subject to such fansies, which, the more unsensible
    they seeme, the more fantasticall they are; therefore   *1280*
    this dream is easie:

1256 *a-beating*: being hammered out   1260–61 *damaske prunes*: damsons   *prest*: glazed
1264 *clunged*: clung, stuck   *raisons of the sunne*: sun-dried grapes   1265 *Jewry*: jury
1266 *mase*: mace   1267 *quest*: inquest   1268 *stones*: a pun on 'stones' = testicles

      To children, this is given from the Gods
      To dream of milke, fruit, babies, and rods;
      They betoken nothing, but that wantons must
        have rods.

DRO: Ten to one thy dreame is true; thou wilt bee
swinged!

RIX: Nay, Gammer, I pray you tell me who stole my
spoone out of the buttrie?

BOM: Thy spoone is not stolne but mislaide;
1290   Thou art an ill huswife, though a good maid;
       Looke for thy spoon where thou hadst like to be
        no maide.

RIX: Bodie of me, let me fetch the spoone! I remember
the place!

LU: Soft, swift; the place, if it be there now, it will bee
there tomorrowe.

RIX: I, but perchance the spoone will not!

HALF: Wert thou once put to it?

RIX: No, sir boy, it was put to me!
    [*Exit* RIXULA.]

LU: How was it mist?

1300 DRO: I'le warrant for want of a mist. But what's my
fortune, mother?

BOM: Thy father doth live because he doth die;
       Thou has spent all thy thrift with a die,
       And so lyke a begger thou shalt die.

RI: I woulde have likte well if all the gerundes had
beene there: *di, do*, and *dum*; but all in 'die', that's
too deadly.

DRO: My father indeed is a diar, and I have ben a
dicer, but to die a beggar, give mee leave not to
1310 beleeve Mother Bombie; and yet it may bee. I have
nothing to live by but knavery, and if the world

1286 *swinged*: beaten   1291 *maide*: virgin   1297 *put to it*: in danger of seduction
1299 *mist*: missed   1302 *die*: dye   1303 *die*: dice   1308 *diar*: dyer

grow honest, welcome beggerie! But what hast thou
to say, Risio?

RI: Nothing, till I see whether all this bee true that she
hath sayd.

HALF [*to* DROMIO]: I, Risio would faine see thee beg.

RI: Nay, mother, tell us this: what is all our fortunes?
We are about a matter of legerdemaine; howe will it
fodge?

BOM: You shall all thrive like coosners,   *1320*
        That is, to bee cosned by coosners:
        All shall ende well, and you bee found
           coosners.

DRO: Gramercie, Mother Bombie! We are all pleasd,
if you were, for your paines.
    [*Offers her money.*]

BOM: I take no monie, but good wordes. Raile not, if I
tell true; if I doe not, revenge. Farewell.
    BOM[bie.]   *Exit*

DRO: Now have we nothing to doe but to go about this
busines. Accius' apparell let Candius put on; and I
wyll aray Accius with Candius' clothes.

RI: Heere is Silena's attire; Lucio, put it upon Livia, *1330*
and give me Livia's for Silena: this done, let
Candius and Livia come foorth, and let Dromio and
mee alone for the rest.

HALF: What shall become of Accius and Silena?

DRO: Tush! theyr turne shall bee next, all must bee
done orderly: let's to it, for nowe it workes.   *Exeunt.*

Act. 4.   *Sce. I.*

Candius.   *Livia.*   *Dromio.*   *Risio.*
        Sperantus.   *Prisius.*
[*Enter* CANDIUS *dressed in* ACCIUS' *clothes and*
LIVIA *dressed in* SILENA'S *clothes.*]

1319 *fodge*: succeed, work out   1322 *and*: if

LIV: This attyre is verie fit. But how if this make me a foole, and Silena wise? you will then woo mee, and wedde her.

1340 CAND: Thou knowest that Accius is also a foole, and his raiment fits me: so that if apparell be infectious, I am also lyke to be a foole, and hee [wise]; what would be the conclusion, I mervaile!

    Enter DROMIO, [*and*] RISIO.

LI: Here comes our counsellers.

DRO: Well sayd; I perceive turtles flie in couples.

RI: Else how should they couple?

LIV: So do knaves go double, else how should they be so cunning in doubling?

CAND: *Bona verba*, Livia.

1350 DRO: I understand Latine: that is, Livia is a good worde.

CAN: No, I byd her use good wordes!

RI: And what deeds?

CAN: None but a deed of gift.

RI: What gift?

CAN: Her heart.

DRO: Give me leave to pose you, though you bee a graduate; for I tell you we in Rochester spurre so many hackneys that we must needs spurre

1360 schollers, for wee take them for hackneys.

LIV: Why so, sir boy?

DRO: Because I knew two hired for ten grotes apece to saie service on Sunday, and that's no more than a post horse from hence to Canterbury.

RI: Hee knowes what hee sayes, for hee once served the post-master.

CAND: Indeed I thinke hee served some poast to his master, but come, Dromio, *post me.*

1345 *turtles*: doves   1348 *doubling*: cheating   1354 *a deed of gift*: a document effecting a gift   1357 *pose*: propose a question to   1359 *hackneys*: horses hired for riding   *spurre*: question, interrogate   1367 *poast*: ? posset (see note)   1368 *post me*: after me

DRO: You saie you would have her heart for a deed?

CAN: Well?   *1370*

DRO: If you take her hart for *cor*, that heart in her
    bodie, then know this: *Molle eius levibus, cor enim*
    violabile telis: a woman's heart is thrust through with
    a feather. If you meane she should give a heart
    named *Cervus*, then are you worse, for *cornua cervus*
    habet, that is to have one's heart growe out at his
    head, which wyll make one ake at the heart in their
    bodie.

    Enter PRISIUS [*and*] SPERANTUS.

LIV: I, beshrew your hearts, I heare one comming: I
    know it is my father by his [coughing.]   *1380*

CAND: What must we doo?

DRO: Why, as I tolde you; and let me alone with the
    olde men: fall you to your bridall.

PRI: Come, neighbor, I perceive the love of our
    children waxeth key colde.

SPE: I thinke it was never but lukewarme.

PRI: Bavins will have their flashes, and youth their
    fansies; the one as soone quenched as the other
    burnt – But who be these?

CAND: Here I do plight my faith, taking thee for the   *1390*
    staffe of my age, and of my youth my solace.

LIV: And I vow to thee affection which nothing can
    dissolve, neither the length of time, nor mallice of
    fortune, nor distance of place.

CAND: But when shall we be married?

LIV: A good question, for that one delay in wedding
    brings an hundred dangers in the church: we will
    not be askt, and a licence is to chargeable, and to
    tarrie til tomorrow too tedious.

DRO [*aside*]: There's a girle stands on pricks till she be   *1400*
    married!

1372–3 *Molle eius*, etc.: see note   1375 *Cervus*: the hart   *cornua cervus habet*: the hart has
horns (see note)   1398 *to*: too   1400 *stands on pricks*: 'who's on tenterhooks'

CAND: To avoid danger, charge, and tediousnesse, let us now conclude it in the next church.

LIV: Agreed!

PRI: What be these that hasten so to marrie?

DRO: Marrie, sir, Accius, sonne to Memphio, and Silena, Stellio's daughter.

SPE: I am sorrie, neighbour, for our purposes are disappointed.

1410 PRI: You see marriage is destinie; made in heaven, though consumated on earth.

RI: How like you them? Be they not a pretie couple?

PRI: Yes: God give them joye, seeing in spite of our hearts they must joyne.

DRO: I am sure you are not angrie, seeing things past cannot be recald; and being witnesses to their contract, will be also welwillers to the match.

SPE: For my part I wish them well.

PRI: And I; and since there is no remedie, I am glad of

1420 it.

RI: But will you never heereafter take it in dugeon, but use them as well as though yourselves had made the marriage?

PRI: Not I.

SPE: Nor I.

DRO [to CANDIUS]: Sir, here's two old men are glad that your loves, so long continued, is so happily concluded.

CAND: Wee thanke them; and if they will come to

1430 Memphio's house, they shall take parte of a bad dinner. [Aside] This cottons, and workes like waxe in a sowe's eare!

Exeunt CANDIUS [and] LIVIA.

PRI: Well, seeing our purposes are prevented, wee must lay other plots, for Livia shall not have Candius.

1421 dugeon: resentment, vexation   1431 cottons: succeeds

SPE: Feare not, for I have sworne that Candius shall
not have Livia. But let not us fall out because our
children fall in.

PRI: Wilt thou goe soone to Memphio's house?

SPE: I, and if you will, let us; that we may see how the   *1440*
young couple bride it, and so we may teach our
owne.

> *Exeunt.*

Act. 4.   Sce. 2.

Accius.   Silena.   Lucio.   Halfepenie.
[*Enter* LUCIO *and* HALFPENNY.]

[LUCIO:] By this time I am sure the wagges have
playde their parts; there rests nothing now for us
but to match Accius and Silena.

HALF: It was too good to be true, for we should laugh
heartily, and without laughing my spleene would
split; but whist! here comes the man.

> *Enter* ACCIUS [*dressed as* CANDIUS.]

And yonder the maide: let us stand aside.

> *Enter* SILENA [*dressed as* LIVIA.]

ACC: What meanes my father to thrust mee forth in   *1450*
another boye's coate? I'le warrant 'tis to as much
purpose as a hem in the forehead.

HALF: [*aside*]: There was an auncient proverbe
knockt in the head!

ACC: I am almost come into mine nonage, and yet I
never was so farre as the proverbes of this citie.

[LUCIO] [*aside*]: There's a quip for the suburbes of
Rochester!

HALF [*aside*]: Excellently applyed.

SIL: Well, though this furniture make mee a sullen   *1460*
dame, yet I hope in mine owne I am no saint.

HALF [*aside*]: A brave fight is lyke to bee betweene a

1438 *fall in*: agree, get on 1452 *hem*: see note 1455 *nonage*: minority 1456 *farre*: off
course 1460 *furniture*: attire

345

cocke with a long combe, and a hen with a long
leg.

[LUCIO] [*aside*]: Nay, her wits are shorter than her
legs.

HALF [*aside*]: And his combe longer than his wit.

ACC: I have yonder uncovered a faire girle: I'le be so
bolde as spurre her. [*To* SILENA] What might a
1470   bodie call her name?

SIL: I cannot help you at this time, I praie you come
againe tomorrow.

HALF [*aside*]: I, marie, sir!

ACC: You neede not bee so lustye, you are not so
honest.

SILENA: I crie you mercy, I tooke you for a joynd
stoole.

[LUCIO] [*aside*]: Heere's courting for a conduit or a
bakehouse!

1480   SIL: But what are you for a man? methinks you loke
as pleaseth God.

ACC: What, doo you give me the boots?

HALF [*aside*]: Whether will they? here be right
coblers' cuts!

ACC: I am taken with a fit of love: have you anye
minde of marriage?

SIL: I had thought to have askt you.

ACC: Upon what acquaintance?

SIL: Who would have thought it?

1490   ACC: Much in my gascoins, more in my round hose;
all my fathers are as white as daisies, as an egge
full of meate.

SIL: And all my father's plate is made of crimosin
velvet.

ACC: That's brave with bread!

1469 *spurre*: question   1474 *lustye*: insolent, arrogant   1476–7 *joynd stoole*: joint-stool (i.e.
made of separate parts)   1478 *conduit*: stand-pipe, fountain (see note)   1482 *give me the
boots*: make fun of me (see note)   1483 *Whether*: whither   1484 *coblers' cuts*: see note
1490 *gascoins*: gaskins, wide breeches   *round hose*: tight stockings of thick thread
1493 *crimosin*: crimson

HALFEPENIE [*aside*]: These two had wise men to
   theyr fathers.

[LUCIO] [*aside*]: Why?

HALF [*aside*]: Because when their bodies were at
   worke about houshold stuffe, their minds were   *1500*
   busied about commonwealth matters.

ACC: This is pure lawne: what call you this, a pretie
   face to your haire?

SIL: Wisely you have pickt a raison out of a fraile of
   figges.

AC: Take it as you list, you are in your owne clothes.

SIL: Saving a' reverence, that's a lie! My clothes are
   better; my father borrowed these.

ACC: Long may hee so doe. I could tell that these are
   not mine, if I would blab it lyke a woman.   *1510*

SI: I had as liefe you should tell them it snowd.

LU [*aside*]: Come, let us take them off, for we have
   had the creame of them.

HALF [*aside*]: I'le warrant if this bee the creame, the
   milke is verie flat! Let us joyne issue with them.

LU [*aside*]: To have such issue of our bodies is worse
   than have an issue in the bodie. [*To* SILENA] God
   save you, pretty mouse.

SIL: You may command and go without.

HALF [*to* LUCIO]: There's a glieke for you, let me   *1520*
   have my girde. [*To* SILENA] On thy conscience tell
   me, what 'tis a clocke?

SIL: I cry you mercie, I have kild your cushion.

HALF [*to* LUCIO]: I am paid and stroke dead in the
   neast. [*To* SILENA] I am sure this soft youth who is
   not halfe so wise as you are faire, nor you
   altogether so faire as he is foolish, will not be so
   captious.

ACC: Your eloquence passes my recognoscence.

1502 *lawne*: fine linen   1504 *fraile*: rush-basket   1507 *a' reverence*: your reverence
1510 *blab*: blurt out   1511 *liefe*: dearly   1515 *flat*: sour   1517 *issue*: discharge
1520 *glieke*: jest   1521 *girde*: gibe   1529 *recognoscence*: recognition

Enter MEMPHIO [*and*] STELLIO [*separately, unseen by the other, at the rear of the stage*].

1530 LU: I never heard that before, but shal we two make a match betweene you?

SI: I'le know first who was his father.

AC: My father? What need you to care? I hope he was none of your's!

HALF [*to* LUCIO]: A hard question, for it is oddes but one begate them both; hee that cut out the upper leather, cut out the inner, and so with one awl sticht two soles together.

[STEL *aside to* LUCIO]: What is she?

1540 [LUC *aside*]: 'Tis Prisius' daughter.

[STEL *aside*]: In good time: it fodges.

[MEMP *aside to* HALFPENNY]: What is he?

[HALF *aside*]: Sperantus' sonne.

[MEMP *aside*]: So: 'twill cotton.

ACC: Damsel, I pray you how olde are you?

MEM [*aside*]: My sonne would scarce have askt such a foolish question.

SIL: I shall be eighteene next beare-baiting.

STEL [*aside*]: My daughter woulde have made a wiser

1550 aunswere.

HALF [*to* LUCIO]: O how fitly this comes off!

ACC: My father is a scolde, what's yours?

MEMP: My heart throbs, [I'le] looke him in the face – and yonder I espie Stellio.

STEL: My minde misgives mee – but whist, yonder is Memphio!

ACC [*to* MEMPHIO]: In faith, I perceive an olde sawe and a rustie, no foole to the old foole. I praie you wherefore was I thrust out lyke a scar-crow in this

1560 similitude?

MEM: My sonne! and I ashamed! Dromio shall die!

1541 *fodges*: works   1544 *cotton*: succeed   1552 *scolde*: one who uses abusive language, a nagger   1557 *sawe*: saying

348

SIL: Father, are you sneaking behind? I pray you
what must I doe next?

STEL: My daughter! Risio, thou hast cosned mee!

[LUCIO to HALFPENNY]: Now begins the game!

MEM: How came you hether?

ACC: Marie, by the waie from your house hether!

MEM: How chance in this attire?

ACC: How chance? Dromio bid me.

MEMPH: Ah, [my] sonne will bee begd for a concealde   *1570*
foole.

ACC: Will I? I' faith, sir, no.

STEL: Wherefore came you hether, Silena, without
leave?

SI: Because I dyd, and I am heere because I am.

STEL: Poore wench, thy wit is improved to the
uttermost.

HALF: I, 'tis an hard matter to have a wit of the olde
rent; everie one rackes his commons so high.

MEMP [*aside*]: Dromio tolde me one shoulde meete   *1580*
Stellio's daughter and courte her in person of my
sonne.

STEL [*aside*]: Risio tolde me one shoulde meete
Memphio's sonne, and pleade in place of my
daughter.

MEMP [*aside*]: But alas, I see that my sonne hath met
wyth Silena himselfe, and bewraid his folly.

STEL [*aside*]: But I see my daughter hath pratled with
Accius, and discovered her simplicitie.

[LUCIO] [*to HALFPENNY*]: A brave crie to heare the   *1590*
two olde mules weep over the young fooles!

MEM: Accius, how lykest thou Silena?

ACC: I take her to be pregnant.

SIL: Truly his talke is very personable.

1570–71 *begd for a ... foole*: see note on line 43   1576 *improved*: raised   1579 *rackes his
commons*: stretches his means   1587 *bewraid*: exposed   1593 *pregnant*: apt, witty
1594 *personable*: handsome (see note)

STEL: Come in, girle: this geare must be fetcht about.

MEM: Come, Accius, let us go in.

[LUCIO *to* STELLIO]: Nay, sir, there is no harme
done; they have neither bought nor solde: they
may be twinnes for theyr wits and yeeres.

1600 MEM [*to* HALFPENNY]: But why diddest thou tell mee
it was [Sperantus'] sonne?

HAL: Because I thought thee a foole to aske who
thine owne sonne was.

[LUCIO *to* STELLIO]: And so, sir, for your daughter
education hath done much, otherwise they are by
nature softewytted inough.

MEM: Alas, theyr joyntes are not yet tied; they are not
yet come to yeeres and discretion.

ACC: Father, if my handes bee tyed, shall I growe wise?

1610 HALF: I, and Silena to, if you tie them fast to your
tongues.

SIL: You may take your pleasure of my tongue, for it
is no man's wife.

MEM: Come in, Accius.

STE: Come in, Silena: I wyll talke with Memphio's
sonne; but as for Risio –!

MEMP: As for Dromio –!

Exeunt MEMPHIO, ACCIUS, STELLIO, [*and*]
SILENA.

HALF: Asse for you all foure!

Enter DROMIO [*and*] RISIO.

DRO: How goes the worlde now? We have all made

1620 all sure;
Candius and Livia are maryed, their fathers
consenting, yet not knowing.

[LUCIO]: We have flat mard all! Accius and Silena
courted one another; their fathers toke them
napping; both are ashamd; and you both shall be
swingd.

RI: Tush, let us alone; we will perswade them

1595 *geare*: business *fetcht about*: done in a roundabout way 1607 *theyr joyntes are not yet tied*: they are not fully mature yet 1626 *swingd*: beaten, punished

that all fals out for the best, for if underhande
this match had bene concluded, they both
had ben coosned; and now seeing   *1630*
they finde both to bee fooles, they may be
both better advised. But why is Halfepenie so
sad?

    Enter HACKNEYMAN [*and*] SERGEANT [*unseen by
the others*].

HALFEPENIE: Because I am sure I shall never bee a
pennie.

RI: Rather praie there be no fall of monie, for thou
wilt then go for a que!

DRO: But did not the two fooles currantly court one
another?

[LUCIO]: Verie good wordes fitly applyed, brought in   *1640*
the nicke.

SERG[EANT *stepping forward and placing his hand on*
DROMIO'S *shoulder*]: I arest you!

DRO: Me, sir? Why then didst not bring a stoole wyth
thee, that I might sit downe?

HACK[NEYMAN:] He arests you at my suite for a
horse.

RI: The more asse hee. If hee had arested a mare
instead of an horse, it had bin but a slight
oversight, but to arest a man that hath no
lykenesse of a horse is flatte lunasie or alecie.   *1650*

HACK: Tush, I hired him a horse.

DRO: I sweare then he was well ridden.

HACK: I thinke in two daies he was never baited.

HALF [*to* DROMIO]: Why, was it a beare thou ridst
on?

HACK: I meane he never gave him bait.

[LUCIO]: Why, he tooke him for no fish.

HACK: I mistake none of you when I take you for
fooles! I say, thou never gavest my horse meate.

1637 *a que*: a 'q', the sign for a farthing   1650 *alecie*: i.e. 'ale-acie', drunkenness
1653 *baited*: pulled up, rested

1660   DRO: Yes, in foure and fortie houres I am sure he had
     a bottle of hay as big as his belly.

    SERG: Nothing else? Thou shouldest have given him
     provender.

    [DRO]: Why, he never askt for anie.

    HACK: Why, doest thou thinke an horse can speake?

    DRO: No, for I spurd him till my heeles akt, and hee
     sayd never a word.

    HACK: Well, thou shalt paie sweetly for spoiling him!
     It was as lustie a nag as anie in Rochester, and one
1670   that would stand upon no ground.

    DRO: Then is he as good as ever he was, I'le warrant!
     Hee'le do nothing but lie downe.

    HACK: I lent him thee gently.

    DRO: And I restored him so gently that hee neither
     would cry 'Wyhie!' nor wag the taile.

    HACK: But why didst thou boare him thorough the
     eares?

    [LUCIO]: It may be he was set on the pillorie,
     because hee had not a true pace.

1680   HALF: No, it was for tyring.

    HACK: He would never tire; it may be he would be so
     wearie he would go no further, or so.

    DRO: Yes, he was a notable horse for service; he wold
     tyre and retire.

    HACK: Doe you thinke I'le be jested out of my horse?
     Sergeant, wreake thy office on him!

    RI: Nay, stay; let him be baild.

    HACK: So he shall when I make him a bargen.

    DRO: It was a verie good horse, I must needs
1690   confesse, and now hearken to his qualities, and
    have patience to heare them since I must paie for
    him. He would stumble three houres in one mile, I
    had thought I had rode upon addeces betweene

1661 *bottle*: bundle   1666 *akt*: ached   1668 *sweetly*: dearly   1670 *stand upon no ground*: i.e.
he was frisky   1673 *gently*: generously, courteously   1685 *wreake*: exercise punitively
1688 *bargen*: agreement to confine him (see note)   1693 *addeces*: adzes, bladed axes

this and Canterburie. If one gave him water, why,
he would lie downe and bath himselfe lyke a
hauke; if one ranne him, he would simper and
mump, as though he had gone a-wooing to a malt
mare at Rochester. Hee trotted before and ambled
behinde, and was so obedient that he would doo
dutie everie minute on his knees, as though everie   *1700*
stone had bin his father.

HACK: I am sure he had no diseases.

DRO: A little rume or pose – hee lackt nothing but an
handkercher.

SERG: Come, what a tale of a horse have we here? I
cannot stay; thou must with me to prison!

RI: If thou be a good fellow, Hacknyman, take al our
foure bondes for the paiment: thou knowest wee
are towne-borne children, and wil not shrinke the
citie for a pelting jade.   *1710*

HALF: I'le enter into a statute marchant to see it
aunswered. But if thou wilt have bondes, thou
shalt have a bushell full.

HACK: Alas, poore ant, thou bound in a statute
merchant? A browne threed will bind thee fast
inough: but if you will be content all foure joyntly
to enter into a bond, I will withdrawe the action.

DRO: Yes, I'le warrant they will. How say you?

HALF: I yeeld.

RI: And I.   *1720*

[LUCIO]: And I.

HACK: Well, call the scrivener.

SER: Heere's one hard by. I'le call him. [*Knocks at*
SCRIVENER's *door.*]

RI: A scrivener's shop hangs to a sergeant's mase,
like a burre to a freese coate.

SCRI[VENER *entering*]: What's the matter?

1697 *mump*: mope   1697–8 *malt mare*: dray horse   1703 *rume or pose*: cold or catarrh
1709 *shrinke*: desert, skip   1710 *pelting*: paltry   1711 *statute marchant*: type of bond (see
notes)   1724 *mase*: mace   1725 *freese*: frieze, coarse woollen material
1726 *matter*: subject (of your visit)

HACK: You must take a note of a bond.

DRO: Nay, a pint of curtesie puls on a pot of wine! In this taverne wee'le dispatch.

1730 HACK: Agreed.

[*All but* RISIO] *exeunt* [*into tavern.*]

RI: Now if our wits be not in the waine, our knavery shall bee at the full. They will ride them worse than Dromio rid his horse, for if the wine master their wits, you shall see them bleed their follyes.

Exit [*into the tavern.*]

Act. 5.   Sce. I.

Dro[*mio.*]   Risio.   [*Lucio.*]   Halfpenie.
[*Enter* DROMIO, RISIO, LUCIO, HALFPENNY,
from the tavern.]

DRO: Everie foxe to his hole, the houndes are at hande!

RI: The Sergeant's mase lyes at pawne for the reckning, and he under the boord to cast it up.

[LUCIO]: The scrivener cannot keepe his pen out of
1740   the pot: every goblet is an inkhorne.

HAL: The hackneyman hee whiskes with his wande, as if the taverne were his stable, and all the servantes his horses – 'Jost there up bay Richard!' – and white loaves are horsebread in his eyes.

DRO: It is well I have my acquitance, and hee such a bond as shall doo him no more good than the bond of a faggot! Our knaveries are now come to the push, and wee must cunningly dispatch all. Wee two will goe see howe wee may appease our
1750   masters, you two howe you may conceale the late marriage: if all fall out amisse, the worst is beating; if to the best, the worst is lybertie.

1734 *bleed*: vent through bleeding   1738 *cast it up*: pun on 'vomit', reckon it up
1743 *Jost*:? mount (see note)   1745 *acquitance*: document of release   1746 *bond*: band, tie

RI: Then lette's about it speedely, for so many yrons
in the fire together require a diligent plummer.
Exeunt.

Act. 5. Sce. 2.

Vicinia. Bombie.

Enter VICINIA.

VIC[INIA:] My heart throbbes, my eares tingle, my
minde misgives mee, since I heare such muttering
of marryages in Rochester. My conscience, which
these eighteene yeeres hath beene frosen with
conjealed guiltynesse, beginnes nowe to thawe in
open griefe. But I wil not accuse myselfe til I see   1760
more danger: the good olde woman Mother
Bombie shall trie her cunning upon me; and if I
perceive my case is desperate by her, then wyll I
rather prevent, although with shame, then report
too late, and be inexcusable. [*Knocks at the door.*
MOTHER BOMBIE *appears.*] God speed, good
mother!

BOM: Welcome, sister!

VIC: I am troubled in the night with dreames, and in
the daie with feares; mine estate bare, which I   1770
cannot well beare; but my practises devillish,
which I cannot recall. If therefore in these same
yeeres there be anie deepe skill, tell what my
fortune shall be, and what my fault is.

BOM: In studying to be over-naturall,
          Thou art like to be unnaturall,
          And all about a naturall;
          Thou shalt bee eased of a charge,
          If thou thy conscience discharge,
          And this I commit to thy charge.   1780

1754 *plummer*: lead-worker, solderer   1762 *trie her cunning*: test her skills   1764 *prevent*:
anticipate, forestall   1772 *recall*: undo   1772–3 *these same yeeres*: i.e. Mother Bombie's
1775 *over-naturall*: unduly affectionate   1777 *a naturall*: an idiot

VIC: Thou hast toucht mee to the quicke, mother; I
understand thy meaning, and thou well knowest
my practise. I will follow thy counsell. But what
wyll bee the end?

BOM: Thou shalt know before this daie end: farewel.

Exit BOM[BIE.]

VIC: Nowe I perceive I must either bewraie a
mischiefe, or suffer a continual inconvenience. I
must hast homewardes, and resolve to make all
whole: better a little shame than an infinite griefe.

1790 The strangenes will abate the faulte, and the
bewraying wipe it cleane away. *Exit.*

Act. 5. Sce. 3.

Three Fidlers. Synis. Nasutus. Beduneus.
[*Enter the* FIDLERS.]

SYN[IS:] Come, fellowes, 'tis almost daie; let us have
a fit of mirth at Sperantus' doore, and give a song
to the bride.

NA[SUTUS:] I beleeve they are asleepe: it were pittie
to awake them.

BED[UNEUS:] 'Twere a shame they shoulde sleepe
the first night.

SYN: But who can tell at which house they lie? At

1800 Prisius', it may be! Wee'le trie both.

NA: Come, let's drawe lyke men.

SYN: Now, tune, tune, I saie! That boy, I thinke, will
never profit in his facultie! He looses his rosen,
that his fiddle goes 'cush, cush', like as one should
go wet-shod; and his mouth so drie that he hath
not spittle for his pinne as I have.

BED: Mary, sir, you see I go wet-shod and
dry-mouthd, for yet could I never get newe shooes

1783 *practise*: deception 1786 *bewraie*: expose 1787 *inconvenience*: misfortune, discomfort
1803 *facultie*: profession, ability *rosen*: rosin 1806 *pinne*: peg (by which the strings are
tuned)

or good drinke; rather than I'le leade this life, I'le
throw my fiddle into the leads for a hobler.   *1810*

SYN: Boy, no more words! There's a time for al
things. Though I say it that should not, I have
bene a minstrell these thirtie yeeres, and tickled
more strings than thou hast haires, but yet was
never so misused.

NAS: Let us not brabble but play: tomorrow is a new
daie.

BED: I am sorrie I speake in your cast. What shall
wee sing?

SYN: 'The Love-Knot', for that's best for a bridall.   *1820*
    Sing.
    God morow, fayre bride, and send you joy of your
        bridall —
    SPERANTUS *lookes out [of an upstairs window].*

SPE: What a mischiefe make the twanglers here? We
have no trenchers to scrape; it makes my teeth on
edge to heare such grating! Get you packing, or
I'le make you weare double stockes, and yet you
shall bee never the warmer!

SYN: We come for good will, to bidd the bride and
bridegroome, God give them joy!

SPE: Here's no wedding.

SYN: Yes, your sonne and Prisius' daughter were   *1830*
maryed; though you seeme strange, yet they repent
it not, I am sure!

SPE: My sonne, villaine! I had rather hee were fairely
hanged!

NAS: So he is, sir; you have your wish.
    Enter CANDIUS.

CAN: Here, fidlers, take this, and not a worde: heere
is no wedding, it was at Memphio's house; yet,
gramercy! your musicke, though it mist the house,

1810 *leads*: roof *hobler*: ? a child's wobbly top 1816 *brabble*: squabble 1818 *speake in your
cast*: interrupt you 1825 *double stockes*: a pun on 'stockings' 1827 *bidd*: proclaim
1831 *strange*: unfriendly

1840

   hit the minde; we were a-preparing our wedding
   geare.
  SYN: I crie you mercie, sir; I thinke it was
   Memphio's sonne that was married.
    [*Exit* CANDIUS.]
  SPE: O ho, the case is altered! goe thether then, and
   be haltered for me!
    [*Exit* SPERANTUS.]
  NAS: What's the almes?
  SYN: An angell.
  BED: I'le warrant ther's some worke towards: ten
   shillings is money in master Mayor's purse.
  SYN: Let us to Memphio's and share equally; when

1850

   we have done all, thou shalt have new shooes.
  BED: I, such as they cry at the Sizes, 'A marke in
   issues, a marke in issues!' and yet I never sawe so
   much leather as would peece one's shooes.
  SYN: No more! – Ther's the mony.
  BED: A good handsell, and I thinke the maidenhead
   of your liberalitie.
    [*They cross the stage.*]
  NAS: Come, here's the house: what shall we sing?
  SYN: You know Memphio is very rich and wise, and
   therefore let us strike the gentle stroke, and sing a

1860

   catch.
   Sing.

      Song
  ALL 3: The Bride this night can catch no cold;
      No cold, the Bridegroome's yong, not old,
      Like ivie he her fast does hold,
 1. FID: And clips her,
 2:     And lips her,
 3:     And flips her too:

1844 *haltered*: hanged 1846 *An angell*: a gold coin of some value (see note)
1851 *Sizes*: Assizes 1855 *handsell*: gift (see note) 1866 *flips her*: smacks ('fillips') her;
possibly 'urges her'.

ALL 3:	Then let them alone, they know what	
	they doe.	
1.:	At laugh-and-lie-downe if they play,	
2.:	What asse against the sport can bray?	
3.:	Such tick-tacke has held many a day,	*1870*
1.:	And longer,	
2.:	And stronger:	
3.:	It still holds too.	
ALL 3:	Then let them alone, they know what they doe.	

This night,

In delight

Does thump away sorrow;

Of billing

Take your filling,

So good morrow, good morrow!   *1880*

NAS: Good morrowe, mistres bride, and sende you a huddle!

[*Enter* MEMPHIO *and* DROMIO *above.*]

MEM [*above*]: What crouding knaves have we there? Case up your fiddles, or the cunstable shall cage you uppe! What bride talke you of?

SYN: Here's a wedding in Rochester, and 'twas tolde me first that Sperantus' son had married Prisius' daughter. We were there, and they sent us to your worshippe, saying your son was matched with Stellio's daughter.   *1890*

MEM: Hath Sperantus – that churle – nothing to doe but mocke his neighbours? I'le bee even with him! [*To* FIDDLERS] And get you gone, or I sweare by the roode's bodie I'le laye you by the heeles!

NAS: Sing a catch? here's a faire catch indeed! Sing til we catch colde on our feet, and bee cald knave tyll our eares glowe on our heades! Your worshippe is wise, sir.

1868 *laugh-and-lie-downe*: a card-game, but see note   1870 *tick-tacke*: tric-trac, a form of backgammon   1882 *a huddle*: see note   1883 *crouding*: fiddling (see note)

MEM: Dromio, shake off a whole kennel of officers, to
1900   punish these jarring rogues! I'le teach them to
stretch theyr dried sheepes' guts at my doore and
to mock one that stands to be mayor!

DRO: I had thought they had beene sticking of pigs, I
heard such a squeaking! I go, sir!
     [*Exit* MEMPHIO *and* DROMIO *above.*]

SYN: Let us be packing.

NAS: Where is my scabbarde? Everyone sheath his
science.

BED: A bots on the shoomaker that made this boote
for my fiddle! 'tis too straight.

1910 SYN: No more wordes! 'twill bee thought they were
the foure waites, and let them wring; as for the
wagges that set us on worke, we'le talke with them!
     Exeunt. MEMPHIO [*and*] DROMIO [*reappear in the
street.*]

DRO: They be gone, sir.

MEM: If they had stayed, the stockes shoulde have
staied them. But, sirra, what shall we now doo?

DRO: As I advised you, make a match; for better one
house be cumbred with two fooles than two.

MEM: 'Tis true: for it beeing bruted that eache of us
have a foole, who will tender marriage to anie of
1920   them, that is wise? Besides, fooles are fortunate,
fooles are faire, fooles are honest.

DRO: I, sir, and more than that, fooles are not wise: a
wise man is melancholy for moone-shine in the
water; carefull building castles in the ayre; and
commonly hath a foole to his heyre.

MEM: But what sayest thou to thy dame's chafing?

DRO: Nothing, but all her dishes are chafing dishes.

1906 *scabbarde*: i.e. violin-case   *science*: sign of his skill   1908 *A bots on*: a plague on   *boote*: leather-case   1909 *straight*: narrow   1911 *the foure waites*: town musicians   *wring*: take the blame   1918 *bruted*: noised abroad   1919 *anie*: either   1924 *careful*: full of care   1926 *chafing*: bad temper

MEM: I would her tongue were in thy belly.

DRO: I had as liefe have a rawe neate's tongue in my
stomacke. *1930*

MEM: Why?

DRO: Marie, if the clapper hang within an inch of my
heart that makes mine eares burne a quarter of a
mile off, do you not thinke it would beate my heart
blacke and blew?

MEMP: Well, patience is a vertue, but pinching is
worse than any vice! I wil breake this matter to
Stellio, and if he be willing, this day shall be their
wedding.

DRO: Then this day shall be my libertie. *1940*

MEM: I, if Stellio's daughter had beene wise, and by
thy meanes cosned of a foole!

DRO: Then, sir, I'le revolt, and dash out the braines
of your devises.

MEMPH: Rather thou shalt be free.
Exeunt.
[*Enter*] SPERANTUS [*and*] HALFPENIE [*on one side*],
PRISIUS [*and* LUCIO *on the other*].

SPE: Boy, this smoake is a token of some fire; I lyke
not the lucke of it. Wherefore should these
minstrelles dreame of a marryage?

HALF: Alas, sir, they rustle into every place; give
credit to no such wordes. *1950*

SPE: I will to Prisius: I cannot be quiet – and in good
time I meet him! God morrow, neighbor.

PRI: I cast the morrow in thy face, and bid good
night to all neighborhood.

SPE: This is your olde tricke, to pick one's purse and
then to picke quarrels: I tell thee, I had rather
thou shouldest rob my chest than imbesell my
sonne.

1929 *neates*: ox's   1932 *clapper*: tongue   1936 *pinching*: fault-finding   1943 *dash out*, etc.:
ruin   1946 *smoake*: i.e. the wedding serenade   1949 *rustle into*, etc.: are here, there, and
everywhere   1957 *imbesell*: embezzle, cheat

PRI: Thy sonne? My daughter is seduced! for I hear
1960   say she is marryed, and our boyes can tell. [*To*
        LUCIO.] How sayest thou? Tell the truth or I'le
        grinde thee to pouder in my mill! Be they
        marryed?

[LUCIO:] True it is they were both in a church.

PRI: That's no fault; the place is holy.

HALF: And there was with them a priest.

SPE: Why, what place fitter for a priest than a
        church?

[LUCIO:] And they tooke one another by the hand.

1970 PRI: Tush! that's but common curtesie.

HALF: And the priest spake many kinde wordes.

SPE: That shewed hee was no dumbe minister. But
        what sayde they? Diddest thou heare anie wordes
        betweene them?

[LUCIO:] Faith, there was a bargaine during life, and
        the [clerke] cryed, 'God give them joy!'

PRI: Villaine! they be marryed!

HALF: Nay, I thinke not so.

SPE: Yes, yes! 'God give you joy' is a binder! I'le
1980   quickly be resolvd! Candius, come forth!
            Enter CANDIUS.

PRI: And I'le be put out of doubt. Livia, come forth!
        [*Enter*] LIVIA.

SPE: The micher hangs downe his head!

PRI: The baggage begins to blush!

HALF [*to* LUCIO]: Now begins the game!

[LUCIO:] I beleeve it will be no game for us.

SPE: Are you marryed, yong master?

CAN: I cannot denie it, it was done so lately.

SPE: But thou shalt repent it was done so soone!

PRI: Then 'tis bootlesse to aske you, Livia.

1990 LIV: I, and needlesse to be angrie.

PRI: It shalle passe anger; thou shalt finde it rage!

1979 *is a binder*: clinches the matter   1982 *micher*: rascal

LIV: You gave your consent.

PRI: Impudent giglot, was it not inough to abuse me,
but also to belie me?

CAN: You, sir, agreed to this match.

SPE: Thou brasen face boy, thinkest thou by learning
to persuade me to that which thou speakest?
Where did I consent? When? What witnes?

CAN: In this place yesterday before Dromio and
Risio.   *2000*

PRI: I remember we heard a contract between
Memphio's sonne and Stellio's daughter; and that
our good wils being asked, which needed not, wee
gave them, which booted not.

CAN: 'Twas but the apparell of Accius and Silena; we
were the persons.

PRI: O villany not to be borne! [*To* LUCIO] Wast
thou privie to this practise?

[LUCIO:] In a manner.

PRI: I'le pay thee after a manner.   *2010*

SPE [*to* HALFPENNY]: And you, oatemeale groate!
You were acquainted with this plot!

HALF: Accessarie, as it were.

SPE: Thou shalt be punished as principal! Here
comes Memphio and Stellio; they belike were
privie, and all theyr heads were layde together to
grieve our heartes.

  Enter MEMPHIO, STELLIO, [DROMIO *and* RISIO].

MEM: Come, Stellio, the assurance may be made
tomorrow, and our children assured today.

STEL: Let the conveyance runne as we agreed.   *2020*

PRI: You convey cleanely indeede, if coosnage bee
cleane dealing, for in the apparell of your children
you have convaide a match betweene ours, which
grieves us not a little.

MEM: Nay, in the apparel of your children, you have

1993 *giglot*: hussy   1994 *belie me*: tell lies about me   2004 *booted not*: signified nothing
2008 *practise*: deception   2021 *convey*: cheat, steal

discoverd the folly of ours, which shames us
overmuch.

STEL: But 'tis no matter; though they bee fooles they
are no beggers.

2030 SPE: And thogh ours be disobedient, they be no fools.

DRO [aside]: So now they tune theyr pipes.

RI [aside]: You shal heare sweet musicke betweene a
hoarse raven and a schritch owle.

MEM: Neighbours, let us not vary: our boyes have
playd theyr cheating partes. I suspected no lesse at
the taverne, where oure foure knaves met together.

RI: If it were knavery for foure to meet in a taverne,
your wor[ships] wot well there were other foure.

STEL: This villaine cals us knaves by craft!

2040 [LUCIO:] Nay, truly, I dare sweare hee used no
crafte, but meanes plainly.

SPE: This is worse! Come, Halfe[penie], tel truth and
scape the rod.

HALF: As good confesse heere beeing trust, as at
home with my hose about my heeles.

DRO: Nay, I'le tell thee, for 'twill never become thee
to utter it.

MEM: Well, out with it!

DRO: Memphio had a foole to his sonne, which

2050 Stellio knew not; Stellio a foole to his daughter,
unknowen to Memphio; to coosen eache other,
they dealte with theyr boyes for a match; we met
with [Lucio] and Halfepenie, who told the love
betweene their masters' children, the youth deeply
in love, the fathers unwilling to consent.

RI: I'le take the tale by the end, — then wee foure
met, which argued we were no mountaines; and in
a tavern we met, which argued we were mortall;
and everyone in his wine told his daye's worke,

2031 *tune theyr pipes*: get attuned to each other   2033 *schritch*: screech   2034 *vary*: differ
2044 *beeing trust*: having my clothing 'trussed up', i.e. while I'm still dressed   2049 *to his*:
as his   2057 *no mountaines*: see note

which was a signe we forgot not our busines; and 2060
seeing all our masters troubled with devises, we
determined a little to trouble the water before they
dronke; so that in the attire of your children our
masters' wise children bewrayed theyr good
natures; and in the garments of our masters'
children yours' made a marriage. This all stoode
uppon us poore children, and your yong children,
to shewe that olde folkes may be overtaken by
children.

PRI: Here's a children indeed! I'le never forget it. 2070

MEM: I will! Accius, come forth!

STEL: I forgive all! Silena, come forth!

    [*Enter* ACCIUS *and* SILENA.]

SPE: Neighbor, these things cannot be recald,
therefore as good consent, seeing in all our
purposes also we mist the marke, for they two will
match their children.

PRI: Well, of that more anone — not so sodainely,
least our ungratious youths thinke we dare do no
other; but in truth, their love stirres up nature in
me. 2080

MEM: Come, Accius, thou must be marryed to Silena.
How art thou minded?

ACC: What, for ever and ever?

MEM: I, Accius, what els?

ACC: I shall never be able to abide it; it will be so
tedious!

STEL: Silena, thou must be betrothed to Accius, and
love him for thy husband.

SIL: I had as liefe have one of clouts.

STEL: Why, Silena? 2090

SI: Why, looke how he lookes!

ACC: If you will not, another will.

SIL: I thanke you for mine olde cap!

2061 *devises*: schemes, stratagems 2064 *bewrayed*: exposed 2070 *a children*: i.e. a breed of
children 2079 *nature*: natural affection 2089 *as liefe*: as happily

ACC: And if you be so lustie, lend me two shillings!

PRI [*to* SPERANTUS]: We are happie we mist the
foolish match.

MEM [*to* ACCIUS]: Come, you shall presently be
contracted.

DRO: Contract their wits no more; they bee shronke

2100   close already.

ACC: Well, father, heere's my hande; strike the
bargaine.

SIL: Must he lie with me?

STEL: No, Silena, lie by thee.

ACC: I shall give her the humble-bee's kisse. [*He
kisses* SILENA.]

          Enter VICINIA, [MAESTIUS, *and* SERENA].

VIC: I forbid the banes!

RI: What, doest thou thinke them rattes, and fearest
they shall be poisoned?

MEM: You, Vicinia? Wherefore?

2110   VIC: Hearken! – about eighteene yeeres agoe, I nurst
thee a sonne, Memphio, and thee a daughter,
Stellio.

STEL: True.

MEM: True.

VIC: I had at that time two children of mine owne,
and being poore, thought it better to change them
than kill them. I imagined if by device I coulde
thrust my children into your houses, they should
be wel brought up in their youth, and wisely

2120   provided for in their age. Nature wrought with me,
and when they were weaned, I sent home mine
insted of yours, which hetherto you have kept
tenderly as yours: growing in yeres, I founde the
children I kept at home to love dearely, at first
lyke brother and sister, which I rejoyced at, but at
length too forward in affection; which although

2094 *lustie*: rude, cheeky   2095 *mist*: avoided   2097 *presently*: straight away
2106 *banes*: banns (Risio takes the term as meaning 'poison')   2117 *device*: stratagem

inwardly I could not mislike, yet openly I seemed
to disallowe. They increased in their loving
humours; I ceased not to chastise them for theyr
loose demeanors. At last it came to my eares, that   *2130*
my sonne that was out with Memphio was a foole;
that my daughter with Stellio was also unwise; and
yet beeing brother and sister, there was a match in
hammering betwixt them.

MEM: What monstrous tale is this?

STEL: And I am sure incredible!

SPE: Let her end her discourse.

ACC: I'le never beleeve it!

MEM: Holde thy peace!

VIC: My verie bowels earned within me that I shuld   *2140*
be author of such vilde incest, an hinderance to
lawfull love. I went to the good olde woman,
Mother Bombie, to knowe the event of this
practise; who tolde mee this day I might prevent
the danger, and upon submission escape the
punishment. Hether I am come to claime my
children, though both fooles, and to deliver
[yours], both loving.

MEM: Is this possible? How shall we beleeve it?

STEL: It cannot sinke into my head!   *2150*

VIC: This triall cannot faile. Your sonne, Memphio,
had a moale under his eare: I framed one under
my childe's eare by arte; you shall see it taken
away with the juyce of mandrage; beholde nowe
for your sonne's: no hearbe can undo that nature
hath done. [*Shows* MAESTIUS' *mole.*] Your
daughter, Stellio, hath on her wrist a moale, which
I counterfeted on my daughter's arme, and that
shall you see taken away as the other. [*Shows*
SERENA's *mole.*] Thus you see I doe not dissemble,   *2160*

2134 *in hammering*: being hammered out   2136 *incredible*: incredulous   2140 *earned*:
yearned   2141 *vilde*: vile   2143 *event*: outcome   2144 *practise*: deception *prevent*: anticipate, forestall   2151 *triall*: examination of proof   2154 *mandrage*: mandragora (see note)

hoping you will pardon me, as I have pittied them.

MEMP: This is my sonne! O fortunate Memphio!

STEL: This is my daughter! More than thrice happie Stellio!

MAEST: How happie is Maestius, how blessed Serena, that being neither children to poore parents, nor brother and sister by nature, may injoye their love by consent of parents and nature!

ACC: Soft; I'le not swap my father for all this!

2170 SI: What, do you thinke I'le bee cosned of my father? Methinkes I should not! Mother Bombie tolde me 'my father knew mee not, my mother bore mee not, falsely bred, truly begot,' – a bots on Mother Bomby!

DRO: Mother Bombie tolde us we should be founde coosners, and in the end be cosned by cosners: wel fare Mother Bomby!

RI [to DROMIO]: I heard Mother Bomby saie that thou shalt die a beggar: beware of Mother Bomby!

2180 PRI: Why, have you all bene with Mother Bomby?

[LUCIO:] All, and as farre as I can see she foretolde all.

MEM: Indeed, she is cunning and wise, never doing harme, but still practising good. Seeing these things fall out thus, are you content, Stellio, the match goe forward?

STEL: I, with double joye, having found for a foole a wise maide, and finding betweene them both exceeding love.

2190 PRI: Then, to end all jars, our children's matches shall stand with our good liking. Livia, injoy Candius!

SPE: Candius, injoy Livia!

CAN: How shall we recompence fortune, that to our loves hath added our parents' good wills?

2173 *a bots on*: a plague on 2176 *be cosned*, etc.: i.e. deceived by Vicinia 2183 *cunning*: learned 2190 *jars*: discord

MAEST: How shall wee requite fortune, that to our
loves hath added lawfulnesse, and to our poore
estate competent living?

MEM: Vicinia, thy fact is pardoned, though the law
would see it punisht. Wee be content to keepe   2200
Silena in the house with the new-married couple.

STEL: And I doo maintaine Accius in our house.

VIC: Come, my children, though fortune hath not
provided you landes, yet you see you are not
destitute of friends. I shall be eased of a charge
both in purse and conscience: in conscience,
having revealed my lewd practise; in purse, having
you kept of almes.

ACC: Come, if you bee my sister, it's the better for
you.   2210

SIL: Come, brother, methinkes it's better than it was:
I should have beene but a balde bride. I'le eate as
much pie as if I had bene marryed!

MEM: Let's also forgive the knaverie of our boyes,
since all turnes to our good haps.

STEL: Agreed: all are pleased nowe the boyes are
unpunisht.

> *Enter* HACKNEYMAN, SERGEANT, [*and*]
> SCRIVENER.

HACK: Nay, softe, take us with you, and seeke
redresse for our wrongs, or wee'le complaine to the
Mayor.   2220

PRI: What's the matter?

HACK: I arested Memphio's boye for an horse. After
much mocking, at the request of his fellowe
wagges, I was content to take a bonde joyntlye of
them all: they had me into a taverne; there they
made me, the scrivener, and the Sergeant dronke,
paunde his mase for the wine, and seald mee an

2199 *fact*: crime, evil deed   2207 *lewd practise*: low deception   2212 *balde*: barren, useless
2215 *haps*: fortunes   2227 *paunde his mase*: pawned his mace

369

obligation nothing to the purpose: I pray you,
reade it. [*Hands* MEMPHIO *the bond.*]

2230 MEMP: What wags be these! Why, by this bond you
can demand nothing; and thinges done in drinke
may be repented in sobernes, but not remedyed.

DRO: Sir, I have his acquittaunce: lette him sue his
bonde.

HACK: I'le crie quittance with thee!

SER: And I, or it shall cost me the laying on freelie of
my mase!

SCRI: And I'le give thee such a dash with a pen as
shall cost thee many a pound, with such a *Noverint*
2240 as Cheapside can shew none such!

HALF: Doe your worst; our knaveries will revenge it
upon your children's children!

MEMP: Thou boy! [*To* HACKNEYMAN] We wil paie
the hire of the horse; be not angrie: the boyes have
bene in a merrie cosning vaine, for they have
served their masters of the same sorte; but all must
be forgotten. Now all are content but the poore
fidlers: they shal be sent for to the marriage, and
have double fees.

2250 DRO: You need no more send for a fidler to a feast
than a begger to a fayre.

STEL: This daie we will feast at my house.

MEM: Tomorrow at mine.

PRI: The next day at mine.

SPE: Then at mine the last day, and even so spend
this weeke in good cheere.

DRO: Then we were best be going whilest everyone is
pleasd: and yet these couples are not fully pleasde,
till the priest have done his worst.

2260 RI: Come, Sergeant, wee'le tosse it this weeke, and
make thy mase arest a boild capon.

SER: No more words at the wedding! [*Aside*] If the

2233 *acquittaunce*: document releasing Dromio   *sue*: pursue, serve   2239 *Noverint*: let all
men know, i.e. a writ   2260 *tosse it*: toss the drink down, get drunk

Mayor shuld know it, I were in danger of mine
office.

RI: Then take heed how on such as we are you shew
a cast of your office.

HALF: If you mace us, wee'le pepper you!

ACC: Come, sister, the best is, we shall have good
chere these foure dayes.

[LUCIO:] And be fooles for ever.   *2270*

SI: That's none of our upseekings.

[*Exeunt.*]

FINIS

2265–6 *shew a cast*: give a specimen   2271 *upseekings*: i.e. we didn't choose to be fools

NOTES

The following abbreviations are used in the notes:

Bond *The Complete Works of John Lyly*, ed. R. Warwick Bond, 3 vols., Oxford, 1902.

OED *A New English Dictionary on a Historical Basis* (the 'Oxford English Dictionary').

Robinson *The Works of Geoffrey Chaucer*, ed. F. N. Robinson, 1933; second ed., 1966.

All references to Shakespeare's plays are taken from *William Shakespeare: The Complete Works*, ed. Peter Alexander, London and Glasgow, 1951.

JACKE JUGELER

1, s.d. *Enter the* Prologue: though there must always be strong doubts as to whether the Epilogue represents an original or a supplementary part of the extant text (see note on line 992, below), the Prologue certainly serves as a useful prelude to the main action. It is written in the so-called rhyme-royal, a favourite verse-form of fifteenth-century English poets.

1–2. *Interpone tuis*, etc.: 'Now and then introduce some enjoyment into your serious concerns/ To ensure that you can then submit to any toil willingly.' The quotation comes from Book III, 6, of the *Disticha de Moribus ad Filium*, a collection of maxims supposedly by Dionysius Cato, but erroneously attributed to Cato the Elder (234–149 BC). (See Wayland Johnson Chase, *The Distichs of Cato*, Madison, 1922.) The work, which in fact dates from the third or fourth century AD, was highly popular in the Middle Ages, and is alluded to by Chaucer; Caxton published a commentary on 'Caton' in 1483, Richard Taverner's English translation appeared in 1540, Benedict Burgh's in 1557, as an appendix to Isocrates' *Admonition to Demonicus*, the first book for which William Copland, publisher of *Jacke Jugeler*, is believed to have obtained a licence.

372

3. *Doo any of you knowe*, etc.: the self-important tone of the knowing schoolboy is beautifully captured in this and the succeeding lines.

4. *expositorem*: an expositor or interpreter was often present at mummings, street-pageants, and other dramatic entertainments to explain the significance of the dumb-shows, devices, banners, etc.

5. *per sensum planiorem*: 'by way of a more intelligible meaning'.

13–21. *Emongs thy carfull busines*, etc.: cf. the Induction to *The Taming of the Shrew*, II, 131–8, quoted in the Introduction.

27. *Quod caret*, etc.: 'Whatever is deprived of restful intervals is not long-lasting', Ovid, *Heroides*, IV, 89.

32. The rhyming line which should follow is missing.

41. *Plutarke*, etc.: several of the works of Plutarchus, the Greek thinker and biographer who lived from AD *c.* 46 to *c.* 120, were translated into English during the first half of the sixteenth century, but the dialogues of Plato (AD *c.* 429–347), which feature Socrates, were late in being rendered in a similar way.

44. *Of an Honest Man's Office*: Cicero's *De Officiis*, written for his son Marcus, contains the statement that 'Nature has not brought us into the world to act as if we were created for play or jest, but rather for earnest purposes and for some more serious and important pursuits. We may of course indulge in sport and jest (*ludo autem et ioco*), but in the same way as we enjoy sleep and other relaxations, and only when we have satisfied the claims of our earnest and serious tasks' (I, xxix, Loeb ed., p. 105). Robert Whittington, the Tudor grammarian, translated the 'thre Bookes of Tullyes Offyces' in his parallel edition of 1534.

50. *the old commedie*: Cicero's words are 'There are, generally, two sorts of jests: the one coarse, rude, vicious, indecent; the other, refined, polite, clever, witty. With that latter sort not only our own Plautus and the Old Comedy of Athens (*Atticorum antiqua comoedia*), but also the books of Socratic philosophy abound . . .' (I, xxix, ed. cit., p. 107).

64. *Plautus' first commedie*: since the chronology of Plautus' plays can only be approximately estimated, there is no positive evidence that the *Amphitruo*, on which *Jacke Jugeler* is loosely based, was his first dramatic effort, or even the earliest which survives.

65. *the first scentence*, etc.: i.e. 'he would in no way claim that he was writing to serve some higher purpose'.

80. *actours*: the second Quarto of *c.* 1565–9 reads 'Players' at this point, but the significance of the alteration is not obvious.

82. *intoo your presens*: this may be a hint that the original audience for the interlude had assembled for some other purpose, such as a feast.

106. *Jake Jugler*: the name implies not the modern stage entertainer, but a trickster or con man.

112. *You all know well*: a common dramatic device for drawing an audience into the action.

117. *London Wall*: the metropolitan setting, emphasized here and at subsequent points in the text, is an obvious key to the play's provenance.

123. *Nother ... knoweth me verie well*: this qualification is obviously necessary to secure the audience's acceptance of the deception practised on Jenkin Careaway.

135. *buklers*: a buckler was a small round shield, chiefly used to parry the blow of an opponent's weapon; 'to play at bucklers' was thus a phrase frequently employed to denote a fencing-match.

148. *potstike*: a potstick was a familiar kitchen tool of the period, but the oath is curious; since 'postic' appears in later times as an adjective meaning 'hind' or 'posterior', it is tempting to think that the expression was originally 'By God's precious buttocks!' and was later euphemized in the form given here (cf. line 1217 of *Roister Doister*).

156. *in his sleve*: the wide sleeves of the doublets of the early Tudor period were ideally suited for concealing objects of all kinds.

159. *faryng at all*: fare was a popular dice game of the period.

174. *This garments*, etc.: the audience is clearly not meant to inquire too closely into the ease with which Jack Juggler can procure clothing identical to that of Jenkin!

200. *hei hey*: possibly these words belong elsewhere in the line, but they could equally well be extra-metrical, as the editors of the Malone Society reprint suggest, and thus not affect the rhyme-scheme.

217. *Saint Loy*: it may be relevant that St Eloi or Eligius (AD 588–659) was the patron saint of goldsmiths (see line 218).

231. *a galiard*: a lively joyful dance with rapid complicated steps, composed in triple time. Of Italian origin, it was extremely popular during the sixteenth century.

233. *devyd a fart*: the Malone Society editors suggest that the verb should be 'denye', but in its sense of 'give forth in various directions' (*OED* sense 8c), 'devyd' seems entirely appropriate.

235. *paratt Poppagaye*: the term 'popingay' or one of its variants was used early in its existence to mean a parrot; by the sixteenth century the word conveyed the notion of a conceited, vain, or talkative person.

244–7. Sosia, the servant in the *Amphitruo*, plans to invent a story to satisfy his mistress Alcumena, and rehearses it much as Jenkin Careaway does in lines 252–303. (See Plautus, *The Pot of Gold and Other Plays*, Penguin Books, 1964, pp. 235–7.)

296. *But yf you now*: the Quarto texts here read 'That yf you now', but the Malone Society editors suggest 'But' as the correct reading.

318. *jeoperd a joint*: a common phrase, but cf. *Thersytes*, line 435: 'I wyll joparde with it a joyte.'

323. *swete mete woll have soure sauce*, etc.: 'pleasure must be paid for', a common proverbial phrase.

331. *Soft thy knoking*, etc.: more in keeping with Mercury's encounter with Amphitruo at his own door, rather than with Sosia: cf. ed. cit., p. 272: '... you mustn't go knocking doors down like that ...'

335. *as small as fleshe too pote*: J. W. Robinson discusses this very common phrase in *Folklore* 80 (1969).

348 *His arse makith buttens*: a graphic proverbial description of spastic constipation.

364–71. *Now fistes, methinkithe*, etc.: cf. Mercury's exchange with Sosia in *Amphitruo* (ed. cit., p. 239):

MERCURY: Come, fists of mine, it's time you found some meat for my stomach. You've done no work since yesterday, when you left four men flat out and stark naked.
SOSIA: Four men flat out. And I'm the fifth. From now on my name's Quintus.

379. *I have supped*, etc.: cf. *Amphitruo*, ed. cit., p. 239:

MERCURY: The first man I meet gets this fist in his mouth.
SOSIA: Not me. Not at this time of night. I've had my supper, thanks. Give it to someone who's hungry.

385. *Our Ladye boons*: since the rhyme is defective here, perhaps the phrase should be 'Our Ladye's bandes', although this was of special application to the pangs of women in labour. If 'boons' is retained, it may imply dependence on the Virgin's grace or favour (cf. 'boon').

418. *thes ten bons*: the bones of the thumbs and fingers (cf. line 559).

445. *I wolde it were true*, etc.; cf. *Amphitruo*, ed. cit., p. 242:

> MERCURY: ... I tell you I am Sosia.
>
> SOSIA: I wish you were, by all the gods, then you'd be getting the beating.

451. *saucye*: from Q 2; Q 1 has 'fancye'.

463. *Helpe, helpe, help!*: again extra-metrical (see line 200 and note).

484–97. *But, syr, might I*, etc.: cf. *Amphitruo*, ed. cit. p. 243:

> SOSIA: Look, mister, could I have a few minutes' peace to speak to you, and no more beating?
>
> MERCURY: An armistice perhaps, if you have anything to say.
>
> SOSIA: Nothing short of peace, or I won't talk. You've got the superior weapons.
>
> MERCURY: Say what you want to say. I won't hurt you.
>
> SOSIA: Promise?
>
> MERCURY: Promise.
>
> SOSIA: And if you break it?
>
> MERCURY: Then may all the wrath of Mercury fall upon Sosia.
>
> SOSIA: Well now, listen. Now I can get a word in – the fact is, I *am* Amphitryo's slave, Sosia.
>
> MERCURY: That again!
>
> SOSIA: Now, now. Pax. I've signed the treaty. And I'm telling the truth.
>
> MERCURY: For which I'll thrash you.
>
> SOSIA: Just as you like; I can't stop you. But whether you do or not, that's the truth and I'm sticking to it.

498. *This bedelem knave*: the name of the celebrated lunatic asylum established in the fourteenth century in the priory of St Mary of Bethlehem, just outside Bishopsgate in London, became contracted to 'Bedlam' and then applied as both noun and adjective to those suffering from forms of mental illness (cf. 'Tom O'Bedlam', etc.), especially those like Diccon in *Gammer Gurton's Nedle*, who roamed the countryside in search of relief (cf. line 975, and Introduction, pp. 28–9).

535. *here they bee yet*: Jack Juggler has been able to provide himself with a supply of apples to match those hidden in Jenkin Careaway's sleeve, and so add to his confusion.

568–87. *I se it is soo*, etc.: cf. *Amphitruo*, ed. cit:, p. 245:

SOSIA: Now I come to look at him, and look at myself – I mean I know what I look like, I've looked in a mirror before now – he *is* very like me. Hat ... clothes ... he might easily be me ... leg, foot, height, haircut, eyes, nose, mouth, cheeks, chin, beard, neck ... the lot. There's no denying it. If he's got a back striped with whip scars, he's me. But I can't understand it ... I'm sure I'm the same man I always was. I know who my master is. I know this house. I can think ... and feel ... Well, damn it all, I don't care what he says. I'm going to knock at the door.

592. *wine shakine*: the Malone Society editors advocate amending this to read 'wind shakin', i.e. 'wind-shaken', but it is far more apt to have Jack Juggler suggest that Jenkin is too drunk to know who he is or where he lives, echoing the attitude adopted towards Sosia in the *Amphitruo*. Jack has already accused Jenkin of drunkenness at line 441, and the idea is repeated by Jenkin himself at line 612, by Dame Coye at line 708 and by Bongrace at line 788.

637, s.d. *Enter from the house*: as implied in the Introduction (p. 33), the front door of Bongrace's residence opens directly on to the stage.

674. *breched in such a brake*: the phrase obviously indicates that Careaway's wits are in a state of confusion, but the Malone Society editors suggest that the phrase may mean 'broken in a snare'. However, I wonder if the phrase refers to the 'brake' or rack, on which his mind has been torn apart.

733. *dullnes*: the text reads 'dulines' but this appears to be simply a printer's error.

741. *rekine better*: 'work out a more suitable punishment'.

751. *canvased*: the word can mean 'beaten', but since it is here associated with the word 'tost', it obviously indicates tossing in a sheet or piece of canvas, a device often used for punishment as well as for sport or as a party game; cf. the tossing of Mak the sheep-stealer in the *Secunda Pastorum* of the Wakefield (or Towneley) cycle sequence: 'For this trespas / ... cast hym in canvas' (lines 624, 628).

774. *Why then, daryst*, etc.: cf. *Amphitruo*, ed. cit., p. 250:

AMPHITRYO: You're a fine rascal, you are.
SOSIA: Me, sir? Why, sir?

AMPHITRYO: Telling me a lot of things that never are and never were and never will be true.

784–6. *Why, thou naughtye vyllayne*, etc.: cf. *Amphitruo*, ed. cit., p. 251:

AMPHITRYO: Are you making fun of your master, rope's-end? Have you the face to tell me something no one has ever seen on this earth and never will — one man in two places at the same time?
SOSIA: I'm only telling you the plain facts ...
AMPHITRYO: The man is obviously drunk ... Where have you been drinking?

840. *as a bere in a cage*: presumably a pun on 'fast' in its dual sense of 'speedily' and 'secure', cf. Lewis Carroll, *Through the Looking-Glass*, Chapter 8:

'... it took hours and hours to get me out. I was as fast as — as lightning, you know.'
'But that's a different kind of fastness,' Alice objected.

866. *Many here smell strong*: the most pointed and effective, if least flattering, allusion to the audience's presence made during the course of the play. (See Introduction, pp. 31–2).

884. The preceding line, which should rhyme with 'harde', has dropped out.

886. *a grote*: the groat, first minted in England in 1351–2, was traditionally equal to four pence. (Cf. notes to line 331 of *Gammer Gurton's Nedle* and line 2011 of *Mother Bombie*.)

900. *How I dyd*, etc.: in his anxiety to justify his claims, Jenkin is naïvely betrayed into revealing his dereliction of duty.

904. *aby*: Quarto 1 has 'have by'; the Malone Society editors suggest 'aby'.

926. *no fault therof*, etc.: a nicely hypocritical touch which well characterizes Dame Coye (cf. lines 644–7, 650–57, 668–9).

933. *pigesnie*: see note to *Roister Doister*, line 460.

974. *Calycow*: an English corruption of Calicut or Calicot, the name of the important port on the coast of Malabar in SW India (now Kozhikode), from which the cotton fabric known as calicut (or calico) cloth derived.

975. *Bedelem*: see note to line 498.

992, s.d. *Enter the Epilogue*: although the speaker of the Epilogue is made to address the audience as does the actor delivering the Prologue, some commentators regard the lines assigned to him as a later addition to the main text. Although the speech conforms to the Prologue's rhyme-royal, its metrical clumsiness, laborious didacticism, remorseless parade of saws, and repetitious moralizing suggest that it is the work of another hand. Furthermore, as David Bevington points out in arguing that the Epilogue was added for publication under Elizabeth, it could scarcely be the work of the original playwright, who 'so heatedly denied topical meaning, for it openly indulges in allegorical sleuthing' (*Tudor Drama and Politics*, Cambridge, Mass., 1968).

994. *the catte winked*, etc.: a common proverb, sometimes appearing as 'It was not for nought that the cat winked when both her eyes were out', roughly equivalent to 'there's more in this than meets the eye'. (See note to line 1019.)

1005. *saye the moune is made*, etc.: proverbial for 'affirm something blatantly untrue'.

1007–9. *might ... Dothe ... defeate ryght*: the notion that 'Might is (or overcomes) right' goes back to classical times, but the English formulation is medieval.

1019. *saye the croue is whight*: another proverbial phrase akin to that at line 1005; it occurs in Alexander Barclay's *Shyp of Folys* (1509) and in Sir Thomas More's *Dialogue concernynge Heresyes*, Book III, where the proverb at line 994 is also to be found.

ROISTER DOISTER

1–28. The Prologue's speech is printed as a continuous whole, but it can in fact be divided into four seven-line stanzas in rhyme-royal, a favourite verse-form of the fifteenth century, and the same as is employed for both Prologue and Epilogue to *Jacke Jugeler*.

8. *For Myrth prolongeth lyfe*, etc.: cf. the Induction to *The Taming of the Shrew*, II, 131–8, quoted in the Introduction.

19–20. *neither Plautus nor Terence*: on the contemporary popularity of these Latin playwrights, see Introduction.

23. '*Royster Doyster*': the name appears to be a recent coinage for a blustering bully; T. W. Baldwin (*Shakpere's Five-Act Structure*, Urbana, 1947, pp. 381–4) finds significance in the fact that the term 'roisters' as analogous to 'fighters' is first found in Thomas Wilson's *The Rule of Reason: conteining the Arte of Logique* (1551) (see

note to lines 1126–60). Baldwin believes that Wilson and Udall discovered the French word 'ruistre' or its anglicized form *c.* 1551, possibly during their association with Calais. Although the character is obviously modelled on the *miles gloriosus,* some contemporary application may be intended.

29, s.d. *Mathewe Merygreeke*: although the name appears to be Udall's own coinage, 'greek' is probably related to 'grig' which can indicate a dwarf, a hen, an eel, and possibly a cricket! In conjunction with 'merry' or 'mad' it often denotes a lover of fun or mischief. The figure's link with the classical parasite is discussed in the Introduction.

31. *the grassehopper*: the fable of the provident ant and the prodigal grasshopper occurs in Aesop's *Fables,* a work studied in the original by most Tudor schoolboys, and therefore a popular source of allusions.

40–56. *Where to be provided...of meate and drinke*: the strictly pragmatic outlook of the parasitic character is brought out here and elsewhere in Merrygreek's lines, but generally he has a more purely mischief-making role than is usual in the parasites of classical comedy.

45–54. *Lewis Loytrer*, etc.: the proper names in these lines and elsewhere (e.g. Tibet Talkapace, Gawyn Goodluck, etc.) closely parallel those in other medieval and Renaissance works in which the surname indicates the bearer's occupation or character. Lines 659–82 of *Thersytes* contain many examples, including 'Peter Pybaker', 'Nycholl Nevergood', and 'balde Bernarde Braynles'.

48. *Tom Titivile*: this name appears to be related to that of Titivillus or Tutivillus, the medieval devil traditionally charged with collecting up the words and syllables skimped by the priest in celebrating divine service and the idle chatterings of inattentive worshippers. He appears as a character in the fifteenth-century morality play *Mankynde* and in the Wakefield Cycle play, *The Harrowing of Hell.*

55. *shootanker*: 'shute' or 'shote' anchor was the common form of the term until the seventeenth century; its derivation is still obscure. It is always taken to indicate the largest of a ship's anchors, used in emergencies, and it seems to have been used figuratively, as here, from an early date.

66. *the Queene's peace*: this may have read 'the King's peace' in some earlier text now lost, especially if the play was first staged before Edward VI (see Introduction p. 24). The revision might then date

from either the reign of Mary I or Elizabeth I, but if Udall himself revised the play rather than the printer, the former date must be accepted, since Udall died in December 1556. (Cf. note on lines 2001–14.)

77. *his nowne*: it was common to elide such combinations as 'mine own', 'thine own', etc., and the form given here developed by analogy, possibly with comic intention (cf. 'my nowne' in line 312).

84. *hold his finger in a hole*: a proverbial remark: 'a foole putteth his finger in an hole'.

97. *suche a goodly person*: this line and line 200 obviously parallel that of Pyrgopolynices in the *Miles gloriosus*: 'It really is a bore to be so good-looking' (Plautus, *The Pot of Gold and Other Plays*, Penguin Books, 1965, p. 155).

105. *the tide...tarrieth for no man*: one of the commonest of English proverbs, which also occurs in the celebrated English morality play of *Everyman* (*c*. 1520) line 144.

121. *Gramercies*: 'Thanks, thank you'; the original form was of course 'Gramercy' (from Old French *grant merci*), but the plural form given here was quite common in the sixteenth century.

122. *speake out like a ramme*: there appears to be no obvious reason for the simile, though there are other notable examples of sheep-imagery in the play (see lines 1628, 1638).

126. *a breast to blowe out a candle*: *OED* suggests that 'breast' here means 'breath', but it seems more likely (if the phrase has any more significance than mere general encouragement) that Roister Doister puffs out his chest at line 125, thus eliciting Merrygreek's pseudo-appreciative comment.

141. *the Toure*: this would appear to be an early instance of the noun alone being used to designate the Tower of London.

148. *The fellow of the lion*, etc.: the first of Hercules' twelve labours was to slay the Nemean lion; he choked the animal to death and afterwards wore its skin as a cloak.

156. *of merchandise*: Merrygreek is expressing scruples about assisting Roister Doister to purchase the services of a mistress, though whether Udall intended this to be viewed as a facet of Merrygreek's character, or merely introduced the point to improve on the Roman authors' less stringent moral code, is a moot point. He can scarcely have been concerned for his players' morals, since they no doubt had read Latin playwrights in the original.

172. *Christian Custance*: W. W. Greg suggests that the name derives

from the French 'coustance' meaning 'expense', her wealth being crucial to the plot. But in Chaucer's 'Man of Law's Tale' his heroine Constance is always referred to as 'Custance', and Udall's heroine's constancy is as vital to the plot as her money.

191. *'Backare!' quod Mortimer*, etc.: a popular catch-phrase, rather than a proverb; cf. *The Taming of the Shrew*, II, i, 73, 'Bacare! you are marvellous forward.'

200–244. *I am sorie God made me so comely*, etc.: it is of interest to compare the similar if terser exchanges between Pyrgopolynices and Artotrogus (the parasite) in the *Miles gloriosus* (ed. cit., p. 155) with the whole of this passage:

ARTOTROGUS: Need I say, sir – since the whole world knows it – that the valour and triumphs of Pyrgopolynices are without equal on this earth, and so is his handsome appearance? The women are all at your feet, and no wonder; they can't resist your good looks; like those girls who were trying to get my attention yesterday.

PYRGOPOLYNICES: What did they say to you?

ARTOTROGUS: Oh, they pestered me with questions. 'Is he Achilles?' 'No, his brother,' I said. And the other girl said, 'I should think so, he's so good-looking and charming; and hasn't he got lovely hair? I envy the girls who go to bed with him.'

PYRGOPOLYNICES: Did they really say that?

ARTOTROGUS: They did; and they begged me to bring you past their house today – as if you were a travelling show!

PYRGOPOLYNICES: It really is a bore to be so good-looking.

ARTOTROGUS: I'm sure it is. These women are a perfect pest; always begging and wheedling and imploring for a chance to see you. They keep asking me to arrange an introduction; I simply can't get on with my proper work.

208. *Malkyn*: a derogatory name usually applied to a wanton slut or a scarecrow, and therefore taken by some editors to be an exasperated expression of distaste for Roister Doister spoken by Merrygreek under his breath. I prefer to regard it as a further piece of ingratiation on Merrygreek's part as he applies the word to those shameless 'Malkyns' who press forward to admire the military hero.

212. *Sir Launcelot du Lake*: the outstanding knight-hero of the Arthurian literature of the Middle Ages, whose name was a byword for

chivalric prowess; he committed adultery with Arthur's queen Guinevere, and his defection led to the break-up of the Order of the Round Table.

213. *greate Guy of Warwike*: a hero of highly popular medieval legends of knightly prowess; Guy's adventures are retold in a number of literary texts in both verse and prose. His deeds of arms were mostly undertaken in the name of his love for the daughter of the Earl of Warwick, the most famous being the killing of a Danish giant named Colbrand or Colbronde (see line 217 and line 116 of *Thersytes*). Cf. *Henry VIII* v, iv, 20–21:

> I am not Samson, nor Sir Guy, nor Colbrand,
> To mow 'em down before me ...

214. *the thirtenth Hercules' brother*: cf. ' "Is he Achilles?" "No, his brother," I said', in the quotation above under lines 200–244.

215. *Hector of Troy*: eldest son of King Priam and the legendary champion of the Trojan army during the siege, Hector was eventually slain by Achilles (see note to line 220).

217. *Goliah*, etc.: the giant Goliath killed by the young David (see 1 Samuel xvii); Samson's life and deeds of strength are described in the Book of Judges xiii – xvi; for Colbrande see note to line 214.

218. *Brute of the Alie lande*: in the Middle Ages it was commonly supposed that Brutus or Brute, the great-grandson of Aeneas, the legendary founder of Rome, was the first British king and the founder of the British race. His story is told in Book I of Geoffrey of Monmouth's *Historia Regum Britanniae* (*c*. 1135). However, it is likely that here the term is simply used to denote a hero or champion. 'The Alie lande' may mean 'the Holy Land' although that term occurs as early as 1297, and *OED* cites no other instances of the 'Alie' form. Brutus traditionally lived in Greece before landing in Britain. It is tempting to wonder if 'Alie' is somehow related to 'Albion', but there is little support for the notion. (Cf. line 280 and note.)

219. *Alexander*: Alexander III of Macedon (356–323 BC), famous for his feats of conquest in Asia Minor and beyond, was also the hero of a number of medieval romances (see note to line 220).
Charle le Maigne: Charlemagne (AD 742–814), King of the Franks and created Holy Roman Emperor in 800, became the subject of a series of romances and *chansons de geste* in the later Middle Ages (see note to line 220).

220. *the tenth worthie*: i.e. an addition to the original nine mentioned in line 222; they were the pagans Hector, Alexander, and Julius Caesar; the Jews Joshua, David, and Judas Maccabaeus; the Christians Arthur, Charlemagne, and Godfrey of Bouillon.

223. *the thirde Cato*: the first two were Marcus Porcius Cato ('Cato the Censor') (234–149 BC), and his great-grandson, Marcus Porcius Cato Uticensis (95–46 BC), the Stoic philosopher and opponent of Julius Caesar.

250. *having money inowe*: an obvious lie!

253. *By Cocke*: a common distortion of the oath 'By God!' though probably not intended as a euphemism.

280, s.d. *Annot Alyface*: it has been suggested that 'Alyface' means 'Holy-face' (cf. 'Alie lande' in line 218), but this seems somewhat incongruous; the first element may derive from 'aloe', a bitter purgative drug, or possibly from 'ale'.

282. *stale ale*: ale which has stood long enough to be free from impurities, hence strong, vintage ale.

291–2. *whip and whurre*, etc.: M. P. Tilley's *Dictionary of the Proverbs in England* cites this under W 304 as its only example of the saying.

294. *Soft fire*, etc.: a common proverb of the time, counselling caution.

301. *sirrha*: although the term had 'sir' as its root, and was therefore usually applied to men and boys, it could still be used for women: the note of contempt, reprimand, or superiority was still present.

307. *ye will drinke anon*: i.e. be punished (cf. 'drinke withoute a cup' at line 309)

323. *Olde Trotte*: a common term of disparagement for an old woman (cf. 'Dame Trot', etc.)

331. *Pipe, mery Anot*: a popular song of the time, or a variation upon it.

371. *husbande*: not of course a married man, but a husbandman, either a farmer or a householder with duties to attend to.

379. *chad not so much*: this conventional mode of representing rustic dialect on stage will be familiar to many from its adoption by the disguised Edgar in *King Lear*, IV, 6. 237–47; it is used in other plays of the period, but this is a very early example of its employment. See the Appendix on the use of dialect forms for rustics, pp. 427–9. (Cf. lines 483 and 493 for further examples.)

384. *Why shoulde I feare you?*, etc.: Tibet's answers to Roister Doister in this and subsequent lines show a strong affinity with those of

Jaquenetta when addressing Don Armado in *Love's Labour's Lost*, I. 2. 126–37.

390. *when dyd you last kisse your cowe?*: a favourite witticism (cf. *Gammer Gurton's Nedle*, line 564), often encountered in proverbial form as in Thomas Wyatt's lyric, 'I have sought long with stedfastnes', lines 21–2:

> For fansy rueleth, tho right say nay,
> Even as the goodeman kyst his kowe ...

> (*Collected Poems of Sir Thomas Wyatt*, ed. Muir and Thomson, Liverpool, 1969, pp. 51–2.)

396. *They that lust*: 'there's no accounting for taste'.

402. *A mischief on all loutes*: Tibet curses Roister Doister for distracting her from her allotted task.

406. *commaunde me to you*: in her confusion Madge appears to mistake 'commends her to you' for the remark she utters. It is of course patently untrue that Christian Custance greets Roister Doister (cf. line 409).

418, s.d. *Here lette him tell hir*, etc.: one of the few descriptive stage directions in the whole play.

418, s.d. *and another servant*, etc.: although the heading to the scene only mentions Dobinet Doughty and Harpax, it seems clear from lines 422–3 that Harpax is not the only other servant on stage at this point, and that he has a 'fellow'. This character doubtless appeared as one of the 'foure men' required to sing Roister Doister's 'obsequies' in III. 3. 994–8.

430. *With Nobs nicebecetur miserere fonde*: it is tempting to dismiss this as a piece of pure nonsense, but it can be made to yield some kind of sense. 'Nobs' is used by John Skelton and other contemporary writers to mean 'darling'; 'nicebecetur' means a fashionable or attractive woman: 'miserere' is Latin for 'have mercy'; 'fonde' is 'foolish'; thus the whole may mean 'with foolish "Darling sweetheart, have mercy upon me"'.

431. *be ye spedde alredie?*: 'have you already succeeded in your aim?' For several lines Merrygreek deliberately pretends that Madge is Roister Doister's beloved.

436. *mocke muche of hir*: the substitution of 'mocke' for 'make' seems deliberate and yet rather pointless, since the mockery derives from Merrygreek, not Roister Doister, whose solicitous deference to Madge Mumblecrust is most marked (cf. line 1196).

442. *She is but a gristle*: cf. *Thersytes*, line 391 '. . . it is but a grestle'.

460. *pygsnie*: literally 'pig's eye', a term of affection much employed in the sixteenth century with the meaning 'precious little eye'; cf. 'the apple of my eye'.

466. *a whole pecke of argent*: the peck was a unit of measurement employed for grain, hops, or other dry goods; it was the equivalent of a quarter of a bushel.

482. *Blanchepouderlande*: blanche powder was a white powder sprinkled on food, especially fruit, when preparing it for the table.

484. *the last elephant*, etc.: cf. *Miles gloriosus* (ed. cit., p. 154):

ARTOTROGUS: . . . I was thinking about that elephant in India, and how you broke his ulna with a single blow of your fist.

490. *he knew his match was in place*: 'he recognized that he had met his equal'.

491. *the King of Crickets*: the tone here begins to resemble that of *Thersytes*, whose hero runs away from a snail (see Introduction, p. 22).

494. *Belzebub*: Beelzebub, one of the chief devils, traditionally carried a club as a weapon. (Cf. *Gammer Gurton's Nedle*, line 831 and note.)

495. *Mumfision*: there seems to be no clue as to the significance of this proper name, nor of the context of the allusion in which it features. 'To bear the lantern' (line 496) is to show the way as leader.

545. *I wrote it ech whit*: a seemingly unimportant detail which is to have far-reaching consequences by the time Act III scene 4 is reached.

557. *shall win her?*: Manly proposes 'will win her?' for the Quarto's 'is well enough?'

567. *spouse*: obviously not used in the sense of 'husband' but in that of 'fiancé'.

573. *pecke of golde*: see note to line 466. Madge has transmuted Roister Doister's 'argent' to gold!

574. *lacke of a pynte*: either 'it will be a pint short' or 'it won't amount to even a pint'; a pint could of course be used as a measure for dry as well as liquid substances.

591. *Up before day, sirs*: an acknowledgement of the presence of spectators.

603. *recorder*: this popular wind instrument, possibly of English origin, was greatly in vogue in the Tudor period.

608. *Jacke Raker*: said by Boas to be a proverbial instance of a bad poet, though I have not met with examples of the allusion elsewhere.

610. *Foolishe Marsias*: Marsyas was a Phrygian satyr who challenged Apollo to a contest in music, playing the flute while the god played on the cithara; the Muses adjudged Apollo the winner, and as a punishment for his presumption, Marsyas was flayed alive. His story is told in Ovid's *Metamorphoses* vi, 382–99.

623. *I bring hir a ring*: a ring also features as a token in the *Miles gloriosus*.

630. *a charme*: i.e. a 'magic token' acting as a warning against future misconduct.

648. *one Lumbarde's touche*: Italian goldsmiths, money-lenders, and bankers, especially those from Lombardy, were famous in the Middle Ages; their London centre is still known as Lombard Street, and retains its banking associations. Dobinet trusts that Truepenny will display one of the traits of a Lombard, the ability to accept the golden ring from him, and convey it to Christian Custance.

656. *'In docke, out nettle!'*: a proverbial phrase signifying inconstancy and instability, derived from the charm originally spoken when someone wished to ease a nettle sting by rubbing the place with a dock leaf.

677. *But ye roile abroade*: Tibet envies Truepenny's freedom to rove outside Dame Custance's house, by virtue of his role as messenger. He retorts that, in order to chide him for being outside, Tibet and Annot also have to leave the house!

689. *Frenche hoodes*: female head-dress based on a curved framework instead of the angular 'gable' style. The hood (often of black velvet) fell in vertical folds down the wearer's back. Popularized by Anne Boleyn and Catherine Howard, it was later worn by both Mary I and Elizabeth I.

691. *ferdegews*: the farthingale (or verdegew) introduced to Britain from Spain by Catherine of Aragon; modelled on a canvas petticoat, it was stiffened later by hoops of whalebone to produce the desired cone-shaped silhouette. Over this foundation, several petticoats were worn, a corset giving the slender waist so much admired.

692. *sutes of chaunge*: Tibet imagines either that each serving-maid has fourteen different outfits or that each change of clothing has seven double layers of fabric.

696. *prickmedaintie*: 'to prick' can mean 'to dress up elaborately', so the term means someone affectedly fastidious about their dress.
come toste me a fig: 'Who's getting ideas above their station?' Cf. *Look Back in Anger*, II, i: 'Pass Lady Bracknell the cucumber sandwiches, will you?'

735. *Trill on the berie*: J. Q. Adams suggests 'Twirl (or whirl) on the mound', but *OED* cites several examples supporting the meaning 'pass round the wine', 'berie' carrying the meaning that 'the grape' sometimes does today. One of the sources cited is line 658 of *Thersytes*: 'synge tyrle on the berye'.

752. *a tomboy*: the text reads 'a Tom boy' and *OED* cites this as its earliest instance of the term in its modern sense.

760. *Why did ye no?*: the text reads 'No did?' Greg suggests 'Did ye no?' in its place.

763. *naughty*: this word has a range of meanings from 'immoral, wicked' to 'disobedient, wayward, mischievous'; the contexts suggest that Christian Custance uses it in the latter sense at line 763, while Tibet at line 774 comes nearer to the more pejorative meaning.

786. *Paule's steeple*: until 1561 when it was struck by lightning, the tower of Old St Paul's was topped by a wooden steeple measuring some 150 feet or more and forming a well-known landmark. Funds were collected for its restoration, but it was never replaced. The Cathedral itself burnt down in the Great Fire of London in 1666. (See S. Schoenbaum, *William Shakespeare: A Documentary Life*, Oxford, 1975, p. 98.)

838. *after the olde rate*: 'go on much as I did before'; 'feel just about the same as usual'.

842. *make but one sleepe*: i.e. enjoy undisturbed slumbers, unlike the conventional sleepless lover.

852. *as loving a worm againe as a dove*: 'he (poor worm) returns your love as much as the traditionally amorous dove does'; the dove was a conventional symbol of devotion (cf. line 1798).

878. *But by imagination*: 'only from the mental picture I've formed of him'.

893. *play choploge*: 'engage in hair-splitting arguments (chop-logic)'.

894. *the devill in the horologe*: the word 'horologe' was applied to any

type of instrument for recording the time; the proverb is used to indicate that kind of disruptive activity which disturbs any smooth-running system. Cf. 'to raise Cain', 'to create merry hell', etc.

908. *Juno sende me*, etc.: a possible trace of the classical background to the play lingering on in Udall's mind.

912. *in poste against you*: Merrygreek puns on the notion of running post-haste to meet Roister Doister (*OED* sense I. 5), and running up against him physically.

914. *bycause I cannot be had*: Tilley (op. cit.) suggests that the proverb should be 'I am sad because I cannot be glad' which implies that Roister Doister is parodying a well-known catch-phrase; Tilley offers only two indirect parallels to his example from *Roister Doister*.

920. *a lilburne ... a hoball ... a lobcocke*: the *OED* throws a little light on the last pair of these colourful synonyms: 'hob' is related to the name Robert or Robin, and appears in 'hobgoblin'; 'lob' is paralleled in a number of modern European words for 'clown' or 'oaf' and is related to 'lubber'.

926. *a good gander*, etc.: part of the *miles gloriosus* tradition is that he can be frightened by domestic animals, insects, etc. (cf. Thersytes and the snail; see also lines 1775–8, and note).

955. *Placebo dilexi*, etc.: here begins one of the most notable features of the play, based on a parody of the Roman Catholic funeral rite, containing fragments of services for the dead, as laid down in the liturgy. Skelton in *The Boke of Phyllyp Sparowe* (*c.* 1508) makes similar use of funeral phraseology, but in neither case should it be assumed that this constitutes evidence of pro- or anti-Catholic feeling.

The Church observed two funeral rites: a two-part *Officium pro defunctis* (an evening Vespers, with Matins and Lauds the next morning), followed by the Funeral which included Mass, after which the cortège proceeded to the grave for the burial. Allusions to these services are made between lines 955 and 1000 as follows: Line 955, *Placebo domino in regione vivorum* (Vulgate Psalm cxiv, 9): 'I will walk before the Lord in the land of the living', the opening of the antiphon (or introduction to the psalm) to Vespers in the Office of the Dead, a service which became known as the 'Placebo'.

Line 955, *Dilexi quoniam* (Vulgate Psalm cxiv, 1): 'I am well pleased that the Lord hath heard the voice of my prayer'; Psalm cxiv followed the antiphon.

Line 967, *Nequando* (Vulgate Psalm vii, 2): 'Lest he [i.e. God] devour my soul, like a lion, and tear it in pieces'; this antiphon precedes the third psalm at Matins, prior to the Mass.

Line 968, *Dirige, Domine* (Vulgate Psalm v, 9): 'Make plain before me thy path, o Lord my God'; it forms the first antiphon at Matins, and gave the service as a whole its name of 'Dirge'.

Line 971, *A porta inferi*: 'from the gate of Hell rescue their souls, o Lord', part of a versicle and response at the end of the third psalm at Matins, which also occurs as an antiphon to the fourth psalm at Lauds.

Line 973, *Requiem aeternam dona eis, Domine*: 'O Lord, grant them eternal rest'; adapted from Esdras ii, 34, this phrase recurs throughout the funeral services.

Line 979, *Audivi vocem de caelo*: ('I heard a voice from heaven saying unto me, Write, Blessed are the dead which die in the Lord ...') Taken from the Book of Revelation xiv, 13, these words come from the versicle and response which follow the fifth psalm at Lauds.

Line 999, *Qui Lazarum resuscitasti*: ('You who raised Lazarus from the dead') begins another versicle and response, that which follows the second lesson at Matins.

Line 1000, *In Paradisum deducant te Angeli*: ('May angels lead thee into Paradise') these words are taken from the anthem sung during the funeral service proper when the body was borne to the grave for burial.

956. *Maister Roister Doister*, etc.: the text from this point until line 989 of the present edition creates certain problems. Line 956 is followed in the original with the words '*ut infra*' (as below), which refer the reader to the last three printed pages of the book where 'Certaine Songs to be song by those which shall use this Comedie or Enterlude' are set out. Here are printed 'The Seconde Song' ('Whoso to marry a minion wyfe') (lines 531–42 in the present edition); 'The Fourth Song' ('I mun be maried a Sunday') (lines 1065–88); 'The Psalmodie' beginning with *Placebo dilexi* and line 956 quoted above; 'The Peale of belles ...' (lines 994–8). '*The Psalmodie*' consists of twenty-three lines, some of which are original, some of which are repeated in the main body of the text, but whose sequence does not always conform to that followed by the

main text. In 'The Psalmodie' the four lines beginning 'But in spite of Custance' (lines 961–4) *precede* the three beginning '*Dirige.* He will go darklyng to his grave' (lines 968–70), although lines 969–70 as given in 'The Psalmodie' vary slightly from those incorporated into the main text, reading '*Neque lux, neque crux, nisi solum* clinke / Never gentman so went toward heaven I thinke'. In the main text the four lines in question do not occur until after 'Our good maister here will no longer with us dwell' (line 976 of the present version), where they are immediately succeeded by '*Audivi vocem.* All men take heede by this one gentleman' (line 979). 'The Psalmodie', however, includes a couplet (printed as lines 977–8 of the present edition) which does not appear at all in the main body of the text. The interruption at lines 985–6 does not occur in 'The Psalmodie', which concludes with lines 987–9 of the present text.

The difficulty is to decide how the lines should best be arranged to maintain the most satisfactory progression of ideas. In trying to determine the correct position of the competing lines, I place considerable emphasis on line 964 with its reference to 'Some parte of his funeralls let us here beginne', which seems less justified in its main text position after line 976 than where I have placed it, since the 'funeralls' are well under way by this point. Therefore, concluding that lines 961–4 are wrongly placed in the main text, I have treated them as continuous with the first lines of 'The Psalmodie'. I have retained lines 977–8 which only appear in 'The Psalmodie', but adopted the wording of the main text at lines 969–70. By this method, a reasonably coherent pattern of development seems to emerge from the confusion.

958. *tomorow John*: it would be helpful to be able to read 'John' as 'none' here, since a satisfactory explanation of the proper name is hard to come by. A 'John' can signify a butler, footman, or waiter, but none of these seems relevant in the present context.

970. *unknowing to God*: probably 'unknown to God', though 'ignorant of God' is also a permissible interpretation.

975, s.d. *Evocat servos militis*: the reference to Roister Doister as a soldier (*miles*) is retained in this stage direction and at line 992.

988. *knap*: editors have tended to suggest that 'knap' equates with 'knave' or 'rogue', but it is possible that, linked to 'Good night', it should be taken in the sense of 'nap', meaning 'take a short sleep'. There is a further complication that lines 987–8 do not rhyme, so

there may be some textual corruption here. I also wonder if the Latin phrases at line 989 are an integral part of the original text, for they only appear in 'The Psalmodie', yet line 988 in the main body of the text is followed by the words '*ut infra*' ('as below'), and to reprint the Latin phrases given 'below' is the sole means of complying with the rubric.

993, s.d. *Enter the parish clerk*: the only indications that this figure appears are Merrygreek's remark at line 991, and the fact that five men are required to ring the 'peal of bells' which probably took the form of a sung round or canon.

1008. *Armes! What dost thou?*: Merrygreek clearly takes the opportunity to assault Roister Doister in the pretence of ministering to him in his languishing state.

1016. *Good happe is not hastie*: apparently proverbial for 'success cannot be hurried', but not cited in the main collections.

in space comth grace: another common proverb.

1041. *Backe, Sir Sauce*: Merrygreek is imagining the presence of an importunate onlooker who is impeding Roister Doister's progress through the streets.

1049. *Ye were take up for haukes*: 'you would be seized and slaughtered to feed hawks', i.e. Roister Doister would be ruined by Dame Custance if he were once married to her. Cf. 'she'd have your guts for garters'.

1062. *no grasse on my heele*: Merrygreek uses a familiar phrase for making good speed, which is repeated by Truepenny at line 1550.

1094. *in schooles*: i.e. in the university 'schools'.

1098. *haze*: F. S. Boas in his World's Classics edition hazards the view that 'haze' equals 'have us', but since the meaning 'scold' or 'chide' exists, it seems quite as meaningful to take 'haze' in this sense.

1109. *dyd I not?*: the line succeeding this which should rhyme with it is missing.

1126–60. *'Sweete mistresse ...'*, etc.: this, one of the most elaborate verbal jokes in the whole of Tudor drama (cf. Quince's Prologue in *A Midsummer Night's Dream*), became one of the play's most famous features early in its existence. Both the mispunctuated and correctly punctuated versions figure under the heading 'Ambiguitie' in the third edition of Thomas Wilson's *The Rule of Reason: conteinynge the Arte of Logique set forth in Englishe* ... published in 1553, where they are introduced with the words:

'An example of soche doubtful writing, whiche by reason of poincting maie have double sense, and contrarie meaning, taken out of an entrelude made by Nicolas Udal.'

The fact that the passages do not appear in the 1551 or 1552 editions of Wilson's book may indicate that it was in 1552–3 that *Roister Doister* was first written, published, or performed.

1162. *By the armes of Caleys*: Calais was in English hands from its capture by Edward III in 1347 until its re-conquest by the French in January 1558, a loss said to have hastened the death of Mary I later in that year. The Marches of Calais were in fact the last piece of French territory held by the English in Europe. T. W. Baldwin states that Udall was there in 1551.

1168. *I wrote it myne owne selfe*: i.e. the scrivener composed the wording of the love-letter, but Roister Doister copied it before the letter was delivered to Christian Custance. (Cf. lines 1275–7.)

1187. *Art thou to thine harmes.* etc,: 'Are you so determined to do yourself an injury?'

1189. *Canst thou not lub dis man*, etc.: a curious and inexplicable anticipation of the usual manner in which the White man represented negro speech in the nineteenth and twentieth centuries.

1217. *By Cock's precious potsticke*: see note to line 148 of *Jacke Jugeler*; for the suggestion that the verbal parallel is possibly significant, see under Dudok in the *Guide to Further Reading*.

1220. *scribler*: both Adams and Boas (eds. cit.) think that Roister Doister mistakes the term 'scrivener' for 'scribbler', but there is no need to assume that he is not simply insulting the man whom he thinks has 'marde' his chances with Christian Custance.

1228. *legions*: not used with any precise meaning, but simply to indicate hosts of armed men, a multitude of soldiers.

1265. *Phariseys and Scribes*: a common pejorative combination by this time, one of earliest English instances appearing in lines 6889–93 of the Middle English translation of *Le Roman de la Rose*, commonly attributed to Chaucer. Here Matthew xxiii, 2 (Authorized Version) is translated: 'Uppon the chaire of Moyses . . ./Sitte Scribes and Pharisen', and the text goes on 'That is to seyn, the cursid men/Whiche that we ypocritis calle' (lines 6894–'5).

1346. *sette lyght by hir*: 'make no account of her'.

1356. *Neptune's mightie godshyp*: possibly another deliberately classical touch (cf. line 908).

1380. *Howe doth mine owne Gawyn Goodlucke*, etc.: the immediacy of

Christian Custance's warm concern for her fiancé makes a striking impression in her favour.

1389. *their best Christmasse chekes*: the precise significance of 'Christmasse' in this context is obscure, though the general meaning is not affected by it; the phrase is striking in its own right. (Cf. line 973 of *Gammer Gurton's Nedle*.)

1401. *Let us hearken them*, etc.: Sym Suresby repeats line 1395, possibly a printer's error.

1403–12. *Sirs, see that my harnesse*, etc.: cf. *Miles gloriosus* (ed. cit., p. 153):

PYRGOPOLYNICES: My shield, there – have it burnished brighter than the bright splendour of the sun on any summer's day. Next time I have occasion to use it in the press of battle, it must flash defiance into the eyes of the opposing foe …

1489. *out of thy sty*: the text here reads 'house', but in view of the necessity to rhyme with 'by and by', Greg proposed the reading 'sty' which certainly makes good sense in the light of Roister Doister's raging temper and his contempt for the woman who has refused him.

1499. *Anon*: 'Coming!' 'Be with you right away!' A familiar cry from Tudor tapsters, drawers, and waiters in response to a request for service (see *1 Henry IV*, II. 4. 16–77).

1513. *paishe of God*: if this is in fact a shortened form of 'Passion' like 'pashe' at line 1696, it appears peculiar to *Roister Doister*; the phrase 'for the passion of God' occurs at line 1491. However, it is possible that both 'paishe' and 'pashe' are forms of 'Pasch' meaning 'Passover' or 'Easter' (cf. French *pâques*) and, if so, this would mean that they need no longer be regarded as isolated examples of an otherwise unknown abbreviation.

1517. *sirra*: see note to line 301.

1536. *skimmer*: a perforated kitchen implement often of metal, for skimming off foreign matter from liquids.

1537. *fireforke*: a metallic fork-like poker for raking or poking the fire with.

1538. *spitte*: the pointed rod of metal or wood used to pierce joints of meat, etc., when they were to be roasted at the fireside.

1540. *For my parte*, etc.: Tibet appropriately succeeds in having the last word!

1550. *no grasse hath growne*, etc.: cf. line 1062 and note.

1555. *by your going*: 'from the speed at which you walk'.

1602. *for altogether*: 'once and for all'.

1604. *nor tost so hot*: a fine example of bathos, following as it does on 'bore so brymme'.

1623. *to take dishonestie*: 'to lose my reputation'.

1628. *a sheepe's looke full grim*: an apparent contradiction, for the sheep is proverbial for its timidity and vulnerability; however, 'a sheepe's looke' may be a reflection of Roister Doister's amorous proclivities (cf. 'making sheep's eyes'), and 'grim' is less odd if we take it to mean 'bold' rather than 'fierce'.

1630. *pitche a fielde*: 'engage him in battle'.

1638. *a Cottsold lyon*: the Cotswold hills were noted for their long-haired sheep, humorously referred to as 'Cotswold lions'. It is again of interest that *Thersytes* (line 124) contains a similar reference: 'Now have at the lyons on Cotsolde.' A timid person was said to be as 'valiant as an Essex lion', i.e. a calf.

1646, s.d. *Two drummes with their Ensignes*: this indication of personnel does not appear until the heading of Act IV, scene 8, but it would seem clear that the drummers are part of Roister Doister's 'army', and enter with the rest of the company; the 'Ensignes' are probably 'banners' rather than 'standard-bearers'. Adams (ed. cit.) suggests that each 'army' has a drummer, but I think it unlikely that Dame Custance could enlist such a recruit.

1656. *I am a lad*: 'a man of spirit', an early usage of a now common definition of 'lad', appearing in such phrases as 'one of the lads', 'a bit of a lad', etc.

1694. *the armes of Caleys*: see line 1162 and note.

1696. *the pashe of God*: see line 1513 and note.

1706. *collocavit*: the Latin verb *collocare*, 'to place or position', of which this is the third person singular perfect, seems to have little to do with this coinage, which probably derives from the word 'collock' which means a tub or a pail. One suspects the presence of a piece of schoolboy slang here, linking a familiar domestic term with a Latin verb-ending.

1742. *will ye thus forgo*, etc.: Merrygreek is anxious not to have his sport with Roister Doister prematurely terminated.

1756. *harquebouse*: the harquebus (various forms) was a light portable field-gun.

1760, s.d. *Fires his gun*: this stage direction is not found in the original text, but unless Merrygreek does something of the kind, Christian Custance's remark at line 1762 seems unmotivated.

1763. *Ah sirrha!*: see line 301 and note.

1776–8. *I will turne hir loose*: again this recalls the braggart soldier of the *Thersytes* tradition, scared of harmless creatures (though a goose in full cry is not to be trifled with!).

1785. *queane*: although the term could simply mean 'a woman', it early developed its pejorative sense of a rude or forward woman, and later came to designate a prostitute. Its use here is not, I think, intended to convey more than Dobinet's view that Tibet is a troublesome and vindictive 'madam'.

1787. *Mounsire Graunde Captaine*: an allusion to Roister Doister's militaristic pretensions.

1799. *so soone hotte, so soone colde*: a proverbial phrase, especially when applied to love, as aptly cited in *The Works of Sir Thomas Malory*, xviii, 25 (Oxford Standard Authors, p. 791): '... ryght so faryth love nowadayes, sone hote sone colde. Thys ys no stabylyté. But the olde love was nat so ...' (Cf. 'Hot love is soon (will soon wax) cold'; see *Mother Bombie*, lines 433–4.)

1802. *mankine*: assumed by some editors to refer to Christian Custance's 'mannishness' as evinced by her leadership in the recent 'war', 'mankine' simply means 'mad with rage', deriving possibly from 'mankeen': 'fierce' or 'savage'.

1804. *hir other husbande*: Roister Doister still seems convinced that he is either already betrothed to Christian Custance or about to be so.

1838. *All things that shineth*, etc.: a rendering of the familiar proverb 'All that glitters is not gold': the lack of agreement between noun and verb is common throughout the sixteenth century.

1855. *I heare of your doings to me*, etc.: three meanings are possible: 'I hear strange things about your behaviour towards me'; 'I hear that you have acted in an unfriendly [strange] manner towards me'; 'I hear news of your actions, which strike me as being very uncharacteristic of you'. I personally feel that the first interpretation is to be preferred, but there is no decisive argument to support it.

1874. *better (they say) a badde scuse than none*: curiously enough, this proverb also features in Wilson's *Rule of Reason* (1551), the book cited in notes to lines 23 and 1126; it appears on sig. S 6, and reads 'This is as thei saie in English, better a badde excuse then none at all, in Latine it is called, *non causa pro causa posita* ...'

1883. *O Lorde, howe necessarie*, etc.: a notable change of tone is evident in this speech, with Christian Custance's sincerity and weighty language contrasting with the general tenor of most of what has gone before. The sentiments are not unlike those in the Epilogue to *Jacke Jugeler*, or those of the falsely accused Susanna in Thomas Garter's play cited in the note to line 1893.

1891. *the advoutresse*: this could be an allusion to the prostitute Mary Magdalene, who became one of Christ's most devoted followers after her repentance and conversion, or to the celebrated figure of 'the woman taken in adultery' who features in St John's Gospel viii, 3–11, to whom Christ offered the chance of amendment of life after the humiliation of her accusers. Her story forms the subject of Play 24 of the N-Town Cycle sequence.

1893. *Susanna, wrongfully accused*: the wife of Joacim or Joakim in the Apocryphal History of Susanna (Daniel and Susanna in the *New English Bible*), who was falsely accused of adultery by two elders of the people who themselves lusted after her; the prophet Daniel was able to demonstrate that their accusations did not tally, and they were stoned to death. The incident formed the subject of Thomas Garter's *The Commedy of the Moste Vertuous and Godlye Susanna*. Cf. 'The Man of Law's Tale' (Robinson, II, 639–40): 'Immortal God, that savedest Susanne/Fro false blame'.

1895. *Hester*: Esther was a beautiful Jewess married to 'King Ahasuerus' (in fact the Persian Emperor Xerxes, 485–465 BC) in the Old Testament book which bears her name. When the evil counsellor Haman sought to destroy all Jews in the kingdom, she defended her people so eloquently that the king ordered Haman to be put to death instead. Her story was dramatized in *Godly Queen Hester*, an anonymous play written *c*. 1527, published in 1561.

1898. *yll report*: Ill Report actually features as a character in Garter's play about Susanna (see note on line 1893).

1949–50. *Why, suche a foole it is*, etc.: cf. Terence, *Eunuchus* (in *The Brothers and Other Plays*, Penguin Books, 1965, p. 82):

GNATHO: In return I offer you both – Thraso: for the laughs and everything else you can get out of him.

1960–63. *But when I sayd your anger to favour*, etc.: cf. *Eunuchus* (ed. cit., p. 82):

GNATHO: ... I only had to reveal your true character and praise you according to your deeds and merits, and it was easy.

1964. *no man, woman, nor childe can hate me long*: cf. *Eunuchus* (ed. cit., p. 82):

THRASO: ... I must say I've always found myself exceedingly popular wherever I've been.

1975. *the Eschequer*: the court of law known as the Court of the Exchequer evolved from the judicial aspect of the work of the King's Exchequer which concerned itself with matters pertaining to the royal revenue. Its jurisdiction came to cover cases other than those involving purely financial considerations.

2000, s.d. *Here they sing*: no words are given for the song, but it is at least possible that it simply consists of the lines 2001–14.

2001. *our most noble Queene*: see notes to line 66 above and line 2007 below.

2007. *the Gospell to protect*: Greg, the Malone Society editor, suggests that this phrase is more likely to apply to Elizabeth I than Mary, but his view seems to be based on the assumption that 'Gospell' is used to mean 'the Protestant system of worship and belief' rather than 'the integrity of the Scriptures'. Perhaps if the play was originally composed for Edward VI, and then revised at some point during the reign of Mary I, the changes from 'king' to 'queen' here and at line 66 were made without much thought for the precise sense of 'Gospell', or perhaps it was never used with its specialized meaning in mind. Alternatively, the amendments could have been made if the play was revised prior to its publication *c.* October 1566, when the specialized meaning could again be relevant as Greg suggests. But the whole work cannot be assigned to Elizabeth's reign on the strength of line 2007; there is ample evidence for ascribing the play to Udall, and to a date between 1552 and 1553.

GAMMER GURTON'S NEDLE

Cast-list: *the Bedlem*: see note on line 498 of *Jacke Jugeler*. Diccon's mental condition is touched on in the Introduction.

Mutes: silent performers who perhaps sang in the tavern scene, acted as supernumerary villagers, or played music at the end of Act II.

4. *her needle*: although the piece depends on the 'storm in a teacup' motif, it is worth remembering that a needle represented an expensive and valued item in the sixteenth century.

8. *gossyp*: originally applied to a sponsor at baptism, the term then came to mean a close friend or neighbour (as here), then a female crony, and so to its present sense of a tattler or chatterer (cf. line 23 and elsewhere in the play).

10. *at Masse*: a possible indication of a composition date in the reign of Mary I or less probably Henry VIII, when the Mass was celebrated; it may, however, be another 'historical' allusion. (See Introduction.)

18. *out of his bottocke*: Tudor audiences (like medieval ones) seem to have had no objection to the revelation of the play's *dénouement* in a prologue, or similar form of introduction such as 'banns'.

20. *good nale*: the habit of attaching an 'n' to any noun beginning with a vowel is not uncommon in this period; here it was possibly the result of the existence of the phrase 'at an ale', i.e. tavern, or drinking-session.

30. *within this house*: see remarks on stage-settings in the Introduction, pp. 31–5.

32. *a trump*: in view of the game of 'Trumpe' played at the opening of Act II, scene 2, one might assume that a card or even the game is referred to here, the phrase possibly being intended as 'lost at trump'. However 'trump' can mean a trumpery or trifling article, and unless the phrase is to be amended, this seems the likeliest interpretation.

42. *a slyp of bacon*: according to line 307 the bacon hung behind the door.

50. *a bearward*: the supervisor of one or more performing bears.

60. *pacthreede*: sturdy thread or twine used to sew up packs or bundles.

70. *taken with*, etc.: 'bewitched by fairies or some demon'.

75. *Tome Tannkard's*: cf. the descriptive surnames noted in *Roister Doister*, lines 45–54.

76. *halfe aker*: a small field attached to a farm, suitable for grazing.

78. *'Tphrowh hoore!'*: Hodge's own patent cry to startle the cow.

92. *a noddy*: the first Quarto reads 'at noddy' here, almost certainly an error, and possibly arising from a card-game called Noddy.

105. *sayth she*: the text's 'sayth' may be intended to mean 'she says', but it is unusual, and I have ventured to insert the pronoun, which the rhythm also seems to justify.

108. *a noble*: a medieval gold coin, originally worth 6*s.* 8*d.* (cf. 'angell' in *Mother Bombie*, line 1846 and note.)

115. *The Devill, or els his dame*: a popular alliterative combination, possibly meaning 'the devil or something worse', i.e. his mother or his wife.

117. *pes*: a word of East Anglian origin, which may bear on the origins of the play, its author, or its setting. (Cf. 'Saint Sithe' in line 152 and note.)

thy breeches: presumably Hodge has two pairs of breeches, one in use, the other being mended when the catastrophe occurs. (See Introduction.)

119. *leares*: does Tib intend an insult here, or does she use the term in its earlier sense of 'look obliquely, give a sideways glance'? The general tone may support the modern signification.

122. *the towne*: an enclosed yard attached to a single dwelling-house was known as 'the town'.

126. *never the nere*: 'no nearer being fit to wear'.

129. *in twenty devils' way*: 'in the name of twenty devils'. Hodge's disrespectful tone to his mistress makes him sound more like a husband than an employee, but his grumpy tone masks affectionate concern, as did John Brown's when scolding Queen Victoria.

137. *fooles will be fooles styll*: a proverbial phrase; cf. 'Once a fool, always a fool'.

139. *hoore*: not to be taken as 'prostitute' but simply as abuse.

141. *roking*: Boas suggests a variant form of 'rucking' meaning 'crouching', but a variant of 'raking' seems less strained, and compares well with line 191: 'Rakyng ... amonge the asshes'.

146. *loes your ars*: cf. *Jacke Jugeler*, line 619.

152. *Saint Sithe*: Saint Osyth, or Osgyth, was said to be the daughter of a Mercian chieftain, married against her will to King Sighere of the East Saxons; she became a nun and was murdered by Danish pirates *c.* 675 at Cicc or Chich in Essex, where a priory dedicated to her was founded in the twelfth century. The place then took her name. Like 'pes' at line 117, the reference to a local saint may indicate the playwright's antecedents or the play's setting.

158. *foure of you*: Hodge includes the cat in the security force! (Cf. line 128.)

167. *Set me a candle*: Tudor cottages were dim and gloomy, and on the assumption that the play's action takes place one summer evening, a light would be a necessity in looking for a needle.

175. *Ye must have a crier*: 'it would take a town crier to get you to shift yourself'.

176. *no fier*: i.e. to light the candle at.

181. *our*: thus the printed text, but it may be that an 'e' has fallen out, so that the phrase should read 'over and over againe'.

202. *The fier was sure bewicht*: Hodge's belief in the supernatural has already been demonstrated in lines 80 and 91, and is skilfully built up now to its farcical culmination in Act II, scene 1.

213. *patch*: a fool, called so on account of his traditional parti-coloured clothing.

222. *A candell shall they have*: this reference to burning a candle at the shrine or before the statue of a saint is a further indication either that the play was composed under a Roman Catholic sovereign, or that a historical setting is implied.

235. *Our candle is at an ende*: it is not made clear when it was actually lit!

237. *Backe and syde*, etc.: Brett-Smith prints a fuller version of this song from Alexander Dyce's 1843 edition of Skelton's poems; the sentiments are curiously akin to those of Gus Elen's music-hall song 'Half a Pint of Ale'.

244. *him that weares a hood*: some see this as a reference to a monk, but since many of the laity wore hoods, I take the phrase to mean 'I'll have a drink with anybody'.

267. *a mault worme*: literally 'a weevil that infects malt', but then applied to anyone with a passion for 'the malt'.

275. *scowred boules*: i.e. 'licked them as clean as if scoured'.

281. *true mayde*: presumably a joke, 'mayde' meaning 'virgin' or 'young girl'. Diccon intends to flatter, or to wax ironic.

283. *my naked armes to defende*: 'to protect my bare arms'. Bedlamites often went half-naked and inflicted injuries on their naked flesh; cf. *King Lear*, II. 3. 14–16:

> Bedlam beggars, who ...
> Strike in their numb'd and mortified bare arms
> Pins, wooden pricks, nails, sprigs of rosemary.

287. *where Dyccon will dyne*: cf. Merrygreek in *Roister Doister*, lines 39–42.

293. *barly bread*: at this time, when wheat was not plentiful, bread was often made of barley.

294. *well to fare*: i.e. 'fare well', '*bon appétit!*'

295. *smelled*: a common usage for 'caught the drift of' (cf. line 327).

298. *yawle crawle*: an effective combination to portray hunger's pangs.

301. *spittlehouse ... castel's ende*: 'castle' here must signify 'village'; Hodge suggests his guts should be set as widely apart from one another as possible.

309. s.d. *Which bacon*, etc.: an interesting stage-direction, indicating that readers rather than performers were chiefly in the mind of whoever prepared the text for the press. (Cf. the direction at line 1028.)

311. *rose not on thy right syde*: an early instance of the saying 'you got out of bed the wrong side', used to account for irritability during the day.

329. *crown*: French gold 'crowns of the sun', or écus, were current in England in the fifteenth century, but in 1526 Henry VIII introduced the first 'crowns of the rose'; silver crowns (value 5*s*.) were minted from the reign of Edward VI (1547–53) onwards.

331. *a new grot*: a coin of modest value current all through the later Middle Ages, the English groat was traditionally valued at four pence, but successive devaluations meant that 'old groats' were worth more than new ones.

352. *By the crosse*: possibly an allusion to the cleft in Diccon's buttocks, though this may be over-ingenious.

361. *conjure up a spreete*: the farcical approach anticipates that of Marlowe in the comic scenes of *Dr Faustus*, involving Wagner, Robin, and devils.

364. *prety charme*: not 'attractive token' but 'clever spell'.

369. *this cyrcle plat*: it was common to trace a circle on the ground before summoning up devils; the title-page of the 1624 Quarto of *Dr Faustus* shows Marlowe's hero conjuring within such a circle.

383. *The matter is no worse*: 'it won't be any more terrible than I've suggested'.

385. *beraye the hall*: Hodge's threat suggests that the playwright has momentarily forgotten his imagined setting, the village street, and alluded instead to the place of performance. (See Introduction.)

391. s.d. *Exit Hodge*: it is at this point, I believe, that Hodge must change into his second pair of breeches. (See Introduction.)

394. *a clenly prancke*: obviously ironic: 'clenly' can mean 'neat, dex-

trous, smart', but the inappropriateness of its primary meaning at this juncture is perfect.

401–3. *make a playe*, etc.: an early example of a device made use of by later Elizabethan dramatists, a reflection of the relative sophistication of a college audience, and of the increasing self-consciousness of the Tudor stage.

402. *nede no worde*: 'could transcribe it literally without emendations'.

412. *maketh no great daunger*: Brett-Smith suggests 'makes himself at home', but this seems a needlessly complicated rendering.

414. *at Trumpe*: this game (also known as Triump or Ruff) was a precursor of whist.

421. *Sim Glover's wife*: the sense of a close-knit community is neatly conveyed by making Sim Glover the tradesman who lends Hodge the thong (see line 503).

424. *our dere Lady of Bullaine*: there was an important shrine to the Virgin Mary on the site of the present Church of Notre Dame at Boulogne.

425. *Dunstone ... Donnyke*: St Dunstan (924–88) was an English saint who became Archbishop of Canterbury in 961, St Dominic (1170–1221) founded in 1215 the Dominican Order of Friars, the 'Black Friars'.
the three Kinges of Kullaine: the Magi or Wise Men; their bones were said to be deposited in Cologne Cathedral.

479. *Ye know your harm*: 'you recognize the injury done you'.

473. *before the smoke arise*: 'before the trouble starts' (cf. *Mother Bombie*, line 88).

475. *what lieth in both their harts*, etc.: 'you'll certainly discover their innermost feelings'.

507. *a litle romth*: this remark provides another key to the original manner of presenting the play: spectators are requested to clear a space to enable Gammer Gurton to enter. Even if the request is not literally necessary, it helps to suggest the presence of an audience crowding close to the acting area. (See Introduction.)

512. *Cham lost, man; fye, fye!*: the rhyme line which precedes or follows this appears to be missing.

515. *sporyar's*: probably 'made by a spurrier' rather than 'used by one' although guilds of spur-makers were sometimes those of the saddlemakers too. Brett-Smith suggests that spur-straps needed to be sewn with a stout needle.

518. *all is save*: the forms 'safe' and 'save' were interchangeably used at this period.

529. *post haste*: the term derives from the instruction placed on urgent letters carried by courier or 'post': 'Haste, haste, post haste'.

532. *lose it*: to preserve the rhyme the words should be 'lese it'; the 1575 printed text clearly reads 'lose it', however.

544. *even to dresse you so*: 'that's precisely how she'll treat you'.

565. *thonge*: the text reads 'thynge' here, which may be correct.

566. *bald curtal*: a 'bald' horse was one with a white stripe down its face; a 'curtal' was one with a docked tail.

568. *his naull*: cf. note on line 20; here possibly the 'n' derives from 'an awl'.

gyb: Brett-Smith sees a reference here to a ship 'cramming on all sail', the 'jib' being of course a triangular stay-sail. However, Tudor vessels seem to have carried neither fore-sail nor jib-sail, and 'gyb' is probably a variant form of 'job', though this is not an entirely satisfactory explanation.

590. *Fryer Rushe*: a figure in German medieval folk-lore, Bruder Rausch was a devil who became a friar and wrought havoc in a monastery; his adventures were translated 'nto English and printed in 1568.

591. *Painted on a cloth*: Tudor rooms were often hung with 'painted cloths' depicting scenes of various kinds; cf. *As You Like It*, III. 2. 258: 'I answer you right painted cloth'.

617. *How should that thing be knowen?*: 'how do you make that out?'

625. *A bag and a wallet!*: a difficult phrase to interpret, since 'a bag' and 'a wallet' were virtually synonyms, though the latter was mostly associated with pilgrims, pedlars, and beggars. The phrase 'to turn to bag and wallet', however, meant to become a beggar, and Dame Chat may simply be repeating the insult she uses in line 613.

A carte for a callat!: prostitutes were often whipped at the tail of a cart as it trundled through the streets.

638. *in the darke*: a further reminder that the play's action takes place during the course of an evening.

650. *tarlether*: literally a strip of salted, dried sheepskin, used as a thong; Brett-Smith's old-world courtesy leads him to remark 'Gammer Gurton was not in her first youth'.

what longs to it: 'I'll show you what's what!'

657. *chwarde*: possibly a misprint for 'chware', 'I would be', though strict consistency in spelling 'Mummerset' terms is not obligatory.

663. *shrive*: another indication that Roman Catholic practices were observed at the time of the play's composition, or at the period in which the play is set (cf. line 1202).

675. *cham not well at ease*: 'I'm anxious', 'I'm not easy in my mind' (cf. line 739).

682. *plucke up your hart*: 'cheer up', 'take courage'.

704. *rake her*: a term in farriery used to define the process of relieving a constipated horse by scraping out its fundament with the hand.

712. *bought and sòlde me*: the addition of 'solde me' to the reference to Christ makes little sense, but may be intentional; 'bought and sold' was a synonym for 'ruined'.

720. *ought to get*: possibly 'anything to eat', though the allusion is vague.

749. *gaffer*: a term of respect here, unlike its use in line 418 of *Mother Bombie* (cf. line 1142).

786. *Saint Charitie*: not a 'Saint', of course, but 'Holy Charity', said by E. K. in glossing Spenser's *Shepheardes Calender* (1579) to be the 'Catholiques comen othe'.

795. *by him were knowne*: 'could be traced back to him'.

797. *of your and my degree*: Diccon generously equates the educated Dr Rat with himself in matters of probity!

813. *catch some good*: 'shall do well out of it' (said ironically).

831. *the master devil Belsabub*: Beelzebub ('Lord of the Flies') is designated 'prince of the devils' in Matthew xii, 24, though he is often given a subsidiary position to that of Satan. (Cf. line 517 of *Thersytes*: '... Beelzebub the mayster devyll as ragged as a colte'.)

839. *the ruste*: the chickens roost inside the house, as was common at the time; see Skelton's poem 'The Tunnynge of Elynour Rummynge', lines 190–92: 'The hennes ... go to roust/Streyght over the ale joust [the beam under which the ale vats are kept].'

864. *take my trumpe*: clearly an image from card-playing (cf. line 32 and note).

890. *Sir John*: the most celebrated instance of this nickname for a priest is found in the mouth of Chaucer's Host in *The Canterbury Tales* (see Robinson, VII, 2810): 'Com neer, thou preest, com hyder, thou sir John!'

896. *for his order*: because of his clerical status.

911. *in al the fault*: 'completely to blame'.

922. *Or wold you kepe him out*: from Dr Rat's reply the word 'or' here must have its modern meaning, so the text's 'Or you wold kepe . . .' appears to be in error, and has been amended.

937. *to kisse the stockes*: i.e. to have a spell in the stocks; cf. 'kiss the rod'. (Cf. line 999.)

945. *go wype your nose*: 'put that in your pipe and smoke it'.

946–50. One should note that the rhyme-scheme changes briefly here to ABABB; it is tempting to argue that lines 947 and 948 are simply out of sequence were it not that line 950 provides a third '-urder' rhyme, suggesting that the writer momentarily dropped the couplet form.

947. *shuld him much misorder*: 'did him great harm', 'behaved badly to him'.

973. *beshrew thy smothe cheekes*: possibly 'damn your plausible manner!' but probably an unspecific oath (cf. line 1389 of *Roister Doister*, for an alternative version of the same curse).

986. *Onely upon a bare 'Nay'*: 'merely on the strength of a simple denial' (i.e. with no evidence to back it).

1001. *so bleared be your eyes*: a common phrase for being deceived (cf. 'having the wool pulled over one's eyes').

1028. *a pad in the straw*: a favourite term for a toad was 'paddock', and the fear that toads were venomous led to the formulation of this phrase, akin to the modern 'snake in the grass'.

1036. *the devil in thy cote*: 'perhaps the devil was pretending to be you'.

1143. *a sport alone*: 'nothing but a practical joke'.

1161. *lift the pot*: Diccon suggests that Rat is a habitual drinker.

1175. *a coxe*: a cokes was a fool or ninny, the term possibly deriving from 'Cockney' which originally indicated a milksop or someone 'cockered'; however, it is not impossible that it derives from the word 'coxcomb' as applied to a simpleton rather than to a professional fool.

1176. *The cat was not*, etc.: an allusion to a familiar anecdote of Reynard the fox who lured the cat into a trap in a priest's barn by saying that mice were to be caught there (see Caxton's *Historye of Reynart the foxe*, ed. N. F. Blake, EETS, 1970, pp. 19–22).

1180. *leape at a dasye*: the phrase dramatically conveys the image of a criminal leaping into thin air from the gallows.

1181. *In the King's name*: see introductory note, pp. 211–12.

1185. *by All Halowes!*: 'by all the saints!'

1197. *Thou lier lickdish*: one of the few (perhaps subconscious) references to Diccon's partial function as the parasite of classical
comedy (cf. line 287 and note).

1199. *Hobgobling*: a mischievous ugly imp, hence a fearful apparition.

1205. *my fee is twenty pence*: the Bailiff is evidently accustomed to levy
a fine of twenty pence in any affray in which blood is spilt.

1219–32. The penalties enjoined on Diccon are all entirely farcical
of course, and in keeping with the play's reconciliatory conclusion.

1253. *this*: the function of this word is not clear: Boas suggests a
statement broken off, Brett-Smith a misprint for ''tis'.

1265. *springing of the game*: an image taken from the act of flushing
out partridges from cover; here applied to flushing out the needle.

1276. *As proude coms behinde*: a proverbial phrase (sometimes with
'stout' substituted for 'proud'), meaning that social inferiors are
often no less self-satisfied than their superiors.

MOTHER BOMBIE

3. *a foole to my heire*: from its appearance in line 1925, one suspects
that this may be proverbial, but perhaps the literal sense alone is
sufficient here.

5. *maladies*: the first Quarto (Q1) reads 'malaladies', probably the
result of a line division; the Quarto of 1598 corrects it.

9. *tread out*: a verb often used for the copulation of birds.

11. *bite hot on*: Bond suggests 'border close on', but the *OED* definition supports the notion that Dromio's solutions will only
exacerbate Memphio's sufferings.

13. *hornes*: i.e. if he maltreated her, Memphio's wife would only cuckold him.

22. *cockescombes*: a term taken from the traditional headgear of the
professional fool which was shaped like the comb on a cock's
head.

37. *a faire babie*: all prior editions follow Q1's 'a faire ladie' here, but
Bond was attracted to P. A. Daniel's proposed emendation, which
I accept. In Heliodorus' romantic tale *Aethiopica*, Persina, queen
of Ethiopia, tells her white daughter Chariclea that she was conceived at a time when her coloured mother could observe a picture
of the naked Andromeda rescued by Perseus.

43. *beg him for a foole*: if at this period the mentally deranged owned

property, they were made wards of court, along with minors and heiresses, but those willing to assume responsibility for them (and to control their property) could petition the Court of Wards to be granted the wardship (cf. lines 1570–71).

46–8. *thou shalt eate*, etc.: Q1 here reads 'thou shalt eate, thou shalt sweate ...'; Bond's emendation backed by Daniel's quotation from *Euphues* would appear to be correct: 'these Abbaie lubbers ... eat til they sweate, and lay in bed till their boanes aked' (Bond, I, 250–51).

77. *mewed up*: a mews was originally a cage for a hawk where the bird was confined from time to time, especially when 'mewing' or moulting.

82. *by conference*: the likeliest meaning is 'through the act of conferring together' or 'through conversation or discussion' which of course cannot be permitted to Accius and Silena.

85. *A singular conceit!*: 'A strange stratagem!' This may be intended to be an aside.

88. *keepe my house from smoake*: i.e. 'she'll make it hot for me'. Bond compares a common proverb found in 'The Wife of Bath's Prologue' in *The Canterbury Tales* (see Robinson, III, 278–80) where smoke is equated with 'droppyng [dripping] houses' and 'chidyng wyves' in making men leave their homes, but Memphio's remark is surely metaphorical.

106. *hundreth*: a common form of 'hundred', though not its primary one, 'hundreth' deriving from Old Norse analogues.

116. *Expellas furca*, etc.: the saying derives from Horace's *Epistles*, 'To Aristius Fuscus' (I, 10, 24) where it applies to Nature's ability to survive even in urban environments.

118. *thrust up*, etc.: I take this to mean 'though your son's folly is exalted by marrying him and making a cuckold of him, yet his idiocy being native to him will eventually manifest itself' ('his' here = 'its').

126. *I apply it fit*: Risio 'applies' Stellio's analysis 'fittingly' by saying that Silena gets her amiability from one parent, her folly from the other, but carefully omits to identify the respective sources!

132. *How likest thou this head?*: Bond makes the plausible suggestion that Stellio here produces a miniature of Silena to back his description, but there seems to be no warrant for this use of 'head'; however, Risio may be taking Stellio's word as 'proposition' and applying it literally to Silena's features.

NOTES

139. *I, and so cunningly*, etc.: i.e. Stellio still retains his own foolish nature.

141. *Quod natura*, etc.: 'Because nature bestowed it, nobody can take it away'. I have been unsuccessful in tracking·down the source of this quotation, which does not appear in the standard classical concordances.

142. *fee-simple*: i.e. Silena's folly is absolute and permanent. Property held in fee-simple belonged to the owner and his heirs in perpetuity and in their own right, without any conditions or restrictions being imposed on the inheritance.

162. *with a payre of compasses*: Risio's pun suggests that the youngsters brought together and left to their own devices will soon find a way to mate.

188–9. *wring me on the withers*: an ill-fitting saddle which twists or wrenches the ridge between a horse's shoulders – its withers – produces extreme pain (cf. *Hamlet*, III. 2. 237: 'Let the galled jade wince, our withers are unwrung'). In *Euphues and his England*, Lyly himself wrote 'wring not a horse on the withers, with a false saddle' (Bond, II, 34, 9–10).

197–8. *no better bread than is made of wheat*: a proverbial phrase to indicate someone who is over-fastidious in his tastes. The phrase appears in the 'Epistle Dedicatorie' to *Euphues*: 'English men desire ... to eate finer bread then is made of Wheat, to weare finer cloth then is wrought of Woll' (Bond, I, 181, 17–19).

209–10. *thou hast the palsy*: the term 'palsy' is applied to various disorders of the nervous system, some of which produce an involuntary quivering of the limbs; it is one of the symptoms of Parkinson's disease.

212. *cog*: Sperantus puns on 'cog' in the sense of 'cheating at dice'; Prisius' hands are too unsteady to throw the dice to secure the desired result.

228. *he hath wit at wil*: 'he's got his wits about him', 'he's never at a loss'.

235–6. *as goodly a youth*, etc.: cf. *A Midsummer Night's Dream*, I. 2. 88: 'a proper man, as one shall see in a summer's day'.

237. *as ever went on neat's leather*: i.e. wearing shoes of ox-hide. Cf. *Julius Caesar*, I. 1. 26: 'As proper men as ever trod upon neat's leather.'

240. *my pretie elfe*: several meanings are possible here: it may be that Livia's mischievousness, or her diminutive stature, or the fact that

409

Prisius views her as a child, is alluded to; possibly, like 'worme' in line 656, 'elfe' is simply used to mean 'poor creature'.

242–3. *Made marriages*, etc.: there is a proverbial ring to this sentence, but it does not appear in any of the main collections.

288. *cough mee a foole*: 'make a fool of himself'; cf. line 890 of *Roister Doister*: 'he shall cough me a mome'.

290. *broad-stitch*: probably a variant of 'brede-stitch' (i.e. an interlinked stitch like braid), or else referring to something stitched on broadcloth.

294. *pievish*: meanings for this term include 'foolish', 'spiteful', 'obstinate', and 'ill-tempered', but Livia's succeeding remark suggests 'perverse' as the most relevant equivalent.

299. *joynter*: the holding of property by a husband and wife jointly, with provision made for the latter upon being widowed or, by extension, an estate left to a wife to enjoy during widowhood.

312. *pap with a hatchet*: the title of Lyly's contribution to the 'Martin Marprelate' controversy of 1587–9 was *Pappe with a Hatchet*, a well-known proverb meaning 'to exercise cruelty in a situation where kindness is more usually expected', either by hiding the weapon or wielding it behind a façade of concern.

317. *cammocke*: the word occurs several times in Lyly's works, e.g. in *Euphues*: 'the Cammocke the more it is bowed the better it serveth' (Bond ed., I, 196, 1–2) and *Euphues and His England*: 'serching for a wande, I gather a camocke' (Bond, II, 169, 23.)

332–3. *cowslops and lillyes*: lilies are white (Latin *candidus*), cowslips yellow; the link with Candius' name is obvious, that with Livia obscure, '*lividus*' meaning 'blue, bluish'. Probably only a matter of initials is involved.

334. *turtles and sparrowes*: doves and sparrows were traditionally associated with Venus, the former for its constancy, the latter for sexuality, often equated with lechery.

335. *the foxe and the ermin*: the fox is famed for its craft and stealth, the ermine or stoat for its handsome white winter coat.

336–7. *the cockle and the tortuse*: Venus's emblem was a scallop-shell, on which she stands in Botticelli's celebrated painting, but she was also sometimes depicted accompanied by a turtle or tortoise.

338. *vine ... elme*: vines were often trained about elm trees; cf. *The Comedy of Errors*, II. 2. 174: 'Thou art an elm, my husband, I a vine.' It was frequently used as an image of mutual dependence.

339. *abeston*: Lyly elsewhere describes the property of this fabled stone: 'the stone *Abeston* being once made hotte will never be made colde' (*Euphues*, Bond, II, 191, 32–3).

343–4. *knowes her lerripoope*: in early academic dress the liripipe was the long tail on the graduate's hood; it came to denote knowledge or learning. The modern equivalent might be 'she knows her stuff' or 'she's done her homework'.

348. *a fine pleasant poet*: Ovid (43–18 BC).

354. *Principio quod*, etc.: corrected from Ovid's *Ars Amatoria*, lines 35 –8, leaving out *Qui nova nunc primum miles in arma venis*. The whole may be rendered: 'The first task is to strive to seek out the one you wish to love, [you who come to fight in this novel type of battle for the first time;] the next is to obtain the girl you fancy; the third is to ensure that love lasts for a long time.'

369. *Non caret effectu*, etc.: corrected from Ovid's *Amores* II, 3, 16, rendered in Christopher Marlowe's translation as 'What two determine never wants effect.'

378–9. *I was worth the bidding to dinner*, etc.: i.e. 'I was worth inviting to the meal afterwards, but not the discussion itself.'

383. *in love is no lacke*: a common proverb meaning 'love doesn't go short of what it requires'.

385. *cunning*: 'cleverness' probably used in a double sense to convey both 'academic knowledge' and 'ability to deceive'.

399. *finde them*, etc.: the change of subject from singular to plural is not unusual in Elizabethan English.

413. *capon*: castrated cocks were often confined to the coop to make them plumper for the table (cf. line 21).

415. *holde the ploughe*: i.e. become a ploughman. Don Armado in *Love's Labour's Lost*, V. 2. 71–2, pledges himself to hold the plough for three years for love of Jaquenetta.

424. *break the lawes of nature*: i.e. Sperantus will disinherit Candius, so treating him unnaturally, unless he follows his father's desires.

430. *I'le take an order*: 'I'll see that arrangments are made'.

433–4. *hot love wil wax soone colde*: cf. *Euphues* (Bond, I, 197, 33: '*Philautus* . . . whose hot love waxed soone colde'; ibid., I, 218, 32: 'hot love is soone colde') and *Roister Doister*, line 1799 and note.

443. *Obviam dare Dromio*: Bond suggests that the idiom should be *obviam ire* (or *fieri*) and that Lyly may have made a deliberate error.

452. *to wake our wits*: 'rouse our minds to action'.

453. *Hem quam opportune*: 'look, how conveniently (it turns out)!'

455. *Lupus in fabula!*: literally 'the wolf in the tale!', a proverbial phrase found in Terence's *Adelphoe* ('The Brothers'), rendered in W. A. Oldfather's translation as 'The wolf! Just as we were talking about him!' (*Latin Literature in Translation*, ed. Kevin Guinagh and Alfred P. Dorjahn, New York, 1942.)

476. *tempered*: several meanings are possible here, but the general sense is 'worked up, concocted'.

481–5. *the foole bestride ... tantonie pouch*: a typically elliptical statement, which appears to mean 'Together we'll get Accius to woo (?) Silena, and then lay claim to a reward from our master's pigskin purse, which hangs by his dagger which is thrust through the cord holding it to his belt.' A dudgeon-dagger was one with a boxwood hilt, a 'tantonie pouch' was one associated with St Anthony, possibly because he was often shown wearing one, or equally possibly because he was the patron saint of swineherds, and the purse was made of pigskin.

488. *snaphance*: originally a term for a highwayman, the word then became applied to the flintlock on a musket or pistol, and so to the firearm itself.

489. *a purse with a ring*, etc.: Bond cites Fairholt's reference to a purse closed at the mouth with a thong, and a motto engraved round the ring at the neck, cursing whoever threatened to steal it.

496–7. *decimo sexto ... folio*: bibliographical terms to denote two contrasting formats of book. A folio is a largish volume where the page units are made up of single sheets folded once; one in sextodecimo is much smaller with sheets folded to produce a gathering of sixteen leaves. In Marston's *The Malcontent* (1604) (see note on line 514) the Children of the Queen's Revels are referred to as actors 'in decimo-sexto'.

498. *currant*: applied both to up-to-date news as well as to 'current' coinage (cf. line 1638). Halfpenny exploits the latter meaning with his reference to 'counterfeit'.

504. *slips*: coins of brass were often silvered over and passed off as genuine; referred to as 'slips', they were commonly exposed as bad by traders nailing them to the counter or the wall.

506. *never slip string*: a further reference to the gallows.

508–9. *my hand on my halfepenie*: a proverbial phrase for being preoccupied or 'in a brown study', though in the context I suspect the presence of a sexual pun.

512. *my head is full of hammers*: the notion of ideas being hammered into shape on the mind's anvil is a common one; see the Earl of Surrey's tribute to Sir Thomas Wyatt, lines 5–7:

> A hed ...
> Whose hammers bet styll in that lively brayn
> As on a stithe ...
> (*English Poetry 1400–1580*, ed. Tydeman, 1970, p. 117)

514. *malcontent*: a frequent figure in Jacobean and late Elizabethan drama was the disillusioned and world-weary cynic, who gives his name to Marston's play, whose hero is Malvole, dispossessed Duke of Genoa.

525. *the hen that sits next the cocke*, etc.: possibly equivalent to 'even the experts can't tell'.

529–30. *as full for my pitch*: 'as artful for my size'.

558–9. *Cum mala*, etc.: from Ovid's *Remedia Amoris*, line 92: '(the medicine is prepared too late) when the sickness has gained in strength through long delay'. Of course, in speaking this line, Halfpenny points to the taller of Dromio and Risio as the 'least ass' and to the shorter as the 'mor as'.

561. *bite thee for an ape*: the general sense is clear enough, 'bite' being employed in the sense of 'speak sharply to, censure', but there may be a link with the proverb 'a bit and a bob [blow] as men feed apes'.

567. *Non enim*, etc.: adapted from Ovid, *Metamorphoses* x, 396: '*non est mea pigra senectus*' ('I am not without wit, old as I am').

570. *pudding*: not a sweet course at a meal, but the stomach or other entrail of an animal stuffed with meat, pork fat, oats, barley, etc., as in the modern haggis or black pudding.

571–2. *a right Tunbridge case*: Lucio is presumably thinking of completing a sheath or case containing knives (punning on 'knaves') and other useful implements, by becoming the bodkin (a short dagger or stiletto). Risio answers that the bodkin (Halfpenny because of his size) is already present. The 'Tunbridge case' is puzzling: Tonbridge in Kent (Lyly's home county) was not associated with the metal industry, though there was an Elizabethan iron foundry there, nor does leather-work appear to have been carried on.

576. *must boare them*: Halfpenny here reminds his auditors that the bodkin could be employed for making holes in cloth, etc.; Bond suggests the implication is that the other three pages are criminals whose ears must be pierced as such, and quotes line 1676–9.

577. *Mew thy tongue*: see note on line 77.

586. *a messe*: in this context a group of four diners at a meal, sitting together and being served from the same dishes. Bond compares *Love's Labour's Lost*, IV. 3.203: '...you three fools lack'd me fool to make up the mess'.

599–600. *Ela ... Gam ut*: in the old musical scale known as the hexachords, a unit of six consecutive notes was used, running *Ut – re – mi – fa – sol – la* (cf. the *Doh – ray – me*, etc. of the tonic sol-fa system). In the hexachord scheme the scale begins on the note G (referred to as 'Gamma' or 'Gam'), and ends on E, hence Dromio's remark. Bond compares the Prologue to Lyly's *Midas*, lines 7–8: 'Aske the Musicions, they will say their heads ake with devising notes beyond Ela.'

603–4. *shake three trees at once*: Bond detects an allusion to the three pieces of wood making up the gibbet.

606. *the bush*: it was common for a tavern to display an ivy-bush at or over its entrance to advertise its identity (cf. 'Good wine needs no bush').

608. *Inter pocula*, etc.: probably derived from a discussion in Plutarch's *Quaestio Convivium* I, 1, 'whether it is possible to philosophize amid drinking-vessels'.

649. *a grape owle*: a lover of wine who prefers to stay up at night to indulge his taste. (Cf. 'mault worme' in line 267 of *Gammer Gurton's Nedle*.)

660. *Argentum potabile*: Bond points out that *aurum potabile*, gold melted in oil, was a favourite elixir of the alchemists, but here of course Prisius is speaking humorously of Lucio's habit of turning silver into liquid refreshment.

663. *be as bee may*: 'it's no curse [ban] to let things happen as they will'. Bond suggests the proverb applies where affairs are going well enough to require no special effort; other sources suggest that the inference is more that consent is unwillingly given to something unavoidable (cf. 'it's no use crying over spilt milk', 'what can't be cured must be endured'). The former seems more in keeping, however, with Sperantus' over-sanguine remarks at this point in the play.

667. *pigsnie*: see note to line 460 of *Roister Doister*.

673. *a dodkin*: a coin of Dutch origin, worth an eighth of a stiver, but used loosely to indicate a minute sum.

675. *banquetting for thether Halfepenie*: a difficult phrase to interpret, Bond arguing that the context seems to require 'banquetting' to mean 'gambling' and citing the Italian 'banchetto' ('little table') to back the possibility. The phrase may simply denote that the small Halfpenny by feasting and drinking is trying to develop into a full penny! (Cf. lines 1634–5.)

676. *He must needs goe*, etc.: a familiar proverb found in many sixteenth-century authors.

695. *coming*: all the early editions read 'if I her cunning' here, and it was Bond who proposed the introduction of the word 'find': he only cited Dilke's suggested substitution of 'coming' for 'cunning' in a footnote. 'Cunning' ('knowing', 'smart') is certainly not an impossible reading, but 'coming' makes an apter contrast with 'coy' at line 694.

701–2. *as ever trode on shoo sole*: cf. note at line 237; Silena's part abounds in popular clichés and catch-phrases of the period, often absurdly misapplied. (See Candius' comments in lines 763–8.)

707. *Love and beautie*, etc.: a scholarly allusion to Aristotle's argument in the *Ethics* I, 7, 4–5, that while virtue represents a mean between two extremes of vice, happiness is a goal sought in its own right, and therefore not a 'middle way'.

716. *your name were Geoffrey*: apparently another catch-phrase, possibly related to the parting-shot 'farewell, gentle Geoffrey', which occurs in the morality play *Mankynde* and elsewhere.

732. *And so tell your master*: another pert colloquialism, as in line 749, 'well seene in crane's durt'.

735. *are you there with your beares?*: explained by *OED* as originating in the remark made by a man who, having disliked a sermon on Elisha and the bears, chose to attend another church the following Sunday, only to find the same preacher there delivering the same sermon.

739. *in your tother hose*: 'not if I know it'; 'sez you!'

746. *line of life ... Venus' mount*: terms applied by palmists to features of the hand: the Mount of Venus is the bulge at the base of the thumb, with the Line of Life running around it.

773. *fulsome*: one may compare *Euphues* '. . . the great dislykinge they

415

hadde of theire fulsome feeding' (Bond, i, 266, 10–11).

774. *Sil.*: Q1 has 'LIV.' at this point, probably mistakenly carried over from line 770.

774–5. *never lesse wit in a yeere*: a proverb meaning 'fools were never less favourably regarded than now'; cf. *King Lear*, I. 4. 164.

790–94. Q1 prints Mother Bombie's prophecy as prose, as in every other case.

799. *farewell frost*: another piece of proverbial cheek, similar to the modern 'good riddance to bad rubbish'.

825. *I prae, sequar*: taken from Terence's *Andria*, I. 1. 171: 'You go first; I'll follow shortly.'

827. *and his k*: the Elizabethan equivalent of 'minding one's p's and q's'.

842–2. *a good winde*, etc.: not found elsewhere to my knowledge.

846. *Gascone wine*: Gascony was the old French province lying at the extreme south-western corner of the country.

847. *sack*: the general name for white wines from Spain and the Canary Islands.

849. *the Queene's subsidie booke*: a list of rich persons liable to pay tax or 'subsidy' on lands and movables when called upon to do so.

862. *Rufus*: William II, who ruled England from 1087 to 1100.

866. *caudle*: a thin gruel mixed with ale or wine and flavoured with sugar and spice, often served to sick people.

872. *spigot ... faucet*: Bond suggests that the faucet is the pipe and the spigot the tap which controls the flow of liquid; the parallel statements imply that one is attached to a beer-barrel, the other a wine-cask, but the terms are often met with in conjunction.

874. *blacke boule*: a drinking vessel of black leather.

876. *stand ... hogs-head*: again the distinction is not crystal clear, but a stand seems to have been a small cask holding thirteen gallons, a hogshead a much larger barrel holding sixty-three gallons.

896. *heere in Kent*, etc.: this, the first reference to the location of the play, might suggest Ashford, fourteen miles from Canterbury and nineteen from Maidstone, as the setting, but subsequent allusions (especially lines 1216, 1756, 1885) make it clear that Rochester is intended. Lyly was probably a native of Canterbury, some twenty-six miles away.

898. *Cerere*: Q1 prints 'Cere', corrected by Dilke. The proverb occurs

in Terence's *Eunuchus*, IV.v.6, with 'Libero' for 'Bacchus' (Liber being the old Italian God of agriculture, identified with Bacchus).

912–13 *my clothes ... tenters*: Bond inferred from this and line 1962 that Prisius runs a fulling-mill where cloth is beaten and pressed to thicken it.

926. *modestie*: this is the only citation given in the *OED* for this meaning.

944–5. *the greater the kindred*, etc.: cf. *Hamlet*, I. 2. 65: 'A little more than kin, and less than kind.'

965–70. *You shall be married*: again, Q1 prints this speech as prose.

966. *good Nature*, etc.: I am reluctant to tamper with Q1's 'good nature' which makes perfect sense if Nature is personified; Mother Bombie does not evoke the deity elsewhere in her prophecies. On the other hand, Q2's amendment 'God, Nature' must carry some weight.

980. *that stoole*: presumably this article remained on stage outside Mother Bombie's house door throughout the action.

985. *bewraie*: Bond argues that this must mean 'abandon' here, but the sense seems perfectly clear as it stands.

991. *Ingenium*, etc.: from Ovid's *Amores* III, 8, 3–4 (line 4 corrected by Bond); Thomas Nashe used part of the second line as the epigraph to his *Pierce Penilesse His Supplication to the Devil* (1592).

998. *rong all out in*: Q1 and subsequent editions read 'rong all in', which Bond interprets as 'abused me'; however, the balance of the sentence seems to require the emendation I propose, which gives the meaning 'elicited what he wanted to know'. One may compare Lyly's *Endimion*, V. 3. 102–6: '*Endimion* as full of arte as witte ... by questions wrunge out that, which was readie to burst out.'

1009–10. *evax*, etc.: Latin expressions of joy, surprise, etc. Bond cites the authorized Latin grammar of the day, *A Shorte Introduction of Grammar*, first compiled by John Colet and by William Lily, the playwright's grandfather. (See Foster Watson, *The English Grammar Schools to 1660*, 1908, pp. 243–59.)

1011. *conjunctions*: presumably a pun on the grammatical term and the word for a number of linked exclamations 'in conjunction'.

1030. *Accius' apparell*, etc.: Dromio plans to substitute Candius for Accius, Lucio Livia for Silena, but as Bond points out, there is strictly no necessity for Accius and Silena to dress as Candius and

Livia. This 'device' was perhaps dictated by Lyly's love of symmetry, or by his anxiety to make it clear that Memphio and Stellio in Act IV, scene 2, mistake the fools for 'Prisius' daughter' and 'Sperantus' sonne' if only briefly.

1046–7. *wrought two daies over*: I take this as an image taken from the working of yeast; the *OED*'s quotation from Barnaby Googe's 1577 translation of *Heresbach's Foure bookes of husbandry* (IV, 183b) seems relevant: 'The Hony . . . is suffered to stand uncovered a fewe dayes tyll it have wrought, and cast up a lofte all his drags.'

1049. *whitled*: it is possibly only coincidence that someone drunk is now said to be 'cut'.

1076, s.d. The Quarto text at this point has '*Memphio and Stellio singing*' followed by '*Act. 3 Sce. 3. Memphio and Stellio.*' The song is of course omitted, but when it appears in Blount's edition it is assigned to Memphio and Stellio instead of Silena and Accius. Fairholt and subsequent editors have adopted the emendations followed in the present case; I have assigned the final couplet to both singers as a kind of symbolic coda.

1099–1100. *Accius' tongue shall tie*, etc.: cf. *Euphues and his England* (Bond, II, 220, 20–21) '. . . knit that knot with our tongues, that we shall never undoe with our teeth'. Bond in his notes on *Mother Bombie* cites the proverb, but not the reference from Lyly.

1106. *lapwing-like*, etc.: a well-known fact of natural history. Bond cites the 'Epistle Dedicatory' to *Euphues and his England* (Bond, II, 4, 17–20): '. . . the Lappwing, who fearing hir young ones to be destroyed by passengers, flyeth with a false cry farre from their nests, making those that looke for them seeke where they are not . . .'

1124. *the packe*: i.e. the bundle of Livia's clothes which Rixula as her maid-servant has been entrusted with.

1127. *Omne solum*, etc.: from Ovid, *Fasti* I, 493.

1127–8. *in Christendom*, etc.: a proverbial phrase, allegedly alluding to either Kent's early conversion to Christianity by St Augustine or its later apostasy. Cf. Wyatt's satire beginning 'Myne owne John Poyntz', line 100: 'But here I ame in Kent and Christendome' (*Collected Poems of Sir Thomas Wyatt*, ed. Muir and Thomson, Liverpool, 1969, p. 91).

1129. *Patria ubicunque bene*: Cicero quotes this line in his *Tusculanae Disputationes* v, 37, possibly from Pacuvius: '*Patria est ubicumque est bene*'.

1136–7. *no goose so gray*, etc.: cf. 'The Wife of Bath's Tale' (*The Canterbury Tales*)

> Ne noon so grey goos gooth ther in the lake
> As ... wol been withoute make.
>
> (Robinson, III, 269–70)

1146. *verie pleasurable*: the generally insulting tone of Halfpenny's remarks suggests that this should mean 'easily pleased'.

1147–8. *foule water will quench*, etc.: cf. *Euphues and his England* (Bond, II, 156, 36–7): 'Hoat fire is not onely quenched by yᵉ cleere Fountaine, nor love onely satisfied by the faire face.'

1153. *thou beatedst hempe*: beating rotted hemp (to obtain the fibre) was a common punishment for criminals.

1154. *it was crabbs*: crab-apples were 'stamped' to make verjuice (Thomas Tusser's 'vergis'), a liquid much used in cooking or as a medicine. Cf. with Lucio's remark that of Sordido in Thomas Middleton's *Woman Beware Women*, III. 3. 53–4: 'having a crabbed face of her own, she'll eat the less verjuice with her mutton'.

1162. *now shee's in*, etc.: 'now she's into her stride she won't give over'.

1175. *such fidling varlets*: the musical analogy is kept up by the pages; 'fidling' may also have the sense of 'fussy'. The earliest citation of 'fiddle' meaning 'to cheat' in the *OED* is dated 1604, but the sense is not impossible here.

1177. *foure together*: Rixula anticipates the arrival of Dromio and Risio.

1180. *'Phip, phip'*: the traditional manner of representing the chirp of a sparrow (cf. the dove's 'coo, coo').

1182. *the Parrot that holds tack*: parrots were often taught to cry 'Rope!' (i.e. a hangman's rope); cf. *The Comedy of Errors*, IV. 4.40: 'to prophesy like the parrot, "Beware the rope's-end".' Bond suggests that 'holds tack' means 'as it is appropriate', but it seems clumsily expressed, even if the bird is often associated with trickery.

1185. *stands the wags*: another example of a singular verb with a plural object.

1188. *every man his baggage*: Bond suspects the presence of a proverb meaning 'you're all in the same boat', but Rixula may simply be referring to the four 'packes' of clothing the pages carry.

1254–6. Printed as prose in Q1.

1256. *a-beating*: cf. 'a match in hammering' in lines 2133–4.

1282–4. Once again, Q1 prints the prophecy as prose, as it does lines 1289–91, 1302–4, 1320–22.

1300. *want of a mist*: i.e. 'there was nothing to conceal the fact that it had gone'.

1305. *all the gerundes*: all Latin verbs have a gerund form, which compares roughly to the English verbal noun ending in '-ing'. Its case-endings are *-dum, -di, -do*, hence Risio's schoolboy joke.

1324. *if you were*: Bond's note suggests that Dromio means 'we should be pleased if you were found to be a cozener (or became cozened yourself)', but this hardly accords with his thanks or offer of money. He appears to mean 'If you were happy to tell our fortunes, we are thankful for the trouble you took.'

1342. *and hee wise*: Q1 reads 'and hee wist', almost certainly an error.

1362–3. *ten grotes apece ... to saie service*: clerks received payment to conduct church services; Canterbury is just over twenty-six miles from Rochester.

1367. *poast*: none of the possible meanings to 'post' yields entirely satisfactory sense here, and I am forced to suggest that 'poast' may be an unrecorded form of 'posset' or a misprint for 'posat', i.e. a warming drink.

1372–3. *Molle eius levibus*, etc.: adapted from Ovid's *Heroides* xv, 79, and corrected by Bond; the original appears in Sappho's letter to Phaon:

'*Molle meum levibusque cor est violabile telis*' ('My heart is soft and vulnerable to [love's] light arrows').

1375–6. *cornua cervus habet*: Elizabethan dramatists appear to have found irresistibly comic any remark connected with 'horns', the traditional identifying mark of a cuckolded husband.

1380. *coughing*: Q1 reads 'comming' here, and Bond takes Dilke to task for making the change to 'coughing' (which could be spelt 'coffing' at this time). Yet Sperantus and Livia in I. 3 both speak of her father's cough. The main objection, however, to 'comming' is that it is an untypically clumsy repetition of the word in line 1379, and I have sided with Dilke in accepting the amendment he proposes.

1382. *let me alone with*: 'I'll cope with'.

1397. *dangers in the church*: 'the risks attendant on the asking of the banns' (Bond).

1398. *askt*: have the banns called.

1430. *Memphio's house*: Candius still pretends to be Accius, Memphio's presumed son.

1431. *cottons*: derived from the manner in which strands of wool or hair matt or cling together.

1431–2. *waxe in a sowe's eare*: this phrase sounds as if it should be a common proverb, but it is not found in the principal proverb collections.

1452. *a hem in the forehead*: Bond wonders if 'hem' is a corruption of 'horn' (see note to lines 1375–6 above), but Halfpenny's reply indicates that Accius has 'knockt in the head' the 'auncient proverb' 'As fat as a hen in the forehead' which is proverbial for thinness, not lack of purpose.

1463. *cocke with a long combe*: i.e. a coxcomb (see line 22 and note).

1463–4. *a hen with a long leg*: the *OED*'s earliest instance of 'hen' = 'woman' is dated *c*. 1626.

1468. *uncovered*: this may be intended as a malapropism for 'discovered', or a permissible extension of the meaning 'to expose, lay bare'.

1473. *I, marie, sir!*: roughly 'How about that then?'

1476–7. *a joynd stoole*: cf. *King Lear*, III. 6. 51: 'Cry you mercy, I took you for a joint-stool', 'a taunting apology for overlooking a person' (M. P. Tilley, *Dictionary of Proverbs in England*, Ann Arbor, 1950, under M 897).

1478–9. *conduit or a bakehouse*: typical settings for slanging-matches.

1480. *But what are you for a man?*: cf. *Much Ado About Nothing*, I. 1. 45–6: '. . . but what is he to a lord?'

1482. *give me the boots*: the phrase occurs again in *The Two Gentlemen of Verona*, I. 1. 27: 'Nay, give me not the boots!'

1483–4. *right coblers' cuts*: Bond suggests 'odds and ends'. i.e. coblers' off-cuts, which well describes the disjointed exchanges between Accius and Silena, but the sense of 'cutting remarks' may also be present.

1500–1501. *household stuffe . . . commonwealth matters*: I can only interpret this as meaning 'while their bodies were engaged on domestic business, their minds were on affairs of state (so that their lack of concentration brought forth idiots)'.

1506. *you are in your owne clothes*: another pert rejoinder, meaningless, like line 1511, except that Silena can cap it.

1523. *I have kild your cushion*: though Silena may intend to say 'missed your cushion', a reference to the target in archery – cf. *Euphues*,

Bond, I, 237, 22, 'Truely *Euphues* you have miste the cushion' – 'I kry you mercye, I kylled your cussheyn' does appear in Palsgrave, *L'Eclaircissement de la langue francaise*, 1530, p. 501, but without any clarification of the phrase being offered.

1539–44. The speech-prefixes for these lines were muddled until Bond restored the correct order; his note (III, 549) is worth repeating: 'Each parent expects to find, not his own child, but some one personating his child; and each, being behind his child's back, asks who the personator is, and does not recognize that only the clothes are changed, until the children speak or turn round.'

1546–50. *My sonne would scarce*, etc.: the inference is that Memphio and Stellio consider that the presumed impersonators of their children make them out to be more stupid than they really are.

1558. *no foole to the old foole*: a proverbial remark which, as Dilke first observed, is somewhat too astute for Accius; Bond suggests that it might be attached to Stellio's line which precedes it. However, this would destroy the symmetry of Memphio's and Stellio's parallel speeches, and the 'sawe' does possess a kind of unwitting irony on the lips of Accius.

1578–9. *the olde rent*: Halfpenny's joke depends on the knowledge that 'improving' was a term for putting up rents.

1593. One might expect a question for Stellio to follow, i.e. 'Silena, how lykest thou Accius?'

1594. *personable*: meaning 'handsome', though since the word is usually applied to people, there may be some comic misapplication intended.

1601. *Sperantus' sonne*: all editions prior to Bond's print 'Prisius' sonne' at this point. The confusion is accounted for easily enough, but it may be related to a degree of textual corruption here (see note to line 1604).

1604. Lucio's remark hints that a question from Stellio preceded it, parallelling Memphio's inquiry at line 1600; it also provides further evidence that the text is probably corrupt at this point.

1638. *currantly*: another joke based on the notion of money 'currently' in circulation (cf. line 498 and note).

1644. *sit downe*: Dromio puns on 'arrest' and 'a rest'.

1663. *provender*: i.e. dry food such as corn, oats, etc.

1666. *I spurd him*: a pun on 'spurred' and 'questioned' (cf. line 1359).

1674–5. *neither would cry 'Wyhie!'*: Bond compares the proverb 'It's an ill horse can neither whinny nor wag his tail.'

1676. *boare him*: Bond argues that since this practice was often carried out to identify a horse from others, Dromio intended to steal the one he hired, but line 1679 makes it sound more like a punishment for his deficiencies.

1684. *tyre and retire*: i.e. 'he'd tug and back away'.

1688. *bargen*: probably resulting from a pun on 'baild' in the sense of 'confined', i.e. 'next time I'll see him in gaol first'.

1693–4. *betweene this and Canterburie*: cf. lines 1362–3 and note.

1698–9. *trotted before*, etc.: i.e. 'his front legs would trot, and his back legs saunter'. Cf. Orlando Gibbons's fantasia on London street-cries:

'... a gray mare with a long mane and a short tayle, she halts down right before and is stark lame behind ...'

1709. *towne-borne children*: cf. *Euphues*, Bond, I, 199, 21–4.

'*Philautus* being a towne borne childe ... crepte into credite with ... one of the chiefe governours of the citie ...'

1711. *statute marchant*: a form of bond under the Statute of Merchants (1285) recording a debt which gave the lender the right to seize the lands of the debtor if he failed to repay the loan within a certain period.

1728. *a pint of curtesie*, etc.: this has a proverbial ring, but is not found in any of the principal collections; cf. 'Everie fox to his hole', etc. at line 1735.

1743. *Jost*: possibly from the dialect verb 'joss' meaning 'to mount'; in Lyly's native Kent a mounting-block was known as a joss- or a jossing-block.

1745. *acquitance*: a document absolving Dromio from his debt for the horse.

1775–80. Q1 prints as prose.

1806. *spittle*: presumably the player spat on the pin in order to get it to turn more easily when the violin was being tuned.

1809–10. *I'le throw*: a reading from Q2 replacing the 'I' of Quarto 1. *into the leads*, etc.: Fairholt took 'leads' to mean 'gutter' in this context, on the assumption that a 'hobler' was a wooden post with a coin on top which was pitched at in a children's game, but the use of the plural form 'leads' must indicate 'the roof', and I incline to the view that the disgruntled Beduneus threatens to throw his fiddle up on to the roof just as a child might pitch a wobbly spinning top at a mark known as the 'Hobler's hole'. Cf. Ben Jonson's *A Tale of A Tub* (1633), III. 4. 43–4: '... I had whipp'd 'em all, like tops/In Lent, and hurl'd 'hem into Hoblers-hole...'

1811–12. *There's a time for al things*: an ancient proverb, traceable at least as far back as Ecclesiastes iii, 1, 'To every thing there is a season ...'

1816–17. *tomorrow is a new daie*: a common proverb for putting something off for the present.

1820, s.d. *Sing*: much scholarly ingenuity has gone to explain why neither of the Quarto editions nor Blount's *Six Court Comedies* provides a song here, despite the apparent instruction 'Sing' which is admittedly printed in the same typeface as the dialogue in Q1 (unlike that at line 1860 which is in italic). Fairholt was, however, almost certainly right in thinking 'Sing' to be a stage-direction rather than part of Synis' lines, and this appears to create the problem. The simplest and most obvious explanation for the absence of a song is that line 1821 represents the first line of a song which is cut short by Sperantus' angry intrusion. Thus the answer to G. K. Hunter's query in *John Lyly: The Humanist as Courtier*, pp. 370–71, as to why Blount failed to supply the song is that he recognized that no such song existed or was needed at this point.

1835. *So he is, sir*: Nasutus seems to treat 'hanged' here as meaning 'tied up' or 'hooked'.

1839–40. *wedding geare*: Candius is keeping up the pretence that he is not yet married, and is prepared to follow his father's wishes.

1842. *Memphio's son*: Synis unwittingly furthers Candius' deception and convinces Sperantus that all is well.

1845. *What's the almes?*: i.e. 'What did Candius give you?'

1846. *angell*: the old English gold coin, properly known as the angel-noble, and first coined by Edward IV in 1495, was originally valued at 6*s*. 8*d*. but under Henry VIII it rose to 7*s*. 6*d*., and then 8*s*. In 1552 it was re-valued at 10*s*. (Cf. lines 1846–7, and *Gammer Gurton's Nedle*, line 108 and note.)

1848. *money in master Mayor's purse*: i.e. 'even a rich man would think that was worth having'.

1851–2. '*A marke in issues*': the court's pronouncement of a fine or 'issue', a mark being equivalent to 13*s* 4*d*.; Beduneus' punning interpretation is of course 'a mark in his shoes'.

1855. *handsell*: possibly an 'advance' or a 'first instalment' rather than a 'gift'; the reference to 'maidenhead' (suggesting that this is the first time Synis has ever parted with any money, or that Beduneus hopes that it is a token of more to come) contains both possibilities.

1868. *laugh-and-lie-downe*: possibly intended literally as a children's game, but with more than a hint of *double-entendre*, as with 'ticke-tacke' in line 1870.

1882. *a huddle*: usually applied to a gaggle of old men (cf. line 486) but in this context 'a baby in shawls' or even 'a brood of children' seems a more likely interpretation of the term.

1883. *crouding*: from the Welsh *cwrth*, a form of violin. Sir Philip Sidney in his *Apologie for Poetrie* speaks of 'the old Song of *Percy* and *Douglas*' 'sung but by some blinde Crowder, with no rougher voyce, then rude stile'.

1894. *the roode's bodie*: the body on the rood, i.e. Christ on the cross.

1897–8. *Your worshippe is wise*: obviously ironic.

1908. *A bots on*: the botts was a disease in animals caused by parasitic worms or maggots, and the phrase came to be used much as 'a murrain on . . .' (cf. lines 2173–4).

1923–4. *moone-shine in the water*, etc.: proverbial for 'longing for the unattainable' (cf. 'castles in the ayre' in line 1924).

1925. *a foole to his heyre*: cf. note to line 3.

1927. *chafing dishes*: dishes with the base filled with burning charcoal to cook food at a gentle heat, or to keep it warm once cooked.

1928. *her tongue*, etc.: according to Bond, Memphio wishes his wife's tongue would restrain Dromio's appetite, but this seems a far-fetched view of a remark which is probably a mere riposte to Dromio's reference to 'chafing dishes'.

1972. *dumbe minister*: possibly 'senseless cleric', but I suspect an allusion to an absentee incumbent, though without any evidence to support the notion.

1976. *the clerke cryed*: Q1 reads 'clocke' but the use of 'cry' for the pealing of a bell, even in figurative terms, seems unlikely, and is not attested elsewhere, so I have accepted Dilke's conjectural emendation to 'clerke'.

2011. *oatemeale groate*: possibly 'profligate small coin'; early in the seventeenth century 'oatmeal' certainly meant a swaggerer, but there appears to be no instance of its usage as early as 1594.

2040–41. *hee used no crafte*: Lucio puns on 'craft' meaning 'deception' and 'skill in narration'; in other words the old men really are knaves!

2057. *no mountaines*: proverbial usage: 'Friends may meet but mountains never greet.' Bond compares 'Though mountaines meet not, Lovers may' in a poem from Davison's *Poetical Rhapsody* of 1602, possibly by Lyly.

2062. *trouble the water*: cf. *Euphues and His England*, Bond, II, 143. 14–15: '. . . the Camill first troubleth the water before he drinke'.

2089. *one of clouts*: i.e one made of old clothes, a 'dressed-up dummy'.

2092. *If you will not*, etc.: another common proverb, often followed by 'so are all maidens married'.

2093. *mine olde cap*: presumably 'thank you for nothing'.

2154. *mandrage*: mandragora or mandrake was mainly used for its narcotic properties in the Tudor and Stuart periods, chiefly in sleeping draughts and pain-killers. It was also believed to be of assistance in helping women to conceive and in preventing impotence in men.

2212–13. *eate as much pie*: potato-pie was often served at weddings, according to Bond, but since the plant was not cultivated widely in Britain until the eighteenth century, it would seem unwise to see this reference as anything other than a very general one.

2239. *such a Noverint*, etc.: legal writs usually began with the words '*Noverint universi*' ('Let all men know'), and the term then became slang for a writ. Cheapside was the home of the Court of Arches in the Church of St Mary-le-Bow, from which legal summonses were sent out.

2271. *none of our upseekings*: a phrase not found frequently, but one suspects the presence of a final trite commonplace to round off the action.

APPENDIX

The Use of Dialect

The evolution of 'Mummerset', that well-known rustic idiom still used for stage, screen and radio purposes, forms a fascinating if elusive subject for study, and *Gammer Gurton's Nedle* and to a lesser extent *Roister Doister* have an important place in the narrative. The employment of dialect forms to indicate regional distinctions seems to have appeared in medieval English literature at a time when differences between the speech traits of one area and another were becoming apparent, and audiences began to possess sufficient awareness to appreciate the implications of the contrast. In fact, four main regional dialects developed during the Middle Ages – Northern, Southern (with Kentish as a distinct subdivision), East Midland, and West Midland – and their characteristics endured even after the emergence of a recognized standard form of the language during the fifteenth century.

In Chaucer's 'Reeve's Tale' (*c.* 1390–1400) we have an early attempt to create humour by linguistic means; the poet gives to the speeches of the two Cambridge students, John and Aleyn, the flavour of the North Country idiom, his heroes hailing from Northumberland. But perhaps the earliest instance of such dialectal humour in an English dramatic work occurs in the first half of the fifteenth century with the 'Second Shepherds' Play', which forms part of the contribution of the so-called 'Wakefield Master' to the Towneley or Wakefield sequence of cycle plays. Here Mak, a sheep-stealer, tries to impress on the stolid Yorkshire shepherds whom he hopes to rob, that he is a messenger from the king, and to do so adopts Southern speech-forms such as 'Ich' for 'I', 'sich' for 'such', 'some' for 'same', 'foore' for 'fare', 'doth' for 'do', and so forth, until the First Shepherd, incensed at his deceit and affectation, offers him the following terse and pithy advice (lines 215–16):

> Now take outt that sothren tothe,
> And sett in a torde!

However, it is not until the 1550s that any effort is found to compose theatrical roles entirely or substantially in rustic dialect, although of course earlier work featuring this device may have been lost to view. Certainly, *Roister Doister, Gammer Gurton's Nedle*, and another piece often assigned to Udall, the political morality *Respublica* discussed in the Introduction, all employ the same set of conventions in characterizing the speech of figures from rural backgrounds, whereby a regional impression is conveyed without complete loss of intelligibility. The old nurse Madge Mumblecrust in *Roister Doister* is occasionally assigned utterances of this type; in *Gammer Gurton's Nedle* all Hodge's lines, plus some of Gammer's, Tyb's, and Cocke's, are couched in a similar vein, while the same is true of the semi-comic figure of People 'representing the poore Commontie' in *Respublica*. Since all of these characters can be reckoned to be of peasant stock, their southern (or in the case of *Respublica* south-western) speech is no doubt intended to indicate their geographical and social origins, with the implication that they are socially inferior to those who speak in the more educated manner associated with the 'standard English' of London and the East Midlands.

A brief explanation of the basic ingredients of their language should render their lines relatively simple to interpret. The principal colouring given to their words is that of Southern English, which was a comparatively conservative dialect where change was slow to penetrate, so that its more obvious features were ideally suited to employment for 'Mummerset'. For example, Southern clung to the forms *hi, here*, and *hem* when Northern was developing the equivalents of the modern *they, their*, and *them*; Southern also retained the *-th* ending of the Old English third person plural for verbs in the present tense, which accounts for People in *Respublica* occasionally using 'beeth' for 'are', as in 'vaire woordes beeth but tales' (line 726). Again, Old English *ic* meaning 'I' was modified to *ik* in the North and Midlands, and after about 1400 to *I*, but in the South and West the form *ich* lingered on, particularly before an initial vowel, the pronoun often being reduced to the 'ch' form and elided before verbs beginning with a vowel, an *h*, or a *w*. This accounts for such forms as Hodge's 'cha' or 'chave' for 'I have', 'cham' for 'I am', 'chard' (I heard), 'chope' (I hope), 'chwere' (I were), 'chwold' (I would), and so forth, and for Madge Mumblecrust's 'chad', 'chote' (I wot), and 'chwine' (I ween).

Typical too of the Southern dialect is the tendency to replace long *a* for long *o* as in the examples quoted from the 'Second Shepherds' Play' whereby Northern *stane* and *hame* become *stone* and *home* respectively, and the habit of voicing initial *f* and *s* so that they become *v* and *z*. The latter tendency is found in Hodge's reference to 'vylthy glaye' [filthy clay], his use of 'vast' for 'fast', his swearing 'be'm vather's soul'; Madge exclaims 'zee, law' and 'zo, law', and talks of 'zembletee'. Finally, elision and truncation of words is a common feature of the playwrights' technique in creating rustic-style speech, so we find such forms as 'bem', 'bim', 'bym' used for 'by my', 'geare' for 'give her', 'shase' for 'she has', 'shead' for 'she had', and 'yoush' for 'you shall'.

There is not a great deal of consistency in the way such rustic colouring is employed in the plays, perhaps not surprisingly, since the aim was to create an overall impression of a speaking voice to guide both actor and reader, and there is no doubt that in *Gammer Gurton's Nedle*, as F. S. Boas points out in his *University Drama in the Tudor Age*, much of the vocabulary is Northern in origin. However, these early attempts at 'Mummerset' do add considerably to the liveliness of the characterizations which are such an attractive feature of these Tudor comedies.

GLOSSARY

a have
abering conduct
abeston asbestos
abroade, abrod, abrode at large, generally, out-of-doors
aby, abye pay for (it)
accombred oppressed
acquitance, acquittaunce document of release
acrook awry
addeces adzes, bladed axes
advoutresse adulteress
afine completely
akt ached
alecie drunkenness
alias in other words
allowe, allowen allow, commend, sanction
almes a good deed
amend amended
ameved angered, aroused
amitie friendship
amongs meanwhile
an, and even if, if
angell a gold coin
anie either
anticke grotesque
apaied repaid
aperne apron
apply agree to
appointment dictation
appose baffle, perplex, 'put to it'
araied in trouble, put on the spot
argent silver
arrand arrant
arrierage in arrears, state of debt
arteficiall artful
auctour author, inventor
autentical the genuine article, trustworthy
aventure risk

avise advise (*avise you* consider, think it over)
awreake avenge

backare! get back there!
backside back of the house
backt baked
bagge purse
bagger beggar
baited pulled up, rested
bald hairless one
balde barren, useless
balkes roof-beams
ban swear
bandog chained-up dog
banes banns
banket banquet
bare in hand delude
bargen agreement to confine someone
bauderie hanky-panky
bave behave
bavins bundles of brushwood
bawawe beware
be by
bedlem, bedelem bedlam, inmate of Bedlam, mad
begrime smear all over
beldam hag, witch
beldame aged woman, 'granny'
beleve by-leave, permission
belie tell lies about
bell, beare the take the prize
beraye, bewraie, bewray (i) besmirch, disfigure, foul (ii) betray, expose, reveal
beseme, besime become, beseem, suit
beshrewe curse
bet beat, beaten
bidd proclaim
billiments ornamental headdresses
bine, byn, byne been

bitchfox vixen

bite hot smart painfully

blab (verb) blurt out; (noun) 'blabbermouth'

bleard blinded, dimmed, made bleary

bleed vent through bleeding

blesse beat (ironic)

blinde meaningless

boare bore

bodelouse a louse on the body

bonable abominable

bond band, tie

booking studying

boord make advances to

boote leather case

boots not, it it's not worth it, it doesn't pay, it signifies nothing, it is useless

borde (i) jest (ii) meal-table

borde, in jestingly, lightly

boroue, borow surety

bots on! A A plague on!

bottle bundle

bouncing 'thumping good'

boxes blows

brabble squabble

brag, bragge (adj.) lively, pleased with oneself; (noun) demeanour

brainpan skull

brave fine

brawle brat

breach breeches

breafast breakfast

breake broach, impair, interrupt

breched broken

brewish bread soaked in broth

brim, brymme (adj.) fierce; (adv.) furiously

brinch drink to

broacht embarked on

broad-stitch ? braid-stitch

broche rod for roasting with

broching piercing

broke injured

brusten broken, burst

brute 'devil'

bruted noised abroad

buckle encounter

bukler small shield (*playing at the buklers* fencing)

bungling blundering

burbolt blunt-headed arrow

burnt mulled

bush tavern

business distress, trouble

buske bush

but, but if unless

buy-worde by-word, pet phrase

by and by here and now, immediately, straightaway

by zemblelee apparently

callet whore

calphe, calfe calf, twerp

cammocke crooked stick

canvased tossed about

cape cap

cape-cloke cloak with cape attached

capon castrated cock, fool, 'the stupid one'

captine captain

carefull full of care

cariage burden

carouse booze (*carousing* toasting)

case, in if

cassocks long gowns

cast (noun) characteristic style, contrivance, sample, skill, specimen, tactic, trick; (verb) assess, calculate, contrive, give birth prematurely, guess, think of

cast up (i) reckon up (ii) vomit

caudle a warming drink

chafed glowing with anger

chafing bad temper

charme (noun) ? magic power; (verb) subdue

chayre seat

cheekes side-posts of a door, uprights

chise cheese

chist chest

cholar anger

choploge chop-logic

clapper tongue

clinke the sound of a bell

clocke cloak

close secret

clout, cloute, clowte garment, patch, piece of cloth

cloyed filled to bursting
clunged clung, stuck
cocke young blade
Cocke, Cocke's God, God's (*Kock's nownes!* God's wounds!)
cockescombe fool
cockring pampering
cog cheat at dice, play on words, quibble
cold could
collop piece, slice
colorable plausible
colt, coult cheat, cheater
combat fight over
coming eager, forward, willing
commons means
commontie the common people, the commons
commyn common
complot combined conspiracy
conceit fancy (*conceited* clever, witty)
conduit fountain, stand-pipe
coney rabbit (term of endearment)
conjure deceive
connyng see 'cunning', etc.
conster construe
conveiaunce, conveyance ? cunning, expression, manner of delivery
convey cheat, make over by law, steal
coosned, cosned cheated, deceived (*coosnage* deceitfulness)
cosin cheat
corrasive caustic medicine
costard, costarde, costerd large apple, 'head'
costes discredit
cosune friend
cotton succeed
coulour colour, excuse
councel (in) in confidence
counger conjure, constrain
countenance show of regard
counterfeit fraudulent
coure cower
course curse
course, out of abnormal
coustrelyng attendant, lad
cowslop cowslip
coxe cokes, nitwit

coyle thrash
coystrel rogue
crab crab-apple
crack-halter gallows-bird, rogue-like
craking boasting
cresie unstable
crimosin crimson
crosse amiss
crouding fiddling
croue crow
crust ? beat to a crust
cullyon rascal, term of abuse
cumbre distress, perplex
cungere baffle, bewitch
cunning, cunnynge, connyng (adj.) clever, knowledgeable, learned, skilful, skilled; (noun) cleverness, knowledge, magic art, skill
currant in general circulation
curried, curryed beaten, thrashed
curst shrewish
curtal horse with docked tail
cust kissed
cut fashion, style
cut, kut 'bitch'

daintrels delicacies to eat
damaske prunes damsons
dandle pamper
dapper 'sharp', smart
dastard (adj.) sneaky; (noun) coward
daunger damage, mischief
dawe fool, oaf
day, the last yesterday
deadly excessively
debare denude, strip
dell bit, deal, piece (*everie dell* every detail)
device, devise scheme, stratagem
diar dyer
die (noun) dice; (verb) dye
diligence care
discovered 'let out'
disgest digest
distempered disturbed, troubled
doale charity
docke backside
dodge prevaricate
dodkin doit, small coin

doge dog
do of take off
doon oon dressed, put on
dotage infatuation, insanity, madness
dote act strangely
doubling cheating
doubtfull ambiguous
doubtlesse without doubt
douke duck
drab slut
drawen out extended in length
dreadfully full of dread
dress 'do over', sort out
dressed, drest arrayed, covered, placed, scolded, set, treated
drift intention, plan
dugeon resentment, vexation
dullness stupidity
dumpe depressed mood, perplexity
dumps mournful tunes
durst dare
durt excrement, mire
dyet feeding habits

ear before, ere
ears, eares, be by the quarrel
earned yearned
earnest important
e'en truly
eft again
eke also
emongs amongst
endite set down, compose (*endityng* writing out)
ensured engaged, pledged to
entwite rebuke
erre ere
Eschequer Court of Exchequer
estate position (in society)
event outcome
everychone everyone
exceedingly surpassing others
eyen eyes

face it brazen it out
facing bragging
fact crime, evil deed
facte fact
facultie ability, profession

fadge, fodge come off, succeed, work out
fal occur
fall in agree, get on
farde fared
fare far, far off
farre off course
faryng playing at Fare
fast intent
faucet tap
faut fault
feache collect, fetch
feare scare
fee-simple absolute right of possession
feind fiend
fell feel
fell of fell to
felloneus atrocious
ferdegews farthingales
fet, fete, fette bring (back), carry, fetch, restore, seize, take away
fetcht about done in a roundabout way
fey, in in faith
fidging moving restlessly
fidling fiddle-playing
fier fire
firret ferret
fist, fyst hand, handwriting
fit, fitte song
flat absolute, sheer, sour (of milk)
fling, flyng dash out
flip smack, ? urge
flocke despise
floure floor
foile defile, soil
fole, folle fool
fond foolish, stupid
force, no no matter, who cares?
forfende forbid
for that since
founde encounter, meet with
fraile rush-basket
fray, fraye disturbance, scrap, turmoil
freese frieze (coarse woollen material)
freind friend
freuter fruiterer
froe from
fulsome cloying, loathsome
fume angry mood

433

furder further
furniture attire
furre furrow
fysking whisking

gaffer (i) 'old fellow' (ii) term of
 respect
gamesome playful
gascoins gaskins (wide breeches)
gaudyng frivolous nonsense
geare, gere affair, business, matter,
 tackle, to-do
gently courteously, generously
get jet, strut
giglot hussy
Gigs, Gys Jesus
gill wench
gird, girde (noun) gibe (verb) mock
girdle waist-belt
gitterne guitar
glase glass, mirror
glaye clay
glieke jest
glommyng frowning, sullen look
glosier flatterer, sycophant
glosing, glosynge (adj.) deceitful,
 specious; (noun) smooth talk
Godg's, Gog's God's
God's good yeast
goo walk
good goods (*a good* thoroughly)
Gosse God
gossip, gossop, gossyp crony, friend,
 female neighbour
gozelyng gosling
graffe graft
graft scion, 'sprig'
gree agree, accord
greefe, greeve anger, grievance, injury,
 wrong
gristle tender or feeble person
grosse meat flesh of large animals
ground basis
grutch complain, grumble
gyb cat
gyce guise, habit

hackney horse hired for riding
halse neck

haltered hanged
handsell gift
hangeupe one fit for the gallows
hape chance, luck
happelye, happily fortunately, luckily
haps fortunes
hard, harde heard
harde (adj.) essential, very
hardely, hardelye boldly
hardly bravely, by all means,
 certainly, truly
harme injury
harnesse armour
hast haste
haze scold
head ? main proposition
hear, her here
heare, here hair
hennes from here, hence
hether hither
hoball fool
hobler ? child's wobbly top
hoddypeke blockhead
hold, holde bet, wager
hold tack hold one's own
holy holly
homely (adj.) intimate; (adv.) familiarly
honestie, the honourable folk
hooke fellow, lout
horesoon, horeson, whoreson rogue; term
 of abuse
horologe clock
hoxe cut off the knuckle, hamstring
howlet owl
hoyse hoist
hoysted elevated
hucklebone haunch-bone
huddle ? a baby in shawls ? a crop of
 babies (*huddles* miserable old men)

I Aye
il evil
imbesell cheat, embezzle
improved raised
incontinent, incontynente immediately,
 straightaway
inconvenience discomfort, misfortune
incredible incredulous
innosaintes innocents

inow, inowe enough, enow
insurance engagement
intents intentions
inward indoors
irketh, it it annoys me
ise ice
issue discharge
ivy-bush tavern
iwis indeed, truly

jagges tattered clothes
jakes ? excrement, privy
jars discord
jeoparde, jeoper, jeoperd hazard, risk
jetting strutting
Jewry jury
joll bang, bash
jost ? mount
joynd stoole joint-stool
joynter jointure, settlement
jugling deceptive
just regularly
jutte shove

ka indeed, quótha, 'you don't say?'
key colde cold as a key
kite 'shark'
ko quoth
Kock see 'Cocke'
kosse kiss
kut see 'cut'
kynde, of by nature, natural
kype keep

lade load
last daie yesterday
late recently
lawne fine linen
leade cauldron
leads roof
lease, lese lose
leasing lie
least lest
leasune lesson
leere learning, lessons
lees pastures
leese, lese, lesse lose
lesing losing
leive dear

lerripoope lesson
let (noun) obstruction, restraint; (verb) fail, hinder, hold back, prevent
levie break up camp
lewd low
lickdish sponger
liefe dearly, happily
lift left
light (i) alight (ii) wanton
lilburne lubber
lily lovely
live, on alive
lobcocke clown
loitersacke idle rogue
loke luck
lookes locks
looke wel about be on guard
losell, lozell scoundrel, wretch
lout mock
low, lowe admit, approve
lub, lubbe love
lurden beggar, rascal
lust desire, wish
lustie, lustye arrogant, bold, brave, cheerful, insolent, pleasant, robust, valiant, vigorous
lyne cease
lysse lose
lyther wicked

madde madness
maide virgin
maintaine keep on good terms with
maker author
making literary composition
malcontent a discontented man
malison curse
Malkyn term of derision
malt mare dray horse
malypert impudent, malapert
mandrage mandragora
mankine furious, insane
marchent merchant, i.e. 'chap'
marcye mercy
mare mar
marie, mary marry (exclamation)
marybones knees
mas, mast master

mase mace
maship mastership
matiers matters
matte ? Mass
matter subject
mault-worme a lover of malt-drink
mawe gullet, stomach
maystrie, for the to the utmost
meane middle course
meat met
meave move
mede reward
mel occupy oneself
mend amend
mentainyth defends, supports
mery marry
mesars bounds, measure
messe a group eating together
met meat
metely sufficiently
metter metre
mew imprison (*mewed up* shut up)
mickle much
micher petty crook, rascal, truant
   (*miching* playing truant)
minde, mynde intention, way of
   thinking, wish
minion (adj.) dainty, pretty (noun)
   darling, gallant, girl-friend,
   'precious'
misdeem, misdime misjudge
misse uncertainty
mist avoided, missed
mo more
modestie confusion, shame
moke mock
mome clown, 'dope', fool
moneth month
monstrous abnormal, unnatural
motche much
mote may, might
motion propose
moull mole
moune moon
moyling agitation, 'fuss'
mumblyng chewing
mump mope
mun must
murryon (adv.) infected, plaguey
   (noun) murrain, plague

murther murder
mysimithe it seems to me, meseemeth

nale ale
namelie especially, particularly
naturall (adj.) foolish; (noun) an idiot
nature natural affection
naughtinesse untoward conduct,
   wickedness
naughty wayward, worthless
naull awl
ne nor
neast nest
neate smart
neate's ox's
neele needle
nere never
nice reluctant, shy
niddes, nides necessarily, needs
noble a gold coin
noddle brain, head
noddy fool
nonage minority
nons, noons, for the for the purpose, if
   you like
nource nurse
Noverint a writ
nowle 'drunkard', head
noyce noise
noye harm
noyse band, company of musicians
nycely cautiously, pleasantly
nyght night (*starke night* dead of
   night)

oft anything, aught
on one
ons at one period, once
open reveal
or before, ere
other either
ought aught, owed
our hour, over
over-naturall unduly affectionate
over-reach get the better of, go too far,
   pull a fast one, say too much
overtaken overcome with drink

pace parse
packe ? bundle, plot

pad toad

paishe, pashe ? Passover

paltered babbled, mumbled

pangues pangs

pap baby food, pulpy food

paps breasts

parages descent, rank

parboile half boil

pardee by God, truly

pastance, pastaunce amusement, pastime, sport

patch fool

patins clogs, pattens

paunde pawned

pelting paltry

pende griped, pained

peradventure perhaps

percace perhaps

perfit perfect

personable handsome

pes cushion, hassock

pesynge 'piecing'

phantasye ingenious notion

philup fillip, smart blow

picke clear off

pievish perverse

pigesnie, pigsnie, pigsny, pygsnie darling, sweetheart

pike clear off, pick

pike-staffe metal-pointed stick

pild hairless

pinching fault-finding

pinne peg

pissing while, a brief space, short interval

planly plainly

plat patch of ground, plot

plauditie, plaudytie request for applause, round of applause

plaunche clap on

playe trick, 'way of going on'.

pleasurable ? easily pleased

plummer lead-worker, solderer

poast ? posset

polling extortion

portely imposing

pose (noun) cold or catarrh; (verb) propose a question to

possing tramping in mud

potgunne 'pop gun', short gun

pouder pickle, preserve, salt (*poudred* salted)

poulter poulterer

poumile pummel

powpte cheated, deceived

poynte respect

practise deception

prancome peculiar happening, trickery

prankicote show off, swagger about

pregnant apt, fertile, witty

presently straight away

prest glazed

prety clever, pleasant

prevent anticipate, forestall

pricking pressing forward

princockes saucy youth

prive prove

probation proof

proctor advocate, attorney

proofe, of proven, tested

propre perfect

propretie character, good name

prycked up dressed up, tricked out

pudding, puddynges entrails, guts, 'haggis-style' food

pullaine poultry

put of took off

put up lock up

pylorye pillory

quadrapertit composed of four parts

que (i) cue (ii) farthing

queane 'hussy', 'little cat', whore

quesie unsettled

quest inquest

quier choir

quietnes, a ? peaceful settlement

quite (adv.) completely, free; (verb) pay back

quod quoth

racke (noun) neck, etc., of pork or mutton; (verb) stretch

rage (noun) state of madness; (verb) lose one's wits, rave, run mad

rake scrape out a horse

rakes dissipated woman

ramp charge about, on the rampage

rampe 'fish-wife'

randevous rendezvous

rape rap

rather earlier

ray line of battle, martial order

read, reade, red, rede (noun) advice (verb) advise

rechlesse regardless of consequence

recognoscence recognition

recreate refresh or amuse oneself

reed cross, rood

reformed assuaged

refuse reject

rehersed, rehersid gone through, played, quoted

rekine reckon

remitte pardon

repreefe reproof

rewerd reward

richesse wealth

right proper

rode, roode cross, rood

roile rampage, roam

roisting riotous

roking ? raking

romth room

rong out extracted, found out

rosen rosin

round hose tight stockings of thick thread

rouse encourage, stir up

route assemble

roweringe roaring

roysting blustering, riotous

rude uneducated (*rudenesse* uncouthness)

ruffler braggart

rume cold

run lapse, ride

rundlet runlet, small cask

ruste roost

rustle into to be here, there, and everywhere

ruth sadness

ryg harlot

sad solemn, sorrowful (*sadder* more sober)

sadly seriously (*sadnesse* seriousness; *in sadnesse* for a serious reason, in honesty, solemnly)

sance sans, without

sarve serve

sawe maxim, saying

scacelye scarcely

scalde, skald (adj.) scabby; (noun) scurvy character

scapt escaped

schritch screech

scolde nagger

sconce brains, head

scource reckoning, score

scuse excuse

sectour executor

seene in, well an expert on

semple simple

sence, sens already, since, since then

set provide with

sete sat down, set

setting-on 'standing treat'

shamefast bashful, modest

shent blamed, disgraced, punished, ruined, scolded

shiere shire

shoinghorne appetizer

shootanker sheet-anchor

shreve, shrive (adj.) absolved, shriven; (verb) to hear confession and absolve

shrew (noun) villain; (verb) curse

shrinke desert, 'skip'

shyte shut

sike seek

sillie, silly foolish, helpless, simple

sithe seeing that, since

Sizes Assizes

sizing sizzing, yeast

skill of cope with, understand

skinckers drawers and servers of wine

skrine screen

slepe, slype neglect, slip

slip at slip the leash at

slips spurious coins

slipstring one fit for the gallows

slyp long narrow slice, sliver

slype sleep

smell detect, guess

smolders smothers

snache seize

snaphance flintlock on a musket

sod soaked

438

sone soon

sonets songs

sonne, white blue-eyed boy, favourite

sooth encourage, flatter, humour by supporting, support

sops food moistened with wine

sore fierce

sort, sorte company, crowd

sory solemn, wretched

sossing splashing

sote sot

sound swoon

sourges surges

souse thump

sowing sewing

speede (noun) success; (verb) proceed successfully, succeed

speet punish, spite

spigot tap

spill, spyl damage, destroy (*spilt* ruined)

spiteth offends

spittlehouse hospital

sporyar spur-maker

spoyled injured, robbed

spreete devil, spirit

spurre interrogate, question

squrt diarrhoea, 'the squitters'

stacke stowed, stuck

stanch satisfy, staunch

stand cask

staye halt, standstill

stayers stairs

stell, stelle steal

stert distance

sticke hesitate, scruple

stifelie stoutly

stockes stockings

stoding reflecting

stoke stock

stole stool

stomacke, stomake be offended by, resent (*to have a stomacke* to be valiant)

stoppe check

stound, stounde ? attack, time of trouble

straight narrow, urgent

strange distant, unfriendly

streake strike

stripe wound

stronge arrant, brazen

succes outcome, upshot

sue pursue, serve

sweetly dearly

swil tub tub of pig-swill, wash-tub

swinged beaten, punished, thrashed

swite sweet

switeharte sweetheart

swyncke labour, toil

swythe swiftly, vigorously

sykerly certainly

syller silver

syne observed, seen

sythe since

taken, token (noun) sign, token; (verb) signify

take up grasp, realize

tame docile, meek

tarlether 'skinny old bag'

tatche fasten

tender cherish

tenters frames for stretching cloth

terani tyranny

tergat buckler, small shield

than then

tharte the heart

then than

thether the other

thir their

this thus

throte boule Adam's apple

throwly thoroughly, totally

thrust out ? let loose

time thyme

tite, tyte quickly

to also, too

togather together

tombled mixed up, upset

tooke brought

tosse it get drunk

tossing 'dancing' (*tost* tossed aside)

toste piece of toast

towne yard

toy, toye device, trick

travell labour, travail

tread out beget

tredging trudging

triall examination of proof

tricke smart

trie demonstrate, prove, test the veracity of (*trien* proved)

trim 'cut down to size', reprimand

triple treble

trot dame, old woman

trow believe

trowle pass across or around

trump playing-card, ? 'trumpery' article

Trumpe a card-game

twaye two

twit, twite taunt

two too

turtle turtle-dove

tykled tattled, whispered

unhappy mischievous

unneth scarcely

ure, put in put into practice

vary differ

vengeable, vengible awful, extraordinarily, revengeful

venter venture

verament truly

vere spring

viage journey, undertaking

vilde vile

vou vow

voydeth casts out

wage wag

wagepastie, wagpastie mischievous rogue

wagging chattering

wag-halter gallows-bird

waghith 'spars', wags

waites town musicians

walke his/thy cote beat, make sore

wand, wande cane, rod, switch

warbelith wobbles

ware beware

warke work

warrantise guarantee

warte wert

washical 'what's-it-called'

wealth prosperity, well-being

wede clothing

weete know, learn

weke, in by the madly in love, over the moon

wene reckon, ween

were weary

wesen windpipe

weste wist

whan when

where whether

whether whither

whippet bustle about

whirle fly-wheel, whorl

whiskyng whirling around

whistle mouthpiece

white dearest, spotless (*white broth* phlegm; *white sonne* blue-eyed boy, favourite)

whitled intoxicated

who whoever

whooreson see 'horeson', etc.

whose who's

whurre haste, rushing about

wike week

winch wince

wine believe, reckon, ween

wist knew

wit cleverness, intelligence, sense

wite wit

without outside

woe woo

woll wool

wood, for in a fury, madly

world, a a marvellous experience

worme 'poor thing'

wot, wote know

wreake exercise punitively

wring take the blame

wrong wrung

wrought fermented

yawle scream out

ye yea

ye, yes eye, eyes

yeede went

yelde, yld recompense, reward

ynow enough

ywis certainly, indeed, truly

MORE ABOUT PENGUINS,
PELICANS AND PUFFINS

For further information about books available from Penguins please write to Dept EP, Penguin Books Ltd, Harmondsworth, Middlesex UB7 0DA.

In the U.S.A.: For a complete list of books available from Penguins in the United States write to Dept DG, Penguin Books, 299 Murray Hill Parkway, East Rutherford, New Jersey 07073.

In Canada: For a complete list of books available from Penguins in Canada write to Penguin Books Canada Ltd, 2801 John Street, Markham, Ontario L3R 1B4.

In Australia: For a complete list of books available from Penguins in Australia write to the Marketing Department, Penguin Books Australia Ltd, P.O. Box 257, Ringwood, Victoria 3134.

In New Zealand: For a complete list of books available from Penguins in New Zealand write to the Marketing Department, Penguin Books (N.Z.) Ltd, P.O. Box 4019, Auckland 10.

In India: For a complete list of books available from Penguins in India write to Penguin Overseas Ltd, 706 Eros Apartments, 56 Nehru Place, New Delhi 110019.

The Penguin English Library

FOUR MORALITY PLAYS

THE CASTLE OF PERSEVERANCE/MAGNYFYCENCE/KING
JOHAN
ANE SATIRE OF THE THRIE ESTAITIS

Edited by Peter Happé

These four major morality plays, written between 1400 and 1562,
are in the mainstream of the development of English drama. In a
period of increasing professionalism they combine drama. In a
with a subtle awareness of the nature of drama and stage technique. The earliest, *The Castle of Perseverance*, gives a general account
of the struggle for salvation. Skelton's *Magnyfycence*, Bale's *King
Johan* and Lindsay's panoramic *Ane Satire of the Thrie Estaitis*
more political purpose, and use allegory and satire as
weapons.

The complete texts are accompanied by an informative introduction, notes, a glossary and two appendices.

Ben Jonson

THREE COMEDIES

VOLPONE/THE ALCHEMIST
BARTHOLOMEW FAIR

Edited by Michael Jamieson

As Shakespeare's nearest rival on the English stage, Ben Jonson
has both gained and suffered. Productions of recent years have, as
it were, rediscovered him as a comic dramatist of genius and a
master of language. This volume contains his best-known
comedies.

Volpone, which is perhaps his greatest, and *The Alchemist* are both
tours de force of brilliant knavery, unflagging in wit and comic
invention. *Bartholomew Fair*, an earthier work, portrays Jonson's
fellow Londoners in festive mood – bawdy, energetic, and never
at a loss for words.

The Penguin English Library

THREE JACOBEAN TRAGEDIES
Edited by Gāmini Salgādo

Renaissance humanism had reached a crisis by the early seventeenth century. It was followed by a period of mental unrest, a sense of moral corruption and ambiguity which provoked the Jacobean dramatists to embittered satire and images of tragic retribution.

John Webster (*c.* 1570–1625) in *The White Devil* paints a sinister and merciless world ruled by all the refinements of cunning and intrigue, whilst in *The Revenger's Tragedy*, one of the most powerful of the Jacobean tragedies, Cyril Tourneur (*c.* 1570–1626) displays in a macabre ballet the emotional conflicts and vices typical of the age. *The Changeling* is perhaps the supreme achievement of Thomas Middleton (1580–1627) – a masterpiece of brooding intensity.

FOUR JACOBEAN CITY COMEDIES
Edited by Gāmini Salgādo

The idiom of these Jacobean comedies is everywhere that of the bustling and bawdy metropolis; and the gulling of dupes and the seduction of women and the activities of sharpers and rogues are presented with irresistible vivacity. London and its court appeared to these dramatists as a striking and comprehensive image of human appetite and folly. However, though satire may dominate, the moralist's censure is often tempered by an affection for the richness and variety of city life.

Other Penguins of interest

SHAKESPEARE'S TRAGEDIES
AN ANTHOLOGY OF MODERN CRITICISM
Edited by Laurence Lerner

Shakespeare's tragedies have always been fertile areas for comment and criticism. The same dramas which inspired Keats to write poetry appealed to A. C. Bradley – or to Ernest Jones, the psycho-analyst – as studies of character, and where the New Criticism has been principally interested in language and imagery, other critics in America have seen the plays as superb examples of plot and structure. Most of Aristotle's elements of tragedy have found their backers, and – as the editor points out in his introduction – these varying approaches to Shakespeare are by no means incompatible.

In what *The Times Literary Supplement* described as an 'excellent collection' Laurence Lerner has assembled the best examples of the modern schools of Shakespeare criticism and arranged them to throw light on individual plays and on tragedy in general.

THE ELIZABETHAN WORLD PICTURE
E. M. W. Tillyard

The Elizabethans took from the Middle Ages a modified view of the universe which, Platonic and Biblical in origin, radically differed from our own. For them all creation was ranged in an unalterable order from the angels down to man – for whom the world existed – and thence to the beasts and plants.

In this short study Dr Tillyard not only elucidates such fairly familiar – though often mystifying – concepts as the four elements, the celestial harmony of 'the nine enfolded Sphears', or macrocosm and microcosm: he also shows how this world picture was variously regarded as a chain of being, a network of correspondences, and a cosmic dance. Such concepts were commonplace to the Elizabethans. By expounding them the author has rendered plain, and not merely picturesque, a host of contemporary passages.

'A new and exciting book ... Dr Tillyard adds a new incitement to the adventure of reading the Elizabethans' – *The Times Literary Supplement*

THE NEW PENGUIN SHAKESPEARE
General Editor: T. J. B. Spencer

All's Well That Ends Well Barbara Everett
Antony and Cleopatra Emrys Jones
As You Like It H. J. Oliver
The Comedy of Errors Stanley Wells
Coriolanus G. R. Hibbard
Hamlet T. J. B. Spencer
Henry IV, Part 1 P. H. Davison
Henry IV, Part 2 P. H. Davison
Henry V A. R. Humphreys
Henry VI, Part 1 Norman Sanders
Henry VI, Part 2 Norman Sanders
Henry VI, Part 3 Norman Sanders
Henry VIII A. R. Humphreys
Julius Caesar Norman Sanders
King John R. L. Smallwood
King Lear G. K. Hunter
Macbeth G. K. Hunter
Measure for Measure J. M. Nosworthy
The Merchant of Venice W. Moelwyn Merchant
The Merry Wives of Windsor G. R. Hibbard
A Midsummer Night's Dream Stanley Wells
Much Ado About Nothing R. A. Foakes
Othello Kenneth Muir
Pericles Philip Edwards
The Rape of Lucrece J. W. Lever
Richard II Stanley Wells
Richard III E. A. J. Honigmann
Romeo and Juliet T. J. B. Spencer
The Taming of the Shrew G. R. Hibbard
The Tempest Anne Righter (Anne Barton)
Timon of Athens G. R. Hibbard
Twelfth Night M. M. Mahood
The Two Gentlemen of Verona Norman Sanders
The Two Noble Kinsmen N. W. Bawcutt
The Winter's Tale Ernest Schanzer